REBEL HARD

A HARD PLAY NOVEL

NALINI SINGH

ISBN: 978-1-942356-67-7

eISBN: 978-1-942356-66-0

Cover design by: Croco Designs

OTHER BOOKS BY NALINI SINGH

For detailed descriptions of these books, as well as additional titles,
visit Nalini's website: www.nalinisingh.com

This one's for Kay.
Chocolate brownies, terrifying rappels into underground caves,
endless laughter—our friendship is one of the joys of my life.

REBEL HARD

IN WHICH OUR HEROINE, NAYNA SHARMA, ENTERS THE INDIAN MARRIAGE MART (AND ENCOUNTERS AN ANIMAL OF THE ASINUS VARIETY)

THE ARRANGED-MARRIAGE MART GOT OFF to an inauspicious start.

The prospective groom and his parents were late because their Jaguar'd had a flat tire. Nayna knew their car was a Jaguar because they mentioned it approximately five times in the first ten minutes. The rest of the time, they spoke about how their one and only child, their "ek lota beta," was a prodigy at his job as a lawyer and would "surely, surely" be partner in only two or three years.

"You mark my words," Mrs. Kapoor said with a wave of a hand bejeweled to within an inch of its life, "my Dilip will be winning all the cases at his firm. He's smarter than the partners, but you know the politics. He has to spend time as a junior."

While Nayna's parents tried to get a word in edgewise, Nayna glanced at Dilip Kapoor. She expected to see a familiar, embarrassed look on his face. Parental bragging was pretty much status quo when Indian families got together. The children generally grimaced and bore it while exchanging "I can't stop them" shrugs and commiserating grins with one another. With this being an arranged-marriage introduction, the stakes were even higher.

However, the man who'd ended up Nayna's first introduction—courtesy of a few words dropped in Nayna's parents' ears by a helpful auntie—was smiling with the kind of smarmy self-appreciation Nayna had previously only seen on the faces of Bollywood movie villains.

Not only was he not embarrassed, he broke into the conversation to say, "The senior partners come to me for advice. Everyone knows it, but..." He tapped the side of his nose while braying out a laugh that grated like nails on a chalkboard.

Nayna sat back in the sofa. As far as possible. Any farther and she'd be in the kitchen.

Beside her, her grandmother murmured near silently, "Nayna, bitia, if you accept this donkey, I'll have to disown you."

Nayna barely stopped herself from snorting out a laugh. She couldn't look at her aji or she knew she'd lose it. Barely holding herself together, she poured more chai for Mrs. Kapoor when the woman imperiously held out her cup for a refill.

"We're really looking for someone fairer for Dilip," Mrs. Kapoor was saying. "But with your daughter being an accountant, we thought we should give her a chance." Her tone was magnanimous.

Other women might've been insulted, but Nayna was

overjoyed. Her college-professor father adored his own dark-skinned bride and would allow no disrespect. Which meant she wouldn't have to come up with reasons to reject this match on the horrific chance that her parents liked him. Or were desperate enough to grab at any opportunity.

At twenty-eight and unmarried, Nayna was a cause of constant despair to her family.

"I thought you were intelligent people," her father said with his usual brusqueness when someone annoyed him. "But clearly I was wrong if you're clinging to outdated standards of beauty seeded in our culture by colonialism. As I have no desire for idiotic grandchildren, let us end this meeting now."

Mrs. Kapoor stared at him with her cup halfway to her mouth. Mr. Kapoor blinked and looked straight ahead—Nayna had the feeling he didn't much talk.

Dilip Kapoor ate a third samosa, the crumbs from the first two littering his shirt, then let out another bray. "Good one, Mr. Sharma."

"Young man, you should see an ear, nose, and throat surgeon as soon as possible. That doesn't sound healthy."

Nayna had to hold her breath to fight the laughter and the tears.

It turned out Mr. and Mrs. Kapoor weren't as dense as their genius son. With a "Come on, Dilip!" they got up in a huff—or at least Mrs. Kapoor did. Mr. Kapoor followed with a weak smile aimed at no one in particular. "We have another meeting tonight anyway. We were only stopping here as a favor to Babita."

Nayna's aji waited until after her father had closed the

door on the Kapoor family to say, "I'm sorry, Nayna. Such a disappointment to you. No little donkeys running around."

Nayna lost it.

A BANDAGE DRESS AND A GOOD GIRL
GONE BAD

THREE WEEKS AFTER THE NIGHT formally referred to as the Donkey Incident in the Sharma household and Nayna was no longer laughing. Four more introductions later and the reality of her situation had hit home.

Ass number 1 had been followed by Asses 2 to 5, but her parents weren't giving up the hunt. She'd crossed her fingers behind her back and hoped they'd surrender, but Gaurav and Shilpa Sharma weren't the giving-up type. And they had something to prove. One daughter might've run off with a boy from college and brought shame on the family, but by God, their other daughter would do everything exactly right.

Education. A good job. Marriage. Grandchildren. The end.

Travel? *Pfft. Do that on your honeymoon.*

Adventure? *Humph. You'll have plenty of adventure once your first baby comes.*

Love? *Oho! You young people, always talking about love-schlove. Love comes* after *marriage, with your husband.*

Telling herself to breathe, that the cage doors hadn't shut quite yet, Nayna smoothed her hands over the dress she'd bought in a fit of Madhuri-induced insanity. Her scandalous older sister, young divorcée and all-around gorgeous glamour-puss, had dropped by for a visit the previous Sunday while Nayna was preparing a traditional meal for lunch for her parents and grandmother.

At the time, Nayna had been wearing old sweatpants and an equally old T-shirt stained with ink from the time she'd broken a fountain pen and sprayed herself a beautiful shade of aqua blue. She'd been perspiring from working at the stove, her infuriatingly straight hair pulled loosely back into a bun that had begun to fall apart.

Madhuri had been curled and perfumed and vivacious.

She'd hugged Nayna and told her she had to look after herself or she'd never find a man to marry. "You think I wake up like this?" A perfectly manicured hand indicating her va-va-voom curvy body in its fitted dress of delicate green lace. "It takes work, Ninu. I woke up at *eight* to give myself a facial and do my hair." Then she'd hopped up on a breakfast stool and begun to touch up her lipstick while asking Nayna if she minded making her a cup of coffee.

Nayna loved her sister, and she was beyond happy that Madhuri was no longer estranged from the family, but sometimes she had to fight the compulsion to strangle her. Surely the judge would rule it justifiable homicide? Or maybe she could use the insanity defense? Speaking of which...

"You must've lost your mind," she muttered, running her hands over the dress again.

It looked like she'd wrapped a wide and lightly shimmering black bandage around herself and called it done. There were even slivers of flesh visible where the bandage crisscrossed her body. Not that it covered much of the rest of her either—the so-called dress stopped high up on her thighs, leaving far more of her legs visible than she'd ever before shown in public.

She ran her hands nervously over her *not*-va-va-voom hips—which the dress managed to make look hot—and felt the heavy line of her panties. She'd already gotten rid of her bra after it proved impossible to either hide it or make it look like she was showing her bra on purpose. It helped that she had small breasts and the dress was tight.

Sad as it was, she didn't have a jiggle problem.

Angling her body, she examined her butt in the mirror. "Damn it." The panties were obvious, and they ruined the line of the dress.

She glanced at the door to her room even though she'd locked it herself. Then she bit down on her lower lip and took off the expensive scrap of nothing she'd bought specifically because it was meant to be "invisible" under clothing. "I want my thirty dollars back," she groused as she got them off over her feet.

To make sure she wouldn't lose her nerve, she threw the panties in with the dirty clothes she'd put in the little laundry basket she kept in her room; she'd chuck it all into the wash tomorrow.

Then she looked at her butt again.

The dress skimmed over her body like a lover's hand —not that Nayna would know anything about that. High school had been a washout. Nerds with flat chests didn't get much action. University had been... strange, her parents jumpy every time she left for a class, always worried she'd randomly decide to run off with a boy.

And Nayna, so fiercely determined to reunite her fragmented family that she'd focused all her energy on that. She'd succeeded in her second year as a university student, brought Madhuri back into the fold—and spent the rest of the time trying to make sure they'd never break again. Following rules listed and unspoken. Not doing anything to hurt her parents.

For a long time, that had been enough. She'd been *so* happy to have her entire family around the table at birthdays and on Diwali and during all the moments small and big that were vitally important in life. It hadn't mattered that she'd traded in her own dreams to glue her family back together. Even to the extent of agreeing to marry a man her parents would choose.

Madhuri was the scandalous one, the gorgeous flirt, Nayna her far more boring shadow. The good girl making up for the sins of the bad girl.

"Not tonight," she vowed to the mirror. "Tonight you're going to be the bad girl. And you're going to break all the rules." Nayna had plans to find some gorgeous man and do all the things she'd never done because she'd been so busy following the rules so her family wouldn't fall apart—because the cracks? They were still there.

But even prisoners got time off for good behavior.

Nayna deserved this night, and she was taking it.

Swiveling away from the mirror on that silent vow, she stuffed her feet into the comfortable professional heels she wore to work every day. Then she pulled on a coat that covered up the dress. She made sure it was buttoned up to the throat and that the lower half didn't split so high as to expose her bare thighs.

She checked herself in the mirror one final time before picking up her small evening purse—that, she could get away with—and unlocking her bedroom door. The sounds of the TV reached her the second she stepped out into the hallway of her childhood home. Her parents were watching their favorite Indian soap opera. From memory, the evil sister-in-law was currently trying to break up the hero and heroine—said heroine was, of course, all things sweet and kind and bashfully lovely.

Nayna's mother liked to relate the ongoing storyline to her.

Walking over to stand in the doorway of the living room, she waited until a dramatic statement that shocked all the characters onscreen—she now had at least half a minute while the reaction shots went on.

"I'm off," she said in Hindi. "I'll be late coming home." She crossed her toes inside her shoes. "Ísa and I are thinking of catching a midnight movie."

Her father frowned through his spectacles. "What about work?"

"Tomorrow's Sunday." Even Nayna drew the line at going in to work on a Sunday.

Grunting, her father settled back down in his prized recliner. After ten years of constant use, it was shaped to his tall and lanky form. As always, he had a half-open book on his lap. Nayna's first memory of her father was of sitting in his lap while he read to her.

"You make sure and say hello to Ísa from us," her mother said with a smile as she rose to kiss Nayna on the cheek. "Have fun."

"Where's Aji?" Nayna's grandmother was usually ensconced in an armchair by the old-fashioned hearth on the far side of the living room at this time of night. She'd read or work on her knitting while offering sharp commentary on the soap opera. She had been known to say that the meek and sweet heroine would probably turn out to be secretly more evil than the evil sister-in-law.

Nayna had a feeling her grandmother was hoping for just such a twist.

"She's making herself a cup of tea." Her mother lowered the volume of her voice. "I wish she'd let me do it."

"You know she likes to make it her way." With milk in the saucepan and plenty of cardamom and sugar. "I'll go say bye to her."

"Shilpa."

Her mother hurried back to her seat at Nayna's father's forewarning. The reaction shots were over, the drama back on. At moments like this, Nayna's heart grew tight. Her parents were such different people—her father curt and intellectual and used to getting his own way, her mother gentle and a little dreamy and kind—but then she'd see them watching this show—or catch them discussing it with utmost seriousness—and she'd see a glimmer of why their marriage had lasted.

It probably helped that Shilpa Sharma believed absolutely that the husband was the head of the household. Nayna had never seen her mother oppose her father on anything that mattered. Shilpa always bent while Gaurav got his way. Nayna had been only fourteen when nineteen-year-old Madhuri eloped with her now ex-husband, but she had no memory of her mother fighting her husband even to see her elder daughter.

Good thing Nayna wasn't planning to ask her mother's help with tonight's rebellion.

Moving from the doorway with an inward sigh of relief at having sold her cover story, she walked back down the hall to the kitchen. Her favorite person in all the world stood in front of the stove, watching a saucepan of chai as she brought it up to a boil. Beside the saucepan was a small frypan on which sizzled wide semicircles of taro, each slice about a quarter of an inch in thickness.

"Nayna, beta." A luminous smile accompanied the affectionate address.

"Aji." Walking over, Nayna hugged her grandmother's soft form. For the longest time, her grandmother had worn a white sari. For her, it hadn't been a simple acknowledgment of her widowhood but a symbol of how much she'd loved her husband and how deeply she missed him. But these days she was starting to change it up.

"I like this tracksuit," Nayna told her. A vivid pink with white stripes down the sides, it was full-on velour and sparkle. "You look like you're about to go break dancing."

Her grandmother wiggled her hips. "I can dance in the rain same as any of those Bollywood heroines. No see-through sari though. Who wants to get pneumonia?"

Laughing, Nayna hugged her again, then snuck a

fresh taro chip out of the small bowl of fried ones. "Mmm, carbs." Crispy on the outside and soft on the inside. Nayna loved salted taro chips even more than she loved fries. "Can't eat any more though—the dress I'm wearing will show every gram."

Aji patted her arm with a soft hand that had soothed many a childhood hurt in Nayna. "Go have fun at the party," she whispered, a willing conspirator. "I'll stay home and supervise your parents. You know they get very excited at their show."

Nayna bit back a grin. "I will."

The twinkle in her grandmother's eye altered, became solemn. "You're sure, beta? That you want us to find a boy for you? If you have someone already, you can tell your aji. I will make it all right."

"I don't have anyone." That was part of the problem; she'd talked herself into the arranged-marriage madness partially by pointing out that she hadn't exactly done better on her own. The constant rejection at high school when added to her inexperience at college had left her floundering out in the modern dating world.

Nayna didn't know how to flirt.

Not unless talking spreadsheets and financial forecasts was sexy.

So she, a woman addicted to historical romance novels, had convinced herself she'd be okay with a "suitable" match. Sometimes she was an idiot. But she'd made a promise and she'd keep it. Her family *needed* her to keep it. They were still so fragile, the hurts and the anger of the past a lingering cloud that had never quite dissipated.

"But," she said to her grandmother, "I think I should have some secrets to take into a marriage, don't you?"

Her grandmother's laugh was a big, warm thing. "Yes, I think so." She lifted a finger to her lips. "But go now. Don't let your parents find out. I love my son, but he was born a fifty-year-old curmudgeon."

In full agreement, Nayna snuck out. Once in her car, she drove down the block, then ditched her coat and the sensible shoes. The heels she slid on were considerably skinnier and sexier, and as for the coat, that was going to stay in the car.

She blew out a breath and put her hands on the steering wheel. "This is it, Nayna. Tonight, you be bad if it kills you." Being a virgin at twenty-eight was one thing —yes, it was unusual, but contrary to what the media might have people believe, she wasn't a unicorn. She knew that because she'd googled it in a fit of midnight desperation.

One study had shown that one in eight of her generation stayed virgins till at least twenty-six. Religion and culture were two reasons why, but shyness played a role for many. It did for Nayna. And like her anonymous brethren worldwide, she kept her mouth shut when others exclaimed over the improbability of a late-twenties virgin. As a result, the vast majority of the populace didn't believe her kind existed.

So yes, she could deal with not having lost her virginity yet.

But being a virgin who hadn't really done *anything*, that sucked.

She'd been *such* a nerd at school and university that boys hadn't seen her as anything but a source of study notes. With graduation had come professional confidence. She was fine with male clients—but that confidence didn't translate to dealing with men on a male-female level.

"Tonight it does." She squeezed the steering wheel. "Tonight you're a fearless femme fatale with no panties and a plan to be bad."

3

WARNING: COLLISION IMMINENT

RAJ WALKED INTO THE PARTY with his friend Sailor by his side. "Thanks again for the company, Sail." He liked the couple giving the party and had wanted to show up for at least a short while but had a feeling the crowd wasn't going to be his usual, so he'd asked Sailor along.

"No problem." Sailor scowled. "It's not like I had anything better to do."

"Still moping about the girl who kissed and ran?" Intriguingly, that was all Sailor had said about the woman responsible for his current mood, but she must've been something special. Because while Sailor was four years younger than Raj, the two of them having met through a social rugby team, the other man was as focused on his business as Raj was on his work.

Those rugby games and family events were about the only times the two of them took off.

"Raj!" His hosts came over.

"Tara, Geoff." He shook Geoff's hand, got a kiss on the

cheek from the statuesque brunette who was Geoff's wife. "How's the house holding up?" He'd worked on this project three years earlier.

"Brilliant! We adore it!" Tara waved her arms open wide. "You and your crew do stellar work. I've just recommended you to two friends of ours, so look out for a call from the Fabers."

Raj allowed himself a quiet smile; it was good to hear the praise after a day spent dealing with a dickhead who wanted Raj's people to do double the work on half the budget. Raj had shut that down hard, but making the dickhead see the light of day had screwed with his entire schedule. All he wanted was a beer and the TV, but he couldn't stand up Tara and Geoff.

"This is Sailor," he said. "He actually did a little work on your grounds while he was apprenticing." Raj's friend was naturally skilled with plants, but he'd needed more experience on his CV before he could pitch himself to clients. "He's got his own company now and does great landscaping if you decide you need a change outside. He's done several homes for us."

"Oh, wonderful. We've been thinking about maybe jazzing things up for next summer." Geoff shook Sailor's hand. "But no work tonight. It's a party!"

"Wait, before you go." Raj showed them an image on his phone. "I built you a replica of that small side table you wanted. I'll drop it off tomorrow." A gift had seemed appropriate since this party was both a pre-Christmas bash and an anniversary celebration.

Tara screamed. "Oh my God! It's perfect!" Another kiss on the cheek on a wave of opulent perfume before the couple dragged him and Sailor off to introduce them around.

As Raj had expected, the crowd was composed of rich people with white-collar jobs; he and Sailor stuck out like toughened steel at a platinum shindig, but they both ended up making a number of good business contacts. Unfortunately, they also attracted women who wanted "a bit of rough" for the night.

Raj had to fight to stay polite while they looked him up and down like a side of meat.

"An hour," he muttered to Sailor after they'd both grabbed a beer.

His friend tapped his bottle to Raj's, his blue eyes piercing. "Lot of women here who seem to be on the prowl. You might find one who leads you astray from the whole marriage deal."

"Yeah, I don't see it." These women saw Raj as a body, nothing more.

And Raj was after something else altogether. For a man who'd been abandoned by his biological mother at four years of age and adopted two long years later at six, family meant everything. The bonds of history and tradition, they anchored him. Where others might rail against those bonds, he embraced them. And it wasn't as if his family was arranging introductions with utterly unsuitable women.

All the women he'd met so far had been sweet and intelligent. But Raj kept saying no. He didn't just want a wife. He didn't want a woman for whom he was just an acceptable choice. He wanted a lover who saw *him* and who would become his in the deepest possible way, a lover with whom he could create a family of their own—

a family she wouldn't mind dedicating herself to loving and raising.

His younger sister called him a throwback, but Raj was open in his desire for the traditional setup, in wanting his children to have a parent around when they came home from school. His mother had been his father's right hand in the family business, but as they'd run it out of their home all through Raj's childhood, he'd had her there always.

To walk in to be hugged in welcome, it had mattered to a boy who'd been unwanted for six formative years. He wanted that same sense of security for his children. Which was why his parents had been seeking out smart but traditionally minded women for him; the last thing Raj needed was to end up with a woman who found his desire for home a regressive imposition. He'd make her miserable, and she'd do the same to him.

One thing you could say about parental matchmaking —it was honest. No setting up disparate types in the hope opposites would attract. That was for the movies and for books. In real life, it was better to lay all your cards on the table.

And Raj's cards said tradition, family, domesticity.

Other people could chase fiery passion and wild adventures. Raj was planning on stability and loyalty.

4

NAYNA & RAJ & CHAMPAGNE

THEY'D ARRIVED.

Opening her door, Nayna glanced over at Ísa—whom she'd picked up on the way to the party. Her gorgeously curvy friend looked at her, swallowed, then gave a nod, the red of her hair vibrant against the rich cream of her skin. She looked stunning, but those same curves, hair, and skin had made her life a misery as a teenager. The queen bitch of their high school had made it her mission to torment Ísa with a side helping of meanness doled out to Nayna.

"Nerd No Tits," that had been Suzanne's loving way of addressing Nayna. Nayna knew Ísa was infuriated at the fact that her chief tormentor and the major-league asshole who'd dumped her in such a cruel fashion in college were getting a happily-ever-after, but personally, Nayna saw no happiness in either one's future. Cody was a sniveling slimeball with no concept of loyalty, and Suzanne was pure, black-hearted evil.

Nayna wished them an eternally hellish life together.

Meanwhile, she and Ísa were going to paint the town red.

Together they stepped out into the balmy night air. December in Auckland was the start of true summer, with the heat building to a searing burn by February. It could still be a little chilly at night this time of year, but they were currently having a run of near-January weather.

The two of them giggled as they walked, neither one used to such thin heels. Nayna caught Ísa trying to tug down the hem of her strapless dress of sequined blue, found herself doing the same.

Ísa's shoulders shook before she hooked her arm through Nayna's. "Devil women," she said. "That's what we are tonight."

"Wild, *wild* devil women," Nayna replied. "Definitely not good girls who do what their families want." She felt a primal desperation inside her that she knew was dangerous, but she didn't care. Tonight could well be her last night of freedom. Her parents had stepped up the speed with which they were arranging introductions— the Sharmas were serious about making sure their youngest daughter settled down.

Sooner rather than later would walk in an eligible man who ticked all the right boxes and didn't alienate her parents, and then Nayna would be stuck.

"I dare you to kiss a random guy tonight," Ísa whispered wickedly. "A gorgeous, ripped guy you'd never normally approach."

"Dare accepted," Nayna said without pause, though she'd never propositioned any man, much less a gorgeous, ripped one.

Liquid courage might be the order of the day. Enough tequilas in her and maybe she'd turn into a siren, luring men to their doom in her arms. Or—more likely—she'd pass out comatose at the feet of the hunk she was attempting to kiss. New plan: she'd just pretend she was someone else and go hell-for-leather.

"Since we'll never again see each other," she said to Ísa on the topic of the poor, ripped man she was planning to accost, "who cares if he thinks I'm a crazy woman?"

A tiny frown between Ísa's brows, as if her friend had picked up on Nayna's *true* level of crazy tonight. "Just tell me if you're going to go off with someone so I don't worry."

"You do the same." Stopping by the open front door, Nayna took a deep breath. "Let's go do bad-girl things."

Ísa, at least, had gotten a start on that with her make-out session with a blue-eyed gardener. Nayna still couldn't believe her buttoned-up and often self-conscious best friend had gotten wild with a man whose name she didn't even know, but she was taking inspiration. If Ísa could jump a gorgeous guy in a school parking lot, surely Nayna could find a likely suspect at a party?

The partygoers were in great form when they stepped inside. Nayna took in the sprawling lounge that opened out into an equally sprawling deck that ran to the edge of a crystalline pool lit from within. Several people swam in it already, splashing one another playfully while in one corner of the lounge, another group danced under shimmering disco-ball lights.

Regardless of race, height, or hair color, it was as if they'd all come out of a catalog titled "Beautiful People with Beautiful Bodies."

More beautiful people mingled in the rest of the lounge.

Nayna wished she'd worn her reading glasses; she didn't need spectacles in normal life, but she could've done with another level of armor. Her face felt so bare, so open to judgment. Fighting the urge to tug at the hem of her dress again, she reminded herself she was a modern woman. Her dress was sexy.

And she had no real breasts to speak of, piped up a morose part of her brain.

"Nayna!" Tara walked toward Nayna, arms open. She was tall, brunette, and looked like a retired supermodel who might still strut the catwalk for the right designer—which was exactly what she was. A regular at international shows these days, often as a judge, Tara was one of Nayna's favorite clients at the firm—Nayna had started doing some work on Tara and Geoff's business account as a junior associate before slowly becoming their main point of contact.

After returning Tara's hug, she gave the other woman the spa package she'd picked up as a gift and received a delighted smile in response. Wealthy as she was, Tara remained cheerfully happy with life, nothing jaded or false about her. It helped that she and Geoff had been together fifteen years and their love showed no signs of waning. Just last week, they'd been snapped indulging in a very public display of affection.

Nayna looked at smart, accomplished, happily in love Tara and saw the woman she wanted to become. "This is my friend Ísa," she said, well aware that she wasn't likely to end up with a man who didn't mind a little PDA. Not that Nayna was as self-assured as Tara about such things, but it must be nice to know your husband loved you so much that he didn't care who saw him adoring you.

Tara hugged Ísa too. "I hope you two brought swim-suits," she said, her tone sinful. "Though"—she winked one lusciously made-up eye—"from the look of it, not everyone is bothering with suits."

Another woman tugged Tara away before Nayna could reply. Ísa and Nayna looked at one another, both of them grinning before they headed directly for the pool. Nayna's heart thumped at the idea of skinny-dipping, but she wasn't ready to be *that* wild. She needed time to build up to such an extreme level of craziness.

Madhuri had probably done it multiple times by now. Only... her sister didn't do things that messed up her hair or makeup, so likely Nayna could be the first Sharma daughter to skinny-dip. On the other hand, how did a woman in an arranged marriage go about skinny-dipping? From her experience so far, men who wanted an arranged marriage tended to be stuck on the stuffed-shirt end of traditional. A man like that would never be her partner-in-crime in throwing off the shackles and breaking the rules.

The only thing such men wanted was a woman who was a paragon of virtue and tradition.

The fourth ass she'd met had actually *rated* the snacks she'd made on a scale of one to ten. He'd given her a five-point-five. "Plenty of room for improvement."

That was when her grandmother had put on her "sweet old lady" face and lied her ass off, saying she'd made all the food since Nayna had been held up at the office. The would-be-bridegroom had frozen while stuffing his face. Horrified at the gaffe, his parents had hustled him away.

Five-point-five. Hah! She'd like to see him make fresh bhajias as good as hers. The only thing he'd probably get a ten out of ten in was eating. Nayna would never judge anyone's weight, but she did judge thirty-year-old men with overhanging beer guts. *Especially* when those men felt free to judge her out loud.

She was not too thin, thank you very much. She was—

Oh.

Her internal muttering came to a sudden and abrupt halt, snagging on a male who was the definition of rugged and ripped and *way* out of her league. He was taller than her by a good few inches, had bronzed skin that glowed with health, and muscles that didn't look real, they were so perfect. Not too big, not too small. Just right.

His black hair was a little messy, his jaw rough with dark scruff.

While his jeans were comfortable rather than ridiculously tight, his T-shirt fit well, hugging his pecs and biceps. The man was just *beautiful.*

"Oh my God." Nayna managed to get out a few words. "Is he even real?" Her mouth went dry; she wished she had the guts to go up to him and haul him down to her mouth for a kiss. What a memory that would be in her wrinkly-old-lady years.

"Go for it." Ísa's voice in her ear. "That's your kiss target right there."

Nayna stared at her friend, wondering when Ísa had lost her ever-loving mind.

"Wild women, remember?" Ísa said pointedly.

"Not humiliated women though." Madhuri had inherited all the sexy induce-men-to-begging genes in their family. "Have you seen the woman he's talking to?" she murmured when Ísa nudged her.

Only then did she realize she was still staring at Mr. Gorgeous.

Flushing at the idea of being caught all but drooling, she looked away and tugged at her dress. She knew it covered her butt—she'd checked in the mirror before leaving home—but she'd never worn anything this short. She kept feeling strokes of cool air where air didn't normally flow.

Jeez, she hoped she didn't accidentally flash someone. With her luck, it'd be a client.

"If he's not taken by that woman," Ísa murmured, undaunted, "and my instincts say he's not, then I think you've got a good shot." Warm encouragement in Ísa's tone, but then, Ísa had always been on Nayna's side. "He was just staring at you."

Nayna wanted to dig a hole and crawl in it. "Probably wondering what a nerd like me is doing in this den of freakily good-looking people." She grabbed her friend's arm. "Come on, let's at least go see some skinny-dipping."

Sadly, it turned out Tara's words had been premature. Everyone was still decent. "We'll be the skinny-dippers," Nayna said wildly, clenching her gut to control the butterflies yet dancing in there—that gorgeous man was not for her, and silly fantasies about him would just lead to torment. "After the lights are off and everyone's gone home."

Ísa's laugh was warm, lighting up her big, gray-green eyes. "Deal."

A waiter paused next to them, flutes of champagne on his tray and a "go on" look on his black-goateed face.

Deciding she deserved a glass of bubbles even if she was going to welch on the dare, Nayna reached for a flute. "You want one?" she asked Ísa, and when her friend nodded, she handed it over. She was about to take one for herself when her fingers collided with a big, warm hand. "Oh, I'm so sorr—"

Nayna froze.

It was him.

The beautiful man. The genuine hunk with the jaw he hadn't bothered to shave and the jeans that had a slight tear on the thigh. Not an artistic these-jeans-cost-five-hundred-dollars tear. No, the rest of his jeans were well loved but whole. It was simply that one spot that was worn away to the point that it had torn.

Why was that so sexy?

"Here." He gave her a flute of champagne with a moment of intense eye contact that had her butterflies swooning. "I'm Raj."

She shot Ísa a desperate look, but her traitorous best friend just gave her a small nod and a grin before melting back into the crowd. And that quickly, Nayna was alone with the hunk. She almost begged the waiter to stay, but he was moving off and then someone else slid past her, bumping her in the back.

Raj's arm came around her. "You won't be bumped here." Before she knew it, he'd moved her so her back was to a wall.

Dropping his hand from her back, he kept enough

distance between them that she didn't feel boxed in. Except he had wide shoulders and he'd angled his body in a way that meant she couldn't be bumped by anyone else—or easily approached.

Like a lion cutting his prey out of the herd.

5

DELICIOUSLY BAD DECISIONS IN THE MOONLIGHT

N AYNA'S THIGHS SQUEEZED TOGETHER.

She should've worn panties. Definitely. Things could get embarrassing if he kept on speaking to her and sending out those male pheromones that were playing havoc with her whimpering body. But of course he wouldn't keep on talking to her. Whatever had caused him to decide to approach her, he'd figure out soon enough that she was no sophisticated and experienced partier—even if she was faking it in this dress.

"What's your name?" His voice was like deep water cascading over her, caressing her in all sorts of impossible places.

"Nayna," she managed to get out past her bone-dry throat. "I'm an accountant." *OH GOD, NAYNA!* She winced inwardly at that silent scream from the part of her that wanted to clamber onto Raj and rub herself all over his extraordinarily gorgeous self. She might as well stamp NERD on her forehead.

That witch Suzanne had written the exact word in

permanent marker on her forehead during a school camp—an act through which Nayna and Ísa had both somehow slept. Probably because they'd been exhausted by the compulsory hiking followed by obstacle course runs that ended with a scramble up a rope fence. As if all teenagers were superheroes who chewed steel for breakfast.

But instead of backing off in distaste or confusion, Raj nodded. "Have you done that test you have to do to become chartered? That's the word, right?"

Nayna blinked at the question that sounded far too serious for a casual party conversation—but at least he wasn't running away. "Yes," she said, and it was more air than sound. "Still so new I'm shiny." She was staring at his mouth, his lower lip fuller than his upper, so she saw that mouth curve.

Just a little. As if he wasn't a man who smiled much. Which made her want to crack his shell until his grin creased his cheeks. He'd go from gorgeous to flat-out heartbreaking, of that she was sure. Maybe he didn't smile on purpose. Must be hard to continuously move swooning women out of his path.

Skin heating when she got caught staring, she looked down... and got hooked on the pecs defined by his tee. "What about you? What kind of work do you do?"

"Construction," he answered shortly but didn't move away.

Nayna swallowed and tried to channel every rom-com and Bollywood romance she'd ever watched. What would one of the heroines do now? Probably not stumble around her tongue, saying, "You build things?" *Smart, real smart, Nayna. You build things?! ARGH!*

"Yeah." A shift in his body, the fresh scent of him washing over her.

As if he'd showered before the party.

He'd probably been all sweaty and dusty from being on a work site. And she *really* should've worn panties.

A taut silence filled with the heat coming off his body.

Raj parted his lips to speak. Loud laughter burst into the void a second later.

Glancing back, he frowned darkly, then turned to her. "You want to walk out in the garden?" Rough words, nothing too smooth or polished or smarmy about him. "Little quieter."

He was asking her to go out with him into the dark, away from the safety of the crowd. Nayna didn't do things like that. Nayna also didn't pick up men at parties. Or go out in public wearing not a single piece of underwear.

Throwing back the champagne, she said, "Yes" just as she heard a distinctive ping.

Reaching into the small purse she wore on one shoulder, she pulled out her phone. "It's my friend Ísa." When she checked it, she saw that Ísa had sent her a message saying she was going off with a blue-eyed man whose picture she'd snapped.

Startled at how quickly Ísa had moved on from the hot gardener—Nayna could've sworn her best friend'd had a *serious* reaction to said gardener—Nayna nonetheless wished her luck, then added that she was with the hunk and about to let him do whatever he wanted to her. "Done," she said afterward, slipping her phone away.

Instead of being annoyed, he raised an eyebrow. "Buddy system?"

"You're a stranger."

He didn't laugh at her dorkily prim statement, his face back to full-on serious. Nayna kept thinking about what all that control must contain... and what would happen if he released the reins.

Raj locked his eyes with hers, his pupils jet black and his irises deep brown with a faint glow of gold bursting out near the pupil. "Are you going to go out into the night with this stranger?"

Bones liquid from the heat in his eyes and nipples hard points rubbed by the deep timbre of his voice, Nayna just nodded.

Raj got rid of their drink glasses, then took her hand into his bigger, rougher one and weaved through the crowd. It was like the waters parted for his big, sexy body. Nayna stayed close to the hard heat of him, her blood roaring so loudly through her ears that she couldn't hear much of the party anymore. Raj didn't take them toward the front or the back door but to a small side hallway and out through a door no one else seemed to be using.

"I helped build this place," he told her as he stepped outside. "Put in this door myself." A pat at the polished wood.

Nayna felt a sense of wonder. "You must feel such pride when you see something you constructed with your own hands."

Tugging her outside, he closed the door. "Yes," he said with a quiet self-possession that sang to everything in her. "I can point out every house I've ever worked on from back when I first became my dad's apprentice."

They stepped off the path... and her heel sank in. "Oh." She stumbled against Raj.

Who caught her with his hands around her waist. "You okay?"

"Yes, just my heels." Pressing a hand against his chest without thought, she lifted a foot up. "I'll take them off so I can walk on the grass." Heat burned her, his muscles flexing as he helped her keep her balance.

She was thinking about panties again by the time she got her heels off, hanging them both on one hand. "Thanks."

Clasping her free hand in his, he led her across the grass. "If you stand here," he said, "you can see a view over the trees and across the water."

When Nayna stopped and looked out along the line of his arm, she saw the moon rippling on the ocean, the sight so unbearably romantic that her heart clenched. She'd read romances since she was a teenager, but never had she dared believe she'd get a kiss in the moonlight from a tall, dark, and fascinatingly intense man.

Raj turned to her even as the thought passed through her mind and, releasing her hand, cupped the side of her face. Her breath caught, her heart thumped. And her lips parted. Zeroing in on that betraying act, he dipped his head and touched his lips firmly to hers. No hesitation for Raj, nothing tentative.

The man knew what he wanted—and it was her.

Nayna dropped her heels to the grass. Pressing her hands against his chest, she rose up on tiptoe. He deepened the kiss, one hand stroking down the curve of her waist to stop on her hip where he found a sliver of skin through her dress. When she shivered, he licked his tongue across the seam of her lips.

She parted them and the kiss turned wet and deep.

His stubble created rough friction against her skin and she thought, "He's marking me."

She didn't care, it felt so good.

A moan sounded and she didn't realize it had been her until he rumbled his approval, his chest vibrating against her fingers. Ready for more, for everything, she pressed in closer. Raj nudged her back, and she had a sudden stab of worry that she'd bungled it—she wasn't exactly an expert on kissing.

But he bit lightly at her lower lip as he continued to walk her back until her butt gently hit a wall. Cornering her again. And oh, it felt *good*. His body was so hot and hard against her own, and he was so overwhelmingly big and strong. As for his mouth—serious, intense Raj knew exactly how to use his mouth to make her embarrassingly wet.

When he ran his hand up her body to close over her breast, she didn't protest.

But he stopped, his hand in her hair, and said, "You with me, Nayna?"

Endorphins flooded her system at the sound of her name on his lips. Licking her lips, she nodded. "Yes. Please don't stop."

Dark eyes flashing, he pressed his mouth to hers once more, the bristles on his jaw scraping at her skin all over again and sending prickles of sensation all through her. More strokes of her body, his hands assured and holding a raw heat. His palms snagged at times on the fabric of her dress, his calluses hard from physical labor. All Nayna could think of each time it happened was what those hardworking and gifted hands would feel like on her naked skin.

She ran her own palms down his chest and up over his arms. Smooth skin and firm muscle, there was nothing about Raj's body she didn't like. And his scent... Nayna wanted to nuzzle and just breathe in, kiss his throat, lick him into her own bloodstream.

Hot breaths, hearts beating faster, bodies pressed closer.

Raj tugged down the wonderfully stretchy fabric of her dress. Her breasts popped out. She would've been mortified that he was seeing the pitiful mounds except that Raj had one hand over her left breast while he'd dropped his mouth to her right one. She whimpered at the first touch, biting back a cry of disappointment when he drew back.

"You're short without the heels," he muttered and scooped her up like she weighed nothing.

Nayna's inner core clenched while her hands gripped at his shoulders. Never in her life had she dreamed she'd be with a man this strong.

Wrapping her legs around his waist was instinctive, his body heavy and solid between her quivering thighs as he pinned her to the wall in a dark corner of a moon-kissed garden. The position pushed up her dress indecently farther, until she was a mere inch or two away from total exposure.

A burst of shyness threatened to strangle her.

"That's better," Raj said roughly before she could surrender to the emotion, and then, one hand spread on her lower back, arched her toward him. He licked her nipple once, paused.

Whimpering, Nayna fisted her hands in his hair and tugged.

He gave her what she wanted, sucking her nipple and part of her breast into his mouth. He scraped his teeth over her flesh. Nayna's head fell back, her breathing ragged. She'd imagined what it might be like, but this... "Raj."

Releasing her breast, he came to her mouth. One hand still on her back, he fisted the other in the straight strands of her hair, gripping it tight. His chest crushed hers as he kissed her deep and demanding, her nipples rubbing against his T-shirt. That he was fully clothed while her dress was crumpled around her waist just amplified the wetness between her thighs.

Nayna kissed him back without finesse, driven by need.

He moved the hand on her back past her hip and to her thigh. Cupping her thigh from below, he stroked her skin as he kissed her like she'd always wanted to be kissed.

"You taste so good," she blurted out when they came up for air, and wanted to wince at her lack of sophistication.

But Raj kissed her again, as if in reward for her confession. His bristly jaw continued to be rough against her skin, his hand even tighter in her hair. The small tugs sent pulses right to her clit, the tiny bundle of nerves aching for his touch.

Though if he did go there, Nayna wasn't sure she'd survive it.

The next time Raj broke the kiss, he moved his hand back up to her breast, squeezing and petting it while he held her gaze. "I like how tight and firm you are," he murmured. "Like biting into a just-ripe peach."

Her skin flushed, her throat dry.

"What do you want?" A rough rumble of a question as he ran the pad of his thumb over her engorged nipple.

Her toes curled, her breath catching. "Take off your T-shirt."

He rubbed the pad of his thumb over her nipple again. It was a jolt through her entire system each and every time. Eyes hooded, he watched himself touch her, distracted from her request by the visual eroticism.

So Nayna, bad girl to the core tonight, pulled at his T-shirt.

He got the hint, kissing her hard one more time before he reached down to tear off the T-shirt and drop it to the grass—while keeping her exactly where she was using the pressure of his body. Then she was skin-to-skin with him and he was kissing her throat while making rumbling sounds in his chest, and Nayna decided this was it. *He* was it.

The man to whom she'd give her virginity.

Never, *never* had she thought she'd find a man who made her forget to be self-conscious and just enjoy herself. Yet here she was, half-naked and with no panties and she was ready to keep going as long as he kept touching her.

It felt like she'd been thirsty all this time and he was the rain.

Nibbling his way up her throat, he used his grip on her hair to angle her head to claim another kiss. Nayna wasn't about to resist. For Raj, she was easy. When he stopped and nipped lightly at her lower lip, she opened her eyes to find his looking into hers.

Her breath caught, her gaze his prisoner.

6

REASON #1 WHY ALL NAYNAS SHOULD
INVEST IN RUNNING SHOES

B RACING ONE HAND AGAINST THE wall beside her head, Raj squeezed her breast as if he had every right to fondle her.

Nayna shivered, unable to look away from the penetrating darkness of his eyes. He was the one who looked down... to focus on his hand on her breast. Teeth sinking into her lower lip, she followed his gaze and her thighs clenched around him.

His hand was marked by multiple nicks and scars, his nails cut bluntly. Veins stood out on the back of his hand and along his arm, and she had never seen anything sexier than Raj's hand on her breast. She watched, barely able to breathe, as he rotated the pad of his thumb over her suddenly excruciatingly sensitive nipple.

She dug her nails into his shoulder.

Lashes rising, he leaned in closer and said, "Do you like rock climbing?"

Dazed and aroused, Nayna had to decode the roughly spoken words one by one. "I've never been rock climbing." It was surreal having this conversation while he was fondling her breast and she was petting his chest like it was her most favorite thing on the planet. "You must be good at it. You're so strong."

"Climbing's not just about strength, it's about strategy too." Serious words followed by a line of suckling kisses down her throat, complete with a light graze of teeth. "Like this," he said after kissing his way back to her mouth. "To please you properly will take time. I'll have to learn what you like. You don't build a house on faulty foundations."

Nayna was caught by the blazing intelligence in his eyes as he spoke. She'd known from their first minute together that he was no vacuous hunk; there were too many layers to him, his unsmiling shell hard and armored and fascinating beyond compare. This was not a man you could get to know in a single night, or even in a single year.

Raj was a mystery a woman would only solve if he decided to let her.

Nayna wanted him to let her.

A second after that thought passed through her mind, she mentally shook it away in panicked desperation. If Raj was smart as well as gorgeous and sexy, she might not be able to walk away, and she *had* to walk away. Her parents were looking for a "suitable" boy for her. So far, that had meant two other accountants, one lawyer, one high school teacher, and one financial advisor. Clean-cut. Besuited. Strictly white collar.

Construction workers need not apply.

Frantic to stop him talking because with each word he spoke, he became ever more attractive, she kissed him.

Desperate and needy and wanting him to be hers for this one night.

But Raj was like a force of nature. He took the kiss, stroked his hand back down her body to grip her under one thigh, and said, "Do you like Egypt?"

"What?" Nayna couldn't think when he had his hand that close to her naked core—a couple more inches and he'd discover her lack of panties. "Egypt?"

He began to move one finger in a stroking movement so close to the crease of her thigh that she held her breath, waiting for him to discover that she was his for the taking. But he stopped. When she opened her eyes, she was caught once again by the dark intensity of his.

"The art gallery has an exhibition on Egyptian art," he said, serious and intent even though his cheekbones were flushed with color and his pulse hammered in his neck.

Nayna realized she had her hands in his hair. "Kiss me," she said, because it was all she could say that wouldn't break the dream.

Pushing back with both hands braced on the wall on either side of her head, he said, "Answer first." No give in his voice, nothing but a quiet resolve that was like a hurricane.

Nayna loved everything about Egypt. She wanted to visit the pyramids one day, was fascinated by the hiero-glyphics and the architecture, had even done a history minor at university just so she could take the classes on Egypt. And *none* of that mattered because her path was set—and it didn't involve Raj.

Leaning in, *she* kissed him again. Nayna might not be a femme fatale, and Raj might be a stubborn rock of a man, but Nayna was good at picking up new things. She'd learned how Raj liked to kiss and now used that new knowledge ruthlessly to distract him. Of course by then his fingers were playing along the crease between her thigh and the heat between her legs and her head was buzzing.

No one had told her sex could be this stressful. If he didn't touch her there soon, she was going to start begging.

But Raj broke the kiss to say, "Is that a yes on Egypt?"

On the razor edge of need and desperation, Nayna snapped. "Be quiet!" She couldn't take him wanting her enough to ask her out; this fantasy night was supposed to be a treasure to look back on over the cold, practical years to come. It wasn't supposed to break her heart by showing her a man who made her body sing and intrigued her mind and who *liked* her. "I just want your body! Nothing else!"

Sudden winter between them, Raj's face going glacial.

If she'd thought he was difficult to read before, it now became impossible.

Nayna wanted to crawl into the dirt. *What had she just said?* Throat dry, she went to try to say something, anything, else when Raj set her down gently on her feet. Then he turned away, put his hands on his hips, and took long, harsh breaths. She could see those breaths but not hear them, the music from the party spilling out to flood the garden.

His shoulders were rigid, the muscles of his arms tightly clenched.

Someone pushed open another set of doors at that instant, and the flood of music turned into a deluge.

Face burning and ice in the air, Nayna fixed her dress with shaking hands, then searched desperately for her shoes and purse. *There.* The purse was right where he'd pinned her up, and there were the shoes. Out of Raj's line of sight.

She grabbed them, then made her getaway, her feet silent over the lush grass.

Where had she parked the car?

For a moment she couldn't remember, and panic beat at her throat like a trapped creature. Then her eyes snagged on her cherished lime-green MINI Cooper. Face flushing to scalding, then to freezing, she hotfooted it down the drive to get in. She slinked down into her seat the instant she was inside. Raj was unlikely to come after her, but she wasn't about to risk it.

Only when she was certain the coast was clear did she turn on the engine and carefully reposition the car for a quick escape. *Oh no, was that Raj?* She slinked back down in her seat, relieved she'd turned off the engine and the lights only moments before. Barely able to see from her position, she nonetheless quickly realized the man walking to a nearby Mercedes wasn't Raj. Her shoulders slumped. He'd probably gone back to the party.

Where he certainly wouldn't have trouble finding a woman to lick his wounds.

Great, now she could torture herself with that lovely image.

Her face was stinging hot when her phone pinged with a message from Ísa: *Where are you?*

In the car, hiding, Nayna admitted.

The last thing she expected was for Ísa to slam into

the passenger seat only minutes later and say, "Drive!" She sounded as desperate as Nayna felt.

Not hesitating, Nayna started up the car and zoomed out. "Oh thank God," she said once out on the road.

Ísa spoke the same words at the exact same time.

7

NAYNA'S SECRET DIARY (PASSWORD: L3TTH3CR4Z3OUT)

THINGS THAT HAPPENED TONIGHT:

1. No panties.
2. Ísa went skinny-dipping with the hot gardener (aka Sailor). Only, he has AWFUL taste in friends. He was there the night Cody the Slimeball publicly dumped Ísa, and Ísa is totally confused and disoriented. She's making up conspiracy theories that it's all a way to humiliate her again, but really she's afraid of trusting her instincts. I wish I could kick Slimeball's ass for making her doubt herself.
3. Dad was waiting up for me. Good thing I fixed my hair and makeup at Ísa's apartment. People at work can't understand how I still live at home, but this is my reality. All my cousins

still live at home too. Moving out is "a waste of money," as said by every Indian parent ever—and why would you want to move out unless you were "up to something"? Only Madhuri gets a pass. I'm considering marrying the donkey just so I can divorce him and gain my freedom.

4. Raj. Raj happened.

8

NO SEX THINGS

NAYNA BARELY SLEPT THAT NIGHT, tormented by dreams of an angry man with intense brown eyes who'd left stubble burn on her throat and whose hand she could still feel on her breast.

Gritty-eyed, she handled Sunday—and Madhuri chirping on about the "cute blue sofa" she'd just bought for her apartment.

She had a slight breakdown on Monday night. Thankfully, Ísa was on hand with ice cream and stories of the Slimeball's face getting punched. Even better, said punching had been done by the hot gardener.

"At least one of us might have a chance at a happily-ever-after," Nayna muttered to her spreadsheet on Tuesday afternoon.

Unfortunately for her, that spreadsheet was simple. She still had enough work to take her through to Friday and the mandatory two weeks of Christmas vacation, but none of that work was complex. It left her with far too much time to think... and to remember. How Raj's hands had felt on her body, how his mouth had tasted, how she'd wanted to rub herself all over him.

She jumped when her mobile phone rang. Seeing it was her grandmother, she picked up at once. "Aji, hello."

"Nayna, beta," her grandmother said, her voice upbeat. "Is this leopard cologne popular with men these days?"

Leopard cologne?

"Do you know the name of it?"

"It's the one on television with the oiled men spraying themselves and the big black cats and the girls clawing the men like she-cats."

Nayna's cheeks heated at the memory of how she'd clawed Raj. If he'd left her with stubble burn, she'd left him with a few marks of her own. She wondered if he'd thought about her, winced immediately. If he did, it would be to freeze her to the spot with an icy glare. Raj hadn't struck her as the forgiving type.

"Oh, I know the cologne you mean," she said to her grandmother. "But if you're thinking of buying a gift for Dad, he doesn't use that one."

"It's not for him," her grandmother said airily.

Nayna blinked. "*Aji?*"

"I just think Mr. Hohepa's a nice man," her grandmother answered, coy and nonchalant.

Nayna's mouth fell open. Mr. Hohepa was their new neighbor, having moved in only six months earlier. He and his dog, Pixie, had become firm friends with Aji. The two elders often went for walks together, Pixie bounding between them.

Mr. Hohepa, however, was at least eight years her grandmother's junior.

Nayna narrowed her eyes as she realized her grand-mother had started getting the velour tracksuits around then too—with the excuse that her sari wasn't convenient for walking. "How good of a *friend* is Mr. Hohepa," she asked suspiciously; if that Lothario was leading her grandmother along...

A very un-aji-like giggle. "We don't do the sex things, beta," her grandmother said, turning Nayna's ears red. "But I'm not dead and he's a fit young man. I'm going to buy him the leopard cologne."

Nayna sat staring at her phone a long time after her grandmother hung up. "Aji has a boyfriend." She wrote it down on her notepad, stared at it, wrote it again, and still couldn't get it to settle in her brain.

"Nayna?" One of her more senior colleagues stuck his head inside. "I'm doing a coffee run," Douglas said. "You want your usual?"

"I think my seventy-five-year-old grandmother has a boytoy boyfriend."

"Well, dayum! Good on your grandma!"

Yes, Nayna thought after her workmate had left, good on Aji. She'd loved Nayna's grandfather, of that Nayna had not a single doubt, but she'd also been widowed for ten long years. She deserved fun and joy and romance.

How about you, Nayna?

The voice came from deep inside her, and it was of the fourteen-year-old who hadn't been allowed to go to dances, or to wear makeup, or to be anything less than perfect. That fourteen-year-old looked at her grand-mother, living life more joyously and wickedly than she ever had, and it could be that was the straw that broke the camel's back.

47

Or it could be it was the most recent evidence of Madhuri's carefree life that pushed her over the edge. Highly likely it also involved the reason for her semi-breakdown last night: realizing on Monday morning as her father laughed at something her sister had said that Madhuri would always be his favorite. It didn't matter what Nayna did—she'd never be good enough, perfect enough. Her family would be fine if Nayna was no longer around; it was Nayna who had to be ready to suffer the repudiation.

Then there was Raj.

The idea of allowing a shadowy "suitable match" to put his hands and mouth on her as Raj had done, it made her shudder. "No more introductions, no more trying to impress assholes and idiots," she said in a strangely calm tone.

Nayna was done.

SHE HAD THE WORDS TO her bombshell decision all worked out by the time she left the converted villa that functioned as their offices that night. An urgent client request had come in, and Nayna had volunteered to handle it just to give herself a couple more hours to build up to the confrontation. It was as she was packing up that her father called and asked her to be home by eight thirty for a surprise.

"I'm almost done," she told him and was about to ask about the surprise when he hung up.

Most likely they had an unexpected guest from Fiji. Many of their extended family still called the tiny island nation home, and while her parents had left it more than three decades earlier, they remained deeply connected to people there. Nayna had last visited two years ago, when she'd taken Aji over for a catch-up with her younger sister.

The two older women had laughed and told her stories deep into the humid tropical night as they sat on a porch screened against the mosquitos. Nayna had seen small fruit bats take off from the breadfruit trees during the dark orange of sunset, heard the sounds of the frogs croaking their courtship songs, and felt her skin settle into the easy rhythm of life in a rural town far from Fiji's cosmopolitan resorts and hotels.

That night she'd been in charge of keeping up the supply of tea and snacks, those snacks mostly consisting of mango slices cut before the fruit was fully ripe, then rubbed with a little fresh chili pepper before being sprinkled with salt. It was rare to find unripe mangos in New Zealand, since the fruit didn't grow here, but the rare times she did, the taste immediately brought back the memory of that hazy, lazy night.

Smiling, she wondered if Aji would like to go in the new year sometime. Her grandmother had decided not to accompany Nayna's parents on their upcoming trip, saying "husbands and wives should have time alone." Everyone had scratched their heads over that, as Aji usually chose to stay with her sister while Gaurav and Shilpa went around on their own, doing as they pleased, but Aji had been adamant.

"Old age," Nayna's mother had whispered to Nayna. "It happens to all of us."

Yeah, right. Nayna had a feeling her grandmother's odd decision had far more to do with being free from watchful eyes while she carried on with Mr. Hohepa. "I can't believe my *grandmother* has a more scandalous love life than I do," she muttered as she left the office, but her lips curved.

She'd cyberstalked Mr. Hohepa after her grandmother's call, and it appeared he was exactly who he said: a widower who had four children and three grandchildren. Still, Nayna was going to keep a close eye on the situation, just in case Mr. Hohepa was a gray-haired Don Juan with a woman in every neighborhood.

The light mood fostered by thoughts of her grandmother's romance was long gone by the time she arrived home. She'd practiced how she'd tell her parents of her decision to pull out of the marriage deal over and over again in the car, the words a heavy rock in her gut. If the surprise wasn't a guest, she was going to tell them straightaway.

The longer she waited, the worse it would be.

No unknown car sat in the drive, and she saw no shoes on the front stoop that she didn't recognize. No guest then. Walking in, she girded herself to jump right into the flames.

Her mother pounced on her before she was two feet inside; Shilpa Sharma's face was flustered and happy. "There's a boy coming, beta!" she blurted out before Nayna could speak. "He works late too, so we and his parents made the arrangements for a quarter to nine. Hurry, hurry, change quickly and freshen up!"

Plans shattered in an instant, Nayna walked into her bedroom and just stared at the wall for a minute before full panic screamed into her mind and she grabbed her phone and a paper bag, then went to hide in the bathroom to call Ísa. What the hell was she going to do? She breathed into the paper bag while desperately hoping her best friend would pick up her phone.

She did—and was calm in the face of Nayna's hyperventilating panic. "Just do the same thing you did with the other five. Tell your folks you have nothing in common with him and can't see a marriage working out."

"The other five were asses." Nayna breathed into the paper bag again. "My family didn't like them either. What if this guy isn't an ass and my parents and grandmother love him?" It would be just her freaking luck that guy number six was the charm, a suitable boy with no flaws. "What if I'm trapped in a marriage I don't want?"

"Look," Ísa said firmly. "This is *your* life. Your family can't force you to the altar."

Nayna put down the paper bag, her heart squeezing. "I love them, Ísa." It was as much a truth as her stick-straight black hair and dark brown skin. "No matter what, I love them. I can't be like Madhuri and risk being cut off." And their relationship wasn't a simple equation where she didn't feel loved in return.

Six months ago, her mother had spent three days hunched over with needle and thread, repairing Nayna's favorite salwar kameez—a long tunic paired with thin pants cut close to her legs. An unfortunate incident featuring a badly maintained fence and darkness had left the tunic part of the outfit with a gigantic tear in an awkward spot—and destroyed the beaded pattern. Unexpectedly, her father had turned up with a handful of tiny, shimmering beads to match the ones lost in the darkness. He'd asked a colleague who did crafts for the name of her bead supplier, then personally gone and found matching beads.

Just like two years earlier he'd found a replacement for the fountain pen that had broken.

Her parents might have their blind spots, and they were driven too much by the pain of the past—pain not caused by Nayna—but she could never doubt that they loved her.

As for Aji, her love was a flame that would never go out. Madhuri had hurt their grandmother so much; Nayna had never seen her so wounded. She hadn't understood why her cherished granddaughter hadn't confided in her—and yet, despite that, Aji had sent money to Madhuri to help her out. A teenaged Nayna had helped her fill in the forms for the money transfer. Aji would've probably even gone to see Madhuri if Nayna's sister hadn't eloped all the way to Perth, Australia.

Nayna's parents would've never let her go, and Aji didn't like to fly alone.

Thankfully, Ísa understood what it was to love family even when they drove you to the edge of madness. She loved her mother even though multimillionaire CEO Jacqueline Rain—aka the Dragon—was the least maternal person Nayna had ever met. "How about if..." A small pause before Ísa's voice brightened. "Say that during your private talk, you discovered that he's a little dim in the brain department."

Nayna's eyes widened.

"Knowing your folks, he's likely to have a degree or two, so maybe also hint that perhaps all isn't kosher there," Ísa suggested with a deviousness that would've delighted the Dragon. "Or that you got the impression he barely scraped by."

"Oh God, you're a genius, Ísa!" Scrunching up the bag, Nayna lifted the fist of victory. "My parents are already planning for grandchildren with doctorates—a less-than-intelligent son-in-law will *not* do."

And no, she didn't feel guilty besmirching a random stranger's intelligence. Not when she'd be saving them both from the horror of wriggling out of an arrangement that had no chance in hell of success.

This was war.

TEN MINUTES LATER, SHE RUBBED her damp palms over her pale pink tunic top. The color, which reminded her of the lotion her mother had slathered on her when she had chickenpox as a child, did awful things for her dark complexion. That was why she'd specially dug out the salwar kameez from the back of the closet where she'd shoved it after a relative gave it to her as a gift.

Her mother, usually keen for her girls to treasure any gifts, had taken one look at the salwar kameez and sniffed. "You'd think she didn't like you. Probably she's just used to her fair daughters. Not my beautiful Nayna who shines in jewel colors and looks like a queen in gold."

God, she loved her mother.

Shilpa Sharma bustled in right then, all beaming smiles... until she set eyes on Nayna. A muted shriek. "Why are you wearing that ugly thing?" Shilpa threw up her hands before running over to fix the long pink dupatta Nayna had slung carelessly around her neck;

usually she'd have pleated and neatly pinned the gauzy scarf over one shoulder.

No way to remove her makeup without letting on that she wasn't making an effort on purpose, but she'd "forgotten" to wear any jewelry and her hair was in a bedraggled bun. She'd also thrust on the black-framed reading glasses she used at home.

"Ugh! Why aren't you showing your pretty hair?" Her mother unraveled her bun before Nayna could stop her and quickly brushed the strands down to the middle of her back, then nudged her out the bedroom door. "Take off your glasses."

"No, I feel better with them on."

Giving up, her mother said, "It's too late to change. Don't keep him waiting."

Nayna resisted. "Him?" Usually the two families met first, the male sitting in and the girl coming out with tea and snacks at a certain moment. A few minutes of privacy would be offered the couple later on if the initial meeting went well.

A dance with which Nayna was intimately familiar.

Today's snacks included seinas her mother must've fried. Her mother and grandmother made and steamed the rolls every so often, then froze them so they were easy to pull out, slice, and fry for unexpected social events. Ísa called the savory the "spicy Swiss roll" because it looked so much like the cake except that it was created of taro leaves and a specific lentil paste mixed with spices. Every time Nayna took a batch into work, they were gone within the hour.

Her mother had also magicked up slices of vanilla cake from a neighborhood shop. If Nayna was lucky, she'd be rejected out of hand for not making every morsel.

A girl could hope.

"Yes," her mother said, breaking into her thoughts. "Your father's given permission for you two to talk alone for a few minutes right at the start." A delighted smile as she fussed with the dupatta again. "Gaurav's very impressed with this young man—he's running a big family business, and so well that his parents retired early and spend half the year in Fiji! And he's only twenty-seven!"

"He's younger than me?"

"Only by less than six months." She pushed again. "Go, go."

This was worse than she'd believed. Her parents *liked* him. Enough to drop the supervision requirement. And he clearly wasn't stupid if he was running a business, so Ísa's wonderfully devious plan wasn't going to work. It was up to Nayna. She'd have to pull every trick in the book to nip this in the bud. Maybe she'd pick her nose during tea and snacks time.

Buoyed by the idea, she made her way to the kitchen, then stepped through the doorway between kitchen and lounge. He was standing with his back to her, staring out the large front window. And he was big. Tall. *Wide* shoulders. Heavily—*beautifully*—muscled under the simple white shirt and black pants.

He had a body like Raj. And his cologne... it was so deliciously familiar.

Nayna's throat dried up, her heart hammering.

9

WELCOME TO THE NIGHTMARE OF AWKWARDNESS

FOR A MOMENT NAYNA'S HEAD spun. But this wasn't Raj. White collar was strictly nonnegotiable with her parents. And this man ran a business, wasn't a construction worker who used his hands to create magic out of nothing.

"Um, hi," she said awkwardly while continuing to plan how to horrify him. If her parents liked him, she'd have to get him to do the rejecting. It would be tricky to pull off her actions without being spotted by her parents, but she was patient—she'd wait until the elders were engaged in conversation, then put her mind to making the guy run.

"This is difficult, but I don't want to mislead you," he said without turning around. "My parents set up this meet last minute before I could tell them I was pulling out of having an arranged marriage because—"

Horror curdled her stomach as his voice, deep and a little rough, sank in... and that was when he turned around. Frozen silence, the air molecules glittering ice.

"I thought your name was Nayna?" It came out a growl, Raj's big body held with taut control.

"Middle name. Everyone uses it." Her parents must've introduced her using her official first name: Heera. Why they did that, she had no idea—they always ended up explaining that they only ever referred to her as Nayna because Heera was her aji's name and they didn't think it was respectful to use it when Aji might think they were calling her by name.

Raj just stared at her, a nerve jumping in his clean-shaven jaw and his shoulders bunched under the crisp lines of his shirt.

Nayna opened her mouth to explain—though she didn't know what she'd say—when there was a perfunctory knock on the main door into the lounge and her father walked in. "Family time now," he said with a smile. "You two can have plenty of time to talk later."

He'd never smiled at any of the others!

Oh *God*.

Raj's parents walked in behind Nayna's father, with her own mother coming in from the kitchen with Aji.

Nayna somehow managed to keep it together through the introductions before squeaking out something about getting the tea and scuttling back to the kitchen. Where she dug out the paper bag she'd thrown in the recycling basket and tried to relearn how to breathe.

RAJ KEPT HIS FACE CIVIL and pleasant through sheer force of will, while inside, his emotions rocketed from one extreme to another. He'd walked into the room determined to be honest and ensure he didn't create an unintended victim to his decision to not meet anyone until he'd tracked down the temptress who'd left him high and dry on Saturday night.

He'd known she was all wrong for him the instant she'd told him she was a chartered accountant. A woman that qualified wouldn't want to be a homemaker, wouldn't want to be the kind of wife Raj had always envisioned having. But he hadn't been able to pull away from her and the sweet passion of her kiss, the way she'd touched him as if he was her favorite treat in all the world.

He didn't know her, but he'd wanted to—there'd been a spark of *something* between them that niggled at him. Pulling the plug on his parents' search to find him a wife hadn't even been a question after that point. He'd been determined to find his infuriating mystery woman and... Raj hadn't known *what* he was going to do to Nayna, but he'd known he had to answer the question of whether his reaction to her had been nothing but lust... or more. He was too honest to lead on other women while obsessed with one who'd only wanted him for his body.

Fate sure had a warped sense of humor.

His gut clenched... and his cock threatened to twitch. *Fuck.* He might remain furious with Nayna, but he wanted her as badly as he had that night. A single look at her, a single whisper of her scent reaching him across the room, and he had to fight the urge to haul her into his arms and slam his mouth down over hers.

"Yes, I enjoy my work," he said, having somehow managed to keep track of the conversation though his eyes wanted to lock onto the door through which his sneaky little rabbit had disappeared. "I grew up learning to build with Dad, and I've never wanted to do anything else."

Mr. Sharma, who'd apparently become friendly with Raj's father after running into him at a regional soccer game, smiled. "It's a big responsibility to run such a large company. Your parents are justifiably proud of you."

Raj was well aware his status as the company boss was the only reason he was considered an acceptable match for their accountant daughter. He wasn't insulted. That was the way things were—parents tried to match up their kids on multiple levels, including their work. When a cousin of his, a dentist, had gone the arranged-marriage route, his introductions had been mostly to nurses, pharmacists, other dentists, and scientists. Funnily enough, it had been the rogue pick—a lawyer—who'd stolen his heart.

The two were sickeningly happy together. Their happiness was another reason Raj had decided to let his parents have a shot at setting him up with women. But he'd been very open with them from the start—he'd marry the woman he chose and that was nonnegotiable. Raj had no intention of ending up unwanted and unloved ever again. Of course, his folks seemed to have gone totally off script with this introduction.

Not that Raj was complaining: they'd done him a favor. Otherwise, he'd planned to ask Tara about the sexy woman in the skintight dress who'd been a guest at her party. The woman who'd caused him more than one sleepless night and probably a few layers of tooth enamel from the way he gritted his teeth every time he thought about her last words to him at the party.

"Oh, he was running things when he was barely

twenty-three," his father said jovially with a slap to his knee. "Got the business brain." A tap to his temple. "My side of the family."

Raj's heart ached. Never once had Jitesh Sen made him feel any less his son for being adopted. If Raj's father had his way, the subject would never come up, but Raj had run across families to whom it *did* matter that he didn't know his bloodline, or birth date and time, and never would.

Those people believed in matching horoscopes, and Raj's birthdate was approximate. The doctors had estimated him to be four when he was left at the orphanage. Old enough to remember he'd been half-starved and not wanted even a little bit. Old enough to remember the kicks and the cold and the disdain. The last thing he'd accept was to be introduced to a woman who looked down her nose at him and his family.

Which was why he'd made his parents promise that before they went to any introductory meetings, they'd mention his adoption. He would not have his family hurt by someone with an antiquated sense of custom and ritual.

"This family cares only that you're a good son, and of course about your achievements," his father had crowed in the car on the way over. "None of this horoscope-schoroscope nonsense."

"The girl does have a good job," his mother had thrown in. "But the parents are so lovely, and you never know, it could work like it did with your father and me. Working together on the business."

Raj, caught off guard and only coming along to the meeting so his parents wouldn't lose face, had barely been paying attention at the time. He continued to have trouble with his ability to be present. Where the hell was Nayna?

"And he looks after his little sister so well," his mother was saying now, both parents in full boasting mode. "Especially the times when we go to stay in Fiji. Our younger son, Navin, and his wife are there too, but Raj is the head of the family while we're away and the one they all come to."

Navin and his wife could try Raj's nerves, but his younger sister, Aditi, didn't need much looking after—she was seventeen and clever as a cat. But she was also the baby of the family and knew Raj would lay down his life to protect her. As a result, she didn't try to run rings around him. Though he was beginning to worry about the text messages she'd been getting recently that caused her to look a little guilty.

The kitchen door finally swung open, Nayna walking through with a tea tray, her head demurely lowered. Raj scowled while everyone was distracted looking at her. What was she playing at? Yes, she *was* a little shy—she'd been honestly flustered at the party, especially when he teased her—but she'd also had a quiet confidence that was a glow pulling him into her orbit. No way was she the demure, lowered-head type.

And what in all that was holy was she wearing? The pink monstrosity was a muumuu on her sweet little body. The only thing he liked about her look were the black-framed glasses perched on her nose. He could see her wearing those and nothing else.

He shifted on the couch, telling his mind to end that line of thinking. *Now.*

"Nayna, beta." Her grandmother, dressed in a soft white sari, smiled at Nayna as she set down the tray, before the plump elderly lady turned to Raj's family. "My granddaughter makes the best tea," she said in pure Hindi, untainted by slang.

Raj's own paternal grandparents spoke the same way. They were currently in Taupo, visiting with his uncle's family, or they'd have quizzed him about tonight's meeting the instant he got home. Set in their beliefs, his aji and aja still scowled at the idea that the younger son had married before the older and couldn't wait for him to get hitched so that things would be back in balance.

"Our daughter is a good girl," Gaurav Sharma added. "Dedicated to her studies at university, graduated top of her class. And look at her now—she deals with small businesses valued up to a quarter of a million dollars."

The devil took Raj. "These days a lot of young women like going to parties and spending wild nights out," he said solemnly, a worried possible groom. "Is—"

"Oh, our Nayna's not like that," her mother said with a laugh. "She never even went to parties at university."

Her father nodded. "She prefers to spend her free time at home."

"*Oh*," Raj said in a tone that sounded casual enough but that had Nayna's hand tightening on the teapot she'd just picked up.

He didn't know why he'd done it, why he was playing along with this charade that they'd never met. Raj preferred to be blunt and honest in his interactions whenever possible. But that night with Nayna... that was a secret shared between the two of them. Raj found he didn't want to speak about it to anyone but her.

Now, as he watched and waited for a response from this woman who made him act in unfamiliar ways, she poured her grandmother the first cup of chai, exactly as she should. Then she turned to his parents and asked if they'd like sugar. By the time she angled her head toward him, he, a man renowned in his family for his calm under pressure, had to fight not to growl at her.

This modest and meek mouse of a woman was not the siren who'd kissed him so passionately—or who'd told him to shut up because she only wanted his body. That woman who was all wrong for him might've infuriated him, but she'd had a fire inside her, and that fire had warmed the cold places inside him.

"One sugar or two?" she asked in a demure murmur, complete with a shy smile.

Disappointment settled like a rock in his gut. Perhaps this was the real Nayna and the wild, blushing, delicious Nayna who'd scorched and angered him at the party had been nothing but a mirage—a game she'd indulged in for the night. "One," he said, his desire to play a subtle game with her chilled into silence. Just as well. Even as a child, Raj had never been good at play.

His mother had often called him her solemn little man.

Gaurav Sharma asked him a question about the family construction business at that moment, and he became involved in answering it, only turning to take the cup when Nayna said, "Your tea" in that annoying, meek voice that threatened to destroy his memories of the passion he'd found with her.

No woman had ever ignited such fire in him. He'd thought he'd carry the coldness inside him forever. Then had come Nayna. Only that Nayna had never truly existed. She'd disappeared at midnight, taking the warmth with her.

"Thank you." Muscles rigid from the effort it took to sit here and act normal when he wanted the whole thing over with as fast as possible, he took an absentminded sip of tea... and barely saved himself from splurting it out onto Nayna's father's face.

Covering the moment with a cough after managing to swallow the vile stuff, he forced himself to stay put. Not to pick up Nayna and spank her for pouring what felt like half a bag of sugar into his cup. Which he now had to drink or he'd mortally insult her family.

Witch.

And not meek and mild at all.

10

PEACHES AND SCRUFF AND COLD SHOWERS

NAYNA WOKE THE NEXT MORNING with a fuzzy head and no idea what she was going to do.

The previous night, after Raj and his family left, her parents had turned to her, asked her what she thought. It had been obvious exactly how much they —and her grandmother—liked Raj. Both their families had also gotten along like a house on fire. The meeting had raced to over an hour, only wrapping up because the next day was a workday.

She should've said no right then and there no matter how hard it would've been to disappoint them, but the words of rejection had stuck in her throat—because she didn't want to refuse the man who'd made her feel as he had on Saturday night. Even in her confusion about the future she dreamed of for herself, it had felt deeply wrong to do that.

As it was, she'd mumbled something about needing time to think, and her parents had nodded and smiled.

Her grandmother had patted her affectionately on the back of the hand. Everyone probably thought she was overwhelmed—and they were right.

Unfortunately, it wasn't in the way they expected.

Her hormones had danced like crazy around Raj, just as they had at the party. Her fingers had itched to tear off his shirt. And her thighs had squeezed at the thought of being wrapped around him while her mouth watered at the thought of his kiss.

Physical attraction was *not* a problem.

"Argh!" She buried her face in a pillow and reminded herself that it was highly unlikely she'd have to do anything at all. Not only was he furious with her, but physically speaking, Raj was out of her league. The man was flat-out beautiful and she hadn't had the advantage of moonlight last night.

Shoving aside the pillow on that less-than-cheerful thought, she wrenched off the sheets and gathered her towel and everything else she needed for the shower before stumbling out and down the hall to the bathroom she shared with her grandmother. It was bright white and clean and felt blinding to her gritty eyes.

Squinting against the burn, she put her stuff on top of the closed laundry basket, stripped, then stepped under a scalding-hot spray in a vain attempt to wash away the dreams that had tormented her all night long. Of a certain gorgeous, serious man whom she much preferred with a bit of scruff on his jaw rather than clean-shaven as he'd been last night.

Her body shivered in secret, unfamiliar places at the memory of how Raj's stubble had scraped against her when they kissed. He had hair on his chest too. Crisp and silken at the same time. Not too much. Just enough to tantalize a woman into rubbing up against him.

Her clit pulsed.

"You're heading into cold-shower territory," she moaned at herself. "You *hate* cold showers." But even that warning didn't stop her from fantasizing, and she was flushed under the rich darkness of her skin when she stepped out of the shower.

As she rubbed the towel over her skin, she couldn't help but remember how Raj had stroked it, making it patent that he liked it a whole lot. Her nipples pebbled, standing out impudently on the taut mounds of her breasts. He'd liked those too. Tight and firm, he'd called them. Like just-ripe peaches.

Nayna shivered and slathered on the body cream she loved, let it sink in. The rest of her morning routine was fairly quick, and she was soon back in her room, ready to dress for work. Something made her reach deep into her closet to pull out a skirt suit she'd never before worn. She'd bought it on sale because the deep crimson of it looked glorious against her skin—and the fit was flawless off the rack, which never happened with her boyish hips and small breasts.

However, it had always seemed too out-there for an accountant. Today it felt like armor. Because one thing was certain: at some point during the day she'd get a call or a text from her parents saying that Raj had turned her down. Her stomach clenched even though that was what she wanted—for him to be the bad guy. She could then bounce off the rejection—and the sympathy it would engender—to broach the subject of her own change of mind when it came to the plan her parents had for her life.

"Rejection's a normal part of the process," she reminded herself. Even if it would come from the only man she'd ever truly wanted. In some ways the arranged-marriage mart, as she and Ísa had termed it, was far more honest than dating. No sparing feelings, no trying to be kind and accidentally stringing people along. One set of parents would simply tell the other that it wasn't the right match and on it went.

Some people got bent out of shape about it, but Nayna liked the idea of knowing where she stood. And it wasn't as if she'd always been the first one to say no. Three times, the jackasses who'd come to meet her had sent her parents a message before they'd even pulled out of the drive.

"Good riddance," her father had muttered each time and deleted the number from his phone.

Pulling on a fitted white shirt that she tucked into the skirt, she shrugged into the jacket and buttoned it up. It fit as sweetly as it had in the shop, skimming the lines of her body and making her feel sexy even though the pencil skirt was a perfectly respectable length.

"At least I have a butt." She patted the only really curvy part of her, which the skirt gently emphasized.

She decided to accessorize the suit with a pair of small gold earrings that her grandmother had given her when she turned eighteen. Of a rich yellow twenty-two-karat gold, the floral design was distinctively Indian, and it spoke to the part of her nature that had grown up watching Bollywood movies with her mother and going to the temple with her grandmother.

Her hair she brushed and pinned into a neat roll at the back of her neck. Makeup took only five minutes—she had the morning routine down pat. Popping her lipstick in her purse to put on in the car after she'd had breakfast, she slipped on low-heeled work pumps in black patent leather, picked up her work satchel and purse, and walked into the kitchen.

To her surprise, her mother was bustling at the kitchen counter, in the process of making roti, the simple flatbread that it was usually Nayna's job to make. Nayna stuck to cereal or toast in the mornings, but her father and grandmother liked a vegetarian Indian meal. Her mother usually made the vegetable dish while Nayna did the roti.

"Ma." She put her satchel and purse down out of the way. "I was just about to do that." She normally did it before she got dressed, but she was perfectly capable of handling the task by throwing on an apron over her suit.

"Oh, it's fine. You work so hard, beta." Her mother kissed her on the cheek when she neared. "I like the red."

Nayna ran her hands down the front of her jacket. "Not too much for the office?"

"Why not?" Her mother's eyes twinkled. "Today's a special day. That Raj was lovely, wasn't he? So manly and tall—and so dedicated to his family and the business. He's a man who knows how to commit to things, will make a good husband."

A rush of love filled Nayna's heart. Hugging her mother from behind, she said, "He's far too good-looking for me. You know that." Whatever he'd seen in her at the party had been a thing of moonlight and madness; Madhuri was the stunning one in her family, Nayna her plainer shadow.

Her mother's face turned mutinous. "You're my beautiful, smart, funny girl, and he'd be lucky to have you."

Moving to pour herself a cup of unsweetened chai, Nayna smiled. "Unfortunately, not everyone sees me through my mother's eyes."

Shilpa Sharma snorted. "Well, if he doesn't see your beauty, then he doesn't deserve you." With a sniff, she went back to rolling out the roti. "Though I think you're wrong. He couldn't take his eyes off you."

Nayna wondered if she should tell her mother that his eyes had been glaring as he forced himself to drink the overly sugared tea she'd served him in retaliation for his subtle needling. "Well, just text me when you hear from his family."

Her father walked into the kitchen then, and he was smiling too. But he didn't bring up the topic. Nayna knew the reprieve was only temporary. If Raj's family, for some reason, didn't contact her family, then her parents would contact his. No one liked to leave things hanging when there were other possible matches out there who'd appreciate their offspring (as spoken by countless parents, disdainful sniff and all).

Forget about internet dating. All this traditional meet and greet and reject stuff was brutal. At least Raj's parents were lovely and wouldn't be like asshole number 4's parents, who'd told her parents their son hadn't found her "pretty at all" and wanted a more "womanly looking and beautiful" bride.

It wasn't like he'd been a prize himself, the Napoleon-sized mouth-breather.

Her mother was the one who'd taken the call from Number 4's mother. Her response to the nasty rejection had been: "In that case, he should go to the doll shop they show on late-night TV. He won't have much luck anywhere else."

Nayna had almost choked—and then she'd gotten up and hugged her mother. Because the "doll shop" ad that had somehow been given clearance to advertise on late-night local television was about a boutique sex-doll website. Nayna's mother was a very polite and gentle woman, so her fiery response had showcased just how much she'd despised the pompous ass and his parents.

The polar opposite of her reaction to Raj.

Putting down her tea when her stomach twisted again, Nayna said, "Say good morning to Aji for me when she gets back from her stroll. I think I'll go to the office early. I'm hoping to open up some time so I can take Ísa to brunch for her birthday tomorrow." If Ísa's divorced parents held true to form, they'd forget their daughter's birthday.

"Eat some cereal or toast before you go," her mother ordered. "Or at least take one of those bar things you like —I went to the shop and bought a new box for you yesterday. Raj is a big strong man. He won't want a wife who can't keep up with him."

Groaning inwardly at the continued hope in her mother's eyes—echoed by the slight smile on her father's face—Nayna grabbed an apricot-flavored breakfast bar. She was about to escape to the sanctuary of her car when her mother called out, "I'll make a cake for Ísa, one of those small, flourless chocolate ones she likes. You two can share it over brunch."

"Do you want a fancy box for it?" her father grumbled from behind his morning newspaper. "I'll pick one up from John's shop when I go to the office to get some papers."

Love overwhelmed Nayna all over again. "Thank you," she said, her throat thick. "I'm sure Ísa would love that."

Her mind was a whirl of confusion. She did not want to break their hearts. Madhuri had hurt them *so* much—first by running away with her boyfriend, then by staying out of touch for a long six months while they were all frantic. Part of Nayna would never forgive her sister for that selfishness. Their parents had even called the police, they'd been so frightened something had happened to her.

The police had told them that Madhuri was an adult who'd left of her own free will. There was nothing they could do. Nayna could still remember the deep grooves of strain and worry that had marked her father's face, the extreme thinness of her mother. And Aji, who'd prayed night and day for her granddaughter's safety.

No, Nayna couldn't bear for them to be hurt that deeply ever again. She'd lived the life she had, made the choices she had, because of those memories of terrible pain. But more and more, she felt like she couldn't breathe, as if her entire life was a cage. The only freedom she'd found had been that moonlit night in Raj's arms.

She squeezed the steering wheel and thought of the passion and of the man who'd asked her if she liked rock climbing and Egypt. Maybe that could've been something, but she'd wrecked it with words spoken in panic. The chance was gone.

"It was only a fantasy," she reminded herself softly. "For one night only."

11

UH-OH... AND UH-OH AGAIN

NAYNA WAS GRATEFUL FOR THE work she had to clear if she wanted to take part of the morning off tomorrow. It kept her mind from wandering, and one particular project was so absorbing that she jumped when her cell phone vibrated with an incoming text message.

Taking a quick glance to make sure it wasn't a client with an urgent request, she felt her heart kick.

We should go to lunch and have a proper talk. No point trying to make a decision about the rest of our lives based on two short meetings. That is, if you're interested in my brain now. – Raj

Mouth dry and her blood roaring in her ears, Nayna stared at the phone for a long minute before carefully putting it aside and returning to work. She did *not* have the head space to deal with this. Also, how had he gotten her cell phone number anyway? Her parents? Tara?

When Ísa called not long afterward, Nayna spilled all. She also found herself telling her best friend that she was going to accept the lunch offer, though in truth, she wasn't sure. She had no idea what Raj was up to, no idea what she wanted, and no idea what this would cost her.

Putting her head down, she continued to work, well aware she was avoiding the issue.

The shrill ring of her desk phone not long after ten interrupted her in the middle of a complex piece of work factoring in exchange rates and payments made across two continents. She should've already finished this, but she kept glancing at her cell phone, her head tangled up in a chaos of thoughts.

She picked up the receiver while frowning at a spreadsheet laid out across her wide screen. "Nayna Sharma," she said even as her brain attempted to reconcile two figures. The client's bookkeeping staff must've—

"Hello, Nayna."

Her brain froze, her hand clenching on the receiver. That voice... Dark water cascading over her senses. A husky roughness in her ear. A pointed *oh* at the mention of parties and Nayna being a good girl.

Raj didn't balk at her silence. "How many teaspoons of sugar was it?"

"Seven," she said, finding her voice. "Why are you messaging and calling me? It's protocol for the families to touch base." She didn't actually know if that was true, but it sounded right.

"Don't you want to know?" A rumbling question that sounded serious. "Whether we could be something?"

Nayna's hand curled on her desk, the temptation fierce. In her mind rang the advice she'd given her best friend just last night, right at the end of their conversation, while Nayna was hyperventilating in the bathroom.

I've played it safe my whole life, and now I feel like I'm going to shatter if I don't spread my wings. Take a chance. Make that mistake. Even if it hurts... At least you'll have lived instead of being driven by fear.

Strong words. True words. But could she take a chance this big?

"I told my parents no more introductions," Raj said when she remained silent, his voice holding the dark intensity she'd noticed from their first meeting. "I also told them no interference."

Her cell phone buzzed with an incoming text message. It was from her mother:

Raj's parents called. It's very strange, beta, but they said Raj will talk to you himself. It's not how this is done, but I suppose he's more modern. I think maybe he wants to talk properly to you—I told your father it's the way things are now. Okay, tell us when he calls.

Nayna read the hope between the lines, and her heart hitched again. But she knew she couldn't let her parents influence any decision she made. It was her time to live, her time to stretch her wings and fly out of the cage.

A sudden rush of sound from the other end of the phone line, including a voice calling Raj's name. "I have to go. Site manager needs to talk to me. What's your answer?"

It was strange, but his brusque bluntness made her relax. This man wouldn't play games with her. If he broke her heart into a million pieces, it wouldn't be done in malice. With her and Raj, all the cards would always be on the table... and maybe, just maybe, she shouldn't cut off her nose to spite her face.

After all, she'd chosen him first, before her parents and his got involved in the matter. "I'll meet you at one," she said, her heart a pounding drumbeat.

RAJ HAD INTENDED TO CHANGE his T-shirt at least before he arrived to meet Nayna, but an entire wall had threatened to go wrong at the site when an apprentice used the wrong size nail, and he'd spent precious time fixing the error so his builders could complete another part of the job without delay. As a result, he arrived at the nice little café in sophisticated Mount Eden, sweaty and with dust on his T-shirt and jeans. He didn't notice his work boots were edged with dirt until he stepped out of his utility truck.

He *had* washed his face and hands and arms, but he definitely wasn't in any state to be meeting the sexy and beautiful woman who was crossing the road to the café just as he walked up from another direction. She wasn't wearing her glasses, had her hair up. Her skirt suit was stoplight red and hugged her body in all the right places —and he wasn't the only male who had noticed.

He scowled at the blond man nearby who'd pursed his lips in a silent whistle. The guy shrugged sheepishly. "She's hot, man. I can't help my eyes."

That too was true. Nayna wasn't obvious in her sensuality, but it was there, a simmering ember below the surface that made a man want to unlock her, find out how her sleek body would move in bed, over him, under him.

Her beauty was the same—not blatant and in your face, but quiet, lovely, changeable with her moods. He had the feeling he could look forever at her and be fascinated each and every time.

She hadn't spotted him yet, her focus on avoiding being tripped up by a middle-aged lady with three dogs on leashes. Her lips, painted red to match her suit, curved as the tiny dogs attempted to bounce toward her rather than following their owner's commands.

His body hardened. Those lips. Nayna had the most lush lips. "Try anything and I'll break you in half," he all but growled at the blond when the man looked like he was weighing up his chances.

The other man took a good look at Raj and threw up his hands before backing off. "Like I said, hot. You're a lucky guy."

Having successfully bypassed the hyperactive menaces on four legs, Nayna finished crossing the road and looked toward the café. Her smile faded when she spotted him waiting for her, to be replaced by a look he couldn't read. It was only when she reached him that he remembered the height difference between them—and thought immediately of the dreams he'd had that involved lifting her up and wrapping her legs around his waist while he pressed her to a wall.

She'd be the perfect height then. Especially if she was naked.

Not that she was apt to be thinking of getting close to him at the present time. "Sorry about the gear," he said with a wave at the state of his clothing. "I probably stink of sweat so we should sit outside."

"You smell fine." She tugged up the strap of her small

purse. "But we can sit outside if you like. The sunshine's not too much yet."

He watched her mouth as she spoke even though it was a very bad idea. Nayna had a mouth that did things to him without even trying, made him want to act in ways primal and raw that he'd never previously considered.

Raj was a healthy male in his prime, but he'd never had trouble controlling his sexuality. He'd always had very little sympathy for men brought low by their urges. Well, the joke was on him, because Nayna Sharma could bring him to his knees with her mouth alone... and he wasn't sure he liked that. No woman should have that much power over a man.

It made the man far too vulnerable.

"You hungry?" he asked gruffly.

They didn't have a chance to really speak again until they were sitting down with their meals—both of them had chosen sandwiches, though hers was considerably smaller than his.

"Will that be enough?" Nayna frowned. "Don't tell me that's all you eat doing such a physical job?"

Raj felt warmth stab at him, and it unsettled him all over again how quickly she was getting under his skin. Nayna was even more dangerous to him than he'd believed.

"I EAT ABOUT EVERY TWO hours when I'm physically on a site." Raj's face was unsmiling and hard to read, his words almost curt. "I have to spend one day per week in the office to take care of business matters, but I like working on builds much better."

Nayna nodded. "It'd be a waste of incredible skill if you didn't." She'd looked up their company website, seen the jobs on which he'd been listed as the head builder; as she'd experienced herself, Raj was gifted with his hands.

Her skin tingled, and she had to force herself back from falling victim to her physical reaction to him. Wearing a dusty T-shirt and with tumbled hair, his jaw scruffy again, Raj was bone-meltingly gorgeous; it took exquisite control not to crawl across the table and kiss him with slow, deep intensity. "I thought you'd decided against an arranged match?" she said, her voice husky.

He held her gaze with the penetrating darkness of his. "I didn't think it was fair to meet other women when I was haunted by a woman in a skintight dress who only wanted me for my body."

Cheeks hot, Nayna deliberately took a giant bite of her sandwich. Raj didn't fill the taut silence with words—he was, she thought, a man comfortable with silences. Finally swallowing the bite and taking a sip of water to wash it down, she decided he deserved the truth. "You were meant to be my wild fling before I settled down into marriage with a stranger."

A raised eyebrow followed by the faintest hint of a smile. "I wouldn't have thought I'd qualify as a wild fling."

Now that she knew him, she understood why: he was too intense, took things dead seriously, and oh that was far more intriguing than a brainless hunk. "Trust me," she whispered, "you qualified for me."

Their eyes locked again, the air still.

Hand closing into a fist on the table, Raj said, "I want to marry you."

The stark words reverberated inside Nayna's skull, leaving her without a response.

"I can't get you out of my head," he added, not sounding exactly happy about that. "Marriage would let us explore our physical connection without boundaries."

Nayna frowned. "Such romance."

A grim look in return. "We're adults, Nayna. Romance is for children," he said in a tone that was as hard as stone. "And you're unlikely to get a better offer. Your sister's affair with a postgrad student before she ran off with another man is well known in the community."

Nayna's ears burned. The affair with a married man wasn't something any of them ever talked about, but it lay at the root of all the anguish Madhuri had caused her family. At the time, that master's student had been a member of the local Indian community too. As had been his wife and toddler son.

It was the wife who'd turned up at the Sharma residence, sobbing her heart out after discovering evidence of the affair on her husband's phone. Madhuri, a new university student at the time, when confronted about the affair, had yelled that she was in love.

"My sister was eighteen and a half. He was twenty-four. He should've known better." Madhuri wasn't innocent, had been old enough to make the right decision, but Nayna refused to allow the world to cast her in the role of villainess.

"Agreed," Raj said unexpectedly. "*He* was the married one, the one who cheated. But you know how the world works—everyone blames your sister, and that's a stain against your family name." His tone remained hard, unbending. "You're not going to get many marriage offers.

It's not fair, but people assume you'll be as fickle and disloyal as her."

Nayna's hand clenched around her water glass, her vision red. "Are you offering to marry me despite that stain?"

"Yes. We have excellent chemistry, and the rest we can work out."

It was a struggle not to throw the water in his face, but Nayna wasn't about to make a scene. Not for him. "Thank you for your oh-so-kind offer to save me from the curse of singledom," she said very precisely, "but given that you've just insulted my entire family, implied that I'm so undesirable I won't be able to find a man who wants me despite the 'stain' on my family name, *and* acted with the emotional IQ of a block of wood, I'd rather die a shriveled-up old virgin than let you anywhere near me."

NAYNA'S SECRET DIARY (ANGRY RED-INK DAY)

THINGS THAT HAPPENED TODAY:

1. I found out Raj is an <u>ASS</u>.
2. I came home at nine thirty so no one could grill me about that stupid lunch. I should've thrown the water in his face, scene or no scene.
3. Madhuri got two more offers of marriage. "Stain" on our family name, my posterior.
4. My body still gets wet thinking about him. My body is an idiot.
5. Oh fuck! I just realized I told Raj I was a virgin. Great. Just great.

SOMEONE IS GETTING NAKED
(OOOOOOOH)

NAYNA WAS STILL FUMING WHEN she met Ísa for brunch on Friday morning, but she didn't want to put a damper on her friend's birthday so kept the topic of Raj off the table. When Ísa brought him up, she just said, "He's an idiot and I'm not ready to talk about it."

"You sound like you want to bite his head off," Ísa commented.

Nayna growled under her breath. "No comment. Is Catie all right?" Ísa's younger sister had ended up in the hospital earlier this week.

"She bounces back like a rabbit," Ísa said proudly. "Tough as nails, that's my Catie." She ate a bite of the cake Nayna's mother had made. "Since the topic of the hunk is off the table, how about you give me the scoop on that wedding you mentioned."

"It's going to be a big, fat, OTT Indian shindig," Nayna told her best friend, delighted to have an utterly innocuous topic on which to focus. "You know Pinky? You met her at that festival we went to."

"Gold girl?"

"Yes, that's her." Pinky Mehra never left home without layers of gold and diamonds. "They hired a white horse for the groom to ride in on. And there's a tabla band direct from India." She drummed against the table using the flat of her hands. "Oh, and the bride's wedding suit features thousands of hand-sewn crystals—store-bought 'just wouldn't do.' Makeup artist flown in from Los Angeles because 'no one in New Zealand understands the latest trends.'"

"At least her parents won't be bankrupted by her demands."

"True." The Mehras were filthy rich, and Pinky was their only daughter. "They seem fully on board. If she wants a full-sized aquarium at her reception, she'll get it." Nayna was actually enjoying the over-the-top madness. "They did draw the line at the tiger she wanted."

Ísa spread her hands apart. "Doesn't everyone have a tiger at their wedding?"

Laughing, Nayna ate more of the cake before saying, "And the hot gardener? How's that going?"

Ísa's cheeks went bright red.

Mouth falling open, Nayna pointed the cake fork at her friend. "You got naked with him, didn't you?" she said, a little envious. "And it wasn't for skinny-dipping this time."

"Shh!" Ísa looked around them before leaning in, her voice lowered and her face glowing. "It was wonderful. We had an indoor picnic."

Nayna sighed. "That is so incredibly romantic." A fact Raj would never understand. "So you two are serious?"

Ísa bit down hard on her lower lip. "He's amazing, Nayna. Loves his family, is dedicated to his friends, has so much passion for his work."

Not many people would've heard what Ísa didn't say, but Nayna had known Ísa since they were thirteen. There was a reason Nayna's mother knew that Ísa liked this cake and a reason her father had made the effort to make sure it was boxed up nicely—and a reason her grandmother had added the gift of a gold bangle from her private collection, which would otherwise pass on only to her granddaughters.

Ísa had celebrated more birthdays with Nayna's family than she had her own parents.

"Are you worried he won't have time for you?" she asked, gentle with her friend who had spent far too much of her childhood alone. The birth of her sister, Catie, when Ísa had been fifteen, had assuaged some of her loneliness for family, but Ísa had always been the adult in that relationship.

No one in Ísa's family looked after her; Ísa was the one who took care of everyone else.

Turning her lips inward, Ísa nodded. "The project he has coming up, it's critical to the future of his business and it's going to consume him." The bangle glimmered on her wrist when she lifted her hand to push back her hair. "But it won't just be one project—he has too much drive to stop there. And the thing is, I like his drive, I admire his passion. I just…"

"I know." Nayna closed her hand over the one Ísa had on the table. "You shouldn't ever have to be second best,

Ísa." It was a fierce statement. "Sailor would be privileged to be loved by you." Ísa Rain loved her people without limits, would do anything for them.

Ísa's smile was a touch shaky. "I adore being with him. I'm not ready to make a decision yet."

All Nayna could do was tell her friend she was there for her if she needed to vent. The final decision on her relationship would have to be Ísa's. As for Nayna, she'd made her decision already, and tonight she'd share it with her parents. It would be hard because she wasn't going to share what Raj had said—she would *not* do that to her parents—but she'd make it clear he wasn't the kind of son-in-law they'd want.

Then she'd tell them she was done.

Yep, it was going to be a stellar day for Nayna Sharma.

AS HER BRUNCH WITH Ísa had gone a little long, Nayna was still in the office at six. Her last colleague had left at around five thirty, locking the front door behind him for security, and she planned to finish up and be out of there by seven. She wanted to speak to her family over dinner.

When the doorbell rang, she wasn't startled. With it being summer, it was still sunny outside, and more than likely a courier driver was trying his luck by attempting to deliver a package. The local drivers all knew Nayna and one of her other colleagues often worked late and would be around to sign for things.

Rising, she made her way to the front door. She looked through the peephole out of habit, her hand already on the door handle... and froze. It wasn't a courier driver outside, shifting impatiently on his feet as he waited for a response. No, this man was bigger, and he stood absolutely still.

She should've turned around and walked away, but she wanted to know what the hell Raj thought he had to say to her. Wrenching open the door, she folded her arms. "Did you forget an insult?"

No expression on his face. "I wanted to ask if you'd read this." He held out what looked to be a couple of sheets of paper folded over.

"What? Am I living Lizzy Bennet's life?" She kept her arms folded. "I highly doubt you have anything to say that I want to hear."

Raj frowned. "I don't know who that is, and I can't force you to read anything. All I can do is ask." Then he put the pages on the small white table they had on the porch of the villa. Surrounded by three chairs made of the same wide slats of wood, it was occasionally used for meetings with clients in the summer.

Nayna didn't move as Raj turned and walked down the three steps to the parking lot level. He'd parked his black utility truck beside her MINI, the big bruiser of a vehicle currently sporting a ladder on the roof. In back was a pallet of tiles tied down by ropes. She could also see toolboxes through the back windows.

The display of rugged manliness might've melted her on the spot if she hadn't been so angry with him.

He backed out and around before pulling out into the traffic on the wide road that fronted the villa that had been converted into offices for their boutique firm. Nayna still didn't move. Not until a gust of wind threatened to lift the pages off the table. She grabbed them before they could be stolen away, the action instinctive. Her raging curiosity wouldn't allow her to just leave it.

That and the hollow in the pit of her stomach filled with a deep sense of loss.

Stepping back with the pages in hand, she locked the door behind her, then walked into the little kitchen in the villa and poured herself a fresh cup of coffee from the carafe she'd put on earlier. Only once she was fortified with caffeine did she walk back into her office and take a seat at her desk.

"If you insult me again, I'll hunt you down," she muttered, unfolding the two sheets.

It was handwritten, Raj's scrawl generous and taking up far more room than it should.

Dear Nayna,

I was a complete bastard at lunch. I can't go back in time and fix that. What I can do is tell you why I acted the way I did. I'm not great at words—English was never my favorite subject at school. So I'll stick to the facts.

I'm not sure if your parents told you, but I was adopted at six years of age from an orphanage in India. I was abandoned there at four years of age. I knew I was unwanted, but I didn't know how unwanted until I was twenty-one and the orphanage had to turn over my records when I requested them.

I didn't want to find my birth parents. I have clear memories of being kicked and left alone in dark rooms. I knew they weren't people who loved me. But I wanted to have a sense of my history.

Usually the records are pretty bad. Mine was too, but someone had saved the letter with which I'd been left. It was written in Hindi, and since I never learned the written format, I had to translate it piece by piece using the internet.

It said: Boy was from my first husband. First husband was a drunk and he's dead. I have a new husband now, and I'm going to have a new baby. I don't want my first husband's ugly-faced son and my new husband doesn't either. Boy will probably end up like his father—no good to any woman and not even able to feed his own family. Will probably live on the hard work of some unlucky woman. I don't care what you do with him.

I hope you'll keep that to yourself. I haven't even told my parents, and I never will. It would cause them a lot of hurt.

Nayna's tears rolled down her face, her heart breaking for the solemn twenty-one-year-old boy who'd gone looking for his history and found only rejection, but she forced herself to read on.

I'm not telling you this as an excuse—what I did was inexcusable—but so you'll understand what it does to me to be around a woman who could have a great deal of power over me. I don't, as you might guess, deal well with rejection when it's people who matter. And I think if I let you in and you rejected me, you could break me.

It makes me afraid down to the core—and because of that, I acted like a complete bastard to you. I was trying to find a way to be the one in control so you wouldn't have that power. I'm sorry for what I said, and I'm sorry I made you feel anything but beautiful. You are the sexiest, most fascinating woman I have ever met.

Raj

Nayna stared at the closing paragraphs, reading them again and again and again. Her hand trembled as she raised it to thrust her fingers through her hair, unraveling it in the process. What was she going to do? Because in his unadorned words, she'd read the thing he *hadn't* written: that he might be incapable of ever truly letting any woman in... letting Nayna in.

If she took a chance on him, she did it knowing that he might keep a part of himself forever separate. Such a relationship would destroy her. Because Nayna didn't love halfway. And Raj... he'd angered and hurt her because he already mattered. If they went further, this wasn't a man she could keep at arm's length.

He could break her too.

TEN O'CLOCK AT NIGHT AND Nayna sat in her bedroom, staring at the letter as she'd been doing for what felt like hours. The truth was, she'd had to go out for a couple of hours to attend a ceremony in the lead-up to Pinky Mehra's wedding, but mentally she'd been here the entire time.

She needed to talk to Raj. Picking up her phone, she

sent him a message: *Meet me in the small park a few minutes down from our house.*

He replied within seconds: *I'll meet you by your house. Don't walk down to the park alone.*

Since the perfectly lovely family park could appear creepy at night, Nayna agreed. *Leave your car down the road.* If her parents spotted him, the shit would hit the fan.

I'll message you when I'm there.

Nayna took the time to get out of her pj's and into jeans and a T-shirt. Then she tiptoed through the house, Raj's letter in hand. Her parents had turned in, but Aji busted her in the kitchen.

"Are you going out?" she whispered from the stove where she was heating up some milk in the saucepan.

"Just to talk to Raj about something. He's waiting outside."

Her grandmother frowned. "Be careful, beta. I think he's a good boy, but... I don't want you to be hurt like Madhuri."

That was another thing they didn't talk about; how Madhuri's husband had abandoned her for another woman after two years while Madhuri was scraping by in a minimum-wage job. If Aji hadn't sent through enough money for airfare, Madhuri would've been stuck on the far side of Australia with no way home.

"I'll be okay, Aji." Nayna hugged her grandmother's comforting form, the velour of Aji's yellow tracksuit still not as soft as her grandmother's skin. "I know you'll always have my back."

She kissed her grandmother on the cheek... and

caught a whiff of masculine aftershave. "Were you with Mr. Hohepa?" she asked on a gasp.

Her grandmother's eyes twinkled. "We took a walk through our gardens. He's growing zucchinis the size of watermelons!" She waved a hand. "Shoo. Go have a walk with your young man. Every girl should have some romance."

Romance is for children.

Nayna didn't think Raj had been acting the bastard there—that was what he actually believed. While she had a stash of romance novels that kept growing. But she didn't say anything to her grandmother and went out the back door. Unlike the front door, it didn't squeak or make other betraying sounds. Probably the reason why her grandmother used it to sneak out with Mr. Hohepa after everyone else was in their rooms.

Raj was waiting for her at the end of their drive, his body obscured by a tree until she was close to him. He stirred before she reached him, an intimidatingly large male silhouetted against the night. Nayna wasn't afraid—not physically anyway. Raj didn't strike her as the kind of man who'd ever hurt a woman.

When they'd been together, he'd been rough but in a sexy way. Never hurting her even though he was so much stronger. His hands had been careful on her skin, on her breasts, and she thought if they'd gone all the way, he'd have taken care entering her.

Her skin prickled, her thighs clenching.

14

SUBURBAN PARKS ARE A HOTBED
OF SIN

D ESPITE HER VISCERAL AND IMMEDIATE reaction to Raj—would it always be like this, a conflagration?—Nayna managed to keep it together until they were in the privacy of the park. Since this was a suburban area filled with families, there was no one else there tonight, the children's play equipment their only companions.

"Here." She thrust out the letter toward him.

His hand came up instinctively to take it, the look he shot her hard in a way she was starting to realize didn't mean anger. "You didn't read it."

"Of course I read it," Nayna said. "I'm a woman, not a paragon of self-control." She folded her arms. "I just thought you should have it so you never have to worry that it might fall into someone else's hands." He'd shared an intensely private truth with her, and Nayna would never speak about it, but she wanted him to have this insurance as well.

Folding the pages, Raj put them in the back pocket of

his jeans. "Will it help if I apologize again? I was an ass. I'm sorry."

Nayna puffed out a breath. "Apology accepted."

Raj had opened a vein for her when he was a man who fiercely guarded himself and his privacy. It had crumbled her anger to the earth, left her floundering. And as far as apologies went, she liked his blunt way of accepting that he'd fucked up and needed to apologize.

He stared at her for long minutes, as if trying to read the meaning beneath her equally frank words. "So, where does this leave us?" he asked, his muscles still tense and his gaze making her want to shiver for all the right reasons.

Turning on her heel before she surrendered to the raw physical pull between them, Nayna went to sit down in a swing. It was meant for older kids, so her feet didn't drag too much.

Raj followed, coming to stand behind her. "Lift your feet."

When she did, he pulled back the swing and let go. Nayna whooshed through the summer night air, her hair flying back from her face and a smile creasing her cheeks. Raj pushed her when she reached him again and she flew a second time, then a third and a fourth, her smile turning into a grin of delight. "I haven't done that in forever," she said to him afterward, her legs a little wobbly as she got up. "It was fun."

Unsmiling, Raj cupped her cheek, and for the first time since she'd known him, his actions were tentative. When she didn't pull away, he ran the pad of his thumb over her cheekbone and stepped closer until her breasts pressed up against his chest. She hadn't put on a bra under her navy T-shirt, and her nipples felt like tiny bullets sizzling against the heat of him.

The kiss was slow, deep, demanding, one of Raj's hands in her hair, the other one plastered flat to her back to press her against him. The thick ridge of his erection pushed into her abdomen, causing inner muscles to spasm in need. A whimpering sound escaped her, her hands sliding up his chest to link around his neck as she rose on tiptoe in an attempt to get closer.

Raj's chest rumbled... and a car went past on the road, the beams of its headlights momentarily flashing past them. Jerking, Nayna put at least a foot of distance between them.

"We can't do this." It wasn't fair to Raj. "Not when I'm not even sure I want to be married anymore."

Lines forming on his forehead. "What's changed?"

Nayna told him the unpalatable truth. "I realized that my life isn't mine. I'm allowing everyone else to drive it." It was about damn time she took control. "And as for us..."

Uneasiness bloomed in her stomach at the memory of his letter, of her understanding of his wariness against the kind of love and trust she'd need to have in a man to walk into marriage. "I don't want to end up living the same life for decades to come. I don't want to end up resentful toward my husband. I have dreams that don't involve living in a suburban house and raising babies. At least not yet."

Hands on his hips, Raj watched her with those eyes, so serious and intent. "Will you trust me with your dreams?"

Lips twisting, Nayna spoke quietly. "They're nothing

extraordinary. Things millions of people do every day. Travel, adventure, being free to make my own choices." She pushed her fingers through her hair. "You know how my parents said I didn't go to parties as a student?" Her breath came faster now, her chest heaving. "It wasn't a choice. I haven't had a lot of choice since I was fourteen and Madhuri ran away. Now... sometimes I feel as if I can't breathe."

RAJ DIDN'T STAGGER UNDER THE weight of Nayna's words. He'd braced himself for the worst, and though what she'd said wasn't good, she'd kissed him back as passionately as she had at the party. So he hadn't fucked up to the point that she found him repulsive now.

Relief a cold rain in his blood, he said, "Meeting and kissing a man in a park after dark, does that count as adventure?" He needed direction here; Raj was used to laying straight lines and using a level to get it exactly right. But clearly Nayna wanted to go off-plan.

She looked intrigued at his question. "It's definitely not a good-girl thing to do."

"Then how about you give me—*us*—a chance to figure this out?" Raj was a builder, a fixer, and already his mind was trying to work out ways to fix this so that Nayna saw a future in them. "Don't end us before we begin."

"*Raj.*" Her teeth sank into her lower lip, causing his body to harden all over again.

He moved closer because she reacted to his body, and he'd use every advantage he had to fight for her. Whatever this was between them, this thing that had scared him with its potential power, it wasn't a thing that came around every day. "I don't want to be kissing any other woman. Do you want to be kissing another man?" The last words came out a growl.

"Ugh!" With that infuriated sound, she hauled down his head and kissed him with a ferocious kind of fury. "Fine, I won't call off the entire thing yet. But you should know you're fighting an uphill battle."

"I know." It had taken him a while to work through her words, but he got it now. Nayna wanted no more bonds after a lifetime of being held prisoner to the bonds of family.

Yeah, he damn well knew the battle he'd have to fight. And fight it he would. Because this was a war he intended to win. He wanted Nayna to love him as fiercely as she loved the family for whom she'd swallowed her dreams. "I looked up Lizzy Bennet." It had been an eye-opener.

A blink, followed by a twitch of her lips. "Oh?"

"Does that make me Mr. Darcy?"

Nayna snorted. "You can only wish." A glance at the night. "I should get back."

Walking her home, Raj said, "Do you like that book? *Pride and Prejudice*?"

"It's one of my absolute favorites," she said before adding, "along with a zillion historical romances."

Raj took the blow she hadn't realized she'd thrown. He had a very clear memory of telling her romance was for children. It was what he'd always believed—that it was commitment and hard work that mattered to hold a relationship together. Romance was fluff and daydreams and disappeared liked cotton candy under the first rain of reality.

His brother, Navin, was a case in point. He'd fallen

head over heels for Komal in college, sending her roses and chocolates, writing bad love songs that he recorded for her, spending hours mooning over her on the phone. Navin had waited only until he and Komal had both graduated and he had a job before he asked her to marry him.

Raj's parents had been surprised, but since there was nothing objectionable about Komal, a nurse who had a position at the city's major hospital, they'd celebrated the wedding with fanfare. Raj had been happy for his brother too, had cheerfully helped with anything the couple needed for their wedding.

Two years on and Navin was ducking his wife more often than not.

As for Komal, she'd become impossibly more shrewish.

Raj was glad every single day that he didn't live in the large family home with the rest of the Sens. The flat he'd built for himself at the far end of the garden was close enough to his parents and sister that he was there for them whenever they needed him, but far enough from Navin and Komal that he didn't get caught in the cross fire of their disdain for each other.

Poor Aditi often hid out in his flat too.

"Romance doesn't last," he said to Nayna, unable to be dishonest about something so fundamental. "It fades. Loyalty lasts. Fidelity lasts."

Nayna stopped at the end of her drive, her dark eyes holding his. "Do you know what my father did a month ago? He drove an hour to find the perfect cream buns my mother was craving. Romance lasts if you want it to last."

Raj scowled. "That's not romance. It's just listening to your wife and being a good husband."

Tilting her head to the side, Nayna gave him a considering look. Then, without warning, she walked back to him and crooked a finger. Frowning, he bent his head... and she kissed him all soft and slow, her hand on the back of his neck. A hand with bones far more delicate than his, but he couldn't have broken her hold if his life depended on it.

He was still standing there on the sidewalk long minutes after she'd disappeared into the house, utterly befuddled about what he'd done that had earned him that kiss. Whatever it was, he had to figure it out quickly. Because he wasn't about to lose a woman who looked at him that way, who touched him that way, who knew his secrets and hadn't used them to hurt him.

15

THE MALE POINT OF VIEW

Nayna went into work on Saturday to clear a few final things before she shut down for summer vacation. It felt strangely quiet after the emotional upheaval of the previous day, so she was glad to pull into her drive around three to see her grandmother and Mr. Hohepa heading off for a walk, Pixie happily nosing about in front of them. Aji wore a blue velour suit with white racing stripes while Mr. Hohepa wore tan slacks and a light blue polo shirt, the hat on his head rakishly perched and his cane a glossy black.

As if the two had coordinated their outfits.

Aji was chattering away animatedly to him, and every so often, he'd laugh a big belly laugh, his light brown skin glowing under the summer sunlight.

"Go, Aji." Nayna smiled, but it didn't last long—she spent most of the next two hours avoiding her parents' attempts to question her about Raj. Going out into the garden to hide out on the swing, she stared up at a sky lit with summer sunshine, missing being held against a big, warm body and kissed with an erotic intensity that said Raj was focused on her and only her.

She shivered, thought about calling him, but no, the ball was strictly in his court now. Her lips quirked at the memory of the baffled look on his face after she'd kissed him last night. The poor baby hadn't had any idea what he'd done. But the way he'd scowled and said that it was all about listening and being a good husband, that had hit every one of her romance-hungry buttons.

It had also chipped away at her walls.

The idea of a husband who listened and gave her what she needed... it was a seductive one. But could Raj give her freedom in the long term, or would the rules change over time? The idea of feeling trapped, of slowly suffocating all her life... No, Nayna couldn't, *wouldn't* do it. Raj had more than an uphill battle ahead of him—he was also fighting to push up a giant two-ton rock while engaging in that battle.

"Nayna!" her mother called out from the back door. "Come and get ready. We have to go to Pinky's!"

"Coming!" Nayna called back, glad to have the distraction of the pre-wedding ceremony tonight. She knew her mother and grandmother had been attending wedding festivities throughout the week, including the ceremony where turmeric paste was rubbed all over the bride.

Nayna wondered if sophisticated "mineral water only" Pinky had enjoyed being turned yellow by gleeful aunties and cousins. Grinning, she walked into her bedroom and pulled out a vivid green sari with gold detailing that wasn't so heavy that she couldn't put it on by herself. The task of turning meters of fabric into an elegant ensemble was one in which Nayna was yet a novice.

Ísa called mid-wrap, and Nayna ended up confessing that she'd kissed Raj. She simply couldn't help herself around him. It was a sickness—and no, she didn't want to be cured. Her heart pounded at the thought of how he'd tasted her with slow deliberation; her skin flushed. Hanging up the call with Ísa before she gave away her current state, she took a couple of minutes to calm down before ensuring her makeup was up to scratch.

She decided to add gold eyeshadow and thicker mascara to jazz things up.

Last was the jewelry. Today she stuck with bangles that matched the gold in her sari as well as dangly gold earrings. At the last minute, she added a gold bindi.

As a single woman of a certain age, she had to go armored.

Yesterday at the Mehras, the assembled aunties had all squeezed her cheeks and told her she was a pretty girl. Then had come the questions about why she wasn't married. "Youth won't last forever" was the sage advice, after which they'd complimented her on her career.

Today Madhuri came to her rescue with one particularly insistent auntie who was crossing the line from nosy to hurtful. "I'm so sorry," Madhuri said sweetly, "but my sari's coming loose at the back and I need Nayna's help."

"You young girls." A shake of the head. "Don't you know how to use safety pins? You have to get the big strong ones. Go, go, fix it!"

After leading Nayna out of sight, Madhuri turned and winked at her. Her pale pink sari with white crystals on it was wrapped perfectly around her tall and voluptuous body. Nayna could tie a sari, but she'd need an hour and at least two boxes of safety pins to put on the slippery, heavy creation Madhuri was wearing. And even then she'd be scared she'd step on it and unravel the entire thing.

"Auntie Babita's such an old bat." Madhuri rolled her eyes. "Even her face is kinda batty looking, don't you think?"

Nayna grinned because this was her slightly wicked older sister, and no matter what, Nayna loved her. "Now I'm going to think that every time I talk to her." She hooked her arm through Madhuri's. "Thanks for the rescue, Maddie."

"What are sisters for?" Madhuri nudged her shoulder. "Ma told me about this Raj guy. He sounds hot."

A sudden, awful lurch in Nayna's gut. Raj hadn't met Madhuri, she suddenly realized. She couldn't help but imagine his reaction when he did. Her sister genuinely looked like a Bollywood movie actress. Fair skinned; shiny, tumbling hair with tousled curls; height enough to match Raj's; and a lush sensuality that drew men like moths to a flame regardless of her status as a young divorcée.

"He is supremely hot." Nayna tried not to feel nauseated at her belated realization, at the knowledge that the man who'd called her beautiful had never met the other Sharma daughter. "But why don't you tell me about your new job?" she said, desperate to get off the painful topic. "We haven't had much of a chance to talk since you started there."

Madhuri squeezed Nayna's arm. "Seriously, Ninu, I

love it *so* much." A glow in her features that made her impossibly more stunning. "I think it's my thing."

Nayna nodded and listened and hoped her sister was right. So far Madhuri hadn't stuck with anything for more than a year. She managed to pay her rent and keep her finances stable only because their parents and Nayna topped her up. Nayna knew Aji gave her the odd monetary gift too. As an accountant, Nayna was well aware they should let Madhuri sink or swim on her own so she'd learn better financial management, but it was highly unlikely Madhuri would do anything but drown.

Her older sister had never been able to handle money.

It felt terribly unfeminist to even think it, but Madhuri had been born with the kind of beauty that usually led to a rich husband who took care of everything. That could still happen; regardless, Nayna would never leave her sister to flounder and drown. "Anyone you liked in the most recent proposals?" she asked.

Madhuri wrinkled up her nose. "Ugh, just flabby oldies. I'm divorced, not desperate."

"One hundred percent true." Nayna spotted the food table, set up for self-service—it was casual tonight with only close family and friends in attendance. "You hungry?"

"Starving. Sugar and ghee, here I come."

Nayna ran into one of Madhuri's closest friends, Anjali Kumar, over the mango barfis and white pedas. Basically sugar and milk and flavor and deliciousness. "Anj," she said with a smile. "It's good to see you."

"Nayna." Anjali gave her a hug and a smile that was ragged at the edges; her makeup was as flawless as always, but she had dark shadows under her eyes. Hardly surprising when she had an eighteen-month-old *and* a new baby. "Where's Maddie?"

"Did someone say my name?" Madhuri popped up beside Nayna, having successfully navigated the savories and come away with a pile of goodies for them to share.

As Nayna put some sweets on her plate, Anjali and Madhuri fell into soft conversation. Their conversation was intimate, with Madhuri asking, "Has Avinesh been helping with the baby more since his parents had that talk with him?"

"I wish," Anjali muttered. "He wakes me up when the baby cries, doesn't know how to change a nappy and doesn't want to learn, and now he's picked up squash. Plays three nights a week, then has soccer on the weekends."

Nayna flinched inside. Three years earlier, Anjali's now-husband had proposed with a plane flying a banner while they had a private picnic on a beach. Nayna had been overcome by the romance of it all, even more so because theirs had been an arranged match turned love match.

"I wish I'd never gotten married," Anjali added bitterly. "I love my two boys, but I'd happily divorce Avinesh now if my parents wouldn't throw a fit."

"I recommend divorce for getting rid of excess baggage." Madhuri's comment made her friend laugh, Anjali's resentment falling away to reveal the pretty young woman she was underneath it all.

"I better go—Mum's waving me over. The baby must be grizzling." She left after exchanging a one-armed hug with Madhuri.

"Well, that was pretty awful to hear," Nayna murmured to Madhuri after Anjali was out of earshot. "Avinesh was so lovely with her."

"All men are before marriage," Madhuri said sagely. "The real trick is finding a man who'll be lovely *after* the rings are exchanged."

On that less-than-cheerful note, they took their plates of snacks and found seats. As the ceremony went on up ahead, they chatted and people-watched and ate too many sweets and savories while discussing which outfit was the blingiest—a serious contest at an Indian wedding —and for a while they were simply sisters again. For one night Nayna wasn't angry at Madhuri for how she'd changed the course of Nayna's life.

When her phone buzzed with a message toward the end of the evening, she checked it to see the words: *I got the* Pride and Prejudice *audiobook and listened to a chunk of it while working on a site today. Mr. Darcy is kind of a dick.*

Nayna's body got all warm, her chest squeezing. That big, tough, physical Raj was reading her favorite Austen book, it chipped away more of her armor. It was better than planes flying banners or grand gestures like elopements. She was glad that Madhuri had gone over to catch up with a friend and quickly typed back a response: *He holds the title of one of the dickiest heroes ever, but there is a redemption arc.*

Raj's response made the warmth inside her turn fizzy: *That Wickham guy is shady. Why is Lizzy being an idiot? No guy goes around spilling his guts like that.*

Nayna held a fisted hand up to her mouth, fighting a laugh. She'd never heard a male point of view on *Pride and Prejudice,* and clearly she'd been missing out. *Lizzy isn't perfect,* she wrote back. *She's the prejudice part of* Pride and Prejudice.

Madhuri bustled over. "Are you messaging Ísa? What's she say?"

Quickly typing, *Have to go,* Nayna slid away her phone —and tried not to think about Raj and Madhuri coming face-to-face for the first time. "Oh, nothing much," she said through renewed nausea. "Did you see Pinky's engagement ring? Enough to take out not just an eye but the entire face."

RAJ PUT DOWN HIS PHONE and was about to start the audiobook again when there was a knock on his door, followed by Aditi's face poking inside. It struck him suddenly that she'd lost the layer of baby fat she'd carried around for years, her facial bones becoming defined and striking. Around that pointed face with large chestnut-brown eyes bloomed dark curls. His seventeen-year-old sister, he realized with brotherly horror, was turning into a pretty woman.

"Hey," she said, wandering in to collapse on the battered sofa he kept to one side of the living area he used as his home office. As with all teenagers, her limbs were liquid, arranging themselves in anatomically impossible ways.

"Here, I got you this." He threw over her favorite chocolate bar, which he'd picked up on the way home.

A small smile, but she put it aside instead of devouring it like she usually did.

Right.

Turning his chair from his drafting desk, Raj rolled

that chair across so he was facing her. "Spill it, Monkey." A childhood nickname from the time she used to clamber all over Raj and cling, giggling and refusing to release him.

"It's nothing." She took out her phone, began to scroll through it. "I just want a break from the parentals."

"Adi," Raj said quietly in a tone she'd never disobeyed.

Lips pursed together tightly, she sat up. Her body was nearly vibrating. "I have a friend who's a boy and he asked me to go to the movies *as a friend*, and you'll all say no and it's not *fair*!"

Raj's entire body had turned unyielding at Aditi's first words, the automatic and protective refusal on the edge of his tongue. It was Nayna's voice that stopped him, the echo of her piercing frustration at the constrained life she'd lived hitting hard. Would she have said yes to him if she hadn't been so strictly caged? Would she be happy instead of bruised inside to the point where she might never trust him to value her dreams and needs?

"What's his name?" he asked calmly.

Aditi gave him a mutinous look. "Are you going to go warn him off?"

"No. But I will Google him."

"Harlow Chan." Aditi folded her arms across her chest. "He won that Crafty Corners internship."

Raj raised an eyebrow. He knew all about that hotly contested business internship because Aditi had seemed fascinated with it. Now he understood why. Even if this boy was just a friend now, Aditi liked him in a deeper way. "He must be smart."

"He is." Though her eyes remained suspicious, Aditi launched into a spiel about the virtues of the boy.

If all of what she said was true, Harlow Chan was exactly the kind of boy his sister should be calling a friend. "When did he want to go out?"

Aditi scowled at him. "Anytime. The internship is really tough, but he has time after work sometimes. And it's vacation, so I don't have to worry about waking up early."

Raj considered it. "I'll talk to Ma and Dad," he said, holding his sister's gaze. "I trust you, Adi, but you have to keep on being honest with me. Keep me updated on your plans and don't try to sneak around." It scared him to let his sister out into the world that might hurt her, but keeping a wild bird in a cage wasn't fair to that bird. "And if you two become more than friends, you tell me that."

Lower lip quivering, Aditi launched herself off the sofa and into his arms. Raj held his baby sister and hoped he was doing the right thing. Especially when, an hour later, his father said a flat-out no to Raj's proposal that they allow Aditi to continue her friendship with this boy. But Raj could out-stubborn anyone in his family, and he got what he wanted: permission for Adi to go on the movie date *after* she'd introduced the boy to the family and he'd been approved.

Harlow Chan would get grilled to within an inch of his life.

After delivering the news to his deliriously happy sister and getting a huge kiss on the cheek and a hug in thanks, Raj walked back to his flat and found himself looking at his phone. Why did Nayna's opinion matter so much? But it did. Again, that power she had over him. Fear gripped at his throat.

There was, he thought, only one way to conquer that fear without hurting her as he'd so stupidly done at their lunch. He had to make Nayna Sharma fall madly in love with him—until she was willing to be his without questions or hesitations. Until he never had to fear that she'd walk away and leave him alone once again.

He picked up the phone and sent a message: *Just a warning—I want you, Nayna Sharma, and I intend to play dirty to win.*

16

PLAYING DIRTY

FTER RAJ'S THREAT, NAYNA WAS on tenterhooks the next day, but it passed disappointingly smoothly. Even her parents stopped their attempts at an inquisition. Nayna got an answer as to why when she accidentally overheard them talking.

"I thought Raj was a good boy," Nayna's father was saying, openly dubious.

"I'm sure he is. I spoke to Babita yesterday at the Mehras. She knows the entire family, and she said Raj is very honest and hardworking. She even tried to set up her own daughter with him, but he said no straightaway. Didn't try to take advantage or lead her on. So if he's still thinking about Nayna, he must be very serious."

"Well," her father mused. "That Babita does know everyone's business. I think she has people's houses wired."

Nayna's lips twitched as her mother laughed. Thank God for nosy aunties like Babita. At least Nayna would have clear air for a while before her father decided it was all taking too long. Tiptoeing away from the bedroom door that had been left slightly ajar, Nayna made her way outside.

She'd thought her grandmother was out here, but there was no sign of her. Frowning, Nayna glanced toward Mr. Hohepa's house. Her lips curved as she spotted them through the window—Mr. Hohepa and her grandmother were dancing, slow and sweet, with proper steps. For a long time, Nayna just watched them, her heart full.

When her mother opened the back door, she called out a loud, "Hi, Ma!"

"Don't wake the whole neighborhood, beta. Come help me in the garden."

Nayna snuck a look at the neighboring window as she walked. The dancing figures had disappeared. Sweetly delighted at being able to help the secret romance along, Nayna took the spare hat her mother had brought out, then got down on her knees in the dirt. Her mind suddenly announced that this would be an excellent position for her and Raj. Her height wouldn't matter then.

Skin burning to ash from the inside out, Nayna told her brain to shut up. The last thing she needed was more sexual frustration. She'd already spent the previous night sweat-soaked and woken with the sheets tangled around her legs, her dreams full of dirty things. If he'd phrased his message to drive her insane, he'd succeeded. Oh, how he'd succeeded.

"Did you see that article your father printed out about Raj's last project?" her mother said. "Such intricate work."

"Yes," Nayna said past the thickness of arousal threatening to choke her. "He's very talented with his hands."

Her breasts ached, wanting those talented hands on them.

She was cursing him under her breath by the time she got dressed for the wedding that night. Tonight was the actual ceremony and she had to bling it up. Anything less than dazzling and her mother would accuse her of making them look poor and hard up—and the assorted aunties would shake their heads at how she was letting herself go. Sure sign she was on the road to spinsterhood.

She was fingering a stunning but heavy sari of a deep burnt orange accented with peacock blue that had been a gift from Aji on her birthday when Madhuri walked into her room. Her sister was already dressed in a shimmering black sari with intricate glass beading of emerald green and white. Hair shiny and healthy—and tousled just so— brushed her shoulders. The black kurta she wore below the sari was sleeveless and cut to fit snugly just under her breasts. Black bangles covered her wrists and iridescent black jewels fell from her ears.

"You look like a movie star," Nayna said, astonished as always that this divine creature was her big sister.

Madhuri beamed. "You're going to knock it out of the park in that sari."

"Hah." Nayna shook her head. "This is *way* too hard for me." Not only was the material a nightmare to handle while pleating, the pattern was such that it had to be wrapped in a specific way. "I'll—"

"No, no." Madhuri halted her when she would've reached for another piece. "We have time. I'll put you into it."

Nayna hesitated, but Madhuri was already in full motion. She pulled out the matching orange underskirt, found the peacock blue kurta, and threw both at Nayna. "Which shoes?"

"Nothing too high," Nayna said. "I'll trip."

"Hmm." Madhuri walked effortlessly across the carpet in her own ice-pick-thin heels. "These?" She held up a pair of low-heeled silver sandals. "Easy to walk in but sari appropriate."

Nayna took a deep breath. "Let's do it."

Stripping to her nude underwear, she pulled on the underskirt and tied it around her waist. Madhuri snorted. "That's not tight enough." She took over.

"You're cutting me in half!" Nayna moaned as her sister pulled the drawstring waist to a vicious tightness.

"The weight of the sari will pull it down, you wuss," her sister said. "It has to start off circulation erasing." That torture complete, she shook her head at Nayna's bra. "That'll show in the kurta. It's got a crisscross back."

Nayna picked up the top, examined it. "Built-in bra." Lucky for her because she hadn't bought a special bra to go under the top. And not even women with small breasts looked good in this kind of kurta without having some structure in that region.

Once she'd put on the kurta—it was about the same length as Madhuri's and fitted as close to her body but had cap sleeves—she stepped into the heeled sandals and the wrapping began. Only neophyte sari-wearers attempted to put on a sari without shoes on. That way led to disaster. Either too short or too long, never just right.

Madhuri tucked and wrapped and pleated with quick fingers, all the while keeping up a running commentary. "Remember when we used to dress in Ma's saris when we were young? You had the yellow one you loved."

"And your favorite was the sparkly pink." Nayna smiled, a poignant sadness in her heart for the past that would never again come. "I'm glad we're all family again, Maddie."

Her sister looked up from her pleating. "Me too, Ninu." A wink, no echoes of the past in Madhuri's voice —she had an enviable way of setting bad things aside and "forgetting" them. "Next time I get married, I'll expect you to walk down the aisle in front of me in a circulation erasing sari."

Nayna laughed and the two of them worked together to finish dressing her. To make it easier on herself, Nayna went for the classic look with the end of the sari pleated neatly across her chest and pinned to one shoulder to fall all the way to her calf. The peacock blue shone against the orange.

"Hair up I think," Madhuri said and fashioned Nayna's hair into a bun at the back of her head with tendrils framing her face. "Unless you want curls? I brought my hair iron in case I needed a touch-up before we left."

"My hair still doesn't hold curls, doesn't matter what product I use." Nayna made a face. "This is nice." Simple but soft. "Let me do my makeup and you hunt for some bangles." As Nayna, Madhuri, and their mother all had the same size wrist, they had a shared collection of bangles in every conceivable color. It had just kind of built up over the years.

Madhuri chatted along about her new job and her

crotchety neighbor and how she was in love with the guy on *The Bachelor*.

Nayna stuck out her tongue. "No way. He's so plastic."

"Whatever, Ninu. You have no appreciation for a nice pack of abs."

Nayna's fingers tingled in sensory memory of a certain chest she'd explored, of the ridged outline of a very nice six-pack that she really, *really* wanted to touch again. Embarrassingly damp between her thighs, she finished putting on her eyeshadow and began with mascara. Behind her, Madhuri gave an exasperated sigh. "You go too light on the makeup."

"I can't stand too much on my skin."

"I'll do it for you next time," Madhuri said before extending her hands. "Here, I found silver bangles, orange ones, and blue. You want to color block or mix and match?"

Nayna went for the silver, adding silver bells to her ears to match and a silver bindi with a center of peacock blue. When she looked at herself in the mirror, she felt pretty damn good. She was no Madhuri, but she looked sleek and, dare she say it, elegant. "Thanks, Maddie," she said while her sister added another safety pin to ensure the sari stayed in place.

"There. Done." Madhuri came up beside her, looking in the mirror to fix her own hair just right. "The Sharma girls are ready. World won't know what hit it."

WHEN THEY WALKED INTO THE grand wedding hall side by side, Nayna saw all eyes go to Madhuri. She wanted to smile. That was the way it had always been and would probab— Her thoughts cut off mid-word, her eyes locking with those of darkest brown across the room.

What was Raj doing here?

"Who is that smoking-hot hunk of deliciousness?"

Madhuri's whisper had Nayna jerking. "Raj," she said through a dry throat, her pulse a panicky beat. Because she knew what happened to men when they saw Madhuri. She *knew*.

"Oooooh." Madhuri's tone was intrigued. "I see what you mean about you two not suiting. He's what, six three?"

It wasn't a dig, was just Madhuri being Madhuri. And it wasn't as if her sister would attempt to poach Raj. Men asked to be with her—she didn't have to steal. Stomach churning and cheeks hot at the scene surely to come, Nayna walked with her sister to take a seat at one of the tables. The centerpiece was created of tea candles and exotic blooms floating in a fishbowl, each place setting perfectly arranged.

There was no assigned seating, but every one of the six hundred guests was guaranteed a seat. This was a *very* expensive wedding. And the back of her neck was prickling. Just her imagination. Raj was unlikely to be staring at her when Madhuri was right next to her.

"Good evening, ladies," a deep male voice said just as Nayna put her purse on the table.

"Hello." Madhuri glowed up at him, her smile luminous. "I'm Madhuri, Nayna's sister."

"Raj." He slipped into the chair beside Nayna, his expression as solemn as always and his body clad in a black suit that was criminal in how it highlighted his rough-edged sexiness. "This wasn't taken, was it?"

"My mother was going to sit there." Nayna scowled at him instead of curling up into a self-defensive ball.

"Oh, Ma can sit by me," Madhuri said airily.

Raj nodded and stayed put, his large body emanating a heat that made Nayna want to cuddle into him and sniff at his scent from the curve of his neck. He rose to his feet only when her parents arrived after making their way through all their friends and greeting everyone. Shaking her father's hand and smiling at her mother, he then sat back down. His own parents soon joined them at the table.

Oh. My. God. The man wasn't just playing dirty, he had declared no-holds-barred war.

She kicked him under the table.

When he gave her a steady, stubborn look, she wanted to strangle him. Despite the black-tie-attired orchestra out front and a gifted singer crooning away Hindi classics as the guests settled in, *every* eye in the place was on them. Single, unattached men did not sit next to single, unattached women unless *something* was going on—or that was the accepted point of view. And no one would've missed that he'd deliberately chosen the seat next to *her*, not Madhuri.

Which... okay, yes, that made her want to kiss him. After she finished kicking him.

Bruised ankles or not, he stayed. And brought her chai. Then got her extra sweets. Her parents and his looked on benevolently.

And it started to dawn on her that this serious man, whom she'd never seen laughing, was playing with her. Her bones threatened to melt—but she still had to grit her teeth to control the urge to pour the piping-hot chai into his lap in punishment for his behavior.

"I wouldn't," he said roughly under the hubbub of conversation. "You might damage parts you like."

"I'm going to kill you," she murmured despite the urge to do highly inappropriate things to his spectacular body.

Music drummed through the huge hall.

The wedding was finally ready to begin two hours after the scheduled time. Which meant it was right on Indian-time. The Hindu priest—the pandit—got up to do a small prayer, then the emcee did an introduction lauding the couple. Their university degrees—in science for the groom, in finance for the bride—were heavily emphasized.

"Is it because I don't have a degree?" Raj whispered, his breath ruffling her ear. "Is that why you only want me for my body?"

"I swear to God, I'm going to murder you in a minute."

His responding look held the faintest hint of a smile, and it was pure provocation. She wanted to rip off his clothes and kiss him all over. Did he realize how madly arousing it was to have him crack his mature, serious shell just for her? It made her wonder if he might be like this in bed sometimes, after they got comfortable with one another.

Nayna's toes curled. Hard.

17

NECK KISSES AND THE ABS OF NAYNA'S DOWNFALL

SPEECH FINALLY OVER, THE WEDDING ceremony officially started with the pandit doing prayers. The groom sat to his left, both of them looking at the sacred fire in the middle. The groom's family had arranged themselves on one side of the brilliantly dressed stage, complete with a wedding pavilion dripping with jeweled ropes, red carpet, and lashings of opulent red roses. All of the pavilion's four pillars were encrusted with crystals that dazzled the eye and threw multi-hued reflections across the hall.

Nayna's favorite part came not long after. She stood with everyone else on the emcee's instruction, smiling up at Raj when he stepped aside and nudged her forward so she'd have a better view of the aisle down which the bride would walk. Only afterward did she realize she'd just added fuel to the fire of speculation around them.

And why did the damn man have to smell so good?

Music sounded as the orchestra launched into a beloved wedding piece and a tiny girl dressed in a glittering pink skirt that touched the floor, paired with a miniature kurta and a sparkly dupatta folded and tucked in like a sari, walked down the aisle, throwing flower petals as she went.

She was *adorable*.

Nayna couldn't help but smile as the little girl did her very important task with aplomb. Behind her came the wedding party. It was all very stately, stiff and expensive silk saris and dark suits. Nayna much preferred it when the wedding party danced in. She'd have that at her own wedding... if she trusted any man enough to tie herself to him for life. If she trusted Raj. Because he was the only man she could now imagine in the role.

The bride's special music filled the air.

Exquisite in her designer red wedding garments, Pinky kept her eyes uncharacteristically lowered in a facsimile of meekness as she carried the garland of flowers she'd place over the groom's head. Gold and red bangles covered her forearms, a heavy gold necklace circled her throat and dripped down her front, hand jewelry highlighted her slender bone structure, and she wore a traditional nose ring attached to her hair by a delicate chain.

Dramatic gold earrings brushed her shoulders.

Her makeup was exquisite and her veil translucent red dotted with tiny mirrors that flashed fire. It had a border of gold velvet and when she passed, Nayna saw that her hair was dressed with flowers under the veil.

She sighed at the beauty and romance of it.

A warm breath against her ear. "Poor groom," Raj rumbled under the hubbub of oohs and aahs over the bride. "By the time he gets all that jewelry off, he won't have the energy to get started on the outfit."

Nayna elbowed him. And came up against rock-hard abs.

Her fingers tingled again.

Thankfully they got to sit down after the garlands were exchanged onstage, and Raj had to behave because everyone had gone quiet. Only once the prayers began again did people slowly begin to talk. As Nayna had told Ísa when her best friend accompanied her to a family wedding, talking wasn't considered rude except at certain points.

Indian weddings were long, some more so than others. It was a big social affair.

She got up midway through to stretch her legs—partly to get away from the gorgeous man who'd decided to play dirty and partly to go pay her respects to the grandmothers. Her own aji sat with them. "How's the gang of grannies?" she asked after kissing her grandmother on the cheek.

The grannies cackled and pinched her cheeks. And congratulated her on her "strapping" young man. Nayna didn't even attempt a protest—no one would believe her. Instead, after spending some time sitting with her grandmother and her grandmother's friends, she got up and looked over toward her table. She had a knot deep inside her because, regardless of his public display of intent, part of her expected to see Raj talking to and falling for her sister, but while Madhuri was talking to a man, it wasn't Raj.

He was nowhere to be seen.

The knot turned into a different kind of tension. Men

left alone with Madhuri tended to capitalize on their luck. But not only was Raj not capitalizing on Nayna being missing, he'd spent the entire night irritating *her*, concentrating on her... playing with her.

"Nayna, beta," her grandmother said just as two giggling children ran past, playing tag among the tables. "Will you get me some more chai?"

"Of course." Nayna asked if any of the other grandmothers would like another cup too. She got six affirmative answers.

Leaving them with a smile, she avoided a toddler dressed in a gorgeous little suit who was crawling happily away from his mother, then headed to the small kitchen area in back of the massive event space that the wedding decorators had turned into a glorious wonderland of shimmer and glitz. As the catering staff had a much larger kitchen area to themselves, no one would care about her being back there. Especially since there was already a bit of a party going on outside and around the corner from the kitchen.

A large wooden tanoa, the traditional four-legged Fijian vessel made for holding kava, took pride of place on the narrow table. The men, many of whom she knew, smiled and asked her where her father was; Gaurav Sharma was known to enjoy a bowl of the cold drink made from the powdered root of a tropical plant.

"I'm sure he'll be by," she said with a smile. "He'd never miss a Kava Konference."

They chuckled and continued on mingling around the beverage that didn't cause drunkenness but a surplus of which could make people excessively mellow and a little dopey. At weddings like this, the latter wasn't a problem. It was more about socializing than serious kava consumption.

One of the oldest of the men jokingly offered her a drink, the bowl he held in his wrinkled hand created from the half shell of a coconut polished until it gleamed a smooth and striated brown. "No thanks, Uncle, I don't want my tongue to go numb."

Good-natured laughter followed her as she slipped into the kitchen. Surprisingly, it was empty. A large kettle of tea sat on the stove, still hot, and when Nayna lifted the lid to peek inside, she caught hints of tea leaves in the mid-brown liquid that wasn't too milky but not too weak either. Obviously the Mehras' caterers had been briefed on the importance of a continued supply of good chai— none of this teabag-in-water rubbish as her aji would say, *proper* chai with boiled milk and loose-leaf tea.

After placing cups on a tray, tea-leaf strainer to the ready—all of which she found in a neat grouping of supplies set to one side of the room for just that purpose —she went to pick up the kettle.

A big male hand, marked by the nicks and scars of hard work, came around her and took over the task. "It's heavy," Raj said, his other hand touching her lower back. "You really like tea, huh?"

"Funny man." Butterflies fluttering inside her, she moved the tray across so he could pour.

When he shifted to press a kiss to the back of her neck before carrying on in his task, she shivered but didn't protest.

"Meet me tonight?" he asked, the playfulness gone, to be replaced by that intense concentration on her and *only* her that made her throat go dry, her breasts ache.

"The wedding will go late." Mind a little fuzzy, she nonetheless located some sugar and added the right amounts to the right cups. At least the cooks hadn't already dumped a ton of sugar in the tea—that was the usual modus operandi at mass gatherings.

Going behind her, Raj put his hands on her hips, his fingers scraping over skin exposed by her sari. Nayna was still trying to process the influx of sensation when he kissed her nape again. "I want to kiss you properly."

Nayna's hand trembled as she closed the sugar container. "I'll message you," she said, her tongue in knots.

Moving away right before someone else entered the kitchen, Raj picked up the tray and carried it out. Nayna knew she was adding fuel to the fire, but she walked beside him—someone had to remember whose tea was whose. Her grandmother and the other grandmothers all cooed over Raj playing her knight. She passed out the tea as fast as possible... then took the tray to return to the kitchen.

"Oh no, please stay," she said to Raj, a sweet smile on her face. "Aji and her friends are really enjoying your company." At which point she abandoned him to the granny interrogation. Raj Sen was proving to be a stubborn, immovable force of a man, but he had to learn that he was never going to win all their battles.

He didn't make it back to the table for a half hour. "I feel as if I just escaped shark-infested waters," he murmured to her, his arm on the back of her seat.

She knew she should tell him to remove that arm, that it was sending all kinds of signals, but what she said was "That bad?"

Raj didn't reply, his attention on her gaze. "What is it?"

So damn perceptive. He'd learn all her secrets if she wasn't careful. "What if it doesn't work out?" she whispered. "All this..." The public declaration that no one could mistake, the expectation.

"I'll be the bad guy," he told her, the words a promise. "I will not allow anything to blow back on you. If I have to, I'll make up a secret girlfriend so everyone thinks I'm a shit."

For some strange reason, she trusted him to do exactly that, to shield her against the gossip and the whispers regardless of the personal cost. "I don't know, it might be interesting for me to have a scandalous reputation."

"You won't," Raj said, his gaze steady and his voice determined. "No matter what I have to do."

"Raj." Her father's voice. "Jitesh was telling me about your latest project."

Switching focus and giving her much-needed breathing room, his arm no longer on the back of her chair, Raj began to talk about the job. She listened and heard a passion in his voice that said he loved his work. He worked hard, and he found pleasure in creating and in giving his clients what they desired.

Nayna had the certainty he'd be as dedicated to giving a woman pleasure. Raj wasn't the kind of man who left anything unfinished. He'd probably consider it a failure on his part if his lover didn't orgasm.

Nayna shivered inside... and continued to enjoy his proximity. Until he disappeared an hour before the end of the ceremony. Leaving her to deal with the fallout.

"Well, Shilpa," the aunties said to her mother, "you didn't tell us your little Nayna was engaged."

"It's not official yet," her mother said, sanguine now that Raj had put his cards on the table. "You know young girls these days, they want the 'proper' romantic proposal."

The aunties all nodded like a flock of wise hens.

She really was going to murder him.

18

RAJ DISCOVERS SEXTING IS A THING

NAYNA ABANDONED HER PLAN TO get back at Raj for his quick exit when her grandmother suddenly started feeling unwell soon after she and Nayna arrived home. Her parents had been invited by the Mehras to an after-party that was no-offspring-allowed, so it was just the two of them.

"Let's go," Nayna said at once when her grandmother complained of chest pains. "I'm taking you to the hospital."

She texted Raj from the emergency room while her grandmother was being examined.

I'll meet you, he immediately replied.

Wait—I'll see what they say first. I might have to ask you to get my parents and bring them here. I don't want them driving this late when they'll be worried.

In the end, it turned out Aji just had a bad case of indigestion.

"All that wedding food," her grandmother muttered as Nayna helped her into bed. "I'm going on a diet tomorrow. Can you tell Tawhiri I won't be able to go for our morning walk?"

It took Nayna a minute to work out that Tawhiri must be Mr. Hohepa. "I will, don't worry."

"And your Raj?" Aji mumbled. "Did you tell him?"

"Yes, Aji." She'd messaged him the instant they found out, then told him to get some sleep.

I'll probably fall asleep on you if we meet now, she'd written.

His responding comment had been Raj-solemn. *If you need me, call me. Whatever the time.*

Nayna had stared at those words for a long time. What would it be like, to have Raj permanently at her back? The idea of it was breathtakingly tempting, but as Ísa worried about Sailor Bishop having time for her, Nayna worried what place she'd have in Raj's life long term. She was a priority now, but what role would she have as the years moved on?

Nayna had been last on everyone's priorities for a long time.

It hurt her heart to think of being delegated to the bottom of the heap by Raj.

"You're overthinking things, Nayna," she whispered. "You promised to give him a chance, so worry about the rest later."

Since it was already four thirty and—thanks to Aji—Nayna knew Mr. Hohepa was usually up around five, she wandered into her room and took her time finally removing her wedding finery and makeup. She'd gotten a few interested looks in the ER from the walking wounded, but she hadn't stuck out the most. That honor had gone to a man in a pink tutu, paper crown, and pink tank top, his black chest hair sticking out everywhere and a bloodied towel held up to his nose.

A bachelor party gone very bad.

The light came on in Mr. Hohepa's kitchen. Time for her to play messenger for these two lovebirds. After she did the promised task—and convinced Mr. Hohepa that his obviously adored Heera was quite fine—she finally fell into bed. But she couldn't sleep, was still awake at five thirty when her parents finally stumbled home.

"Shh," her mother said with a giggle. "We'll wake Nayna and Amma."

Her father's deeper tones answered with something unintelligible, but her mother giggled again before the master bedroom door shut.

"My parents are getting more sexing than I am. The universe is now openly mocking me," Nayna muttered to the ceiling before tugging up her light summer-weight duvet and turning firmly onto her side.

She didn't know when she fell asleep, but she dreamed of kisses on the nape and big hands cupping her breasts... and a man she couldn't reach no matter how painfully she stretched out her hands.

CHRISTMAS EVE MORNING WAS A late start for the entire Sharma family. Nayna had hoped to make her aborted rendezvous with Raj that night, but Madhuri came over with a Bollywood DVD and a hopeful look in her eyes and Nayna couldn't say no—Madhuri was like Teflon; things usually just rolled off her, but this one hurt, it had stuck.

Christmas Eve was the anniversary of the day her

husband had abandoned her in a strange mining town on the edge of nowhere, taking off in their car and with what little savings they had. *I have to be with my sister tonight,* she told Raj. *It's a bad time of year for her.*

Understood, was the single-word response.

Nayna wasn't sure if that meant exactly what it said or if he was annoyed or irritated. She decided on the former. Raj wasn't the subtle or passive-aggressive type when it came to the words he'd written to her. He said what he meant and meant what he said.

Christmas Day also dawned quietly but quickly became busy. For the Sharmas, it was a day about family, and this year Nayna's parents were hosting the annual barbeque for their relations. Even though everyone would turn up with salads, cakes, cooked dishes, and more, Nayna's mother was convinced they had to prepare a million different things.

"Ma, no one will starve," Nayna pointed out while frying the samosas. "You realize we'll have leftovers for a month?"

"Silly girl. You know everyone wants to take leftovers away. We don't want to be the stingy ones who never had any leftovers."

"I wonder if Iosua will bring his trifle," Nayna said. "I wouldn't mind eating a great big bowl of that."

"I told him to bring it," Shilpa Sharma said while busily chopping up vegetables for a fancy salad. "Every time we have a party, I'm so happy your cousin married a dessert chef."

Laughing, Nayna fished out the samosas and put in a fresh set to fry. Meanwhile, her father was outside making sure the grill was all set to go, and Madhuri was doing decorations. Aji sat at the kitchen table, mixing dough for a fried treat Nayna loved—basically sweet, cakey balls with raisins. She'd have no problem cooking those.

And eating them.

"Did I tell you your father invited Raj's family?" her mother said casually just as she was about to scoop out the second lot of samosas.

Nayna's nipples grew into hard little bullets. Pavlov's dogs had nothing on her. "What?" she squeaked out past the thumping of her heart.

"Don't let the food burn."

Nayna worked automatically. "*Ma.*"

"I knew you'd blush!" Her mother grinned—though Nayna wasn't blushing and even if she had been, no one would know. "It's fine. You don't have to worry. They're hosting their own family today or they'd have come— they were so disappointed to turn us down. But we don't have New Year's plans and they don't either, so we'll do something then."

Nayna felt a sudden constriction in her chest, a large weight settling on her shoulders. It was happening, the inevitable closing of the cage. Their families were already starting to make plans together while indulgently "letting" them "decide." It didn't matter that she liked the man in the cage with her—it was still a cage.

And it panicked her.

WHEN NAYNA DIDN'T RESPOND TO his Happy Christmas message, Raj didn't worry about it—if her family was anything like his, it was probably organized chaos right now while the preparations were going on.

Then his father started talking about the New Year's Eve gathering he and the Sharmas had planned. "Just casual," he said. "No stress. Relax and eat and drink."

Raj's muscles went rigid. He'd known when he made his move at the wedding that he was declaring his intent, but he'd made his "no interference" requirement clear to his parents. He needed more time to get under Nayna's skin, more time to assuage her doubts, more time to show her that he could give her the adventure and freedom she craved.

He, a man who'd been old even when he was young, was falling hard for a brilliant wild butterfly. Nayna might not describe herself that way, but that's what he saw—a bright, lovely woman with so *much* life and joy and love inside her. Raj was trying to learn to give her what she needed, but one thing of which he was fully cognizant was that the parental involvement would only push her away.

Since he had no desire to add to the pressure, he didn't message her again. His gut twisted as the hours passed, as he waited to see if Nayna would run.

Aditi, meanwhile, giggled as she exchanged messages with Harlow around the food prep in the kitchen. "Don't worry, bhaiya," she said with an impulsive hug when Raj raised an eyebrow. "We're not doing anything naughty. Harlow's sending me dumb knock-knock jokes."

A minute later, she snapped a selfie while pretending to bite into an entire cake and sent it off. As long as his sister kept the images she sent Harlow Chan G-rated, Raj wouldn't have to find the boy and smash his phone to smithereens.

His own phone finally pinged with an incoming message around five: *Hope you're having a good Christmas Day.*

It was a message that told him nothing, made him feel as if she was distancing herself. Raj's abdomen tensed, his jaw tight. About to reply in an effort to break through her self-defensive walls, he thought of Aditi sending her crush photos, and he thought about how Nayna had touched him that night at the party—and in the park.

Ducking into his flat for a little privacy, he took a photo just for her.

It took him three tries to get it right.

He'd never in his life done anything like this, but the current cock-up called for desperate measures. *I got you a gift,* he wrote, trying to figure out if he was flirting right— he wished she was in front of him so he could kiss her and melt her and remind her that the promise of what they had was worth a little risk.

Oh, you didn't have to do that, she wrote back.

Raj sent the photo of his upper body, adding, *From Santa,* to the message at the last minute.

2.7/10 she replied.

Raj's grin spread slowly across his face. It sure looked like he was doing the flirting right, because her response fairly demanded he avenge his honor. Maybe he'd send her a photo a day. No, one in the morning, one at night so she couldn't forget him even if she tried. More, he'd do everything in his power to throw a wrench in their parents' New Year's Eve plans. He would let no one make Nayna feel hunted.

HAVING STOLEN A MOMENT OF PRIVACY, Nayna fell back in her bed, her phone clutched to her chest and a surely goofy smile on her face. Lifting up the phone, she stared at the photo again, at gorgeous ripped abs and smooth brown skin. He had a small scar on his upper left pectoral that she wouldn't mind licking, and the sprinkling of crisp hair on his chest made her fingers curl into the sheets as her breath caught.

She couldn't help rubbing her thighs together in a vain effort to assuage the ache he'd aroused. "You're a fiend," she whispered to the man who was playing with her again, then carefully made a new folder in her photos just for him.

The panic that had held her captive all day receded a little, but it wasn't gone. She still had the feeling of having boarded a runaway train, and every so often her heartbeat would spike, her skin burning in a way that had nothing to do with pleasure. It didn't help that Madhuri flitted around the Christmas party, carefree and without worries once more.

As if the past had never been.

But it *had* been and it had left scars on all of them. Her father, who patted her on the shoulder and called her a good girl for making sure the food table was never empty but who never hugged her. Gaurav Sharma had stopped being affectionate with her after Madhuri's defection, as if he blamed his occasionally indulgent parenting for having set Madhuri on the wrong path.

Her mother, who smoothed her hair and whispered, "You'll have your own home soon, Ninu, your own family" in a way that told Nayna that, on some level, Shilpa Sharma was aware of her younger daughter's need to break free of this inhibited and stifling existence full of people she loved.

Her aji, who was dressed in a glorious gold-and-pink caftan for this event and who smiled at Nayna and said, "I know I can rely on you, beta," when all Nayna had done was bring out a chair so she could rest her feet. "I know I never have to worry about you not being there if I need you."

And even Madhuri, who hurt one day a year... and who couldn't commit to any man now, though the entire time they'd been growing up, being married and having "tons" of babies had been all she'd talked about.

By the time Nayna turned in that night, she was exhausted both in the body and in the soul.

When her phone vibrated, she picked it up, looked at the message, and moaned. Raj had sent her another photo, this one focusing on his flexed arm, part of his naked chest visible along with half his face.

He was smiling.

Nayna traced the line of that smile, utterly and totally demolished, her heart mush.

3.2/10, she wrote back, and her fingers, they trembled. This man, he was dangerous to her. He could seduce her into abandoning her dreams of freedom to live life in the predefined world that had been chosen for her. And yet she couldn't just walk away. Couldn't give up this serious, often-unsmiling, and rock-solid man who was cracking his shell bit by bit to let her in.

19

HALF-NAKED RAJ (NO FURTHER
ENTICEMENT REQUIRED)

N AYNA ENDED UP OUT OF town the next day when
Aji suddenly asked if she wouldn't mind
driving her to the small coastal town of
Raglan. "My old friend, Parvati, is visiting her younger
son there and then going straight back to Wellington. I
haven't seen her in, oh, twenty years!"

The road trip went fine except for a flat tire on the
return leg that meant they got home after dark. In the
interim, Raj had sent her three ab selfies. He was wearing
a hard hat in one of them, streaks of dust on his chest—
he'd captioned it to tell her he was putting in some time
on a job over the vacation period in order to free up his
schedule for a large project that was looking like it might
be more complicated than initially believed.

*I thought you might like to see me in my natural environ-
ment,* he'd added.

If he'd been standing in front of her, Nayna would've
pounced on him like the she-cats in Aji's "leopard
cologne" ad. Missing him far too much but scared and

confused at the same time, she squeezed her phone and fought the urge to ask him to meet her despite the late hour. In the end, she decided he must already be in bed after pulling a long day—he'd snapped that hard hat photo that was the stuff of her pornographic dreams at around eight in the morning, which meant he must've already been on the site for some time, taking advantage of the summer light.

She fell asleep wondering if he'd mind recreating a live-action version of that image and woke the next morning bad-tempered and wildly aroused. No matter what, she was hunting him down tonight and ordering him to do something about it! It was his fault she was a walking bag of hormones.

The phone vibrated while she was scanning through her private Raj folder.

Tonight?

Nayna bit down hard on her lower lip and almost broke the phone typing back: *Soon as it gets dark. Bring the hard hat.*

That night, fate decided to have another giggle at their expense.

A water pipe broke while she was impatiently waiting for night to fall, and, after turning the water off at the mains, her father said, "Call Raj! He probably knows a plumber who'll come out during the holidays at night!"

Raj turned up himself and crawled under the house to diagnose the problem as something he could fix. He'd brought supplies and was under there for an hour while Nayna's father held the flashlight for him and Nayna despaired of ever getting time alone with him. When he finally emerged, the pipe was fixed and he was filthy.

Nayna wanted to haul him into the shower and join him there. Naked.

But after shaking hands with her father and directing a nod toward her that held none of his playfulness in the messages, he left. Her phone vibrated two minutes later: *I can shower and be back in thirty minutes.*

Nayna's heart pounded. *Meet you then.*

Which was how she found herself literally sneaking out her window. "I can't believe I'm doing this," she muttered as she pushed up the window with care for squeaks. Everyone was still wide awake—and though Aji had given her a measuring look when she said she was tired and turning in early, she didn't think her grandmother had any idea Nayna was about to sneak out.

She hadn't even done that as a teenager.

Lower lip caught between her teeth, she got one leg over, then the next, and dropped easily onto the grass in her tennis-shoe-clad feet. All she wore above that were panties and a strappy sundress over which she'd thrown a light cardigan. It was a very deliberate choice of outfit. Nayna wanted Raj's hands on her body and she planned to be brazen about it—after she finished being flustered by his masculine beauty.

Since she had no intention of leaving the window up as an invitation for any opportunistic burglar who might be wandering the streets looking for a chance, she carefully pulled it all the way down. She'd have to sneak back in via the kitchen door—if Aji could do it without being busted, so could she.

Raj was waiting for her at the end of the drive, smelling of soap and freshness, his hair damp but his jaw still scruffy. Her insides clenched. And clenched even harder when he ran his hand down her back and leaned down to murmur in her ear. "Come for a ride in my truck."

A gorgeous hunk of a man was luring her into his truck in the dark of night while all she wore was a thin layer of cotton and not much else. "Let's go."

He didn't kiss her when he boosted her up into his truck, but his eyes smoldered so hot that she felt singed. Hauling himself up on the other side, he shut the door and pulled out. Throat dry, Nayna rubbed her palms down her thighs as the radio played slow night music, and tried not to wriggle in her seat.

"Nayna." His voice held a warning.

Startled and all but bursting out of her skin, she said, "What?"

"Stop wriggling." The words were *extremely* calm, but a muscle jumped in his jaw.

As Nayna had already learned, Raj wasn't actually calm when he got like this. To test her theory, she crossed her legs, causing the sundress to ride up a little.

He slammed through the gear change, the truck's tires squealing as he turned the corner of a deserted road. Nayna's entire body sizzled. "Where are you taking me?" she asked belatedly.

The muscles in his arms stood out as he spoke, his big body all but humming. "A private place."

It proved to be a hilltop that looked out over one of the wild west coast beaches... and was currently utterly deserted, not another human or human habitation in sight. "How do you know about this place?" It wasn't an official parking lot or route; she'd seen no signs, no street-lights along the last part of the drive.

"I worked on a site not far from here. Found it one day while checking out the area." Turning off the lights and the engine, he opened his car door.

Not sure what he intended, Nayna stayed put until he came around and opened her door. But when she swiveled her legs around to get out too, he stopped her by putting his hands on her thighs and stroking upward. Nayna's panties went embarrassingly damp at the rough caress of his touch and she waited, breath tight in her throat, to see how far he'd go.

To a dangerous edge, then back.

Again and again.

Watching his hands and her trembling thighs the entire time.

When he lifted his head, his gaze was way beyond a smolder. "Wait," he nearly growled, then left her to go get something from the back of his truck.

She sucked in a breath when he rolled out a thick outdoor blanket onto the ground, her heart drumming in her chest.

Raj came to her, put his hands on her waist. "Yes?"

Nayna nodded. Wherever this led, she wasn't about to back away. She placed her own hands on his shoulders, and he swung her down to the ground, then shut the door behind her. Feeling awkward, Nayna turned to him. "What—"

He slammed his mouth down on hers, his hands hauling her hips to close the final distance between them. A second of shocked surprise and then Nayna was rising on tiptoe and kissing him back just as hungrily, her breasts crushed against the hard planes of his chest.

When he rumbled something and took them to the blanket, she cooperated fully.

Then his weight was over her, though he was careful to brace himself so he didn't crush her, and she was being kissed like she was his air and he couldn't breathe. Nayna gripped his hair, stroked his nape, and kissed him back with all the frustrated passion inside her. When she bent one leg at the knee, he took advantage of the position to stroke the back of her thigh, going all the way to the edge of her panties.

Her pulse hitched, her cardigan suddenly stifling. "I have to take this off," she gasped out after breaking the kiss.

Rising off her, he gave her room enough to get the garment off and was back before she could ask him to strip off his tee. God, he was so hot, so hard. His erection was blatant, the hand he ran up her thigh and to her hip confident. Finally breaking the kiss as he played with the lace side of her panties, his chest heaving as hard as hers, he looked into her eyes.

Whatever he saw there had him stroking his hand around her hip and under her panties to cup her bare cheek. Shyness threatened to drench her. She tugged at his T-shirt in a desperate fight to stave it off. Getting the hint, he rose and got rid of it before settling right back into his previous position, her bare cheek in his hand and all.

His fingers moved, stroking.

She swallowed and ran her hands down his chest, glorying in him. When she rose to press kisses across his skin, he shuddered. She loved how he tasted, the inherent masculine scent of him below the freshness of soap intoxicating. Squeezing the part of her he held, he dropped his mouth to her neck, kissing and nibbling his way down.

"I've been dreaming about seeing these breasts again," he said against her skin as he tugged one strap of the sundress over her shoulder.

Her breast popped out, her nipple the picture of enthusiasm.

Raj closed his hand over it, squeezed. When she moaned, he smiled—and oh, that slow, sexy smile was even more glorious than she'd imagined and it scrambled her brain until she forgot to be embarrassed or shy as he tugged off the other strap, then pulled both down her arms, leaving her dress crumpled at her waist.

"I always seem to end up like this around you," she whispered against his throat.

Raj pushed up off his hands with the ease of a man in peak physical condition. "I'm not complaining," he rumbled, his eyes taking in the sight of her laid out like an invitation. "You're fucking beautiful."

The rough-edged comment hit her hard, made her boneless.

When he came back down on her and dropped his mouth to first one breast then the other, she gripped his hair and held on for the ride. Her hips jerked up convulsively against him, but he didn't seem to mind, sliding one arm behind her back and arching her even further for his wet, suckling kisses.

Her breasts would be red tomorrow from the scrapes of his teeth and the roughness of his stubble and she just wanted more. Wrapping one leg around his back, she luxuriated in the feel of his muscles moving underneath, fluid and controlled at the same time.

"Raj," she whispered when the sensations became too intense, a strange emptiness at her core. "I need you."

His mouth was on her own before the sentence ended, his arms wrapping tight around her and flipping them over so that she lay on top of him, her breasts flat against his chest, her dress in danger of totally falling off, his erection a rigid brand against her. Without warning, like a switch being flicked that made her feel buried under a flood of sensation, it was all too much for her starved body and she ducked her head against his neck.

Breath ragged, he stroked her back.

After all they'd done together, it was the kiss he pressed to her temple that made her eyes sting, it was so violently tender. "Sorry," she whispered.

"Why?" Another slow stroke of her back. "Anticipation just makes things better."

His chest vibrated against her as he spoke, and she shivered. Rising up to look down at him, she said, "I thought I was ready." Frustrated and aroused and needy. But it looked like after twenty-eight years of virginity, she needed to ease into the erotic rawness of what happened when the two of them came together.

With him, she had no walls, no barriers.

Just nakedness far beyond the skin. And it terrified her.

"I'm yours whenever you're ready," Raj said, and the words crashed over her like the waves below, powerful and turbulent.

20

THE CONSTRUCTION WORKERS' BOOK CLUB

RAJ ENDED UP HAVING TO work the majority of the next few days, along with a couple of his guys who wanted the extra pay. That night on the cliffs with Nayna, especially the way she'd lain snuggled up against him for over an hour after they called things to a halt, it was the best Christmas gift he could've imagined.

He could've pushed her in the nights that followed, but he'd fought his aggressive instincts and given her the room she needed. She'd come close to panic with him on the cliffs, and he didn't think it had been about sex. It was all happening too fast for her, the nameless thing that burned between them a hurricane.

"Hey, Raj!" one of his men called out. "Gazza says those are lady scratches on your back. He right?"

Raj hadn't realized Nayna had scratched him. Grinning, he said, "No comment and keep your fucking eyes to yourself." A construction site wasn't exactly time for gentle language.

"Hey, Gazza, I think the boss has a girl."

"And you're a bunch of gossips!" Raj yelled back. "I'm paying you to hammer, not chat."

"Hammer! Is that what they call a Freudian slip?" That was from Gazza—currently in the midst of an English literature degree for "reasons." What reasons, he'd never verbalized.

"Gaz!" Raj yelled up. "You ever read *Pride and Prejudice*?"

"Yeah, for class." The other man continued to frame an upstairs window. "That Mr. Darcy is a wanker like the entire first half—if I was that much of a wanker, I'd never get laid."

Nodding because someone finally agreed with him, Raj whacked in another timber before saying, "And what the fuck about Wickham?"

"Dude's a fucking fuckwit" was the concise response.

Tino, who'd started this all off, said, "You two in a book club or something?"

"A club to get girls, dickhead," Gazza responded. "Girls like guys who read."

"Yeah, says who?" Tino demanded.

"Look up 'hot guys reading' online."

When Tino did and went, "Shiiiiiit, why didn't you fuckers tell me this years ago!" Raj went over to take a look.

And saw countless images of men reading in public. Pictures taken by women. Who had then commented with heart emojis and words like *swoon* and "my panties just disappeared."

Hmm.

That night he sent Nayna a shirtless image—of him

sprawled in his bed, reading about that wanker, Mr. Darcy. He'd stolen the print book off his sister's bookshelf for this purpose. It was worth all the work it took to get that shot when Nayna replied with: *I'm dead now, Sen. I hope you're happy.*

Yes, Raj was very happy. Panic or not, she was still talking to him, still reacting to him. The door wasn't quite shut. His butterfly hadn't flown out of his sight.

RAJ FINALLY ADMITTED DEFEAT ON the morning of New Year's Eve. He'd tried everything possible, but his parents would not budge on the "casual" get-together with the Sharmas. "Shilpa and Gaurav will make such nice in-laws," he heard his mother, Sangeeta, say to his father—the two were on the lawn, not far from Raj's flat at the back of the property.

His sister, who was hanging out with him, raised an eyebrow, then began to sing "Here comes the bride" under her breath.

"Quiet, Monkey." He pointed a finger at her.

Unrepentant, she stuck out her tongue. "So, are you going to marry her?"

"That's between me and Nayna." And it was a dream so important that he couldn't share it with anyone until it was real, until she agreed to be his.

"Ugh. Spoilsport." Aditi slumped back on the sofa, her mass of curly hair a halo around her head. She was as tiny as he was big, her face triangular where his was all square lines. And her brain worked completely differently too.

"You still kicking the asses of the boys in your physics class?"

"It's my solemn duty." Still slumped like a jellyfish, she scowled. "God, the mansplaining I got when I started this year. Just because I'm short and female." She sat up. "I hope you never mansplain to a woman."

Raj threw up his hands. "I've been schooled by you since you were four, what do you think?"

Bouncing up, she came over to hug him from behind where he sat at his drafting desk, working out a building problem. "I love you, bhaiya." She smacked a kiss on his cheek. "I'm gonna quiz this Nayna chick. She better be good enough for you."

His admonitions to her to keep her distance were soundly ignored. "That's what comes of being a nice big brother," he muttered to himself when they got to the Sharma house and Aditi attached herself to Nayna like a human limpet.

"Were you speaking to me?"

He shook his head at Madhuri. "No, sorry." He took in her flawless makeup, her tight top that showed a little too much cleavage, her skinny jeans, and had zero reaction. Nayna, meanwhile, was wearing a loose white linen shift with three-quarter-length sleeves, and he wanted to tear it off and lick her up like candy.

"Sooo, you and my sister are serious." A waggle of Madhuri's eyebrows. "I'm happy for Nayna."

He had the feeling she was sincere. He also had a feeling that Madhuri was used to being the center of attention. Even though she was happy for her sister, she kept attempting to outshine her. Not just the clothes and the makeup and the flashy earrings. The charming of his parents, the way she got Aditi away from Nayna by talking hair trends, how she took over a conversation Nayna was having with her own father.

It annoyed him.

Especially when Nayna's entire family didn't even seem to notice, as if the behavior was so normal that it didn't ping on their radar. He scowled, gaining a dark new insight into Nayna's upbringing.

What kept the fuse on his temper from igniting was that Nayna's quiet beauty and inner warmth continued to shine despite Madhuri's flash. Aditi floated back to Nayna, and his parents smiled huge smiles at her as she kept the evening flowing, making sure the music was just right and speaking to everyone with a natural warmth.

Everyone but him. Him, she avoided.

Raj narrowed his eyes and waited for his chance. This was New Year's Eve, and he intended to start the coming year as he intended to end it: kissing Nayna.

RAJ'S BUBBLY LITTLE SISTER CHATTED to Nayna while Nayna refilled a snack plate in the kitchen—and hid from Raj. She was feeling very raw at the moment, having caught sight of Madhuri and her father laughing uproariously at something earlier that afternoon. After which Gaurav Sharma had hugged his older daughter.

It was stupid, but Nayna had felt so left out, so second-best.

Never good enough.

Rebellion had stirred, slammed up against who Raj was becoming to her. If she walked away from him to prove a point to her father, she *would be* stupid. But the idea of falling in with her parents' plans, of being good little Nayna, it grated.

Hence the hiding.

Torn in two directions, she'd taken the mature stance of avoidance.

Aditi, meanwhile, was being very cute, subtly grilling Nayna. She played along. Raj must be a good brother if his baby sister was so protective of him. "Your brother Navin and his wife couldn't come?" she asked during a break in the questioning.

"Yeah, his friends do a party every year." Aditi wandered over to the end of the counter near the fruit bowl.

"You can look if you like," Nayna said, spotting Aditi's curious eyes on a pack of photographs she'd had printed the other day. "It's only photos of family and friends." She turned to find the rest of the sweet chili dip. "We still like to do albums."

"Ma does the same," Aditi murmured, opening the pack.

Aha! There was the dip, shoved behind a giant head of lettuce. Grabbing it, Nayna went to scoop it out into the serving bowl.

"Hey!" Aditi held up a photograph. "Why do you have a photo of Harlow?"

Nayna smiled, remembering the day at Ísa's apartment when she'd snapped the shot. "He's my best friend's brother—stepbrother, technically." Ísa just called Harlow her brother because that was who Ísa was, a woman with an incredible ability to love. "Do you know him?"

Aditi nodded, a shy smile curving her lips. "We met at this thing our schools did together."

"He's lovely, isn't he?" One of the sweetest teenage boys Nayna had ever met.

Aditi's cheeks pinked and she bit down on her lower lip. After glancing out the door as if to check if anyone else was nearby, she said, "We're going to the movies together next week, when he has a little time off from his internship. Just, you know, as friends," she added quickly.

"Do your parents know?" She didn't want this spunky girl in trouble.

But Aditi nodded. "Raj bhaiya spoke to them," she said, using the word for brother after Raj's name—a normal thing for such a younger sibling. To simply say her older brother's name would sound wrong, a harsh scratch on a record.

Aditi gave Nayna a measuring look. "He's always been as strict as them, really overprotective. But... he's changed."

Nayna had to fight not to show her reaction, but the warmth uncurling inside her felt like a living thing. "Has he?" she asked, and it came out husky.

"Yeah," Aditi said. "I mean he's still bhaiya." A roll of the eyes. "So bossy and wants to know every detail of where Harlow and I will be, but it's like he really thinks about what I ask him before he gives an answer instead of just saying no to stuff like this."

Nayna finished preparing the tray, a tightness in her chest. "He sounds like a wonderful brother."

"The best," Aditi said at once. "Even before. Shall I take that tray? And can I keep the photo of Harlow?"

"Thank you, and yes, you can." Nayna handed over the tray, then reached out to fix one of Aditi's curls so that it was no longer bouncing in her eye.

She waited to let out a shaky exhale until after the girl had disappeared into the backyard, where everyone was gathered under colorful lights Madhuri had strung up. Aditi's words, what they implied... they cut her knees out from under her. Raj had *listened* to Nayna. Not only had he listened, he'd understood.

Confusion reigned in her, crashing against the need to break the shackles and a compulsion to shackle herself to Raj.

RAJ SLIPPED INTO THE HOUSE five minutes after he saw Aditi come out and realized everyone aside from Nayna was out on the lawn. He tracked her down in a hallway inside the house. Pinning her between the hands he'd braced on the wall on either side of her, he said, "It's nearly midnight."

"Raj." She pushed at his chest while casting frantic looks around him. "They'll notice!"

"No they won't. Our parents are involved in a heated discussion about that Indian soap opera they all watch, and our sisters are playing a game on Madhuri's phone." He nuzzled her, taking her scent into his lungs, settling the tension wrapped around his gut. "I've never kissed anyone at midnight on New Year's Eve."

Her hands paused pushing at his chest, curled in instead, and he wanted to shudder in sheer relief. "Never?"

"Never." He wondered if he should tell her what other things he'd never done. "Have you?"

She shook her head, her eyes huge and her teeth biting down on her lower lip.

"How about it?" It came out a rough request.

Running her hands down his chest in that possessive petting way that gave him hope, she rolled her lips inside her mouth and when she parted them to speak, they were pink and wet. "Okay," she whispered. "But you have to figure out how."

"Leave me to it." His jeans were ridiculously uncomfortable in the crotch region right now. "I have to go get my cock under control first."

Her eyes dipped to his jeans, and he saw the pulse jerk in her throat. "I can't believe you just..."

Loving her scandalized response when he'd sucked and licked her bare breasts not so many nights ago, he bent close to her ear and whispered, "My cock feels like concrete. It wants to be inside your hot and tight—"

"Nayna!" It was a singsong cry from the kitchen. "I didn't tell the folks you were in here with Raj, but you better show your face soon or you're *busted*."

Raj pushed off the wall. "I'll see you at midnight."

21

HAPPY NEW YEAR

AYNA'S BREASTS WERE SULKING WHEN she walked into the kitchen, so addicted to Raj's touch that the tiny mounds ached at being denied it. "Where's Aditi?"

"Keeping the folks distracted." Madhuri gave her the once-over. "Huh. You don't look like you've been doing anything at all."

It was a good thing Madhuri didn't have X-ray vision.

Her sister's phone beeped before Nayna had to come up with an answer. Pulling it out of her pocket, Madhuri glanced at it. A dreamy look softened her face, her lips curving.

"Who is he?" Nayna asked her sister.

Madhuri was a flirt, had always been a flirt. However, despite what some people might believe, she didn't take it beyond flirting with most men. Regardless, she had a far richer dating history than Nayna.

Which wasn't hard since Nayna had never actually been on a date.

As for Madhuri—Nayna didn't know what their parents believed, but her sister had been dating steadily since the divorce. Madhuri might be commitment-shy, but she liked men, and she liked being around men and being taken care of by men.

Even living alone, Madhuri was never short of male help. The last time Nayna had been over, she'd found Madhuri's middle-aged landlord helping her sort out a problem with her television. And there'd been nothing slimy about it—the man had just been happy to be around Madhuri's effervescent feminine presence.

It had always been that way.

Growing up, Nayna had watched in awe as her sister drew male attention at every wedding and every large party to which they were invited. The marriage offers had begun pouring in the instant Madhuri turned eighteen, but their parents had turned them all down.

"We want our daughter to be educated and able to stand on her own feet before marriage," her father had said to more than one hopeful suitor.

When those suitors had assured Gaurav Sharma that they'd support Madhuri's continued studies even after marriage, he'd shaken his head. "No, this is old-fashioned. Marriage at eighteen is not what we want for our girl. She should have her university years."

That, Nayna thought, was partly why it had hurt their parents so awfully when Madhuri eloped at nineteen. She'd thrown egg into Gaurav's and Shilpa's faces, caused them even more shame in the community than engendered by the affair with the master's student. Raj had deliberately been a bastard that time at lunch, but he was also right: there remained families who wouldn't allow their precious sons within a hundred meters of Madhuri.

Not that Madhuri cared; she had more men in her thrall than she knew what to do with anyway. Six marriage offers had arrived since Pinky's wedding. Two from divorced males, three from never-marrieds, and one from a man who was separated as of a bare two months ago but already looking. He'd gone directly into the discard pile. No one wanted to be with a jerk.

"Look at this," Shilpa Sharma had said when she got a message about one of the never-marrieds. "He's a real estate man, owns that big apartment complex out by where Mina mausi lives."

Madhuri had been intrigued. "He must be loaded."

"Yes, but he's also older than your father," their mother had said, waving her hand. "Why do these wrinkly old men think they can get the pretty girls?"

"Um, have you seen Nita's husband?" Nayna had pointed out.

Their mother had shuddered. "He's going to be dead before she has her first child."

"I don't think that's in Nita's plans." Madhuri's silky voice. "She's waiting for him to pop off so she can live the high life with a stud."

Laughing at the wickedness of Madhuri's words, Shilpa Sharma had moved on to the next offer. "You should go for this Rohan boy instead. The electrician with his own company. Electricians make good money—we had to pay five hundred dollars that time we had the problem! And he's young and fit."

Madhuri, of course, was taking none of the offers seriously—and somehow getting away with it. Every time their parents began to push, she'd say she didn't intend to be a two-time divorcée and planned to take her time choosing the right groom. "Don't tell Ma and Dad," she whispered now before turning her phone around so that Nayna could look at the photograph on it. "His name is Bailey."

Bailey was a surfer dude, complete with a surfboard under his arm and beach-blond hair. His smile was tooth-paste white, his skin like a baby's bottom. "How old is he?" Nayna asked. "*Five*?"

Madhuri giggled. "Twenty-one," she said. "I'm the sophisticated older woman who's teaching him the ways of the world."

Nayna's lips twitched. She had to hand it to her sister—Madhuri knew how to live life. "I'm guessing this one isn't long term?" she said, taking in the pretty cottage behind Bailey the Surfer. It had a name—inscribed on the plaque beside Bailey's right shoulder: *Seagrass.*

Madhuri gave a liquid shrug. "Who knows? We're having fun right now." Shimmying around the kitchen, she added, "Lots and lots of fun."

"When did you go to this cottage? It's pretty."

"Been there a couple of times now. Last was a month ago."

Nayna happened to glance out the window as Madhuri went to reply to Bailey's message, and caught sight of Aji and Mr. Hohepa sneaking off with Pixie as their tail-wagging third. No doubt for a "walk." Turning back on a surge of inexplicable emotion that built inside her like a wave an inch away from breaking, she caught

Madhuri's expression. "Don't look at Bailey's messages around the folks. You have the sex face on."

"I can't help it. He makes me want to strip off my panties and do a pole dance." Her phone beeped again before Nayna could respond.

Leaving her sister to answer it, Nayna walked outside —to see that Raj had already beaten her there. He must've gone out the front door and walked back around the side of the house—as if he'd left to grab something from his truck.

He glanced over when she exited the house, his dark gaze intent. When he raised an eyebrow in a silent question, Nayna wondered what her face betrayed. She shook her head, then carried on doing the small things that needed to be done to make sure this entire thing went off smoothly. It gave her a place for her hands, a way to settle the churning confusion that boiled within.

But she couldn't shut out how well her parents were getting along with Raj's. The four of them were laughing together with an ease that said they were becoming fast friends. And with each burst of laughter, Nayna felt the chains tighten even further. Everything was being put into place, all the pieces slotting in.

Her agreement was just a formality.

RAJ COULD FEEL SOMETHING WAS seriously wrong, but he couldn't pin Nayna down long enough to figure out what. He was good at fixing things—but he couldn't fix what he didn't know was broken. He'd thought they were doing okay when she'd kissed him so passionately, but things had changed by the time he finally trapped her alone against the side of the house out of sight of their families. He couldn't read her at all.

"Less than a minute to go," he said, determined to get to the root of this, determined to fight for his Nayna.

Her fingers brushing over the smooth line of his jaw. "I miss the stubble."

Rubbing his jaw against her palm, he said, "It's growing already."

No smile, her eyes haunted when they met his. "How long do we have?"

"Long enough to kiss at midnight." Aditi was the official timekeeper, and he'd asked her to start the countdown two minutes late; his baby sister had been delighted to be part of the intrigue.

"If someone sets off fireworks at midnight," she'd whispered, "I'll say they're jumping the gun."

Bracing his body even more firmly into Nayna, holding her in the only way she'd let him, Raj said, "Why that look? Are you worried about our parents making plans?" He knew that was part of it, but not all. "I'll handle that. No one will push you into anything until you're ready."

He'd made a mistake in declaring his hand; he'd thought it would ease the obstacles in their path, the two of them no longer watched so closely, but all it had done was scare her. "I'll fix it," he promised her. "Let me."

No answer from Nayna.

Sliding her hand to the back of his neck, she rose on tiptoe. "Hurry," she whispered. "According to my watch, it's three seconds to midnight."

Feeling as if she was water slipping out between his fingers, he kissed her with all the need in his heart, wrapping her in his arms and lifting her off her feet as the sky above them burst with fireworks set off by others in the street.

A new year had begun, but the shadows of the past haunted them both.

22

THE ROLE OF THE DASTARDLY VILLAIN
IS NOW TAKEN

Nayna expected to dream of Raj, her body ached so for him, even as confusion tangled her in a thousand knots. But when she did slip into sleep, she didn't dream sexy, frustrating dreams about a certain hot man in construction. She dreamed of waking in darkness. Heart skittering and breath jagged, she began to walk with her hands outstretched, searching.

Her palms hit a wall.

She followed it, running now, only to hit an edge and another wall. Again and again.

Trapped. She was trapped in a box without light. And now the air was going.

Clutching at her chest, she continued to run, continued to search, but there was no way out and she was suffocating and she couldn't breathe and—

Nayna jerked awake, her heart thumping a million miles an hour and her breath coming in harsh pants. She stared at the door she'd closed before she went to bed and her pulse spiked again. She barely stopped herself from getting up and wrenching it open.

That wouldn't solve the problem.

Throat dry, she grabbed the bottle of water she kept on the bedside table and took a long gulp. Then she sat there and thought of that dark, airless room where she'd been trapped. Her skin grew taut and pinched as her breath began to turn shallow.

No, this wasn't good.

Even the gorgeous photos that Raj kept sending her couldn't help. Nayna's memory of warmth and safety when he held her in his arms didn't help. But she couldn't say no when he asked her if she'd meet him at a café the day after the new year: *My brother and sister-in-law would like to say hello. But Nayna, if you're not comfortable, I'll put them off.*

Her throat got all tight, her eyes burning.

I'll be there, she wrote back, because he was wonderful and siblings were different from parents.

She didn't mention why she was going out when she left the house that afternoon, in no mood for the questions and speculation. When she arrived at the café, she found Raj waiting outside for her. He looked good enough to eat in those well-loved jeans he'd worn to the party, work boots, and a gray T-shirt that hugged his pecs.

He cupped her cheek with one hand when she reached him. "Thank you for coming." Such serious words.

"It's important to you." And he was becoming terrifyingly important to her.

A brush of his thumb over her cheekbone, his gaze potent and unreadable. "Navin and Komal have grabbed a table inside." Pulling open the door of the café, he placed his other hand on her lower back as they walked to the counter and ordered before joining his brother and sister-in-law.

Navin Sen was more slender than his brother and had a bit more curl in his hair as well as a pristinely clipped goatee. His smile was wide when he extended his hand toward Nayna. "It's nice to meet you at last."

"Same," Nayna said, with a smile aimed at both him and his wife.

Komal Sen was... glossy. That was the perfect word. Lovely round face, pouty lips painted to perfection, sleek and shiny hair expertly colored in shades of bronze and brown. Her red dress fit like a glove when she rose to her feet and gave Nayna an air-kiss, and she had Madhuri's kind of curves.

She engaged with the men like Madhuri too, flirtatious with Raj without crossing the line—though from their body language, she seemed to be having a tiff with her husband. The giggles and admiring glances were all shot Raj's way, the curled lip and snarky comments her husband's. Komal's behavior would've been off-putting to many women, but Nayna had grown up with Madhuri.

Compared to Nayna's sister, Komal was a novice when it came to capturing male attention. Nayna found her familiar in a way, and that relaxed her. "How was the party?" she asked after their drinks came.

"Oh, fantastic!" Komal stirred sugar into her coffee. "I danced my feet off."

A tension at the corners of Navin's mouth that told Nayna his wife hadn't been dancing with him. She shot

Raj a quick glance, not about to touch that with a barge pole. He gave the slightest shake of his head.

Taking the cue, she ignored the mounting evidence of marital discord as they continued to talk. Raj had his arm along the back of her chair again, his fingers occasionally brushing her upper arm, and Nayna didn't want to be anywhere else. For a short while, she felt only like a young woman out with her man, the two of them getting to know each other.

No expectations.

No burden of tradition.

No tacit road for them to walk.

"Excuse me for a minute." Rising, Navin headed off toward the restrooms.

Raj's phone went seconds later. "It's a client," he said after a glance. "I'll try to make it quick." A brush of his hand over her ponytail before he stepped outside to take the call.

"Nice to see Raj find someone." Komal's voice dragged her back.

Nayna told herself she was imagining the sudden razored edge in it. "He's an amazing man."

"Yeah, I chose the wrong brother."

Ohh-kay, now they were in incendiary territory.

Nayna took a sip of her mocha, mentally telling both men to hurry up.

"But wow, pretty big sacrifice for you to give up your career after all that work," Komal murmured after another sip of her latte.

Nayna frowned. "Excuse me?"

Tilting her head to the side, Komal blinked innocently. "Oh, didn't Raj tell you?" Syrupy voice, but the nastiness was there in the tilt of her lips. "Navin says his brother's always been open about wanting the full traditional deal. Wife at home cooking the rotis and looking after the kiddies, man working."

Churning in Nayna's gut. "There's nothing wrong with that," she said, not about to let this woman judge Raj; Nayna understood where his desires had been born, why that was his dream.

"Oh Lord, no," Komal gushed. "If Navin earned enough to keep me at home, I'd jump at the chance to join the ladies-who-lunch set. Not sure about the kids though. Raj wants them while he's young, and I prefer keeping my figure."

Oh, thank God.

"I wonder if they sell this coffee by the bag?" Navin said, sliding back into his seat. "It's pretty good."

Raj returned a minute later, and the rest of the conversation was innocuous enough. However, by the end of it, when Nayna was alone with Raj again, she felt no compunction at all in saying, "Your sister-in-law is not a nice woman." Bitch was the word that fit. Nayna never used that word lightly, but Komal had gone out of her way to discomfort her husband, and her digs at Nayna had been subtle but pointed.

Whatever her issue was, it didn't excuse her behavior. The way she was going, she could stand in for the melodramatic "evil sister-in-law" on that soap opera. All she needed to do was stand around reciting her nefarious plans aloud while ominous music built to a crescendo in the background. And the irony of her name being Komal —which meant soft, delicate—was just the icing on the cake.

"No, Komal can be difficult." Raj walked with her out of the café. "But she's Navin's wife, and my brother isn't innocent in the problems between them—but those problems aren't ours." Wrapping one arm around her shoulder, he said, "Want to walk a little? There are a few construction projects going on around here. Competitors."

Nayna slid her arm around his waist and decided to live in the dream. "Yes. Let's go spy on them."

The two of them had far too much fun over the next two hours, with Raj grumbling about how he could've done a better job on the various projects and Nayna playfully saying, "I know, honey" until he kissed her smiling mouth. He was scowling at her teasing, and his stubble prickled, and it was wonderful.

But she had to know if Komal had been telling the truth. The other woman had been attempting to stir trouble, no doubt about that. Which was why Nayna wasn't about to make any assumptions until she had an answer direct from the source. "Raj, did you dream of a homemaker wife and lots of children?"

"I didn't know you then," he said simply. "Now when I think about my future, I see you." A kiss that was rough and tender both, Raj's arms coming around her. "What I wanted before no longer matters."

But it did, Nayna thought as she drove home. Raj's dreams *mattered*. Being abandoned, it had left wounds in his heart that even the love of his parents hadn't fully healed. That cruel letter had reopened what had healed. Raj's dream of a wife content to focus on their home, happy little children, and a husband who provided, it was both simple and profound.

Even more important—above all else, beyond the specifics—he needed absolute, unflinching commitment from the woman who was his. He needed to know she was in this all the way and for the long haul. And for him, that meant marriage. It meant tradition. It meant following the well-trodden path because that path led to community and roots and certainty.

There was *nothing* wrong with that.

But Nayna had no idea what she wanted from life. *Him*, she wanted him. But not the tradition that had begun to feel like ropes around her, cutting off her air. Not the implicit defined patterns of behavior. Not the rigidly limited choices. The very things that centered Raj were her worst nightmare.

Nayna had no right to put her dreams over his.

23

EVERYTHING'S BETTER WITH TEQUILA!!!

NAYNA WENT IN TO WORK again on January third. She'd fibbed and told her family the firm needed her to handle an urgent client request, but she'd just been desperate to be out of the house. She'd come in to work part of yesterday evening too, her intent to keep her mind occupied with things other than Raj and the mess she was making of her life.

When she'd returned home, her sister had been sitting at the kitchen table chatting with their father, both of them laughing and smiling. Madhuri had been waxing lyrical about how her landlord had given her permission to paint a feature wall.

Nayna's stomach tightened.

Putting down the pen, she glanced at the clock. It was seven and she should probably go home. Instead, she picked up the phone and spoke to the married couple who were her bosses. Then, laptop and purse slung over her shoulder, she went on an emergency run to a mall that was still open, grabbing a bite to eat along the way.

After which she drove to Ísa's apartment building and parked in one of the external guest spots.

And just sat in her car, staring at the steering wheel.

Anger and frustration and sadness and raw need churned inside her.

Tap, tap.

Nayna jumped, looked up to see Ísa's face outside the window. Heart thudding, she scrambled out of the car. "You gave me such a fright. I was away with the fairies."

"How long have you been waiting?" Her best friend was dressed in work clothes and carrying her satchel, so she must've only now returned home.

"Not long, just five minutes," Nayna said and the two of them chatted while going up to Ísa's apartment.

Once inside, Ísa made them a pot of tea as they continued to talk. Then her best friend's face took on a stubborn cast. "Now sit," she ordered Nayna. "Talk."

Nayna slumped into the sofa, Ísa beside her. "I need to get away." She hadn't understood that until she'd been sitting in her office, figuring out how she could avoid going home. "You know what I've realized? Raj is obstinate as hell in a quiet way. He's decided on me and he's not budging." It felt so beautiful to be wanted that openly; if only that could fix everything.

"And you're not sure yet?" Ísa asked.

"I want to strip him naked and jump his bones like a sex maniac," Nayna admitted because this was Ísa, from whom she had no secrets. "Plus it turns out I like his brains." She took a big gulp of the tea. "But there's all this other stuff in my head that's making it hard to think."

Unable to sit still, she slammed the cup on the table

and rose, started to walk back and forth. Her breathing came out short and sharp, her blood roaring in her ears. "Last night I got home to find my sister sitting at the kitchen table again, chatting away to my father. I love her, but at that instant I wanted to scream at her for ruining my life."

Her body trembled. "And that was when I realized she hadn't done anything to me." It had been a ringing slap that stunned.

Nayna had walked quietly through to her room and just sat on her bed for ten long minutes, staring at the wall and seeing her own blindness. "This is my life, and I'm the one who's screwed it up." It had been a powerful insight, one that had made her face up to her own mistakes, her own lack of courage.

For better or worse, Madhuri had made her choices.

Fourteen-year-old Nayna'd had good reason to resent her sister. She'd lost her freedom to be a teenager because of Madhuri, had never had the chance to make teenage memories of the kind Madhuri had taken for granted.

But Nayna was an adult now, and she was still blaming her sister for her own life.

That was bullshit.

Slumping back into the sofa, she folded her arms. "I'm taking some extra vacation time, getting the hell out of here so I can clear my head. I've already okayed it with my bosses." With the hours she'd put in pre-Christmas and over the past couple of days, her work was more than up to date and she'd be available to them by phone should they need her; she also had more than enough vacation time banked.

"Where are you going?" Ísa asked, protective as a mama bear.

"Here." Nayna used her phone to forward the booking to Ísa; she did want someone to know her whereabouts should she go missing or get eaten by a possum.

Ísa made sure the details had downloaded before she said, "If Raj tracks me down and asks?"

Nayna had zero self-control where Raj was concerned; he looked at her and she melted. "You know nothing."

"Got it."

After drinking some more of the tea, Nayna raised an eyebrow. "So, you're going camping?" Her friend had messaged her about the family camping trip to which Raj's friend Sailor Bishop had invited her.

"I hate you." Ísa's glare was pure death. "I'm doing it for love."

Snort-laughing and deliriously glad for the distraction, Nayna said, "Don't forget the toilet paper."

They talked more, of fears and hopes and pain. Nayna's heart ached for what Ísa was struggling with when it came to Sailor. He sounded like a really good guy —but one who had dreams that threatened to break Ísa's heart. Nayna's parents might be too involved, but Ísa's were the other extreme. Except for a beautiful and happy few years with her own aji, Nayna's best friend had grown up alone but for a few nannies.

Rain came down in a hard burst beyond the windows, blurring the night.

"Fuck the tea," Nayna muttered on a burst of aggravation. "Where's the tequila? I'll sleep over." She'd bought a small roll-on case at the mall, then filled it with necessary toiletries, a pair of pj's, and a couple of changes of clothes. She had a spare set of canvas trainers in back of her car for when she wanted to run errands after work and didn't want to wear heels. Anything she'd forgotten, she'd borrow off Ísa.

She had no plans to go home again until she'd figured out her messed-up head. She sent through a quick message to her mother to say she'd be spending the night at Ísa's.

"Tequila as ordered." Ísa held up a bottle triumphantly.

Nayna found the salt.

The first shot burned like fire.

The second not so much.

By the third, they were giggling and Ísa was muttering about romantic cactuses.

"It's cacti," Nayna said with a burp. "I think."

"Cac...tiiiii," Ísa sounded out slowly. "Dating a gardener is uh-mazing! He gives me cactuses. Be careful," she said solemnly. "They prick if you're naked."

Nayna wasn't sure if it was after the fourth or the fifth shot, but at some point she dialed Raj's number.

"Hi," she said when he answered. "I want to lick your abs."

"I could be persuaded," he said and she thought he might be smiling. "Especially since I've just showered off the day so I'm clean for your tongue."

"I don't mind sweaty." She crunched a potato chip, then dug her hand into the bag for another one. "How come you're so cute?"

"Mere jaanam, are you drunk?"

"No." She hiccupped, decided to take another sip of

tequila to wash down the potato chip. "Only had a few drinks."

"Of what?"

"You called me your darling." She blew him a noisy kiss. "You're my jaanu too."

"Nayna, baby, what are you drinking?"

"Tequila!" she whooped, and beside her, Ísa gave a battle cry.

"Are you in a bar?" Raj asked, his tone rougher. "Do you two need a ride home?"

She crunched more potato chips. "Will you be half-naked when you come? I want a half-naked taxi driver. With romantic cactuses."

"Cac-tiiiiii," Ísa whispered loudly.

"Nayna, *focus*. Where are you?"

Nayna stuck out her tongue at the phone. "He wants to know where we are," she said to Ísa without removing the phone from her ear.

"Home!" Ísa yelled too loudly toward the phone. "We're at home!"

"See?" Nayna said into the phone. "We're at home like I said." Her brain was a little fuzzy, and she wanted to make sure she didn't forget to tell him the most important thing, so she said, "I want to lick your abs."

"Anytime," Raj answered, and she was eighty-nine percent sure he was laughing. "Can I lick yours in return?"

Nayna pulled up the sleep T-shirt she'd borrowed from Ísa because she couldn't be bothered going down to her car to get her stuff. Above her panties, her belly curved softly. "I don't have any," she said sadly. "It's all soft." She poked at it. "My panties are orange."

A harsh groan down the line. "Jaan, don't drive tonight."

"Duh. I'm staying at Ísa's." Pushing down the T-shirt, she said, "Will you teach me how to have abs?"

"No. I like you soft."

Nayna smiled and kicked her feet... and took the drink Ísa held out. Her friend's face was a little red. Maybe she was drunk. Giggling at the thought, Nayna said, "You're so pretty, Raj. I'm gonna have sex dreams about you."

Then she hung up and threw back the shot.

"Sex dreams!" Ísa fell off the sofa laughing.

Cracking up at her friend's expression, Nayna swigged directly from the bottle of tequila and decided she would lick Raj's abs *twice.*

RAJ STARED AT THE PHONE. "Sex dreams," he muttered. "Nayna Sharma, you will drive me to madness." Then he tore off his towel, which he'd wrapped around his body after he heard the phone come alive with the ringtone he'd programmed for her, and walked back into the shower.

As he stroked himself to release under the heated spray, he imagined Nayna's tongue as she licked her way down his abs and decided to go further. Those soft lips surrounding him, her long, slender-fingered hands on his thighs, her hair falling forward as she—

"*Fuck.*"

He came so hard that his back bowed and white spots flickered in front of his eyes. Slumping back against the shower wall while the water cascaded over him, washing away the signs of his orgasm, he told himself that he had to get a better handle on this. If he didn't, he wouldn't be able to make it good for Nayna when she was ready to let him. And he wanted to make it good for her. So damn good.

Finally getting out of the shower again ten minutes later, his body under control but his mind full of thoughts of her, he checked his phone to make sure she hadn't sent him a message. Nothing.

His adorably drunk Nayna was probably fast asleep by now.

He'd been worried there for a second that she was out somewhere and clearly incapacitated, but knowing that she was with her best friend, the two of them getting drunk safely at home, made him grin. He wondered if she'd remember what she'd said to him when she woke up tomorrow. If she didn't, he'd be certain to remind her. It wasn't every day that a man got told he was cute and that a woman wanted to lick his abs.

Rubbing at his stubbled jaw, he said, "Cute" and chuckled.

He dressed in a pair of jeans and a T-shirt, ran his fingers through his hair, then pulled on his sneakers and padded down the stone pathway that connected his one-bedroom unit to his parents' place.

His friend Sailor didn't get it, how he could still live so close to his folks. Sailor loved his parents, but he'd been out of their place as soon as possible. But this was Raj's normal. As the eldest son, he was expected to live at home—and to bring his bride home too. Raj had never felt like rebelling against that aspect of his culture; he'd grown up in a multigenerational family home, and he wanted that for his children too.

Of course, he'd extend his place to be bigger. The family had the room on their patch of land, and no way was he sharing living space with Navin and Komal. He'd likely have to build a room for Aditi too, or she'd curse him to eternity, he thought with an inward laugh.

Raj, did you dream of a homemaker wife and lots of children?

The memory of Nayna's solemn question made his lingering smile fade. He wanted to get in his truck and find her right now, had planned to track her down after his shower, but she was in no state to talk.

"Tomorrow," he promised himself. He'd find Nayna tomorrow and make her understand that *she* was the most important part of his dreams now. Everything else they could work out. She didn't have to be afraid he'd try to put her in a box. Never would he do that to his bright, brilliant Nayna.

"Tomorrow," he whispered again, and it was a vow.

24

(VERY QUIET WHISPERS ONLY PLEASE)

"NAYNA."

Nayna buried her head under the pillow, wondering why someone was playing the tabla inside her skull. But then a cruel hand came and ripped the pillow away.

"Nayna," the voice said again. "Wake up or you'll miss your flight."

Groaning, Nayna cracked open one eyelid. "I hate you," she said to her best friend. "How can you be so chipper?" As far as she knew, Ísa had drunk exactly as much tequila as she had.

Ísa raised an eyebrow. "Do you remember how I told you not to get started on the half bottle of whiskey I found?"

Nayna scowled. "What bottle of whiskey?"

"Exactly." Throwing the pillow aside, Ísa pointed toward the bathroom. "Shower, then I'll drop you off at the airport if you want."

Usually, if Nayna was traveling within the country,

she just parked her car in the airport's long-term parking lot, but today she nodded. She was going to be gone at least a week, maybe more, and she didn't want to leave her car in the lot for that long.

"I'll go grab your stuff." Ísa picked up Nayna's keys. "And I'll move the car to your parents' place tomorrow."

Staggering into the bathroom, Nayna turned the shower to as hot as she could handle, then stepped in. It was halfway through, as the heat burned away the last of the alcohol fumes that she began to remember. Eyes huge, she slid open the shower door, and yelled out, "Did I call Raj last night and tell him I wanted to lick his abs? And that I was going to have sex dreams about him?"

Given the hysterical laughter that came from the direction of Ísa's kitchen area, the answer was a resounding yes. *Dear God*. Ducking back into the shower as her face flamed, Nayna quickly finished washing up. Ísa had thrown in her overnight bag in the interim, so after stepping out of the shower and drying off, she brushed her teeth using the toothbrush she'd bought yesterday. Technically, she thought, overnight bag wasn't the right term.

It was more a "running away from home" bag.

After slapping on some moisturizer from the hastily assembled bag of toiletries, she put away the bottle, then dug through to find clothes. Panties, bra, jeans, T-shirt, socks, and she was done. She stuffed her heels in one corner of the bag.

Taking it to near the front door, she saw Ísa had found her trainers. She left the bag beside the shoes, brought over her laptop bag and purse from where she'd left them in the lounge the previous night, then joined Ísa at the breakfast counter. Her friend pushed a bowl of porridge toward her. Made Aji's way. And with brown sugar on top. "You're the best," she told her friend. "My abused stomach thanks you."

When her phone beeped, she figured it must be a text from her mother reminding her of her second cousin's son's fourth birthday party—which she was supposed to attend tonight. If she hadn't intended to run away, she'd most definitely have worked late. She loved children, but that four-year-old was a horror. Last time Nayna had been around him, he'd purposefully spit orange juice on her dress while his mother looked on indulgently.

However, it wasn't Shilpa Sharma who'd messaged her. The name on the screen was Raj and the attached image was of his abs with the caption: *Ready to be licked.*

Groaning, she dropped her head to the counter and banged it twice while Ísa grabbed her phone—and began to laugh so hard she nearly fell off her stool.

"Why didn't you stop me?" Nayna said. "Isn't that in the friend code?"

"I was drunk," Ísa pointed out, gray-green eyes dancing. "And man, he does have nice abs!"

"You can lick your gardener's abs. Gimme back mine." She'd swiped the phone into her hand before she realized what she'd said.

Mine.

"Hey," she blurted out in an attempt to distract herself *and* her clever best friend, "you never told me about cactus love."

"Eat your porridge." Ísa shoved a big spoonful into her own mouth.

Nayna didn't think she was hungry, but she got to the

bottom of her bowl. After which she drank a huge cup of black coffee, and then the two of them rushed out the door. Thankfully traffic was light this early in the morning, and Ísa was able to drop her off right in front of the domestic terminal.

Nayna gave her friend a quick hug, grabbed her bag, and said, "Remember, cone of silence." She intended to text both her family and Raj just as she was about to board, let them know she was fine and that she was taking off for a few days. Nayna would never leave them to fear for her safety—she'd experienced that awful sensation herself when Madhuri left; to inflict it on another human being was beyond her.

However, she'd be keeping all details of her intended destination to herself.

Forget about the FBI or the CIA, Nayna's father was part of the CIF aka Concerned Indian Fathers unit. One hint of where she was headed and he'd contact the cousin of someone's uncle's brother's wife's auntie who happened to have a little convenience shop in the nearby town, or it would be a friend of a friend's brother-in-law's daughter who happened to be working the desk at the place where she planned to stay.

And there went her privacy.

Having already checked in on her phone, the first thing she did inside the terminal was go stand in line at the nearest coffee station and get a large flat white. Then she found a seat, glanced at the clock, and began to type a message to her mother.

She was only halfway through when she received a photo that made her lower body clench. Oh, Raj was having far too much fun with this. But she still couldn't help saving the photo, especially since she could see his bed-tumbled hair, his face wearing that slow, sexy grin that undid her.

After pushing Send on the message to her mother, she'd risen to join the boarding line when another incoming message made her want to moan.

Another picture of Raj's abs—this time with the tongue emoji added on.

When Ísa rang right after, she confessed all to her laughing friend. Afterward, she sent Raj a reply: *I'm going out of town for a few days. Talk when I get back.*

She put the phone into airplane mode immediately afterward.

She couldn't talk to anyone, especially not to the man who made her want to forget everything and just be with him; she needed time alone to decide.

On the rest of her life.

RAJ SCOWLED DOWN AT HIS phone. He'd just had a call from a Sharma girl. Too bad it was the wrong Sharma girl. Madhuri had tracked him down after Shilpa Sharma called her and told her that Nayna had run away. Not surprisingly, everyone's first thought was that Nayna had run away with Raj.

Now he rang Nayna's mother directly. "She told me she was going away for a few days. Your daughter is very responsible and intelligent. She'll be fine." It wasn't Nayna's safety that worried him but the thoughts tumbling around in that smart brain.

His heart had been beating hard and rough ever since he'd gotten that message and realized she was distancing herself from him. He couldn't use their physical connection to hold on to her if she'd deliberately traveled far from him. And fuck, that hurt like a kick to the gut.

"She told me she was going away to have some time alone to think!" Shilpa Sharma said. "Why can't she think at home? We have a perfectly good bedroom for her."

A sudden bustle of noise, the voice next on the line a male one. "Raj? What's this nonsense?" Gaurav Sharma demanded. "You're supposed to be her fiancé. Why can't you control her?"

Raj's hand tightened on the phone. "You need to let her have this," he said past his own violent need to see her, hold her. "Nayna is feeling trapped by the idea of marriage. She hasn't had much choice in her life, and now she's being railroaded into marriage." It hurt Raj to say that, to admit that she might decide he wasn't the husband she wanted.

A hesitation in the older man's voice when he said, "Do you think she's gone overseas?"

"No." Nayna was too loyal to her family to go so far out of reach without warning. "I'll deal with this, Mr. Sharma."

"She's my daughter."

Raj rubbed at his forehead. "Do you know her dreams?" he asked, fighting to keep his voice even. "Have you ever asked Nayna what she wants?" Maybe he shouldn't be speaking so bluntly to a man who might be his father-in-law if Raj's dreams didn't shatter, but he was too fucking angry to worry.

The idea of "controlling" Nayna, it made his vision haze red. "Have you ever looked at her and seen *Nayna* rather than a daughter who might turn out to be like Madhuri?"

Gaurav Sharma sucked in an audible breath. "Just bring her back home safe and sound," the older man said before hanging up.

Raj's chest heaved after the conversation, and he had to take harsh breaths of the summer air before he tried to call Nayna. Her phone was either off or she was already in the air. He sent a message, got a response after about two hours: *Yes, I'm safe. If you're the reason my parents aren't hounding me, thank you. I need time to think.*

Raj's shoulders knotted. Despite what he'd told her father, his first instinct was to fight, to push. That was how he'd survived the first six years of his life and the urge had been burned into him. It was what made him such a good businessman and how he'd taken his father's company to the next level.

He called her.

To discover she'd switched off her phone again.

"Fuck." Gritting his teeth, he breathed, just breathed. It was a technique he'd had to teach himself when this happened, when he ran up against a roadblock that no amount of pushing or fighting would conquer. The six-year-old boy inside him began to panic, and it manifested as a tightness in his chest and a rigid tension in his body.

He had a feeling it always would, but he'd learned to think past it.

His breath coming in clearer after several minutes, he sent Nayna another message that would download when she turned on her phone. "Fight for me like I'm fighting for you," he whispered after pushing the Send key. "Want me like I want you."

25

RAJ DECLARES AN AB MORATORIUM

NAYNA ONLY LASTED AN HOUR before switching her phone back on. She didn't want to be out of touch in case of an accident or emergency among the people she loved. Strangely, once again, she had no messages from her family. That was not a natural state of affairs. It had to be Raj. No one else would have the kind of stubborn will to go up against her father and win.

Raj, however, *had* sent her something: Another picture of his abs, but this time he'd blacked out that part of his body as if it were a censored image and written: *No more abs for you.*

Her lips trembled where she sat on the bus she'd taken from Christchurch, where her plane had landed. She missed him. Unbearably. But she didn't reply, couldn't reply. Not until she had more inside her than need and confusion.

After arriving at her cabin on the edge of Franz Josef Glacier Village late that day, she holed up, watching bad reality television deep into the night hours. She just needed something to occupy her brain so it wouldn't go around and around in circles, a dog chasing its own tail.

Part of her kept screaming what are you doing? And what *was* she doing? Raj was the most incredible man she'd ever met. She should grab on to him and never let go. Only... being with her would savage his dreams. He'd never turn his disappointment on her, was too good a man for that, but she'd know and it'd break her. And making his dreams come true would destroy hers.

Yet the idea of walking away stuck like a stone in her gut, unpalatable and brutal.

At least she had time to figure out what the hell she was going to do.

Franz Josef was a resort town of a kind. In the sense that it was near a spectacular glacier and had thermal baths you could luxuriate in, and restaurants and cafés that served world-class food. That was where it ended. The village was pretty much one street surrounded by verdant native forest and looming mountains. Those mountains were beautiful in the morning with the hovering mist a light blanket.

As for the glacier, it was a wonder of blue ice frozen in the midst of what looked like an enormous waterfall, movement forever captured in place.

Since Nayna had a lot of time on her hands—even reality TV could only take up brain space so much of the time—she got a ride out of town several times that week, then hiked across the rocks to the foot of the glacier. She'd made a spur-of-the-moment purchase of proper cross-training sneakers and a light jacket in Christchurch, and they came in handy. Her canvas trainers were just not supportive enough for the rugged environment, and it could get cold in the national park.

It was a good walk, the glacier at the end her reward.

To mix it up, she did a number of the other short hikes through the park, sticking to the well-posted paths —she had no intention of ending up lost in the wilderness.

She also met several lovely people—hikers, tourists, and locals. The bakery a twenty-minute walk away from her cabin recognized her as a regular by the third day. She'd never had such delicious baked goods in her life. Or maybe she was overcompensating with carbs. She didn't really care. Cream doughnuts with raspberry jam were the best doughnuts.

But as she lay in bed on the ninth day since her self-imposed exile, Nayna admitted her intense loneliness. She missed the constant buzz of life in a family home, missed sitting up drinking chai with her grandmother, teasing her mother about the soap opera's latest twists and turns, even missed her father's dry comments from behind his newspaper and Madhuri's giggles when she dropped by.

She missed Raj most of all.

He'd messaged her a photo every day, the fiend. The man was getting very good at shockingly sexy selfies that didn't show his abs. A shirt partially unbuttoned. A towel held casually to block the view. A shot of his back taken in the mirror. More pictures of him reading, along with an update that made her laugh: *Mr. Darcy is finally not being a dick. I might like this guy after all. Tino at work is reading it too now. Mostly in public, where women can see him.*

Nayna saved every single photo and message but didn't reply except for a message every forty-eight hours confirming her status as alive: *The local possum gang hasn't swarmed me yet.*

Lord help her, what was she going to do?

It turned out she was going to switch on the television and watch reruns of a home-renovation show full of men in hard hats. Outside, the quiet darkness shook its head at her, clearly judging her choices.

When her phone lit up with an incoming text, she grabbed it in grateful desperation.

It was Ísa, who Nayna knew was currently camping with Sailor and his family: *How's the whole 'running away to the jungle' thing going?*

A freaking jungle would've been noisier than this, Nayna replied in the midst of the cocoon of silence that surrounded her. *They have baboons in the jungle, right? And baboons are noisy. It's so QUIET here I keep expecting to hear ghostly wails and rattling chains.* She'd never realized how much of a city girl she was until this trip—where were the sirens in the night, the neighbor on their other side blasting his music too loud, or the car backfiring and turning into a drum in her dreams?

Ísa's reply came quickly: *I am currently suffering from the curse of peace and quiet and nature as well. Do you think the ghost will come with a dashing duke to rescue you?*

I'm more into the stubbled-jaw, blue-collar man these days, Nayna admitted. *Do you know what I'm watching right now? A rerun of a home-renovation show full of construction types.* Every time one of them picked up a hammer or began handling lumber, she'd imagine Raj doing the same, his muscles flexing, and then it was all over. *I hate myself.*

Why don't you invite Raj to join you? Have a little fun away from prying eyes.

Nayna stared at her friend's sinful suggestion. And stared.

Ísa was right. Why *didn't* she invite Raj to join her? It was arrogant of her to think she could make this decision alone when the two of them were in this together; whatever happened, the fallout would hit them both. She'd talked to her bosses and was doing some remote work so she could have more time off. Raj might not be in a position to leave his business... but she could ask.

She pushed the Call button before she realized that it was freaking late at night—or early in the morning, depending on your view of things—but it was too late by then because he'd picked up.

"Nayna?" His voice was rough, a sleepy growl.

Toes curling into the sheets, Nayna said, "Sorry I woke you." Actually, she wasn't sorry if that was what he sounded like when he woke up—at least if this all collapsed and she ended up a shriveled old maid just like Auntie Babita had warned, she'd have the memory of this conversation with him.

"Is something wrong? Do you need help?"

The sharp concern in his rapidly awakening voice turned her heart to mush. "No," she said at once. "I just..." A deep breath. "I was wondering if you'd like to join me for a couple of days."

She'd expected silence, shock. Raj's family was pretty traditional, and though the two of them had been plenty naughty together, this was going into more dangerous territory altogether.

But he replied at once. "Where are you?"

Nayna took the risk and told him.

"Hold on." Sounds of movement that had her imagining him rising naked from his bed, his hair tumbled and his eyes hooded with sleep.

A minute later, he said, "I'm pulling up flights on the laptop. I see seats open tomorrow morning to Christchurch. I'll hire a car and drive from there."

Nayna hung up a few moments later so he could concentrate on making the bookings, her heart pounding and her mouth dry. When she could finally string together words, she messaged Ísa to let her know what was going on.

Her best friend replied: *Take my advice and do every dirty thing you've ever dreamed.*

Nayna bit down hard on her lower lip as she responded to her friend, then put her phone on the bedside table, intending to sleep. Of course, her brain wasn't about to cooperate. It raced and raced. Raj was coming to her. And this time there were no parents, no prying eyes, just the two of them in a town of strangers.

No rules. No boundaries.

Nayna dreamed of tangled limbs and sweaty bodies... and the chance to find out who she and Raj could be together when no one was interfering, when the choices they made were theirs and theirs alone.

AFTER A LITTLE HUNTING, RAJ had lucked out by finding an opening on an early-morning flight to Hokitika. His plane had stopped in Christchurch first, before continuing on to the small West Coast town. He'd already booked a rental and picked up the SUV only minutes after landing.

It was a drive of under two hours to get to Franz Josef, but he wouldn't have risked it if he'd felt in any way sleep-deprived. New Zealand roads were well-paved for the most part, but they could be winding and lonely out this way. If he had a wreck, he'd be waiting a hell of a long time for someone to find him.

However, he was wide awake, excitement pumping adrenaline through his veins. When Nayna had throttled back her messages and replies, he'd braced himself for rejection. At the same time, he'd kept up his photo campaign so she wouldn't forget him; it had taken teeth-gritted control not to go any further, not to push as he wanted to push.

But if the reward was this, he'd do it all over again.

Swinging through Hokitika township, he bought a large cup of scalding-hot coffee as well as a bagel, both of which he wolfed down before beginning the drive. It was a smooth one, no gridlock to worry about. Just stunning native forest and a wild coast.

He stopped only once along the way, to help a motorist resecure a couple of kayaks that had begun to slip from the roof of the other man's vehicle. It was just past eleven when he rolled into Franz Josef. The town was wide awake but quiet, the vast majority of those who came here not party people but hikers and backpackers interested in the glacier and the other natural beauties in the national park.

Pulling over, he grabbed his phone and checked the

instructions Nayna had given him on how to get to her cabin. He followed them to the letter and soon found himself going down a narrow pebbled drive surrounded by the dark green of native ferns and trees.

The cabin stood at the end in splendid isolation.

He scowled. She was all alone out here.

Leaving the vehicle, he heard the rush of water and realized there must be a waterfall nearby, but he was more interested in the fact there was no one else within shouting distance. He grabbed his bag from the back seat and shut the car door... just as Nayna opened the front door of the cabin.

26

AUNTIES IN THE PHARMACY WHEN YOU'RE BUYING *CERTAIN THINGS*

H IS HEART KICKED.

She was wearing jeans and a T-shirt, her feet bare and her silky straight hair hanging past her shoulders, and he'd never seen a lovelier woman in his life.

"Hi," she said when he stopped in front of her.

Starved, he cupped the side of her face and dipped his head, kissing her into his bloodstream. She was fire and spice and his addiction. He dropped his bag and, wrapping his arms around her, lifted her up to make the kiss deeper, more intense. She kissed him back as passionately, her arms tight around his neck.

Breaking the kiss only when she gasped for air, he nuzzled her neck. "You smell good enough to eat." He kicked his bag inside, carried her in, then kicked the door shut behind him.

She slid down his body in a luscious rub of soft against hard. "Raj." A whisper of breath against his lips. "I'm so happy you're here."

"Nothing could've stopped me." He'd long ago learned to fight for what he wanted. And in her invitation, he saw hope that she was fighting for him too. It was enough. For now, it was enough.

What happened here, in this cabin, would decide the rest.

Kissing her again, he thrust his fingers in her hair, fisted his hand. The strands were silky and soft and he wanted to feel them all over his body. When she grazed her teeth over his lower lip, he couldn't help the fingers of his other hand from digging into her hip. She didn't seem to mind, snuggling up even closer to him and opening her mouth under his.

Raj was only male.

And this was Nayna. His Nayna.

Making a harsh sound in the back of his throat, he took the invitation and deepened the kiss until it was raw, rough. No way could Nayna have missed his erection—the damn thing was trying to poke a hole through his jeans. But she didn't pull away.

Lifting her up, he said, "Legs around my waist."

Sleek and strong, those legs wrapped around him. Turning, he backed her into the nearest wall. "This is going to be my favorite position for kissing." It put her mouth at exactly the right height, her breasts easy for his hands to caress and handle.

"Kissing only?" Nayna was running her fingers up and down his chest.

"Do you want the T-shirt off?"

"Why are you even wearing it?" was the wicked response, the woman in his arms the same one he'd met that very first night.

A smile uncurling deep inside him, Raj pressed in until his chest crushed her breasts, their breaths mingling. "Maybe I want you to take it off."

Eyes locked with his, she hooked her fingers under the edge of the T-shirt and tugged it up. He cooperated because being naked with Nayna was at the top of his mental to-do list. The physical, this intimacy, it meant something to her.

It did to Raj too.

Dropping his T-shirt to the floor, she shaped his upper body with possessive hands. The sensations went straight to his throbbing cock.

"Nayna." He kissed her throat, sucking a little.

Shivering, she moved one hand up to hold him closer. He could take a hint. He kept on kissing her neck... and found a little spot just behind her left ear that caused her to make a sudden kittenish sound and dig her nails into his nape. His cock jumped. He did it again. She whimpered.

One hand on her breast, Raj squeezed the plump warmth of it before rubbing his thumb over the pebbled nipple. But that wasn't enough. Raj wanted the taut little mounds naked under his hand, under his mouth.

He pushed up her T-shirt.

She raised her arms.

Skin tight, he didn't give her time to change her mind, stripping off the tee and dropping it on the floor beside his. "What is this?" The words came out gritty, barely understandable.

She looked down. "My bra?"

"It's all lacy and see-through and taunting me." He

could see the dark circles of her nipples through the pale peach lace, wanted to suck them into his mouth.

So he did.

She cried out, her fingers gripping at his hair.

His mouth suctioning hard on one pouting nipple, he plucked and rolled the other one between his thumb and finger. When one of Nayna's hands came to his wrist, he realized immediately he was being too rough. He took it down a notch and her breathing sped up. *Got it*, he thought on a fiercely determined surge and kept it at that exact pressure.

He wanted Nayna hot and wild for him.

Tugging at his hair, she pulled him up for another kiss. Their tongues tangled, his chest pressing up against her lace-covered breasts. One hand on the curve of her hip, he leaned in hard and took everything she had to give until she pushed at his chest. Pulling back because he figured he might be crushing her, he went to shift his attention to her throat but Nayna shook her head.

"We need to talk." Her chest heaved, her words breathless.

Talk? Raj barely had a brain at this point. "Now?" he managed to say.

Nayna stared at him. "What the hell am I saying?" Hauling down his head, she branded his mouth with her own.

Raj's hand was back on her breast before he was even aware of moving.

NAYNA HADN'T KNOWN THIS MUCH pleasure could exist. Raj was... She shuddered on another rocking wave of sensation. He could get a little rough, but the instant she let him know, he gentled. That was even sexier than his abs and gorgeously muscular shoulders. It was as if he was learning her, learning what she liked and putting it in his memory banks.

Her serious, dedicated, practical, and *wonderful* lover.

Nayna decided to return the favor. She'd noticed he liked it when she played with his chest, which was a gift from the gods since she *loved* playing with his chest. Now, as he kissed her, his hands braced on either side of her head, she tried different pressures until she found the one that made him groan.

A light scratch across his nipples had him sucking in a breath and looking down to watch what she was doing. Nayna remembered something she'd heard once about men being visual creatures. Raj definitely liked watching her hands on him. All at once, she could imagine him watching her as she gripped the hottest, hardest part of him, and oh, her thighs were clenching so tight around his hips.

Hand fisting in her hair, Raj tilted back her head so he could kiss her again. She continued to pet his chest while he did so, and when he put his free hand on her breast and tugged down the cup of her bra, she shivered but didn't tell him to stop. Breaking the kiss, he looked down again, his hair messy and falling across his forehead and his lips kiss-swollen.

Nayna almost couldn't look down herself, the image was so carnal. But she did, and it was even more erotic than she'd imagined. He was rubbing the work-roughened pad of his thumb gently over her tightly furled nipple, then circling with his nail, the tiny edge causing her to shiver.

He looked up and his pupils were dilated. As if satisfied she was still with him, still enjoying this, he looked down again. Nayna's chest heaved. One hand curving over the back of his neck, she said, "You like to look." It just came out. She couldn't keep the thoughts inside her head when he was doing such delicious, naughty things to her.

"Hmm?" A squeeze of her breast, the calluses on his palm a delicious rasp of sensation. "I guess I do." A slow, devastating smile when he looked up, as if he'd made a discovery. "Are you going to let me?"

She had no idea what wicked things he was asking, but she'd give him anything right now. Aware of the danger, she leaned in and sucked at his lower lip. He let her play, and he played with her. She was pretty sure her panties were well beyond damp at this stage; she could smell her arousal. It might've been embarrassing if Raj hadn't been with her every step of the way.

His own arousal wasn't exactly a secret.

He was big.

Kind of intimidatingly big.

She'd worry about that later.

Right now, she was being kissed and fondled by the sexiest man she'd ever met. His stubble was rough and perfect, and she was totally okay with stubble rash. She'd stocked up on high-strength concealer for a reason.

It was only when he moved them to the bed, dropping her onto her back, that she had a flash of intelligent thought. "I'm not on the pill." Blurted-out words. Important words.

Thrusting his hands through his hair, Raj groaned. "I'm an idiot." A second later, his pragmatic brain kicked in. "Where's the closest pharmacy?"

Nayna pointed to her bathroom. "I went this morning." She'd been sure she'd be busted by some auntie on holiday any second. Her heart had beat like thunder. She'd felt like she was trying to buy drugs instead of protection. "It's in the medicine cabinet."

Raj bounced onto the bed. On his hands and knees above her, he leaned down to kiss her with an open delight that just... turned her into light and fluff and sparkles. She'd *never* seen him like this with anyone. Not his family. Not her family. Not with the people at the party.

Just her.

"One second," he said and got off the bed when they came up for air.

Nayna began to feel a bit awkward a split-second after he disappeared into the bathroom. Pulling up the bra cup he'd pushed down, she swallowed. He entered the bedroom again, the box in his hand.

Lifting it to his mouth, he used his teeth to rip off the plastic. As she watched, he emptied the box onto the bedside table.

"Easy access," he said when she just stared, and then he was over her again, a big warm wall. "I have to tell you something before we do this."

Distracted by his biceps as he leaned on his forearms, she said, "Hmm?"

"Nayna, my face is up here." It was a laughing comment, his shoulders shaking.

Wanting to smile—she'd never thought sex would

include smiling—she looked up. "I'm listening, cutie-pie."

A hint of color on his cheekbones as he said, "I'm going to mess this up." It came out a rough statement. "I want you too much and I'm probably going to lose it the instant I get inside you."

Nayna squirmed, her thighs squeezing tight around an arousal that might send her over the edge before he even pushed in. "That's okay. I'll give you a do-over." If he kept on looking at her as if she was his favorite candy and he was starving, she'd give him as many do-overs as he wanted.

Scowling, he shook his head. "No. This is our first time. We both get to orgasm." No give in his words.

Nayna's mind caught on his phrasing. "It's our first time together," she murmured, trying not to feel jealous of all the women who'd come before her; her shyness and resulting lack of experience wasn't Raj's fault.

"That too."

It took Nayna a minute. Her brain sparked with too many neurons all firing at once. "B-but you're so..." Dumbfounded, she ran her hands over his chest and abs. "How can you have never...?"

"I decided I'd only be with a woman who wanted to lick my abs." He kissed her.

And though she was still caught in a loop of disbelief and wonder, she had no shields against his kiss. Or from his desire. Raj wanted her and he made no attempt to hide it. To hear his breathing go uneven, to feel his chest rising and falling as raggedly as her own, his hands trembling slightly when he touched her—as if he couldn't believe his luck—it made her feel the most beautiful woman on the planet.

She touched him as voraciously; drinking in every drop, savoring every moment, every touch. His body was hot silk and rigid strength, his chest hairs a crisp abrasion against her skin. Then there was the defined vee above his hips—she was going to kiss and lick every inch of the muscles that created that vee.

Don't get her started on the furred trail that led down into his jeans.

Breaking the kiss, she followed that trail with her fingers—and knew he was watching again.

Her breath caught.

Her nipples throbbed.

Reaching the edge of his jeans, she played her fingers near the button above the zipper. She wasn't trying to be a tease. The truth was, her shyness around men had decided to wake up and wave its flag at the worst possible moment. Her throat was dry, her pulse thrumming. "In the movies," she whispered, "they make it look so seamless."

"In the movies," Raj rasped, "the guy never goes off half-cocked." Groaning on those harsh words, he tugged away her hand. "We both have fun on our first time," he repeated stubbornly. "That means you keep your hands away from dangerous places."

Placing his palm on her navel as she fought the sudden wave of self-consciousness, he spread his fingers over her skin. "Let me do this." His eyes holding hers, his pupils dilated. "Let me make you feel good."

27

HEAT WAVE AT THE GLACIER

NAYNA SWALLOWED AND FOUGHT HER nerves by focusing on his erection, the heat flushing his cheeks, the desire in his eyes. Raj wanted her. He wasn't pretending, wasn't disappointed. No, he was all but vibrating with passion.

"Yes," she whispered. "I want this."

Raj shuddered before taking a long, deep breath and lowering his fingers to the button of her jeans. She was the one who watched this time as he undid the button and pulled down the zipper—to reveal the pale peach of her lace panties.

"You bought a matching set," he said, sounding a little choked.

Nayna had to confess. "I was thinking of you when I did it."

He groaned and slipped his hand inside her jeans to cup the hottest, most private part of her. Having not expected the sudden move, Nayna jerked. *Oh, wow.* Exhaling a gusty breath on the punch of erotic sensation, she made herself look down at the sight of his hand—big, brown-skinned, with a few nicks and scars—holding her so intimately.

It fried her senses.

"Tell me what you like." Raj lowered his body so that he was speaking against her ear. "I've never done this before. Help me get it right."

A single motion of his finger across the gusset of her panties had her toes curling and her stomach in free fall. Nayna had been dreaming and aching and fantasizing about him for so long that the simple friction of the lace against her skin as he explored her might well be enough to send her over.

Unable to stop the instinctive motions, she moved against him, rubbing and needy. He made a rumbling sound of approval in his chest, seemingly happy with her nonvocal encouragement.

"I fantasized about this," he confessed as he continued to stroke her between her thighs. "After that night at the party—that night when I was nearly certain you weren't wearing panties."

Nayna shivered. "I wasn't."

A groan. "I dreamed about touching you like this and hearing you whimper. I told myself you'd be wet and silky for me."

He so didn't have to worry about that.

"This is better than my fantasy." He kissed his way down the edge of her jaw to her mouth, at the same time using his free hand to tug down the cups of her bra.

Wrapping her arms around him because she loved kissing Raj as much as he seemed to love kissing her, Nayna jerked her hips against his hand when he stopped his petting. He started up again, going a little faster when she shifted impatiently.

Nayna felt wanton and wild and she loved it.

Suddenly needy for something she couldn't put into words, she pressed down against his touch—he pushed back with the heel of his hand before withdrawing for a second, only to slip his hand inside her panties.

He speared two fingers through her flesh, pinning her clit in between.

Nayna's cry was silent, her nails digging into his neck and the fingers of her free hand clenching on his biceps as her body tried to ride his hand. She should've been mortified and uncomfortable, but she couldn't be, not with him encouraging her with rough whispers and private caresses that followed the movements of her body.

Right at the end, when she couldn't stand it anymore, she gripped his wrist and guided him to exactly where she wanted the pressure.

The orgasm tore her apart. It was nothing like the sharp sweetness she'd experienced at her own hands. This was deeper, harder, a wrenching jolt that flowed over her in luscious, demanding waves.

RAJ KNEW HIS DECISION TO stay celibate until he found the woman who would be his was old-fashioned even in their culture. But as he watched Nayna's face while her body rippled under his touch, her hand gripping convulsively at his wrist, he had zero regrets. It wouldn't have changed anything if she'd been more experienced; it would've still been their first time together.

Exploring this new adventure with Nayna by his side, yeah, that felt good.

His own breathing was a ragged rasp by now, his heart a roar in his ears. He'd never seen anything more beautiful in his life. She was heat and woman, the dark brown of her skin flushed with a fine layer of perspiration, and on his fingers, she moved sweet and slick and goddamn perfect. His fantasies paled in comparison to the reality.

He couldn't understand some of the things he'd heard on the work sites. More than one man had complained about how long it took to make a woman come. Hard work, they'd muttered, to a chorus of agreement. The women on the sites had added their own thoughts—that the vast majority of men were lazy bastards who just wanted to get off and who acted as if making a lover orgasm was a chore.

Raj *loved* watching Nayna lose it. He loved that he'd done this to her. And he loved the idea of learning all the different ways in which he could coax her to pleasure, his confident but shy Nayna with the reading glasses sitting on the bedside table.

Her lashes lifted, revealing eyes deep and dark and fuzzy with passion-drenched shock.

He stopped the motions of his hand even before she tugged at his wrist, guessing that she might be too sensitive now. It was, however, hard to take his hand from her flesh. He'd found his favorite instrument to play, his favorite hobby in which to indulge. He had the feeling he could do this with Nayna all day long.

Except for one thing—his cock was about to snap in two.

And Nayna looked so soft and sexy and erotic that he had no hope of resisting her.

Holding her gaze, he hooked his hands into the sides of her jeans and began to tug them off. She lazily lifted her hips so that he could strip her of the denim. Afterward, he gave himself a second to appreciate how sexy she looked in just her panties and with her nude breasts exposed and deliciously framed by the lines of her bra.

That was about as much control as he had.

Getting up, he tore off his jeans and underwear and threw them to the floor, then grabbed for one of the flat packets on the bedside table. A new awareness came into Nayna's eyes, her gaze going to his as he finally got the damn thing open and began to roll it down his erection. His hands were trembling with need, and he'd been half afraid he'd mess it up.

Chucking aside the empty foil packet the instant he was done, he reached for the sides of her panties. She stiffened and he snapped up his eyes. But she relaxed almost at once and lifted her hips again in silent encouragement.

The scrap of lace joined the rest of their clothes on the floor.

Though he was trembling by the time he came between her thighs, he locked gazes with her once more and said, "Are you sure?" Nayna might want to break the rules, but she'd always before followed the traditional path. If she did this, she'd have to live with it. The last thing Raj wanted was for her to regret their first time together.

Never did he want Nayna to regret being with him.

"I'm very sure." It was a soft statement, but there was

no doubting her resolve, especially when she hooked one of her legs over his waist and arched her body into his.

Soft dampness rubbing against him, a lap of heat and musk.

Muscles trembling from his teeth-gritted attempt at control, he guided himself to the slick heat of her and nudged in.

She made a funny sound, and when he looked up, he saw that she was wide-eyed, her hands braced up against the headboard. "You feel... large."

And even though Raj was about to totally lose his shit, he grinned. "That's it, jaanam. Talk dirty to me."

She laughed, husky and delighted.

On the verge of coming then and there, Raj clenched his jaw and pushed into her as slowly as he could manage. He did everything in his power not to hurt her even though he knew that was apt to be impossible.

When she made a sharp noise at one point, he hesitated, but a second later, she lifted her hips toward him and he just couldn't hold it together anymore. He thrust the final inches into the heated tightness of her body, and when he looked up, her eyes were closed and her spine slightly arched. Lowering his head, he sucked her nipple into his mouth as he withdrew then thrust back in.

Once.

Twice.

And boom.

28

THE WOMAN WITH NO PANTIES

NAYNA LAY ON HER BACK in bed, the sheets pulled up to her neck and her bra straightened. She didn't know why she'd done that when she wasn't wearing panties—or anything else for that matter. Raj lay beside her, the sheets rumpled at his waist and one arm bent above his head. The other one he'd tucked under her head and kind of curled it across her chest.

Nayna liked that. It was cuddling. Even if he wouldn't call it that, it definitely was. She'd been half afraid he'd just turn over and go to sleep, or maybe go into the shower. She'd read all those complaints from women who wrote in to the magazines, but Raj had only gotten up to dispose of the protection—after letting her use the bathroom first.

Then they'd both come back to bed and he'd made sure she ended up cuddled next to his furnace of a body. Only now she didn't know quite what to do. No one ever described what you did *after* sex. Especially when it'd been your first time.

"Did it hurt?"

She jerked a little at Raj's deep voice, her skin heating. But because she could hear the worry in his tone, she gave him an answer. "A tiny bit," she said honestly as she turned onto her side to face him. "Kind of like a deep twinge." She continued to feel him between her legs, as if he'd left an imprint inside her. She wondered how long it would last and hoped it would be a while. She liked the intimate sensation, hugged the erotic knowledge that she'd been with the most gorgeous man she'd ever met. And that she'd been his first too.

"Was it..." She bit down on her lower lip and tried again. "Did you have a good time?"

"Fucking incredible," was the blunt response. "Even though I went off like a rocket."

Nayna's cheeks burned hot at the frank talk, but she liked it. "Me too," she said, after coughing to clear her throat. "I... I liked feeling you move inside me."

Raj's legs stirred under the sheet. "So," he murmured, "when do you think you'll be ready again?"

Nayna's eyes widened, her hand going motionless on his chest—because of course she'd begun petting him. "Do you want to?"

"Nayna, I'm a guy who just experienced sex for the first time—and with the hottest woman on the planet. Yes, I want to."

His stomach rumbled.

"How about we eat something first?" She curled her fingers into the crispness of his chest hairs. "I've got microwave pasta or we can go down to one of the restaurants for a proper meal."

"I like pasta," said the hunk in bed with her. "'I also like you mostly naked."

SHE ENDED UP WEARING RAJ'S T-shirt over her bra. Her panties were a lost cause, and she decided against pulling on a fresh pair when they'd certainly end up as damp. The decision made her feel naughty and sexy—she couldn't wait for Raj to discover her small secret.

Shivering inwardly, she stepped to the kitchenette with his large male presence by her side. He surprised her with how comfortable he was with the preparations. Unlike her father, he didn't simply sit down and expect her to get everything on the table. He actively helped— and it made her wonder what he'd be like as a husband.

Unsettled by the rogue thought, she said, "Will coming down to see me put you behind schedule?"

"If it was for an entire week, yes, but a few days I can catch up over a weekend day or two." After taking a sip of water he added, "I told my parents I was coming to see you."

Nayna winced. "Your folks are very traditional, Raj." She was probably a fallen woman in their eyes now, branded a bright scarlet. "And they've undoubtedly told my parents."

"I'm sure both are deluding themselves that we're just talking," Raj said with that slow smile that made her stomach go into free fall. "That's what I said I was coming to you to do—talk."

Nayna grinned. "Do you think they actually believe that for a second?"

A masculine shrug, accompanied by an even deeper

smile. "It doesn't matter. We're getting married anyway, so everyone's going to look the other way."

A tightness in Nayna's chest, her plastic fork falling to the table. "Raj, just because we were... together doesn't mean I've decided I'm ready for marriage."

No scowl, no anger, just an intensity of eye contact from a man she already knew could be bullheaded when it suited him. "You waited twenty-eight years to sleep with a man. Do you truly believe you're a woman who can take this anything but dead seriously?"

The words shook her. Because they were on the mark.

The idea of being naked with anyone but Raj, it made her stomach roil.

She picked up the fork with care and took a bite, chewed, before answering. "I don't know who and what I am." The words poured out from where they'd been stored for fourteen long years. "All I've ever done is try *not* to be like my sister. Following the rules because she broke the rules. Fighting to make my parents happy because she made them so sad. Doing my best to be a good girl because she was a bad girl."

Her breath turned fast and shallow under the weight of a crushing realization she'd been struggling against for far too long. "I'm a *negative* of a person, Raj. I sometimes wonder who I would've become if Madhuri hadn't run off at nineteen."

She squeezed the fork. "If she hadn't, would I still be this Nayna? Would I be the woman who's never left home even to go on a short trip to another country with her friends? Would I be the accountant who wears boring suits and dresses that aren't too short?" Bandage dress excepted. "Would I be the Nayna everyone can rely on to do exactly as she should?"

Her voice had risen with each word, until she couldn't stand the pressure anymore and rose, began to pace around the room. Plastic fork still in hand, she gesticulated up at the ceiling. "Who the hell am I?" she yelled out to the heavens. "No one knows!" Her gaze connected with Raj's. "Do you see *me*?" Harsh words, but fear tangled around her. "Or do you see the woman you want to see?"

Raj's face was impossible to read, his body held loosely—but she saw the rigidity of his biceps, heard the fierce control in his voice. "What are you going to do?" Soft words, emotion locked down tight.

Nayna wanted to throw the lightweight fork at him, crack that shell. "I hate living alone," she blurted out, gesturing around the cabin. "It'll make me painfully unhappy long term, but I'm going to move out." She hadn't understood until right this instant that she'd made the call.

"I've had the goddamn sword of Damocles hanging over my head my entire adult life! Break a rule and it'll fall." Her shoulders sagged, her next words a whisper. "So let it fall." At least she'd know then. No more wariness, no more toeing the line to stave off rejection.

Surely Aji would still love her, she comforted herself.

A muscle throbbed in Raj's jaw. "Is there room in this new life of yours for me? Or were you telling the truth the night we met and you only ever wanted me for my body?"

He was angry, she realized. Very, *very* angry. She should've felt afraid but she didn't. He had himself ruthlessly in check. And though she wanted to jump on the offer and never let him go, she had no right to stomp on his dreams. "You want a wife, Raj." His assumption that their intimacy could have only one end underlined that searing truth. "You want tradition and marriage and a life rooted in community."

Her eyes burned. "I would make you so unhappy." It sickened her to think of this beautiful bright thing between them going to rot in the face of divergent dreams; she couldn't bear to see Raj look at her in resentment. "We should end this before it hurts any more."

Raj looked at her, all clenched muscles and fury before he rose and went to his duffel. Back to her and breath harsh, he pulled out a fresh T-shirt and shrugged into it. He had his feet in his sneakers and was walking out the door before she knew quite what was going on.

The door shut behind him, leaving her in echoing silence.

Only his scent remained, rich and masculine and clinging to her like a kiss.

Nayna burst into tears.

RAJ HAD NO IDEA WHERE he was going, but he turned left after he came out of the cabin and went down the path marked out by the beaten-down grass. A sign appeared about a hundred meters in. It indicated that this track led to a large waterfall and that it would take him an hour to make the return trip.

He set off, more than willing to burn off his emotions with the physical. Native birds sang around him, and the sun speared through the forest, but he saw none of the beauty, felt none of the calm. His heart was thunder, his skin so tight he felt it would burst if he clenched his muscles any harder.

Nayna had been a virgin. She hadn't slept with anyone all this time—and he'd thought that she was choosing him. And she had, but only for her first time. Not forever. *Fight for me,* he'd begged her silently. But Nayna wasn't trying to hold on to him any way she could; she was ready and willing to walk away.

Fuck, his throat was closing up.

Bending over with his hands on his thighs, he breathed through the burn at the backs of his irises, breathed through the tearing in two of his heart. He'd had to leave the cabin before he splintered right in front of her.

So what are you going to do, Raj? asked the part of him that had come here with the secret, beautiful dream of taking her home as his bride. *Leave her? Try to find another wife?*

Raj rose, shoved a hand through his hair. As if that was even an option. Nayna Sharma was his forever. No woman could make him so happy... or hurt him so badly. She was light and laughter and sinful smiles that held him captive. He couldn't imagine doing with anyone else what he'd done in that cabin with her.

The idea of waking up next to her for a lifetime, it filled all the hollow places inside him.

But to Nayna, was he freedom and love and happiness... or was he a cage?

29

NAYNA SHARMA, THE T-SHIRT THIEF

NAYNA DIDN'T KNOW WHAT TO do.

Her lower lip trembled every time she thought of Raj walking out.

Desperate not to be here when he returned in case he just picked up his bag and left—*like she'd told him to*—she cleaned herself up and put on a fresh pair of panties and her jeans, along with one of her own T-shirts. Raj's T-shirt she folded and was about to put on the bed when she hesitated... and decided to hide it instead.

She didn't care if it was pathetic; she needed a piece of him, needed his scent around her.

Lost afterward, she almost reached for her phone and called Ísa. But she wasn't ready to talk about this, wasn't ready to put this horrible sense of loss into words. Stuffing some money into her pocket, she walked out the door and toward Franz Josef town instead.

Sugar and carbs would help.

Wouldn't they?

Raj RETURNED TO THE CABIN to find it empty. He wasn't exactly surprised.

Leaving the cabin, he didn't try to call Nayna but decided to walk into the town instead and see if he could spot her. While it wasn't a tiny place, it *was* small enough that he could theoretically find her if he went in the right direction.

After reaching the edge of the commercial area, he saw that the restaurants and cafés were bustling. Plenty of people, most of them tourists and hikers. Way more people than he'd expected, but none of them a slender woman with sleek black hair and subtle curves, her eyes sparkling and her lips generous.

A moment's thought before he went with his first instinct and aimed himself toward the bakery he'd seen as he drove in. Its sign—painted a bright pink—stood out against the dark green of the forest all around them. Nayna said he didn't see her, didn't know her, but Raj listened to everything she said—and the things she didn't.

He found her seated outside, finishing off a mug of frothy chocolate. When he slid into the seat across from her, she gave him an unreadable look.

"So, when are you leaving?"

Raj's gut clenched. "I'm not that easy to get rid of," he said, ready to battle for her.

Lower lip quivering, she ducked her head and his heart, it kicked hard.

"Nayna, jaan." Ignoring the others around them and driven by raw protectiveness, he moved faster than he'd ever before done. He hauled her up into his arms and cradled her tight, one of his hands cupping the back of her head and his other arm locking around her.

"Don't cry. Please, Nayna. I'm sorry I left like that." He'd apologize for anything she wanted if she'd just stop sobbing against him as if he'd walked on her heart with steel-toed boots. "I won't ever do it again." He'd been protecting himself, and in so doing, he'd hurt her. "I'll stay and fight with you."

A shuddering sniff, words mumbled out against his chest that he had no hope of understanding, she was still crying so much. Raj held her even tighter, shielding her from the curious gazes of others walking in or out of the bakery. It wasn't too busy, but he didn't like anyone seeing his tough Nayna brought down so low.

"I told you to go," she said, and this time he heard. "I was being self-sacrificing." A hiccup, more tears. "It was stupid."

Wrecked though he was, he felt a smile burn to life on his lips. "You don't want me to go?"

A fierce shake of her heard. "I want to keep you forever."

With those words, she sealed the break in his heart, made it stronger than new. That was the only thing he'd ever needed from her. "Then we figure this out," he rasped against her ear, stroking his hand over her hair. "We make it work. Our way. No one else's."

Another sniff, Nayna rubbing her face against his T-shirt. "I can't walk through town like this."

"Just tuck yourself against me. I'll protect you." Always he'd protect her.

Nayna's ravaged face ripped at him when they reached the cabin.

She took one look at his own face and said, "One minute" in a voice that had gone husky as a result of the emotional storm.

A few steps and she closed the bathroom door behind herself.

When she emerged, he was seated in one of the lived-in armchairs in front of what looked to be a gas fireplace but might've been electrical. He hadn't ever put in one of these models on a project, didn't know the brand name. But he'd worked out how to turn it on, and it was running when Nayna stepped out of the bathroom, as, despite it being summer, the rainforest air was cool.

She'd washed her face, brushed her hair back, and looked bright-eyed.

For him. Because she'd seen what it was doing to him to watch her in distress.

Lifting an arm in invitation, Raj said, "Come here."

She came, curling onto his lap, a small armful of woman who fit him perfectly. The fire crackled next to them in an excellent imitation of a wood-burning unit.

"This cabin is very well built," he told her, finding his anchor in the familiar. "Look at how carefully the beams have been placed, the metal brackets they've used. It was done by a master carpenter on-site, not prefabricated in a warehouse somewhere."

"I've been here over a week and I never noticed any of that," Nayna murmured. "Tell me more of what you see."

So he did, and she asked questions that told him she was really listening and appreciating his point of view. He'd never actually thought about the conversations they might have after marriage—when he'd been hell-bent on marriage—but he should have; Nayna was a white-collar professional, Raj a blue-collar tradesman at heart. He ran the family business, but his passion was in the work itself.

"It doesn't bore you?" he asked.

"Are you kidding?" Nayna smoothed her hand over his pecs. "I failed woodworking class in intermediate school. My custom jewelry box fell apart." Laughter in her words. "I'm in awe of your ability to build things from the ground up."

Running his hand over her hair, Raj said, "Do you enjoy your work?" It was something he hadn't thought to ask until she'd yelled about who she'd have become without Madhuri's shadow over her life.

"I'm an accounting nerd," she said. "I like it. But... the firm mostly has established clients. I'd love to work with a start-up of some kind, help build it, you know?" She sat up in his lap, her eyes shining. "It would be a risk, with no guarantees, but the idea of being part of the genesis and growth of a company, that excites me."

Raj thought of his parents' words the night of the introduction, how Nayna could work for the family business. That wasn't going to happen. Theirs was a strong, stable company, but the accounting work was steady and nothing exciting. Great for them, but stultifying for an intelligent woman who wanted to make her mark.

"Have you investigated possibilities already?" he asked, considering who he knew that might be able to offer her information that could help.

Shaking her head, she leaned one arm on his shoulder. "My parents would've flipped," she murmured with a lopsided smile. "Giving up a good paycheck for uncertainty." Dropping her voice into deeper tones, she said, "We bring you up right, we give you room to study, and this is how you thank us? By throwing away a good job for this rubbish-schwubbish start-up that pays you in peanuts?"

Raj chuckled at her impression of her father. "What else do you dream of?"

"Hiking in the Amazon, climbing the Great Wall of China, spending a night in the Sahara Desert." Laughter spilled out of her. "I want to taste the entire world, Raj!"

A sense of unease fought to settle in Raj's gut, but he nudged it out of his consciousness.

Spotting a strand of hair sticking to her cheek, he pulled it gently away—and Nayna leaned in to nuzzle her nose against his. Her kiss was tender and unexpected, the way she cradled his face in her hands the sweetest touch. Sinking into the armchair, he wrapped her up in his arms and surrendered.

Slow, soft kisses on his mouth, across the heavy dark of his stubble, down along his neck.

"Nayna," he groaned, fisting one hand in her hair.

She slid her hands under his T-shirt, pushed up.

Needing her skin-to-skin with him, he helped her strip him of the cotton, then did the same to her. She was still wearing the pale peach bra that was both an invitation and a seduction. But when he would've bent his mouth to her, she pushed him back. "It's my turn," she murmured... and put her mouth on his skin.

Raj had fantasized plenty during his celibate years. He was a traditional man who'd chosen to wait, not a monk who'd given up the idea of sex altogether. But not once had he dreamed about a woman kissing his chest with utter attention to detail, as if she didn't want to miss an inch.

A flick of her tongue over his nipple.

Raj shuddered and wove his fingers into Nayna's hair again. Then he let her do as she pleased. Because having Nayna adore him like this... Yeah, he could live with it. When she tugged away her head, he thought she wanted to stop, but she simply wanted to change position. To a kneeling one between his legs.

The better to reach his abs.

Dropping back his head, Raj didn't look as she tasted him with small flicks and licks. If he did, he would probably lose it again. Because while Nayna was absorbed in his abdomen, she was also very close to his cock. And that part of his body didn't understand patience. Not after so many years of being deprived.

If he wasn't careful, he'd come in his pants like a hormone-crazed teenager.

NAYNA FLICKED UP HER LASHES and saw that Raj's head was thrown back, his jaw tightly clenched. The hand he'd thrust back in her hair was fisted, and every so often, he'd tug. She had the feeling it wasn't on purpose, more an involuntary action when she hit a sensitive spot.

Every part of her hummed at seeing him like this, so utterly open to her. The way he'd held her, the way he'd kept her protectively close when they walked back, the fact he'd been ready to fight for her even when she'd tried to be silly and give him up... All she wanted to do was show him what he was to her.

Words worked. But for them, so did the physical.

Touches, kisses, caresses, they were two people between whom it could never be casual.

She ran her tongue all the way along one side of the vee.

"Fuck." It was gritted out, his thighs rigid on either side of her.

Her own pulse throbbing in her neck, she took advantage of his closed eyes to look down at the part of his body so very close to her cheek, the denim of his jeans fighting to contain it. And maybe because he wasn't watching, or maybe because they were starting to become each other's on a level beyond anything she'd experienced with another human being, she closed her hand over him.

The cry he let out this time was more of a roar, the hand in her hair pulling almost painfully tight for a second before he let go and grabbed at the arms of the chair. "Nayna." A rasp. "I think we should move to the bed."

Emboldened by his response, her entire self full of a raw emotion that had no name, Nayna glanced up and held his gaze. "No." She tightened her hold a fraction and heard his breath catch. "I'm not sure I'm ready to have this large object inside me again." Her cheeks burned hot, but she didn't look away. "I want to play with it though."

Raj shoved both hands through his hair. "I'm dead. You're looking at a dead man."

Her shoulders shook and she knew—it would only ever be like this with Raj. Leaning in, she pressed a kiss to the spot on his navel where the furred trail disappeared into the waistband of his jeans. His hand came back to her head, this time to curl around her nape. And his cock, it twitched under her touch.

Catching her lower lip with her teeth, Nayna undid the button on his jeans and took extreme care while lowering the zipper. He was wearing black boxer briefs, but releasing his cock from those wasn't in any way difficult—the smooth, hard length was already attempting to escape.

When Nayna closed her fingers gently around him, he went so motionless that she thought he must've stopped breathing. Glancing up, she saw veins popping out on his arms, sweat dampening his chest... but his eyes were open.

Watching, as he liked to do.

Blush or not, Nayna held the dilated darkness of his eyes and decided to have one more lick. This time, it wasn't of his abs.

30

TRUE LOVE HURTS

RAJ SAT ACROSS FROM NAYNA at one of the outdoor tables of a bustling restaurant. The two of them had ventured out when hunger struck. Nayna wore her lightweight jacket, and Raj had thrown on the hoodie he'd packed, but otherwise they were in jeans and T-shirts. The people around them were a wild mix—some dressed as casually as Nayna and Raj, others wearing formal black dresses or crisp shirts.

The staff served everyone with equal cheer under the orange-gold evening sunlight.

"Does this count as a date?" Nayna asked after they'd ordered, her chin propped up on her hands. "I've never been on a date."

Raj bracketed her feet between his sprawled-out legs. "After what you did to me in that cabin, Nayna with the sundar nayna, it can be whatever you like." He was no poet, but she gave a delighted smile at his play on the meaning of her name.

"No one's ever said I had pretty eyes before." She batted her lashes.

"I think you mean 'fine eyes.'"

Her smile turned into a grin at his reference to her favorite book, but their server returned right then with their drinks, and the next minute or two was taken up with getting the drinks placed on the table and taking sips.

"Raj." Nayna's tone had become solemn. "If you support me in moving out, it'll turn my parents against you." A hard swallow. "They love you right now."

"Let me deal with that." Raj had taken on tougher opponents than Shilpa and Gaurav Sharma—and his priority was Nayna. "The most important thing is to make sure you come out of this unscathed."

Nayna's face fell. "Never going to happen." Raw words, not the least bit flippant.

Because Nayna Sharma loved deeply and unconditionally.

Raj wanted that fierce force of love in his life, wanted to be able to take it for granted. Not as her family did, abusing her generous nature. But in a way that was his anchor. Never worrying, because it was a constant.

Until then, until she trusted him enough to give him her heart, he'd hold her declaration about wanting to keep him always, at the surface of his thoughts. No old demons would get between him and Nayna; Raj wouldn't allow it.

"My father will never forgive me for disrupting his plans," Nayna added. "And my mother... she's his wife. She's always stood with him." A deep breath. "Aji will stay in touch, I'm sure." She gave a shaky smile. "She's having a love affair of her own."

Raj tried to imagine the pure-Hindi-speaking, white-sari-clad elderly lady he'd met having a love affair and hit a mental blank. Until he thought of what Nayna might be like at that age, and suddenly it wasn't such a hard thing to visualize. Because Nayna would still be as lovely, as brilliant.

"The first thing we have to do is find you a place," he said as their fish and chips arrived on the table.

HOWEVER, GETTING INTO AN APARTMENT proved easier said than done. The rental market in Auckland was well beyond capacity. Laptop open in front of her as she sat in bed after dinner, Nayna called up landlord after landlord, only to be told there was already a waiting list for the advertised rentals.

Raj, who'd slipped down to lie on his back with one arm bent behind his head and his eyes on the screen of her laptop, frowned. "That's too far out," he said when she pulled up another listing. "It'd add two hours to your commute every day."

"A long commute might be the only realistic option."

Raj was silent for a minute before saying, "I have an idea." After asking her to pass him his phone, which he'd left on the bedside table beside her, he called a number and said, "Ping, how're you doing?"

Nayna listened as he asked the other man about a property that Ping had been rehabbing. "Is it ready for a tenant?" He listened while his friend spoke. "Yeah, I'll vouch for her," he said after about thirty seconds. "That's all?" Another pause. "You give her the place and I'll finish up the job for you at no cost."

The deal was done two minutes later.

Hanging up, Raj said, "You have a one-bedroom unit in Epsom. Two-story place, internal garage below, everything else above. Entire complex only has eight units overall, most of them occupier-owned, and the landscaping is neat and easy-care. Good-sized lounge, tiny kitchen, approximately a ten-minute drive to your office."

Nayna's mouth was dry, her pulse skittering. "What did you promise your friend?"

"Nothing major." He put the phone down on the bedside table on his side. "The deck's unfinished. I can polish off the job on the weekend. Officially, you won't be on the rental agreement until that deck *is* finished, but the house is safe and sound and warm, and Ping's a professional. You won't have to worry about a creepy landlord."

Nayna put down the laptop. "I'm doing this," she whispered, the reality of it coming down on her head like a ton of bricks.

It was time to see the sword fall.

RAJ WATCHED NAYNA SLEEP THAT night and knew he might be the architect of his own heartbreak. The Nayna she was now wanted him, but the Nayna she became as she found her wings... that Nayna might decide a man so rooted in tradition and culture wasn't the man she wanted by her side.

It was possible that she might never fully trust such a man not to turn on her with rules and boundaries and demands that stifled her spirit. Nayna was a woman heading off into the unknown, excited and invigorated by what she might discover... while Raj needed roots, needed an unbroken line from the past to the future.

His chest ached, but he could no more stop helping her fly than he could stop breathing. "I love you, Nayna Sharma," he whispered, the words a secret he couldn't say to her when she was awake.

It would be another kind of pressure.

Nayna knew his deepest hurts, and it would go against every part of her nature to scar him any further. Her heart was too soft, her ability to be loyal too powerful. But even worse than Nayna flying away from him would be a Nayna who stayed only because of a sense of obligation and friendship.

So he would tell her of his love only in the midnight hours, when she slept in his arms. He'd help her fly... and hope she'd choose to fly to him.

31

WEDDING BELLS RINGING

RAJ DROVE NAYNA HOME.

He'd left his truck parked at the airport, and after they landed in Auckland around eight at night, he dumped both their bags in the back seat, then opened the passenger door for her. But before she could get in, he gripped her jaw and initiated a deeply demanding kiss that held all the need he couldn't show her, all the hopes he had to keep under lock and key.

"Now," he said afterward, "let's go pretend we spent the time talking."

She cradled his jaw in one hand, his stubble now more into scruff territory. "I'm so glad you're mine," she whispered and made the knot of tension inside him unravel a fraction.

Just enough that he could smile and say, "Me and my abs?"

"Well, duh." Laughing, she pushed playfully at his chest before getting up into the passenger seat.

Raj closed the door and jogged around to get into the driver's seat—and tried not to imagine what it might be like to do things like this with her every day. Shared rides, casual errands, quick trips. Sweet domesticity was his dream, not Nayna's.

"Rock music okay?" he asked when his usual station came on after he started the engine.

She pretended to play air-guitar before launching into the rock ballad currently playing. Grinning, Raj joined in, and the two of them treated the truck as their own private karaoke studio until he turned into the street on which the Sharmas had their home.

Suddenly Nayna's song cut off. She hugged her arms around herself. "How am I going to do this?" she whispered. "It'll break their hearts."

Raj ran the back of his hand over her cheek. "We'll do it together."

A rub of her cheek against his knuckles. "It's not going to be pretty."

"I can handle not-pretty." Though he'd have to keep a handle on his temper if her family got close to crossing a line. "Visitors?" He nodded at the small red car parked behind the garage.

"Madhuri." Nayna blew out a trembling breath. "I guess she might as well be here for this too."

Raj turned into the drive.

It was time.

NERVES JANGLING, NAYNA GOT OUT of the truck and waited for Raj to grab her bag from the back before the two of them walked around the side of the house to enter through the back door. That door led into the kitchen, where she was sure to find her mother or grandmother at this time of night. Maybe Madhuri and her father too.

The kitchen was the absolute heart of the Sharma home.

The door opened before she reached it, her mother bursting out. "My Ninu, you're home!" A crushing hug scented with a familiar floral perfume before her mother pulled back and said, "I'm so glad you're here." Her smile dazzled as she turned to hug and kiss Raj on the cheek too. "And Raj beta, you too. You would've both missed the excitement otherwise."

Belatedly realizing that Shilpa Sharma's enthusiasm had only a little to do with her return from the South Island, Nayna frowned. "What's happened? And why are you wearing your newest salwar kameez?" A vivid aqua with pink accents, it had been meant for an upcoming sixtieth party.

"Madhuri is engaged!" Her mother clapped her hands in front of her, her eyes literally twinkling.

Nayna's mouth fell open. "*No!*"

"Yes!" Her mother danced on the spot.

Mind snapping to the surfer boy whose photo she'd seen on Madhuri's phone, Nayna said, "Anyone we know?" She wasn't about to accidentally bust her sister if the groom wasn't to be Boytoy Bailey.

"Oh, it's Dr. Sandesh Patel," her mother said. "You know, the one who has his own clinic. Never been married, and he wants Madhuri!"

Nayna's head spun. "Where is she?" She needed to talk to her sister and find out what the hell was going on. From having fun with a surfer boy to getting engaged to one of the most respected men in their community? A man who had always struck Nayna as coldly unbending. Not the kind of husband who'd have patience with Madhuri's quixotic ways.

"She's getting ready in her old room," Shilpa Sharma said happily. "Sandesh is coming over in the next five, ten minutes so we can make it all official—your timing was wonderful!" Her mother tucked Nayna's hair behind her ears with maternal affection. "I mean, Sandesh really should've talked to your father first, but with Madhuri having already been married, and him being older, well... It's all fine. Your father is very happy. *Imagine!* A doctor in the family too!"

Nayna glanced at Raj. No way could she do what she'd planned, tell her family about her decision on a day so joyous for Madhuri.

He gave the slightest incline of his head. "I'll leave your fami—"

But he never got to finish the sentence, her mother waving off his words. "Of course you must stay. You are like one of us." So much happiness in every word, that of a mother who had two daughters safely settled. "I'm sure Sandesh would love to talk to you—you'll be seeing each other quite often now."

Nayna's insides lurched again, but there was nothing she could do at this instant without wrecking Madhuri's day; it would cost her only a few more hours of tangled nerves to give her family this night of happiness. After going inside and saying hello to her father and her grandmother, both of whom welcomed her back with a smile and—from her father—a suspicious lack of questions, she walked down the hallway to talk to Madhuri.

Raj remained in the living room with her father and Aji.

"Maddie," she said with a quick knock on the door before entering. "What the bejesus is going on?" A hissed whisper as she shut the door behind her.

Madhuri looked up from her seat in front of the vanity. She was dressed in what Nayna called a half sari. A flared ankle-length skirt in pale amethyst sprinkled with crystals. A cropped and fitted kurta in the same shade. And a really long dupatta that could be pleated and tucked in to appear as if the woman were wearing a sari, but without the complications of having to handle meters of fabric.

Huge kohl-rimmed eyes met Nayna's in the mirror when Nayna came up behind her sister and put her hands on her shoulders.

"He's a good man," Madhuri said, reaching up to touch one hand to Nayna's. "And I'm getting older, Ninu. I need to settle down and start a family before no one will have me."

Madhuri was only thirty-three, soon to be thirty-four, and looked ten years younger at the very least. "What about the surfer?"

A liquid shrug. "That wasn't serious." Dropping her hand from Nayna's, she picked up the mascara to finish doing her eyes. "And I realized it wasn't going anywhere. When Sandesh proposed... It's the second time, you know."

Nayna raised both eyebrows. "The second time? I never heard about the first time."

"That's because I didn't tell anyone." Madhuri capped her mascara and put it aside. "I knew how the family would react. You've seen what Mum and Dad are like right now. Can you imagine if I'd told them he'd proposed and I'd said no?"

"I see your point." Not only was the doctor hugely respected, he was also incredibly wealthy as a result of a medical invention he'd patented while a student. "But Maddie, he's at least ten years your senior."

"Fourteen," her sister said, correcting her. "He's stable and so mature." In the mirror, her eyes met Nayna's. "I know I'm not the most mature person." A wry smile. "It'll be good for me to have him—and maybe I can loosen him up a little."

Nayna's head was still spinning. "As long as you're sure," she said. "I just want you to be happy."

"He's not as bad as he comes across, you know." A softness to Madhuri's features. "It's going to sound weird with how involved he is in the community, but I think he's shy and deals with social situations by going all stiff —he's not like that with me."

"No, that's not weird at all." Nayna had gone mute herself at times when she was younger; who knew what others had taken from her unsmiling features? At least a few people had probably thought her stuck up and snooty. "Hopefully we'll get to see the man you see once he becomes comfortable with us." She hugged her sister from behind, the crisp scent of Clinique *Happy*, Madhuri's favorite perfume, as familiar to her as their mother's heavier bouquet.

Madhuri touched her fingers to Nayna's again. "If I tell you something, promise me you won't ever tell anyone?"

"Promise," Nayna said at once, because whatever lay between them, they were sisters underneath it all.

"Vinod hit me."

Nayna froze in the hug, her eyes colliding with Madhuri's stark ones in the mirror again. "What?"

Turning sideways in Nayna's arms, Madhuri glanced at the door before whispering, "The first time was three months after we eloped."

"*Madhuri.*" Nayna was kneeling in front of her sister before she realized it, her hands locked with Madhuri's. "Why didn't you say? Why didn't you *call*?" No matter how angry Shilpa and Gaurav had been, they would've brought Madhuri home, of that Nayna had zero doubts. Their parents had their faults, but never would they have stood by while their daughter was being physically abused.

"I was ashamed." Madhuri's hands gripped at Nayna's. "First time in my life," she joked shakily. "I'd chosen him and he turned out to be a violent abuser. But that first time, he told me it was a mistake, apologized, and I forgave him."

Nayna clenched her stomach to quiet her rage. "Did it happen again?"

"Yes. Not all the time. Couple or three months between each time, so I could 'forget.'" She smiled. "I'm not like you, Ninu. You would've kicked ass and taken names. I was too scared of being on my own to walk away."

How very strange that her often flighty sister would say that on the verge of Nayna's decision to step out into the world on her own. "Promise me that if Sandesh ever hurts you, you'll tell me."

"Promise," Madhuri said at once.

"Do you want to pursue anything against Vinod now? A police case?" There probably wasn't much the police could do with the evidence of violence long faded, but laying the complaint could help Madhuri heal.

Her sister shook her head. "No. It probably makes me a coward, but I just want to move on."

"It doesn't make you anything of the sort," Nayna said fiercely. "You have to look after yourself and heal the best way you can."

Madhuri shuddered out a breath, as if Nayna's words had taken a weight off her shoulders. "Ninu? I'm sorry you didn't get to go to parties, or on that exchange trip you earned."

It was an apology that had come years too late, but Nayna had already forgiven her sister, had no more resentment in her heart, only love and hope that Madhuri's second marriage would be as joyful as her first had been horrible. "It's okay, Maddie." She rose onto her knees to hug her sister.

After they parted, Madhuri returned her attention to the mirror to do the final tweaks to her makeup. "This time around, I picked a good man," she said. "Just like you have." Smiling with a determined brightness that thrust the past away, she lifted up her wrist. "Look what Sandesh gave me as a present after I accepted him," she whispered conspiratorially. "I haven't told Ma or Dad. They'd be scandalized." A giggle.

Nayna's eyes widened. "Are those *diamonds*?" On Madhuri's wrist was a bangle that blended in with all the others except that the fire in the stones was icily real while the others were all pretty fakes.

"Of course they are." Madhuri put down her lipstick. "I'm marrying a filthy-rich man. And he knows how to treat me." A frowning glance in the mirror. "Oh my gawd, I just realized what you're wearing. Go, change!"

NAYNA DRESSED QUICKLY IN AN ombré-blue half sari with pearlescent beading, the skirt swirling around her ankles. Though this kurta was longer than her usual preference, it was cut to flatter her figure, and once she pinned the gauzy white dupatta in a front-facing style, the outfit turned quickly elegant.

Hair up in a bun, a dash of makeup, and she was done.

Walking out to the kitchen, she helped her mother arrange the last of the snacks. "Thank you, Ninu," Shilpa Sharma said with a quick side hug. "I don't know what I'd do without you."

Nayna's stomach hurt.

Smiling through it, she picked up the tray of sweets and took it out into the living area, her mother bringing the savories. Raj managed to brush his hand over her hip as he ducked into the kitchen to carry out the tea and cups.

That was when her mother announced that Madhuri's affianced was bringing along his elderly parents as well as two siblings *and* their wives and children.

"Our living room isn't that big," Nayna muttered to Raj while her parents were distracted. "Why is he bringing so many people?"

"Probably because he wants to show off his fiancée." Raj's dark gaze was solemn. "You doing okay?"

She just had time to nod before her mother waved frantically. "I think I hear their cars! Go make sure your sister is ready!"

32

EXTREME DANGER WARNING: DUCK
FOR COVER

NAYNA DIDN'T HAVE ANOTHER CHANCE to talk to Raj in the two hours that followed. Dr. Patel's family exclaimed over Madhuri's beauty with plenty of "Wah, wah, etna sundar" and "Poora film star!" Being told she was as beautiful as a film star was nothing new to Madhuri, but Nayna's sister managed to produce an excellent facsimile of a meek and blushing bride overcome by their compliments.

Nayna elbowed her at one point. "You're laying it on a bit thick, Maddie."

A soft giggle. "I thought about pulling my dupatta across my face, but who wants to get condensation marks on a new silk dupatta?"

Nayna's lips twitched.

Across from them, Madhuri's doctor—a distinguished older man with wings of gray in his hair and a rangy frame—couldn't take his eyes off her. And every so often, Madhuri would shoot him a private look that gave Nayna hope her sister's marriage would be a happy one.

As for Raj, her father introduced him to the guests as his younger daughter's fiancé. Nayna's fingers clenched in the folds of her skirt, but there was no way she could correct her father in front of strangers. Raj captured her eyes in the aftermath, gave a tiny shake of his head, a silent reminder that she didn't have to do anything she didn't want.

Her lungs expanded, her mind clearing.

Just as her father stood up and clapped to bring the meeting to attention—after returning from a private chat with the doctor. "My future son-in-law has asked permission to marry my daughter far more quickly than would usually be acceptable. It turns out he's just been offered a prestigious position at a teaching hospital in London."

Everyone gasped. Madhuri did a good job of appearing shocked and amazed.

Nayna had to bite her lip to keep from laughing.

"However, the problem is that he has just tonight been informed that he must take up this position in two months' time rather than the six months that was initially agreed. He also needs to go over earlier to set up his living situation. As a result, he's asked my permission to have the wedding in the next six weeks."

Everyone gasped now—Madhuri included.

To their father's credit, he did glance at her and got her nod before continuing. "Sandesh has a good friend who owns a large hotel that's used for weddings, and this friend is willing to squeeze us in on a date five weeks from now. The hotel ballroom is more than large enough for our guests, and Sandesh tells me that he also has friends and acquaintances who will step up for the decorations and catering."

Gaurav Sharma shifted his attention to the man who sat in a chair beside Nayna's end of the sofa. "Raj, we might have to ask your help in moving things here and there, and perhaps with building the mandap if we can't hire a nice one in time."

"That's no problem," Raj said at her father's reference to the wedding pavilion in which the bride and groom would sit with the Hindu priest. "Anything I can do to help."

"What about Madhuri's wedding suit?" Nayna asked, well aware of her sister's priorities; Madhuri was nearly bursting with horror at the idea of being married in anything but the latest fashions, but for her to ask now would make her look bad in front of her future in-laws.

Her younger sister asking was another matter altogether—siblings got a much freer pass in such things.

Madhuri shot her a grateful look, mouthing, "Owe you, Ninu."

It turned out Madhuri's doctor was ahead of them. "I've asked a business acquaintance of mine who owns a sari shop to organize a special shipment of designer saris and wedding suits from India," he declared. "You'll be able to choose whichever one you want from among them, and it will be fitted exactly to you."

Madhuri beamed at her suitor. "Oh, Sunny, you're so wonderful," she whispered.

Sunny?

Nope, Dr. Sandesh Patel didn't strike Nayna as a Sunny, but it intrigued her that he was that to Madhuri. The entire Patel family, meanwhile, broke out in huge smiles, utterly charmed by Nayna's sister.

And so it went, until he and his family left.

The rest of them relaxed, talking over the events of the night—with Aji relaying how Madhuri had first shocked them all with the news of Sandesh's proposal. "I nearly fell down dead," their grandmother said, one hand on her heart. "And now the excitement of a wedding so soon!"

"It'll be good practice for Nayna's and Raj's wedding," Shilpa Sharma commented with a laugh. "We'll know what *not* to do by then!"

Nayna looked at Raj. She couldn't stand it anymore, had to clear the air before this went any further or she might find herself in the midst of a double wedding. "I have some news too."

The laughter morphed into Cheshire cat smiles—she knew everyone in her family expected her to announce that she'd formally accepted Raj. "I've decided that before I make any decisions about the rest of my life, I need to find out who I am."

A scowl replaced her father's smile. "What were you doing these past days? Did you not figure all that out already?" A huff of air. "You modern girls. Look at Madhuri. So well settled now."

Nayna didn't even bother to roll her eyes at how quickly her sister had been turned into a paragon. Beside her, Madhuri bit off a squeak. At least her sister found that comparison a little over the top too.

She swallowed hard and continued on into the silence, very aware of Raj seated in the chair next to where she sat on the sofa. His presence gave her confidence as she continued. "I've decided I need to move out and live on my own for a little while."

Chaos erupted. Everybody started talking at once.

Her sister, her father, her mother, even her grandmother. The tone was incredulous in general, and shocked beneath it. Even Madhuri, wild girl that she'd been, looked as if Nayna had dropped a brick on her head.

"No." Her father's voice cut through the din. "This is ridiculous. You're a good girl. You'll get married and have a respectable life." His tone made it clear that was that.

But when he rose as if to leave the room, Nayna said, "I'm sorry, Dad, but I have to do this."

Her father spoke not to her but to Raj. "I thought you were going to talk some sense into her."

Raj got to his feet. "Sir, I don't want Nayna to be my wife if she doesn't want to be my wife. And she needs this time."

Her father's jaw tightened. "Are you telling me you're supporting this nonsense?"

"I'm supporting Nayna," Raj said, still polite but refusing to back down.

"Get out," her father snapped. "I thought you had some spine."

Raj stood his ground. "I'm here for Nayna. I'll always be here for her."

Her father shifted his attention to Nayna, his hard eyes meeting her own. "If you do this, you're no daughter of mine."

Though Nayna had expected as much, it was a kick to the heart nonetheless. Nodding, she rose to her feet, so grateful for Raj's big body right next to her, her shoulder brushing his arm. "I'll pack my things."

"Rubbish!"

Everybody stared at Nayna's mother, who was up on her feet with her hands clenched by her sides. But she wasn't yelling at Nayna. She was yelling at her husband. Nayna's eyes widened. She'd never in her entire existence seen Shilpa Sharma raise her voice to Gaurav Sharma. When she glanced down at Madhuri's seated form, her sister reached up and linked a hand with hers. Madhuri's eyes were as huge as Nayna's felt.

Raj lowered his mouth to her ear. "This wasn't in the script."

Nayna pressed her lips together to keep from bursting into hysterical laughter.

Across from her, her father finally found his voice. "Shilpa?" he asked, not in anger but in stunned shock.

"Nayna, you sit down!" her mother ordered. "Raj, don't you move!"

Nayna sat. Raj didn't move.

"And you, Gaurav Sharma, you listen to me!" Her mother waved a finger in front of his face. "I let you do this the first time and I lost my Madhuri for *six* years." She beat a fist against her chest. "I followed my husband because I was brought up to believe my husband knew best. I was told a good wife stood always by her husband's side. And I missed my eldest for six long years. I cried for her for six long years. Now you want to take my *baby* from me?"

Shilpa put her hands on her hips and shook her head. "No. As long as I live, Nayna will be welcome in this house and she will be welcome to every family event, and if you have any argument with that, I suggest you move yourself to the spare bedroom and stay there!"

Absolute and utter stunned silence.

Nayna didn't know where to look. She kind of felt like she should disappear out of the room, but she didn't want to move and make a sound. From the frozen way Raj was standing and Madhuri was sitting, they felt the same. Only her grandmother continued to rock in her chair, seemingly unconcerned with the explosion from her mild-mannered daughter-in-law.

"Gaurav beta, Shilpa bitia," she said gently. "I think you need to take this somewhere else."

"You both stay here," Nayna's mother ordered Nayna and Raj before she stalked out of the room and slammed into the kitchen, her husband following.

Nayna opened her mouth, shut it again. Raj, who was still standing, ran his hand over her hair. Her grandmother watched him, a slight smile on the seamed lines of her features.

"Well," Aji said, "this is exciting."

Madhuri giggled, and suddenly Nayna was giggling too. Raj looked at the two of them in bemusement, especially when their grandmother slapped her thigh and joined in the laughter. Meanwhile, from the kitchen came silence. After a while, Raj walked back there and leaned against the door while they all held their breath, then came back to tell them, "I think they've gone in the back-yard. Can't hear anything from the kitchen."

That only made the three of them laugh even harder. When it was all over and they'd finally caught their breath, Nayna looked at her grandmother.

"I'm sorry, Aji," she said. "I didn't mean to mess everything up."

Her grandmother waved away her apology. "Oh, mere laal," she said with deep affection, "all I've ever wanted was happiness for you." Her eyes went to Raj. "You're a brave boy to stand up to Gaurav, and you're the kind of boy her father should want for her. He'll realize that when he calms down."

Nayna wasn't so sure, but she didn't interrupt her grandmother.

"My boy has always been obstinate and perhaps a little judgmental," Aji said. "You, Madhuri, didn't help by running off. Why did you ever do such a silly thing? You know if you'd brought the boy home, you'd have eventually talked your father into a proper marriage!"

Madhuri winced. "I was young and stupid," she said, propping her chin in her hands. "It seemed a good idea at the time."

Funnily enough, that was such a Madhuri thing to say that it made perfect sense.

Reaching for the snacks she'd ignored until now, Nayna picked up a samosa that had gone cold. Half-wrapping it in a paper napkin, she handed it up to Raj, who'd perched himself on the arm of the sofa beside her. It put one of his powerful thighs temptingly close, but Nayna behaved herself.

"Eat," she said. "You must be starving." Neither one of them had eaten anything through the entire talk with Sandesh Patel's family.

He accepted her offer, then watched as she took a samosa for herself before eating. The two of them filled their stomachs in silence for a while before Raj said, "So, who do you think will come out the winner?"

"I'm not taking any bets." Madhuri held up her hands, palms out. "I have never seen Ma get this mad. *Never*."

Nayna nodded. "Our mother doesn't get mad," she told Raj. "She gets disappointed or sad or maybe a little bit annoyed, but she doesn't get angry. And she doesn't yell at our father. Ever."

A loud clanging sound reached them just then.

"You go," Madhuri hissed at Raj.

Nayna started to argue, but Raj brushed his knuckles over her cheek, then bravely—and cautiously—went through the kitchen door to find out what was going on.

33

SHILPA SHARMA IS NOT JOKING

RAJ RETURNED WITH THE NEWS that her mother had apparently thrown the lid of a metal trash can at her father. "It looked like it hit the fence and not him," he said. "Your father seems to be trying to calm her down." A pause. "It's not working. Last I saw, she was grabbing peaches from under your tree to throw at him."

Nayna gave him a bhajia to eat while Madhuri, now that she knew the coast was clear, snuck into the kitchen to reheat the chai, and they all had cups of that while they waited. And waited. And waited.

"It doesn't matter what happens, Ninu," Madhuri said at one point, a mulish tone to her voice. "You're going to be at my wedding. If they say you can't be, I'll say I'm not getting married."

Eyes burning, Nayna hugged her big sister.

Aji was smiling widely when they separated. "Shall I bring my boyfriend to your wedding?"

Madhuri almost dropped the teacup she'd picked

back up. "*Aji!*"

Nayna giggled as Aji settled in and regaled her flabbergasted eldest grandchild with stories about her beloved Mr. Hohepa.

"We go for midnight walks some days," she told Madhuri, a twinkle in her eyes. "A good thing about getting old is not sleeping so much."

Nayna thought Aji's eyebrow waggle nearly slew Madhuri on the spot.

Raj, meanwhile, was focusing strictly on the seina Nayna had passed him, as if it was a gourmet delight that required his utter and unflinching attention. Poor Raj. He'd gone looking for a traditional wife and found a drama of Bollywood proportions. But he was still here. Still standing by Nayna's side.

Her parents pushed through the kitchen door while she was fighting the urge to hug Raj. Nayna saw a smile on her mother's face, a somewhat befuddled, dazed look on her father's.

"We will help you move out, beta," her mother said to Nayna, bending down to give her a kiss on the cheek. "Did you already find a place? Tell us all about it."

Feeling a strange kinship with her dumbstruck father, Nayna did.

"Good," Shilpa Sharma said after telling Nayna not to buy towels because Shilpa had tons of brand-new spares. "You're close enough to help with the wedding preparations. I know Sandesh thinks he's got everything organized, but there are a thousand things that go into a good wedding. And my Madhuri, she's going to want a big, fancy wedding aren't you?"

"I've always wanted one of those ice sculptures,"

Madhuri confessed. "Like maybe a giant swan with its wings out. Oh, and gold foil used in the wings so they sparkle."

"Ooooh." Shilpa's eyes widened. "I don't think I've ever seen one of those at an Indian wedding—not even Pinky Mehra had one. And how about that cake you showed me on that Insta thingie? The five-layer one with the roses and the lights and the waterfall?"

"Oh, Ma!" Madhuri all but melted off the sofa "I would *die* if I had that cake! Should I message the baker? Maybe she can fit me in!"

THE NEXT SATURDAY AND NAYNA still had no idea what had happened.

The one thing she did know was that she was standing in her brand-new apartment, boxes around her. Raj was outside with her father and a couple of guys from his crew, doing some work on the deck while her mother and Madhuri bustled about in the kitchen, making some ginger tea for them.

Their grandmother had a slight cold and had requested it—and strangely enough, Madhuri, who was a terrible cook, made incredible ginger chai, beginning with freshly crushed ginger and lots of full-fat milk. The pot was Shilpa's, one of a spare set her mother had given to Nayna. Along with cutlery, glasses, plates, even a rice cooker.

Nayna looked at her best friend, who was carefully unwrapping Nayna's knickknacks. Ísa sat on an old but funky red sofa that Nayna had found online and that Raj had driven forty minutes out of town to pick up for her.

"I did it," Nayna said. "I really did it. I moved out."

"Your father is acting very weird," Ísa whispered after craning her neck around to make sure no one would overhear her, ponytailed red hair swinging against the blue of her top. "Not angry weird. *Weird* weird."

"I think he's in continued shock from my mother's first ever show of temper." To be honest, Nayna hadn't quite processed that herself. "I just..."

Sinking down into the sofa beside Ísa, she whispered, "I never thought she'd fight for me like that." And suddenly her voice trembled, tears closing up her throat. "I always thought I would only be loved if I was perfect. That I *had* to be perfect."

Her friend put her arm around her and hugged her close. "You silly goose." Ísa's own eyes were wet. "My mother is a fire-breathing dragon with a calculator for a heart, and she crisped someone who was trying to cause trouble for me. Your mother is an actual human. Of course she fought for you."

Nayna snuffled, laughing through her tears before quickly wiping her eyes dry on the tails of her checked green shirt so that her mother and grandmother wouldn't worry when they returned to the room. "I just... I saw how she was with Madhuri. She was so sad, but she never went against my father."

"Well, it seems like she learned from her mistake," Ísa said. "I'm proud of her. What she did, it meant going against what she's believed her whole life."

Nayna nodded and leaned up against Ísa again. "She was born on a farm in a rural part of Fiji, did I ever tell you that? Only twenty-one when she married my father, and her parents took her out of school at age sixteen so she could help out on the farm more. My aji used to tell me how shy and sweet she was, how my father had to go with her everywhere for a while until she became used to the hustle and bustle of the city."

"That actually sounds super cute," Ísa said with a grin. "Your dad doing that for her."

"He loves her." Of that, Nayna had never been in any doubt. "It was arranged, their marriage, but Aji says after five other introductions, my father took one look at my mother and he was a goner."

Nayna raised her hand to her face. "Apparently she was considered damaged goods by others because of that burn scar she has on her upper cheek, but he told Aji that she was the most beautiful girl he'd ever seen. And after they got together, he even asked her if she wanted to study some more, and that's how my mother ended up learning how to be an office manager." A position she'd held part-time for much of Nayna's childhood.

"No wonder he's so discombobulated now," Ísa said. "He adores her. And she's mad at him."

"She's *really* mad. I..." Nayna blew out a breath. "Like Raj said, this wasn't in the script." And it had left her with shaky ground under her feet. "It's all upside down."

An engine sounded outside. "Is that another truck arriving?"

"Oh, that'll be Sailor," Ísa said with a sweetly posses-sive smile. "He had to check in on a job, but he's going to help Raj finish up the deck. His brothers are coming over too."

"The Bishop?" Nayna asked, well aware that Sailor's older brother was the lauded captain of the national rugby team.

Ísa nodded. "Gabe's picking up their younger brothers on his way in."

"That, at least, should make my father's day." Gaurav Sharma was a huge fan of rugby and of Gabriel Bishop in particular.

Before Nayna could say anything else, her grandmother returned from the restroom. "Come, Ninu, Isshu," she said, using the nicknames she'd given them long ago. "We must be faster in unwrapping these things."

AFTER EVERYONE ELSE HAD LEFT—post beer and a barbecue—Raj sat down with Nayna's father on the finished deck. While the other man had turned up today, he'd remained quiet and hadn't interacted with Nayna at all.

Raj'd had enough. No one would hurt Nayna on his watch. "She's the most extraordinary woman I've ever met," he said to the older man. "And she's never been given any freedom. All she sees in the idea of marriage is a trap, a cage."

Nayna's father stared straight ahead, a muscle working in his jaw. "I was looking out for her," Gaurav Sharma finally gritted out. "Madhuri ended up abandoned in a foreign city. What kind of life is that for a girl?"

Raj decided not to point out that Gaurav had curtailed Nayna's freedom long before Madhuri's marriage went bad; this wasn't about point-scoring. It was about ensuring Nayna's father didn't hurt her soft heart. "You want to protect her, make sure no harm comes to her."

"It's what a father does."

Pain stabbed at Raj. He wanted children too, but only with Nayna. His wild and blazingly intelligent lover who wanted adventure and a life lived on a sprawling canvas... while Raj was most at home in the familiar and the rooted. "I can't imagine how hard it would be to let my child go into something that could cause him or her harm," he said past the reminder of how Nayna was moving farther and farther from him. "But holding on so securely that they can't breathe... it could break them in the end."

Nayna's father didn't say anything for a long minute. When he did speak, he said, "We should go inside. My mother will want to go home."

It wasn't the end result Raj wanted, but at least Gaurav Sharma said goodbye to his daughter rather than simply ignoring her. And when the older man shot Raj a pointed look for not leaving with them, his wife glared at him, and Nayna's father said nothing—though thunderclouds formed on his brow.

"Well," Nayna said after everyone had gone, "that was a strange, beautiful day."

Yes, that was the way to describe it, but for Raj it had also been a terrible day. The day Nayna took her first step away from him. But for now she was his, and he would drown himself in her.

Pressing his hands to the door on either side of her head, he kissed her.

Making a throaty sound, she rose up toward him at once, wrapping her arms around his neck. And the stranglehold of fear around his heart, it eased a fraction.

34

DREAMS, BEER, AND ICE CREAM (NOT IN THAT ORDER)

T HE FOLLOWING MONDAY PASSED BY at the speed of light.

Nayna's firm had a big meeting to work out their plans and aims for the year to come, and once again, Nayna felt an itch inside her to move beyond the steady, familiar work she was doing there. She was good at it, but she'd never given herself the chance to figure out if she'd be good in a position that required more nimble movements and decisions.

"Nayna." Douglas stopped her after the meeting, his green eyes piercing against the dark brown of his hair. "I've got a major meet with the Barths Tuesday afternoon. You want to sit in?"

The Barths were big clients—and whatever Nayna's future held, any such connections would be a bonus. "Thank you. That'd be fantastic."

The meeting ended up being in the private room of a restaurant, and once it was over, Douglas drove them both back to the office. "I spent Christmas vacation in

Egypt," he told her, regaling her with stories when she admitted her interest in the country. "There's an Egyptian exhibition on at the art gallery," he said as they turned into the firm's parking lot. "Last week before it closes. I'm thinking about going. You want to come?"

The past and the future collided, two very different men asking her to attend the same event. Douglas, of course, was just being friendly. Though he was divorced and currently single, he'd never made any move on Nayna.

"Thank you," she said, "but I'm not going anywhere until I clear my workload."

"Well," Douglas said, "if you change your mind, you know where I work." His grin was wide. "I'll email you a few of my Egypt photos too. I've already bored everyone else with them."

Laughing, the two of them entered the villa and headed off to their separate offices.

In the days that followed, Nayna had to work long hours to catch up after having taken extra time off work. Raj dropped by one night with takeout while she and Douglas were working out a problem.

Delight had her bouncing inside.

She introduced the men and they shook hands. For a second, she thought she was imagining the sudden tension in the air, but Raj's expressions were no longer opaque to her—and the way he was holding his jaw, it didn't exactly shout happiness. As for Douglas, he shot her a huge smile before he left and said, "Don't forget about the Egyptian exhibition. We still have a few days to catch it."

Raj said absolutely nothing after Douglas left the

room, simply helped her set out the takeout on the coffee table in one corner of her office, between two small sofas. Nayna waited until her colleague had exited the villa altogether, driving off in his BMW, before deciding to take the bull by the horns.

"I don't know what that was about," she said bluntly. "If I was going to go to that exhibition, it'd be with you."

Raj gave her an intent look. "I don't think he knew I existed until I walked in." Quiet, potent words.

Nayna frowned. "That's because I don't talk about my private life in the office." She liked her colleagues but didn't consider them close enough friends to chat to them about the problems and joys of her life.

Raj's shoulder muscles remained rigid. "He thought you were single, and he was building up to asking you out."

Nayna snorted. "He's known me since I began working here. He hasn't suddenly been overcome by my beauty." And if Raj didn't stop being so hardheaded about this, Nayna would have a blowup to rival Shilpa Sharma's.

"The man was hitting on you," Raj said without raising his voice. "Or does he stay behind to help out all the people in this office?"

"Ugh!" Nayna hauled Raj's face down to her own, kissing him until his fingers dug into her hips and her heart was thunder. "You're my man, and we're not having a dumb fight over nothing."

Raj's gaze smoldered. He was the one who initiated the next kiss, and that kiss burned through her like hot black fire. She'd already taken off her jacket earlier in the day, and now he unbuttoned her shirt with one hand while tugging up the hem of her pencil skirt with the other.

She shoved her hands under his T-shirt, clawing at his back as he kissed her throat, one hand on the lace-covered mound of her bra. Each squeeze, each brush, it only made her hotter. When he pulled away to spin her around, she instinctively braced her hands on the edge of her desk.

"Raj?"

Shoving up her skirt to her hips, Raj didn't reply as he pulled down her panties. Nayna lifted one foot, then the other so he could get them fully off. The sound of a belt being opened, a zipper being lowered, the crackle of foil.

Her face was hot, her entire body teetering on the cliff of anticipation.

One big hand gripped her hip. "Nayna." A ground-out word that demanded a response.

She lowered herself even farther, arching her back. "Yes," she whispered. "Yes."

He surged into her in a hard thrust that lifted her onto her toes and tore a scream from her mouth. Hands on her hips on either side, Raj thrust in and out in a relentless motion that pushed her over the cliff in a passionate clenching of inner muscles that made him stiffen and let out a loud grunt before he leaned down to press a kiss to her neck.

His breath was heaving bellows, his heart pounding against her back.

Reaching up with one hand, Nayna brushed her palm over his bristled cheek. "You're mine," she said, her voice husky. "I don't want anyone else."

RAJ MET UP WITH NAVIN for a beer the next night, his mood still dark.

He'd been rough with Nayna the previous day in her office, and he wasn't happy with himself about it. He hadn't physically hurt her, and she'd been with him all the way, but Raj wasn't used to losing control the way he had with her.

You're mine. I don't want anyone else.

Nayna believed that now. But how much longer would those words be true?

"Hey." Navin tapped his beer bottle to Raj's. "What's with the tall, dark, and brooding look, bro? I know you're not trying to pick up women."

Raj hadn't even noticed the women in the pub, all his attention on an accountant with dark eyes who filled all the holes inside him but who might only be his for a small moment in time. "It's nothing," he said to his brother. "How are you and Komal doing?" The strain between the two had hit such a fever pitch that Aditi had all but moved into Raj's small flat, making up a bed for herself on his fold-out couch.

Navin shrugged and took a sip of his beer. "She's pissed off at me because I'm 'just' a teacher, can't give her some fancy lifestyle. I don't know what she expected since I was a student teacher when we met."

Raj didn't like his sister-in-law, but he knew this wasn't all Komal's fault. "You're hardly home, Navin. Why the fuck are you out with the boys all hours when you've got a pretty young wife at home?"

"It's not like she's at home either," Navin shot back. "I saw her at the same club I was at yesterday."

Raj's temples pounded. "I don't care who's at what

club," he said. "You two have to figure something out—it's not fair on Mum and Dad and Aditi to have you two hissing at each other like feral cats."

Flushing, Navin ducked his head. "Komal didn't even want to move in with the family," he muttered. "I talked her into it."

That, at least, explained a little of his sister-in-law's behavior when she'd first come home as Navin's bride. "Have you considered moving out?" At this stage, their parents would wave them off with cheerful smiles and offers to load their furniture.

"It's fucking expensive," Navin said, though—despite his complaints—he wasn't hard up. Not only did he have his teacher's salary, he got a percentage of the construction company's profits. Raj had made his father and mother agree to that setup—even though Raj was running the business, he never wanted Navin or Aditi to feel cut out of something their parents had built.

"I can organize more funds," he began.

But Navin shook his head. "I'm being an asshole, bhaiya." Taking another drink of his beer, he put it back down. "I know I'm in a good spot, and I know if you weren't around, the parents would be looking at me to take over the family business—and I'd be miserable." A faint grin that reminded Raj of the small boy who'd once followed him around. "I must've done something good in a past life to end up with you as a brother, though I clearly also did something very nasty to end up with the marriage from hell."

Raj squeezed his shoulder. "Try, Navin," he said quietly. "You loved Komal madly when you two got married. That kind of love doesn't just disappear." His own love for Nayna would be forever a part of him, no matter what happened.

Navin's hand tightened to bloodless whiteness round the beer bottle, and Raj realized his younger brother was fighting a strong surge of emotion. "I think she's having an affair."

The words were a punch to the gut. "Think or know?"

"I don't have any proof." Navin finished off his beer. "Not that I really care. It's not like she loves me anyway."

Raj did what he could for his brother that night, but Navin wasn't talking anymore. He was also drunk when Raj drove him home, then helped him up the internal stairs to his and Komal's part of the house. The house had three master suites, two upstairs and one downstairs. Raj's parents occupied one of the upstairs ones, Komal and Navin the other.

There had previously only been one master suite upstairs, but Raj had added in a second after Navin's engagement, when his brother told Raj he and his new wife would be staying in the family home. He'd done it as a wedding present, never realizing that his brother was trampling on Komal's needs and wants.

Aditi had a single room at the far end of the same hallway.

At the end nearest the stairs was a large rumpus room/lounge, set up with a television and sofas.

Raj and Navin had both had single bedrooms on the ground floor before Navin got married and Raj moved out. At present, one was his mother's sewing room and the other functioned as his father's study. When in town, Raj's grandparents occupied the final master suite on the ground floor. That suite had been built for them so they wouldn't have to deal with stairs.

The main downstairs lounge was where his parents watched their television shows and hosted guests, but there was another, more casual space that flowed off the kitchen and was the lounge Raj and Navin had used most often when growing up. Navin's game system still sat in one corner, dusted off occasionally by Aditi and her friends.

So it wasn't as if this was a small house with people on top of one another. And yet Navin and Komal had managed to permeate the entire house with their dislike of one another.

When he knocked lightly on the door of their suite, conscious of not waking his parents, it was wrenched open from the inside.

"Where the f—" Komal bit off her words when she saw Raj supporting Navin.

Stepping aside with her lips compressed tightly together, she let Raj bring his brother inside and drop him on the bed. Not sure Komal would bother, Raj took off his brother's shoes.

Navin, meanwhile, smiled drunkenly at Komal. "Pretty girl," he slurred. "C'mere."

"Not while you have eau de beer coming out of your pores," Komal muttered before glancing at Raj. "Thank you."

"He should be fine, but just keep an eye on him." Raj went to step outside.

A hand on his forearm, Komal's nails cut short as befit a nurse but her face fully made up despite the late hour. "You're a good man, Raj." Her smile was warm, far softer than he'd seen her direct Navin's way over the past couple of years. "Any woman would be lucky to have you."

Raj broke the physical contact at once. "Good night, Komal."

But she followed him to the door. "If Nayna Sharma's still dangling you like a fish on a hook, she doesn't deserve you. You need to move on before you waste your life waiting for her to make up her mind."

Ignoring the words and glad the commotion of bringing Navin home hadn't woken anyone else, Raj made his way down the stairs and out the back door. He shrugged off Komal's poisonous words as he walked; he understood his Nayna in a way Komal never could. The idea of clipping her wings... No, Raj would never do it.

No matter how much he hurt.

Opening the front door of his flat, he glanced left. A smile formed on his face when he spotted his sister's curls peeking out from under the thick blanket she'd pulled up over herself despite the summer warmth. Walking over, he tucked the blanket in more neatly and wondered what Komal had done that had driven Aditi out here today.

His sister-in-law was still on his mind when he walked into his bedroom and began to prepare for bed. Not in the way she wanted to be, however. In Navin and Komal, he had a graphic example that people changed.

Emotions changed.

Raj knew his stubbornness could be both a gift and a curse. When he claimed people, he held on. Love for him had never been a simple matter. He would love Nayna Sharma always.

"Bhaiya?"

Hearing the sleepy call, Raj pulled on a T-shirt over his sweatpants and wandered out to see Aditi sitting up in bed. "Did I wake you, Monkey?"

A yawning nod. "It's okay. I went to bed at grandma hours." She rubbed at her face. "Want to watch TV and eat ice cream?"

Raj had an early start the next day, needed to get some sleep. However, with his mind tangled up in thoughts of a woman with hair of silk whose body welcomed him with tight heat but who wouldn't wear his ring, he didn't think he'd be sleeping anytime soon. "Sure. You can pick the show."

Aditi chose a baking show. Halfway through her bowl of ice cream, she leaned her head on his shoulder and began to tell him about how Harlow had built her a village. It took him a while to figure out that Harlow had built that village in a game the two played online. "I lost a level because of a dumb mistake and couldn't make my village, so he stayed up like five hours one night to gain the points to gift me the village."

Raj was only half listening to his sister, but when he did finally go to bed, he dreamed of building Nayna a village full of adventures and wonder and showing her that life with him wouldn't be tedium, tradition, and rules.

The problem was, Raj wasn't sure he could pull it off.

As with Mr. Darcy, tradition was woven into his bones.

35

NAYNA UNBUTTONS HER SHIRT

TWO DAYS AFTER THE EROTIC encounter with Raj in her office—she still blushed thinking about it—Nayna had to admit he'd been right. Douglas *was* hitting on her. Nothing creepy or crossing the line, but when he asked her out to dinner while they were both working late, she knew she had to put a stop to it right then.

"Raj and I, we're serious, Doug," she said, calm but firm. "Exclusive."

Unabashed, Douglas kicked back in the chair across from her. "You never talk about him. Can't be that serious."

"I'm not the kind of woman who spreads her private life around," Nayna said, annoyed. "I'd appreciate it if you dropped this. It's making me uncomfortable."

He held up his hands, smile fading. "Hey, sorry. I just... You've changed somehow, Nayna. There's a new brightness to you, and it's attractive as hell. But I won't push where I'm not wanted."

Afterward, back in her office, Nayna found herself annoyed all over again at the memory of what Douglas had said. But what turned her irritation into worry was the memory of Raj's words.

I don't think he knew I existed until I walked in.

She'd taken that as an indication of jealousy, but what if it was worse? What if Raj thought she was deliberately pushing him to the periphery of her world? Was that why he hadn't been in touch since? Was she beginning to lose Raj?

The idea of it caused a deep pain in her stomach, made her breath knot.

Picking up her phone, she called him. "I miss you," she said when he picked up. "Are you working late today?"

A pause before he said, "I can change my plans if you're free."

Her toes curled, but the spreadsheet in front of her mocked her hunger to hold him. "I can't if I want to have any of the weekend free." She had to catch up after her unscheduled time off. "Saturday?"

"Done."

Nayna hung up with her nerves in a knot. Raj was never voluble on the phone, but he'd sounded even more curt than usual. Maybe it was just her imagination and it was only tiredness on his part. He was working long hours too after three of his crew came down with the same cold that had hit her grandmother.

Thankfully, Aji had only had a mild case and was all but fully recovered—helped along by many cups of ginger chai and hours of Indian television dramas. Spoiler: the evil sister-in-law was still trying to cause trouble, and now she was trying to make it look like the younger, innocent sister-in-law was having an affair with the milkman.

But even the thought of that never-ending plotline wasn't enough to distract Nayna from her worry about what was going on with Raj. He hadn't even sent her an ab selfie for days. She picked up her phone to look through her private Raj folder... and felt a stir of wickedness. Not giving herself time to chicken out, she made sure her office door was firmly shut, then quickly undid several extra buttons on her shirt and fluffed at her hair.

It stayed dead straight.

Ugh.

She took the shot regardless, a selfie of her blowing him a kiss while her cleavage was teasing shadows between the sides of her shirt. Only when it was too late did she wonder if Raj would find the shot shocking rather than enticing.

RAJ WAS JUST ABOUT TO turn on the rotating saw when his phone buzzed with an incoming message. Still in a good mood from Nayna's "I miss you," he pulled it out... and was damn glad he hadn't turned on the saw or he might've sliced off a valuable body part.

Her lips were soft and luscious as she blew him a kiss, her barely buttoned shirt taunting him with the secrets hidden within while her shining black hair flirted with the darkness of her skin. Blowing out a long breath and happy no one was close enough to have picked up on his immediate physical reaction, he saved the image in a private folder.

Part of him was fighting a tinge of heat on his cheekbones at being so sensually teased by the woman he loved, but he wasn't an idiot. If Nayna wanted to send him sexy selfies, he wasn't going to tell her no. What he wrote back was: *One more button.*

Her response was: *You can undo that one on your own. xx*

Entire body hot with need, he slid away his phone. And told himself that a ring on her finger didn't matter, not so long as she thought of herself as his. He had to get over that, or he'd wreck what they had between them.

When his parents cornered him that night and asked what was going on with Nayna, Raj said, "We're together."

His mother shared a speaking look with his father before putting a hand on his. "Raj, beta, you know we won't force you into anything, but you've always wanted to get married, set up a family, have children." Worry in every word. "Will this kind of a relationship make you happy?"

"It's Nayna," Raj said simply. "She makes me happy."

His parents didn't appear convinced, but they let it go, and the conversation drifted to Madhuri Sharma's wedding, to which Raj's entire family had been invited. Komal wandered in partway through, dressed in scrubs for a night shift.

After drinking half a cup of tea and listening to the conversation, she said, "You know Madhuri has a history?" An arch tone. "The Sharmas tried to bury it, but I have a friend who—"

"*Komal.*" Raj's father spoke before Raj gave in to his temper. "Madhuri is Nayna's sister, and Nayna is with Raj.

The Sharmas are like family. We don't talk about them behind their backs."

Komal's face hardened. Putting down her mug, she said, "Sure" and left.

Raj narrowed his eyes, not trusting her instant capitulation. He'd have to watch her, make sure she didn't try to foment trouble for Madhuri in the lead-up to her wedding. "Where's Navin?" he asked his parents.

His mother winced. "Out again."

"It's his fault she's like this," Jitesh Sen muttered. "This is what happens when you neglect your wife."

"She was never exactly sunshine," Aditi said, having obviously overheard the last comment as she walked into the kitchen. "But Navin bhaiya isn't helping." She hugged Raj from behind. "Ma, are there any cookies left? I'm legit *starving*."

"Show me your leg again," their mother demanded. "It's definitely hollow."

Aditi laughed and banged at her leg with a hand while making echoing sounds.

As his family moved around him, conversation ebbing and flowing, Raj felt a true hollow inside him. Nayna might never be a part of such conversations, might never sit around a table of an evening with his parents and sister—and possibly Navin and Komal, if the two didn't implode.

That too was a truth he had to accept.

Things came to a head with Navin and Komal the next night, when they had a screaming fight just after Raj pulled into the drive. Aditi waved at him frantically from the front door, and he headed her way instead of back to his flat.

"What's wrong?" he began, then heard the yelling and screaming.

"You're such a mama's boy!" Komal cried. "Anytime anything happens, you run to your ma! No fucking spine!"

"At least she cares about me instead of being a cold-hearted bitch!"

"Go to my place," Raj told Aditi.

His baby sister didn't argue. She just grabbed the spare key to his place from the kitchen drawer, picked up her phone and her math textbook, and hauled ass. Raj, meanwhile, took the stairs up to Komal and Navin two at a time. He found his parents already there, his mother looking shell-shocked and his father pale.

"You bastard!" a sobbing Komal cried. "You slept with that whore!"

"*I'm* not the one who's cheating!" cried a Navin with scratches on his face. "And even if I was, who'd blame me with such a bitch for a—"

"Shut up, both of you!" Raj's voice cut through the caustic mix of rage and pain in the air. "Ma, Dad, why don't you go for a walk?"

When his parents accepted his suggestion in silence, Raj realized exactly how shaken they were. "This is enough," he said quietly to his brother and sister-in-law after the three of them were alone. "I don't care what the problem is between the two of you. You do *not* do this in front of our parents and Aditi."

Navin flushed and Komal wouldn't meet Raj's eyes.

"In fact," he added, "I think you two need to think

about finding your own place. Clearly living here isn't working for you." Not if Komal was accusing Navin of being a mama's boy when Sangeeta Sen made a point of staying out of the married couple's problems.

Komal looked up, glanced at Navin. "I'm okay with moving out," she said, and her tone was relatively calm.

"Why don't you move in with your boyfriend?" Navin said before twisting on his heel and slamming his way down the stairs.

Tears shimmered in Komal's eyes, and when his sister-in-law started crying, Raj could do nothing but hold her. She sobbed against him for a long time before he pulled away.

"I should've married you," she whispered, her eyes red and swollen.

Shrugging away the statement—given Komal's emotional meltdown, she couldn't know what she was saying—Raj nonetheless took another step back. "Do you want me to call your sister?" Komal had stayed with her sibling on more than one occasion when she and Navin had a tiff.

She rubbed off her tears. "No. I have a night shift. Navin will be gone by the time I get home, so I have time to think about what I want." Turning, she glanced over her shoulder at him. "Navin and I aren't suited, were never really suited. But we thought we could make it work. You should think about that."

The bullet hit home, but Raj kept his face expressionless as he turned to leave.

"Raj?" Komal's voice halted him, her next words sharp. "Love marriage or arranged marriage, the commitment has to come from both sides."

Raj left without listening any further. Komal could stir trouble elsewhere. Raj had made his decision and he'd see it through.

He was halfway down the path to his flat when his phone rang with an unfamiliar number. "This is Raj," he answered, figuring it might be a client who hadn't previously called him.

"Raj beta," said an elderly female voice. "It's Nayna's aji. Mr. Hohepa fell on our walk. Can you come drive him home?"

And that was how Raj found himself playing wingman to a dapper sixty-seven-year-old. "Are you sure you don't need to go to the hospital?" he asked Tawhiri Hohepa after successfully getting him inside his home and all set up in bed.

"No, no. It's just a turned ankle. Old rugby injury—a good night's rest and I'll be back up and around." He winced. "Sure wish Heera hadn't seen me fall though."

Nayna's grandmother bustled in then, a mug in hand. "Your favorite herbal tea," she said with a smile. "Let me tuck you in."

Rubbing the back of his neck, Raj got himself out of the room and hoped Nayna's aji couldn't tell he was blushing. She came out only minutes later, gave him one look, and laughed. "You young people. Where do you think you came from, huh?"

"I arrived by stork," Raj said seriously. "My brother and sister by magic."

Tucking an arm through his, Nayna's aji patted at his arm. "You're a good boy to come. I didn't want to call Nayna out so late, and she wouldn't have been strong enough anyway." She beamed up at him. "It's a smart thing I memorized your number from Nayna's phone."

Raj didn't want to ask why. He really didn't. "The back door, Aji?" he said instead, after they were out of Mr. Hohepa's house.

"Let's walk to the park and back," she said, and so they walked under the quiet night sky. "I wanted to talk to you," Nayna's grandmother told him on their journey back. "My Nayna, she's flowering, but some things have always mattered to her. Family, love, a place to call home."

Raj frowned but didn't interrupt.

Aji patted his forearm again. "Before Madhuri did her silly running away, Nayna would talk about traveling and seeing wild places, but she also looked at bridal magazines and planned her own wedding as girls often do."

"People change," Raj said, thinking once again of Navin and Komal.

"Yes. Look at me with a boyfriend at my age." Delight in every word. "But I'm still the Heera my husband married too. Just because we grow doesn't mean we forget our old selves. We are all created of many skins." Waving him down when they reached the back door, she kissed his cheek. "You love her as my Nayna deserves to be loved. Don't lose faith in your own ability to grow."

Raj stared down at the seamed lines of her face, feeling the sense of tightness around his chest snap. "Midnight walks and shared secrets?"

Aji's smile was luminous. "See? You understand." She opened the back door. "Love grows when it is tended."

36

AJI INTERFERENCE IS GOOD
INTERFERENCE

N AYNA'S MOUTH FELL OPEN. SHE'D dropped by her parents' early morning on Saturday to say hello before she went in to work for a few hours to wrap things up. Only Aji was up. "You called Raj?" she squeaked, wondering what her traditional lover had made of her grandmother having a boyfriend.

"Of course I did." Having boiled up the milk and sugar, Aji added the rolled oats. Watery oatmeal was *not* the done thing in the Sharma household; it was proper milk porridge, thick and rich, or it was nothing. "I think I shocked him, but he walked me back and told me to call him anytime I needed him—he also said Tawhiri and I need to walk on better lit pathways."

Nayna's lips twitched and her heart, it expanded. She could just see solemn and serious Raj quietly pointing out the need for safety. "How is Mr. Hohepa?"

"I saw him earlier. He's feeling much better. Here, have some breakfast." Aji spooned her out some of the porridge, and Nayna saw she'd added plump raisins as well.

The two of them ate together, and it was as Nayna was rising to go that her grandmother said, "Nayna, he's a strong man." Her eyes held Nayna in place. "But even strong men need tending. Don't forget that."

Nayna's heartbeat turned into a drum. "Did he say something?"

"Raj isn't the kind of man to talk of his heart to anyone but the woman who holds it," her grandmother chided her. "I'm just saying that love grows when it's tended."

Aji's words swirled around in Nayna's head all morning. The idea of marriage still made her chest constrict, and marriage, she knew, was Raj's dream. But... being rooted mattered to him too. Knowing how things stood was important to him. And Nayna could do something about making sure he had zero doubts about her commitment to him.

She picked up the phone and called Aditi to find out Raj's current whereabouts.

"Yo, boss!" Tino yelled out. "Courier just delivered flowers for you!"

Raj pushed back the earmuffs that protected his hearing from all the noise on a construction site. "What?" he asked, sure he'd misheard. "Did you say flowers?"

Tino held up a bunch of red roses. "Fancy schmancy romancey flowers."

Skin a little hot and a smile weaving through his blood, Raj walked over to take the roses from Tino. The other man tried to peer over Raj's shoulder as he opened the card tucked inside, but Raj blocked him with his shoulders. It helped that he was taller than Tino.

The message was typed, must've been sent through to the florist by email. But it was from Nayna: *Sexy hunk, hot fling, my rock—and my grandmother's rescuer—you're the full package, Raj Sen. I'm crazy about you. ~ Nayna with the pretty nayna*

He was grinning so wide that he probably looked like an idiot. Around him, his men were mouthing off about never getting flowers from their girls.

"Yeah well," Gazza called out to a grumbling Tino, "at least you have a girl now! I told you the book would work."

"Only now I have to read the next one!" Tino yelled back. "Sense and Shampoo or something."

Raj's shoulders shook as he took the roses into the site office. He found an old paint can, filled it with water, and put the roses in, but made sure to grab the card and hide it safely in his pocket. His crew was fully capable of peeking—and ribbing him endlessly about being called a sexy hunk.

He should've remembered that Tino had met the courier.

Sexy hunk and hot fling.

Midday, and that was what he found painted on a piece of tarp his crew had draped over the front of his truck. Raj laughed and took the ribbing in good humor. He'd called work to an end for the day, and everyone was off for the weekend. Including the man Nayna considered a sexy hunk and a hot fling.

Not just that, but her anchor.

He put the roses carefully in his truck for the ride home to shower off the grit and dust from the site. After which he messaged Nayna, signing off with: *From the sexy hunk.*

LESS THAN AN HOUR LATER, Raj brought his truck to a stop in front of Nayna's unit to find her already waiting outside, together with the overnight bag he'd asked her to pack. Getting out, he walked over to steal a kiss, his cells parched for her, and his lips curved in a smile.

"My crew is never going to let me live down being called a sexy hunk and a hot fling."

An unrepentant look from Nayna. "I only speak the truth." The smile she gave him, possessive and delighted, twisted its way around his heart.

He'd do anything if she'd only look at him that way forever.

Lifting a hand, she rubbed at the sides of his mouth. "These look like stress lines. Is it the job?"

"No. We're on track there." Raj pressed his forehead to hers. "It's Navin and Komal. I'm pretty sure a breakup is on the horizon." Right now the two were frigidly ignoring one another.

"I'm sorry to hear that... but they seem pretty toxic together."

Raj nodded. "I'm hoping the damage they've done one another isn't permanent." There were no winners in a situation like theirs. "But today's not about them." He kissed her again. "We need to get going if we're going to be on time."

"I'm trying not to ask where we're going," she said

after she'd buckled into the passenger seat. "But it's making me crazy."

She tried to play twenty questions with him to get some clues, and, hoping he'd chosen the right thing for this woman who wanted to experience life in all its facets, Raj played along. When she asked if they'd be getting dirty, he said, "Highly likely, especially our hands."

Frowning, she tapped her finger against her lip. "Our hands." It was a murmuring thought. "We're going to do pottery?"

Raj groaned.

She threw up her hands. "Pottery might be fun! You could make a pipe to smoke, and I'd make... also a pipe to smoke."

Laughter rippled out of him. "What's your next question now that you wasted that one?"

"Why are we wearing sweatpants and thick socks?"

"Part of the instructions. No jeans allowed. Something about the seams digging in."

That had her thinking for a while. "Is it something scary?"

"Depends if you like heights."

"Okay, that's a solid clue." Nayna bit down on her lower lip, the action catching his eye and threatening to tighten his sweatpants over a certain part of his anatomy, but Raj managed to keep his attention on the road. They were out of Auckland now, sheep and deer farms passing on either side of them. Despite it being summer, they'd had enough rain that the fields were green, the sheep puffy white clouds against the velvet grass.

"I don't mind heights," Nayna said after a while. "Are we jumping off something? Because you know that thing about bungee jumping and retinal detachment, don't you?"

"Damn, the tickets are nonrefundable."

A suspicious silence before she pushed him playfully on the shoulder. "Not funny, Raj Sen," she said, but he heard the smile in her voice.

That smile never faded as the miles passed, the road trip made an adventure by Nayna's interest in everything. He had to stop by an ostrich farm so she could watch the long-necked creatures bob about. Then came the deer by a fence line that she had to photograph.

"Hey, what was that sign?" She twisted around to look behind her as they drove on. "It said we're going in the direction of Waitomo!"

"You're getting warm."

Nayna wiggled excitedly in her seat. "I love the glow-worms," she said. "You were supposed to tell the truth when we played twenty questions. There are no heights involved in the caves."

"Mea culpa," Raj said, and kept on driving.

NAYNA WASN'T SURPRISED WHEN RAJ drove not to the main entrance to the cave system but into a parking lot that had a sign touting adventure tourism. She figured he must've booked them in for a walk/climb through one of the less well-known caves.

While Raj checked them in, she looked at the brochures for all the adventures on offer and felt her eyes go wide. He'd said no when she'd asked if they'd be getting wet, so they couldn't be going on the black water rafting trip. She wasn't sure she was ready for that anyway. From the pictures, a number of the passages appeared extremely narrow. Also, the water looked freezing.

"We're checked in." Raj took her hand in his, led her out to a small private parking lot behind the main building. "This is where we catch our next ride," he told her just as a professional guide came out. Two twentysomething women who'd been loitering outside came closer, and Nayna realized the four of them were going together.

It turned out they'd be driving about fifteen to twenty minutes to reach an isolated cave. The ride was a fun one with all five of them ending up chatting. As they got to know one another, Nayna sat with Raj next to her, his arm casually around her shoulders, and drank in the sensation of being with him among people who saw nothing unusual with an unmarried couple on a date.

Because this was *definitely* a date.

The sense of freedom was exhilarating.

At last their van reached a solid-looking structure in what felt like the middle of nowhere. Behind them was a private farm through which the adventure company had authorized access, but in front of them lay only local forest. Large tree ferns, lots of lush green foliage. Once they were all out of the van, the guide looked each one of them up and down, then began passing out blue coveralls.

They were instructed to put the coveralls on over their clothes and, if they had anything loose in their pockets, to leave it behind in the lockers provided. "I'll take the photos," the guide told them. "Trust me, you do not want to lose your phone down there."

That done, the guide sent them into another part of

the structure to find a pair of heavy white calf-high boots to pull on over the thick socks they'd been instructed to wear. Nayna returned after finding a pair that fit and saw the guide handing out what looked like climbing harnesses.

"Raj." She elbowed him. "Why is he giving those out?"

37

A KISS UNDER STARLIGHT

Her gorgeous, often serious boyfriend gave her a slow, wicked smile. "Trust me, you'll love it."

After the harnesses came helmets that had to be clipped securely under the jaw. All of them ready and safety-checked, they strode off into the untamed landscape. Every so often, a native bird would call out, but otherwise it felt as if they were on the edge of civilization.

Because of rain the day past, the area was a little muddy, and Nayna almost slipped a couple of times, but Raj was always there to stabilize her. They arrived at the start of a small hill and began to go down... and that was when Nayna saw it.

A platform.

Hanging out over the edge of nowhere.

The ground was just suddenly *not there*.

Raj closed his fingers over hers when she sucked in a breath. "Okay?" His eyes held a true question, and she knew he wasn't teasing this time. If she said no, they'd turn around and walk away.

But she squeezed his hand back and grinned. "I'm terrified, but I want to do it."

He laughed, and the two of them went down to the platform built of crisscrossing lines of metal that allowed a dizzying view down into the depths below, the platform literally suspended over thin air. It was as if a giant hand had scooped out a massive hole in the earth, the distance from the platform to the ground so far that their landing spot was shrouded in shadows. A river's roar echoed in the air, but she had to squint to make out any hint of its rushing force.

The guide stood at the far edge of the platform, and behind him was nothing but open space. To their left was a rocky wall lush with moss, to their right a frame from which hung a number of ropes that dropped down into an abyss surrounded by primeval green foliage. Each rope ran through a system of metal brackets and pulleys that made zero sense to Nayna.

All she cared about was that the ropes seemed very secure.

"First thing," the guide said, "we hook you up, so even if you trip and fall off this platform, you'll live to trip another day."

Nervous laughter from one of the other women.

Butterflies danced in Nayna's stomach.

The guide was clipping her by the harness to one of the ropes before she could have second thoughts. Once all four of them were clipped in, he gave them a safety briefing, then it was go time. All of them had to lean back against the very edge of the platform, their backs hanging out into nothing.

"Now, take one foot off the edge."

Squeezing her eyes shut for a second, Nayna did as instructed, then hooked her foot into the rope as they'd been taught. She had her eyes open again by the time the guide told them to take the remaining foot off the edge. Which would leave her hanging over thin air, the next stop a looooooooong way down.

She glanced at Raj, her heart thundering and fear squeezing her chest. "I can't believe we're doing this," she said to him.

A smile lighting up his eyes, he took his other foot off the edge of the platform but didn't drop, controlling his descent with the ease of a man who'd obviously rappelled before. "Do it, Nayna with the pretty nayna," he said. "I'll be with you all the way down."

Taking a deep breath, Nayna surrendered her last footfall on reality. And realized the hardest part had been letting go and leaving the platform. "This is so fun!" she said to Raj. "I'll go rock climbing with you!"

Raj grinned at her reference to their first meeting and kept pace with her, both of them taking in everything around them as they rappelled down while calling out encouragement to one of the others—the most skittish of their group. The woman, a tourist from Norway, kept going, and then they were all on the floor of a huge subterranean cave twenty minutes after stepping off the platform.

Looking up, Nayna saw the sunlit circle of sky rimmed with hazy green from where they'd come. It felt like a haunting alien world down here, even the foliage unique and a little eerie in a beautiful way. And the adventure had just begun.

They climbed over rocks, scrambled down them, and crossed parts where it felt like they could fall into the darkness and never be found. Then they were in the most stygian part of the cave, an area so devoid of illumination that they had to flick on the lights on their helmets.

"It's cold," Nayna said, her breath fogging the air.

"Imagine what the water's like," Raj murmured, referring to the underground river they'd seen after they first landed. "We have to try the black water rafting."

"Did you see some of those photos?" Nayna shuddered. "The roof of the cave was right up against that woman's face."

"We'll work our way up to it," Raj said, and she heard the anticipation in his voice.

Wonder and hope dawned inside her. Raj, she realized, wouldn't belittle her need for a life lived beyond the borders of domesticity. He was a man who liked tradition and roots, but for the first time, she began to see that her needs could coexist with his.

"All right, team," the guide called out, "this is the best part. I want you to come through the small passageway behind me. Be careful, it's pretty narrow. Lights off soon as you exit the passage."

Once on the other side, it took a second for Nayna's eyes to adjust to the absolute blackness you would never find in the civilized world. Down below, far from sunlight, this pitch-darkness was unlike anything she'd ever experienced...

Then stars began to appear against the black. She gasped. "Glowworms."

The others whispered around her.

Raj slid his fingers through hers.

After a while, everyone went quiet, all of them enchanted by the starlit sky deep within the earth, while their breath fogged the air and their chests squeezed. When Raj touched his fingers to her jaw, she angled her head so their helmets wouldn't crash, and they shared a soft, sweet kiss under a subterranean sky.

Nayna was sorry to leave. "It was wonderful," she whispered to Raj, astonished and full of a raw emotion aimed solely at this man who kept surprising her. "Thank you for organizing this."

"We haven't finished yet," he said. "Let's see if you thank me when we get to the end."

She realized what he meant when they stood at the foot of a metal ladder that shot up and up and up and *up* into darkness. That ladder was attached to the wall and was a straight vertical climb. It didn't look so bad—especially after the guide scrambled up, then called out that he was dropping the safety rope for the next person.

Raj had already volunteered to be the last one to go up, the one who'd be left in absolute quiet and silence. The first to climb was the woman who'd been the most nervous throughout. They all encouraged her with shouted calls as she began to climb. She disappeared into the darkness at a certain point, and they watched and waited for the safety line to be thrown back down.

It took a lot longer than it had with the guide.

By the time it came to her turn, she and Raj were the only two left at the bottom. She hooked herself up, and Raj checked to make sure everything was secure. Then he kissed her, their helmets banging this time, and they laughed before Nayna began the climb up rungs slippery from the boots of those who had gone before.

Her muscles began to quiver halfway up.

Pausing, she glanced down. Raj was just a pinprick of light below her, but he called out, "Go, baby! You're over halfway up!"

She smiled, feeling young and pretty and Raj's girl-friend, and carried on. Her helmet hit an edge of rock at one point, and her light went out, pitching her into complete darkness but she didn't panic. She just wiped one hand against her coveralls and turned on her light. Her muscles were beyond quivering by the time she hauled herself up over the edge to join the others.

"Your boyfriend's brave," the Norwegian's Australian friend said. "It must be creepy as hell down there."

"He's amazing," Nayna said, her attention on the safety rope that was being curled by the guide as Raj climbed. Predictably, he arrived far faster than the rest of them, but for the guide. The other man gave him a fist bump, and then they all took turns getting photos. Raj kissed Nayna in theirs, and it was the best thing.

And that night, as Raj moved in her slow and deep, Nayna had the thought that freedom wasn't a sensation you could only experience alone. With the right man, it'd be with her all her life. Part of her wanted to blurt out her love for Raj then and there, but more than two decades of watching her mother bow down to her father's will held her back.

Madhuri's terrible experiences held her back.

The memory of Anjali Kumar's bitterness with her squash-playing and unhelpful groom held her back.

Raj was her boyfriend now.

Would it be the same if he was her husband? Would he take her on dates full of adventure and make love to her with naked passion? Or would everything change, the weight of expectation and culture forcing her into a mold she would never fit?

38

SON OF AN OWL

OST OF THE NEXT THREE weeks were swallowed up by the manic preparations for Madhuri's wedding. The most important of which, of course, was Madhuri's wedding suit. Her sister drove Nayna crazy waiting for the shipment to arrive— and then it did, and Madhuri organized a viewing party. Her, Nayna, their mom, Aji, and two of Madhuri's friends.

Anjali was one, Madhuri's university friend, Jaci, another.

"Can I bring Ísa along?" Nayna asked her sister.

"Issie's welcome anytime!" An ebullient Madhuri wrapped her arms around Nayna and squeezed. "Tell her I expect her to wear a sari to the wedding. I'll pick one for her!"

The store had closed to the public at four, opened at five for Madhuri's viewing party. Once inside, they were treated to chai and coffee as well as sweets and savory snacks hot from the oven. "I think my future brother-in-law must've dropped a hell of a lot of money," Nayna murmured to her best friend.

Ísa nodded wisely and ate another savory before saying, "How is this going to work anyway? The doc who's marrying your sister ordered a whole bunch of things. What happens to the rest, the things Madhuri doesn't want?"

"Well, she'll probably pick a few outfits today. The wedding's over several days—and she might decide to keep something back for an anniversary party next year." Because her sister *would* be having a big anniversary party, of that Nayna was certain. "The rest, I'm guessing that Sandesh is going to resell to the store, probably at a loss. Which is why we're all being treated so well." She didn't think her brother-in-law had any intention of going into the clothing business himself. This was all for Madhuri's benefit.

Ísa nodded. "I guess it's not too bad a deal. He gets a happy wife and they get a profit." She winced. "Oh my God, I just sounded like my *mother*. Profit and loss, all while I'm about to look at wedding clothes."

Nayna patted her friend on the back. "Don't worry, I've seen odd flashes of the Dragon in you through the years, but the fire breathing never takes full hold. Read a few romance novels, throw in a lot of poetry, and you'll come out whole on the other side."

Ísa nodded solemnly at the prescription. The two of them had been swapping novels and poetry books forever. "Did you read that new historical?" Ísa began, but then Madhuri squealed and all heads turned toward her.

The store owner had personally wheeled out the first rack of garments. Nayna's eyes widened at the shimmer and sparkle on display. Each and every one a designer outfit worth thousands upon thousands of dollars. Single pieces of art for Madhuri's delectation.

Everyone gravitated toward the garments, each of them choosing their favorites for Madhuri to try on. A few pieces, Nayna discarded at once.

"Maddie would never wear this shade of red," she said to Ísa. "Says it makes her look like an old tomato."

Ísa pointed to a dark pink outfit. "Not traditional red, but I think your sister might like it."

Nayna agreed. "I'm pretty sure Madhuri is going for knockout, not so much traditional as unforgettable." Her sister had already spoken to a hairstylist about having a "wild" hairstyle—by which she meant something that hadn't already been done but was stunning. Not a flower bun. With Pinky Mehra added in, they'd already been to four weddings this year where the brides had gone for the elegant look popularized by a Bollywood actress.

Madhuri examined each and every garment with care, cooing over the beadwork or the Swarovski crystals or the expensive fabric before finally deciding which one to try first. Most of the garments the doctor had ordered were skirt-and-tunic combos where the tunic didn't display too much flesh—if any. Modesty was applauded in brides. However, he—or the shop owner who'd created the order—had also added a number of designer saris.

"I'll be back soon!" Chosen outfit in hand, Madhuri disappeared into a changing room.

Excited to see her sister all dressed up, Nayna sat down in one of the provided chairs, Ísa on her left and her mother next to Ísa. Her grandmother sat beside Shilpa Sharma while Anjali and Jaci were on Nayna's other side. All of them had champagne in hand—the doctor must've spent *a lot*—and snacks nearby.

"Anjali, how are your boys?" Nayna's mother leaned forward to ask. "Is Avinesh looking after them tonight?"

A curl of Anjali's lip. "Him?" A snort. "He's out having a beer with his squash mates. I dropped the boys off at my parents'." Her smile morphed into intensely real. "Honestly, they are the light of my lives."

They all cooed over the adorable photos of her boys the other woman showed around.

Anjali then dropped into conversation with Jaci while Nayna's grandmother and mother chatted. Nayna wasn't attempting to eavesdrop, but with Anjali and Jaci right next to her, she couldn't avoid overhearing the other woman's continued thread on her husband.

Any love Anjali'd once had for Avinesh appeared stone-dead.

Nayna wouldn't be surprised if she opened the paper one day to find Anjali had murdered her husband using a frypan and a meat tenderizer.

"This is going to be a long haul," she murmured to Ísa, who'd also caught a little of Anjali's discontent. "Thanks for the company."

"Are you kidding? All these gorgeous clothes and the yummy food? I'm so in." Her best friend lowered her voice. "Did she just say her husband eats her head?"

"It makes sense in Hindi," Nayna reassured her while struggling not to laugh—Anjali was now literally translating animal-related Hindi insults into English but replacing harsh swear words with words she clearly found easier to say, with hilarious results.

"Son of an owl?" Ísa repeated, mystified. "Donkey poop?"

Nayna's stomach ached with the force of holding in her laughter.

It was as well that Madhuri walked out in the first outfit at that moment, or Nayna would've lost it. Her sister was ravishing. Everyone gasped and the two store dressers ran forward to arrange the dupatta over her hair, positively astonished by her.

"You look like a movie star!" one of them said. "Madhuri Dixit."

Her friend disagreed. "No, she's Aishwarya Rai in *Jodhaa Akbar*. You know, when she had the brown contact lenses."

Loving the attention, Madhuri showed off by strutting down the room and back. "What do you think?"

The consensus was that she had a winner.

Madhuri laughed. "It's just the first one!" Then she went back into the changing room, calling out, "Ma! Can you come help me?"

Their mother got up at once. Nayna didn't interrupt or offer to assist too. This was important to their mother —she'd missed Madhuri's first wedding, and it was giving her so much joy to be involved in every aspect of the second.

Ten minutes later, Madhuri appeared in another astoundingly beautiful outfit. The gasps were louder this time.

"This one!" Anjali cried. "Lord, Madhuri. You're going to knock Sandesh's eyes out."

When her sister looked toward Nayna, Nayna got up and took her hands, just shook her head at Madhuri's loveliness. "You know you're going to look beautiful in everything," she said, well aware where this was going. That, however, didn't mean she wasn't going to be the little sister who messed with Madhuri. "Maybe narrow down the color range?"

"Are you kidding?" Madhuri put her fisted hands on her hips. "I'm not narrowing down anything!"

Five outfits later—all of them stunning, with Madhuri a vision of beauty in every single one, Ísa picked up a sweet and said, "I see what you mean." She took a bite of the crumbly white barfi, the taste for which she'd picked up over the years while hanging out with Nayna. "I think I'm going to put on five kilos by the time she's done."

Nayna snorted. "You're still thinking too small." Swallowing the last of a peda that appeared to have condensed milk in it, she said, "Ten kilos."

Ísa's shoulders shook, and the two of them shared a laugh before they returned their attention to the next catwalk appearance by Madhuri.

After trying on every single one of the suits, Madhuri began to try on the saris—and Ísa slipped halfway down her seat as if melting into a puddle. Nayna's grandmother and Madhuri's friends all laughed, as did Nayna.

Poking her head out of the changing room where their mother was putting her into a sari, Madhuri said, "What's so funny?"

"I'm trying to slide into another time and dimension where you actually choose a garment before midnight!" Ísa called out.

"Just you wait until it's your turn. I'll be the one calling time," Madhuri threatened, but the response was lighthearted. Madhuri had been missing for a large chunk of Nayna's and Ísa's teenage years. And Ísa was deeply loyal and fiercely on Nayna's side. As a result, she'd always looked askance at Madhuri. However, because they both loved Nayna, the two had come to an accord that allowed such jokes.

"Okay." Nayna's mother bustled out and took a standing position on the other side of the chairs, her face glowing. "Madhuri, we're ready!"

Madhuri stepped out. And the entire room went silent.

Of a luminous shade of gold with a thick gold-on-gold border, the sari caressed Madhuri like a lover without being the least bit indecent. It shimmered like it was lightning given form despite being heavy with embroidery and glittering crystals.

The premade blouse that came with it echoed the embroidered border and fit Madhuri nearly perfectly. A little more taking in at the sides and it would be an *absolutely* perfect fit. It had a scoop neck and a simple back, but the way the sari draped over everything, the exquisite work on it...

Nayna pressed a hand to her heart, her throat thick. "You are so beautiful," she whispered.

Beside Madhuri, their mother was crying. Madhuri's own eyes shone wetly before she took their mum into her arms. "I can't believe I'm going to wear a sari to my wedding," she blubbered out. "God, it's so *traditional.*" Despite her attempt to sound disgusted, it came out delighted and slightly shocked.

But there was no doubt in anyone's mind that this was the one. It took Madhuri's beauty and turned it transcendent. She looked as if she'd stepped out of another time, an Indian princess ready for her prince. Nayna wouldn't be surprised if her sister's wedding photos ended up in a magazine somewhere. Especially as Madhuri had—by working her contacts—found an award-winning photographer to record the event.

When the shop owner finally found his voice again, he tried to steer Madhuri toward the section that sold twenty-two-karat-gold jewelry, but she was having none of it.

"I'll be wearing my mother's, my nani's, and my aji's jewelry," she said with a deep smile aimed at Aji and their mother. Their maternal grandmother, their nani, had passed on, but she'd left her jewelry to her daughter, and so Madhuri would wear both families' histories when she walked to her groom.

Aji dabbed at her eyes while Shilpa Sharma continued to sniffle. Nayna got up and hugged both her mother and sister at once.

"I'm so happy for you, Maddie." Pulling back, she cupped her sister's face in her hands and smiled. This, she thought, *this* was the relationship they would have now.

As adults in charge of their own destinies.

No resentments, no shadows of the past. They were forging into the future in different directions, each choosing her own path but always family, always sisters.

"Ninu," Madhuri whispered in her ear after the tears had passed, "how much has Anjali had to drink? I'm sure she just muttered something about the offspring of a buffalo."

39

BROKEN HEARTS CAN BE MENDED

I T WAS ELEVEN O'CLOCK AT night by the time Nayna finally returned home. She'd offered to take Anjali home, but Madhuri had said she'd look after her friend. Nayna had helped out by parking Anjali's car in the bridal boutique's private back lot for Anjali to pick up when she was sober. She and Ísa had still been giggling over Anjali's repertoire of badly translated insults when they pulled out of the lot in Nayna's car.

"Sad to see a grand romance come to this," Nayna had said afterward.

"I remember you telling me about the proposal with the plane and the picnic." Yawning, Ísa had stretched out her body. "All that is nice, don't get me wrong, but it doesn't sound like the two actually ever had any talks of substance—I mean, she seems completely surprised by who he is."

Nayna couldn't disagree with her friend there.

Once she'd dropped Ísa home and made her way to her apartment, Nayna went to call Raj, she was missing him so, but decided against it at the last minute. He was getting up at the crack of dawn to take advantage of the summer light, and she didn't want to interrupt his sleep. She'd messaged him from the shop earlier, giving him a rundown of events.

He'd been doing paperwork for the business but had paused to send back a sexy photo featuring his face and naked upper body. The sight of his lightly furred chest lovingly caressed by the desk light had curled her toes, but what had made it even sexier was the smile creasing his cheeks. Only Nayna ever got that smile.

She'd all but sighed into a melted puddle... then had to hurriedly hide the photo when her mother sat down next to her. Hugging the memory close, she'd just kicked off her shoes when her phone rang in her hand.

"Raj," she said, answering at once. "I thought you'd be in bed by now."

"I'm at the hospital." A strain in his voice she'd never before heard.

Nayna was already shoving her feet back into her shoes. "What's happened? Are you all right? I'm on my way."

"My father's had a heart attack." Other sounds behind him, machines beeping and the echo of an intercom summoning a doctor. "He collapsed while he and my mother were watching TV. I got him in the ambulance with Ma, and I just arrived at the hospital with Aditi. We don't know anything yet."

"I'm getting in my car. I'll see you soon." Her heart thundered; Raj was as close to his family as she was to her own. If anything happened to his father, it would devastate him.

RAJ WAS WAITING FOR HER near the elevators; Nayna had messaged him when she got into the parking lot, to find out if they were in the ER or had been moved to a cardiac ward. Going straight to him, she hugged him tight. His arms squeezed her with crushing strength, but she didn't care. She was ready to give him anything he needed.

"How is he?"

"In surgery," Raj told her, his voice rasping. "It's bad."

Nayna just held him and let him hold on to her until he was ready to draw back.

"Ma and Aditi are in the waiting room," he said. "Komal was on shift in another ward, but she got her charge nurse to replace her, and she's helping make sure we're kept updated. I haven't been able to reach Navin—he went out for a friend's bachelor party, probably isn't paying attention to his phone."

"I'm sure he'll be here soon." Nayna ran her hand down Raj's back.

He leaned into her for a second before leading her to the waiting area.

Sangeeta Sen took one look at her and burst into tears. Enclosing her in her arms, Nayna rocked the older woman while Raj took care of his baby sister. More family arrived as time passed—Raj's father had two younger brothers, and Raj's mother had an older sister. All but one came with their spouses.

Jitesh Sen's remaining brother was based in Taupo, several hours south of Auckland, and was already on his way—with his wife and Raj's paternal grandparents.

Depending on traffic, they'd reach the hospital in about two and a half more hours.

The only one still in the wind was Navin.

Komal, dressed in the dark blue of a nurse's scrubs, had a pinched look about the eyes when she walked in to give them the news that the surgery was progressing well. "Navin's not replying to my messages," Nayna heard her whisper to Raj. "He's probably drunk. That's what he does when out with that group."

"I'll keep trying to track him down," Raj said. "Give me the numbers you have for his friends. Nayna, do you have a pen?"

Digging one out of her purse, Nayna walked over. He took the pen and pressed a kiss to her temple before returning his attention to Komal, who gave Nayna a jagged look. Then the other woman was passing on the numbers, and Nayna went to sit with Sangeeta and Aditi again. When Raj's sister curled against her side, Nayna threw her coat around the teenager and hugged her close.

Aditi fell asleep for about forty minutes, woke fuzzy-eyed and in need of the restroom.

As she wandered off in the right direction, Sangeeta Sen, her face wan, said, "Raj beta, Nayna bitia, can you find some strong tea?"

The two of them left to see what they could rustle up. Once away from his relatives, Nayna took Raj into her arms again, running her hands up and down the powerful column of his back. She'd noticed everyone leaned on him, the older adults as well as his younger sister. They all looked to Raj as if expecting him to have the answers.

Even the cardiac nurse who was liaising with the

surgical staff spoke to Raj, so the immediate family must've nominated him as their lead contact. Twice, after speaking to the nurse, Raj had taken his mother aside and talked to her alone. Decisions being made, Nayna had realized, the doctors asking for Sangeeta Sen's approval of certain actions.

Sangeeta relied visibly on her eldest son, her hand clenching on his arm, and Nayna had the feeling Raj was the one who'd made the final calls, taking that burden from his mother. If something went wrong because of a certain decision, he'd bear that too.

"You don't have to keep up the front with me," she murmured to him. "I just want you to know that." She'd had a stark display tonight of the position Raj occupied in his family—the anchor, the one who kept the entire family stable. Whether that meant making the toughest decisions of them all, tracking down his absent brother, or running the family business.

He wasn't allowed to crumple. He wouldn't *let* himself crumple.

She wondered if he'd ever trust anyone else enough to be the vulnerable one, trust enough to share the load. "You're my rock," she whispered, "but I can be yours too. Let me."

Raj shuddered out a hot breath that ruffled her hair; his muscles didn't relax, but he said, "I'm so fucking glad you're here."

Nayna's eyes burned as his arms locked even tighter around her.

THEY FOUND THE TEA, GOT enough for the group, and

returned with disposable cups that put a little heat into everyone's bodies. It wasn't long afterward that Raj's father came out of surgery. The surgeon, Dr. Jonathan Olivier, was still clad in his scrubs when he came to talk to them—but he had a smile on the craggy lines of his face.

"A triple bypass is always complicated," he said to Raj and his mother.

Aditi stood between her mother and brother, tucked under Raj's arm, while Nayna stood on his left, her fingers linked to his. Komal stood on his mother's right side. A distraught Navin had finally responded, calling Raj to say he was on his way, but that had only been twenty minutes earlier.

"The good news," Dr. Olivier said, "is that it all went perfectly, and barring any unforeseen complications, Mr. Sen should recover fully."

Raj's fingers squeezed tight on hers even as he calmly asked the doctor more detailed questions about what they could expect going forward. The overriding theme —aside from dietary changes on which they'd be further advised by a hospital nutritionist—was that his father would need lots of care and wasn't to do anything strenuous for a number of months.

"Mr. Sen will also need to manage his stress levels," Dr. Olivier added. "Stress is terrible for the heart, and speaking from two decades of experience, I can tell you it'll impede his recovery."

The doctor, tiredness apparent in his own features, looked around. "Now, I think you should all go home and get some rest. Mr. Sen is in intensive care and will stay there for at least forty-eight hours."

"Dr. Olivier, my mother needs to see my father." Raj's voice was firm.

The doctor took in Mrs. Sen's tear-worn face and said, "Please come with me. For now, you'll be the only visitor." His eyes met Raj's. "The staff will let you know as soon as the rest of your family is clear to go in. It'll be immediate family only until he's out of ICU."

Raj let go of her hand to take care of the goodbyes with his uncles and aunts, promising everyone updates as soon as he had them. Aditi stayed with Nayna. Komal, meanwhile, kept glancing at her watch, then over toward the nearby elevators.

Raj's brother walked out of an elevator ten minutes after the extended family had departed. His eyes were hollow. "Bhaiya?" he said, looking at Raj.

"Dad's fine, recovering in ICU. Ma's with him." Raj squeezed his brother's shoulder. "Komal's been with us all night, decoding the medical jargon."

Navin went immediately to Komal, wrapping her up in his arms. The other woman didn't hesitate to hug him back, and Nayna's heart sighed.

"Maybe we'll get a happy ending for those two after all," she murmured to Raj while Aditi was distracted and collecting her coat from the chair where she'd left it.

Raj took in his brother and sister-in-law in silence before hugging Nayna close. When Aditi came over, the two of them stretched out one arm each and brought her into the embrace. And though Raj held them both, he allowed Nayna to hold him in return. Her big, tough lover let her see his need.

And it smashed another wall in her heart.

40

A SCENE FIT FOR BOLLYWOOD

NAYNA PARTED WAYS WITH RAJ in the hospital parking lot. He was driving his mother and sister home. Komal and Navin were heading out in Komal's car as Navin—afraid he was over the alcohol limit for driving—had caught a ride in with a friend.

After settling his mother and Aditi in his truck, Raj took the time to walk Nayna to her car. Sangeeta Sen had been in full agreement when he stopped Nayna from going off on her own. "It's still dark outside," she'd said sternly. "Aditi and I will lock the truck doors and wait for Raj to return."

The parking lot was awash in light, but Nayna didn't reject the offer. Mostly because she wanted to have a moment alone with Raj. "Get some rest, all right?" she said to him when they stopped by her car.

His hand cupping her jaw, his thumb stroking over her lips. "You'll be okay driving home?" he asked, searching her face. "Not feeling sleepy?"

"I have so much caffeine in my blood that tired is the last thing I feel." Turning her head, she kissed his palm. "I'll be fine. And if your mother and Aditi want me to come over tomorrow, just let me know." She'd work it out with her bosses.

Raj kissed her, the pain in him making her want to give and give—but Raj's family needed him right now. "When you have time," she said against his lips, "I'll be here. Anything you need, Raj."

Another primal kiss before he released her. "Message me when you arrive home."

Well aware of how shaken his heart was right then, Nayna said, "As soon as I'm inside."

Her headlights flashed off Raj's body as he stood watching her leave, and she felt a wild desperation to go back and get in his car, go home with him, hold him. He might never be a big talker when it came to his emotions, but he spoke to her with his body, allowed his shields to fall when he was in her arms.

But going home with him was simply not an option.

Her parents and his parents might be willing to overlook the fact they were spending considerable time together, but neither party would overlook it if she ended up in Raj's bed so close to where his family lived. Not even if she just wanted to put her arms around him while he slept.

It'd be considered disrespectful in the extreme, especially in the current circumstances.

Nayna banged her fisted hand on the steering wheel, frustrated with herself. Because the thing was, she would never do that to her parents *or* his. The freedom to make her own choices didn't mean spitting in the faces of those she loved and respected.

It didn't mean throwing dirt on the tradition that was such a core part of Raj.

The color and the joy of their culture, the huge families and the extended relationships, it all mattered to Nayna and always would. She had a hundred aunties if not more, barely one percent of them related to her by any kind of blood. All those women—Batty Auntie included—would drop whatever they were doing if she ever needed serious help.

Despite all that, today she wished that it didn't matter that she wasn't married to Raj. She wanted the right to be by his side, to curl up around her rock of a man and hold him through the coldest hours of the night.

IT WASN'T UNTIL TWO MORE nights had passed that Nayna saw Raj's father at last. Knowing the doctors wanted to keep Jitesh Sen in as restful a state as possible, she hadn't asked for an earlier visitation. Honestly, his immediate family were likely the only ones he wanted to see anyway.

However, when she dropped by the hospital that evening with some requested takeout for the younger members of the family, Raj—still in his work gear—said, "My dad was asking about you."

"Oh." Nayna put the takeout on a table inside the whānau room—a space designed for families of patients —then went to stand in front of where he sat in a visitor chair.

She ran her fingers through his hair, straightening the wind-tumbled strands. "That's good, isn't it?" Raj had told her that his father had been sluggish and slow for the past couple of days, but that the physicians were telling them it was to be expected after the major surgery.

Wrapping his arms around her waist, Raj laid his head against her navel and let her play with his hair as he exhaled, and her heart, it broke into a million fragments. When it put itself back together, Raj was in every nook and every cranny, the cracks woven back together with his name as the glue.

She loved him. More than she'd ever loved anyone her entire life.

The hole that love put in her defenses, the sacrifices she was ready to make to ensure his happiness, it scared her... but she didn't stop petting his hair.

"Yes," Raj said. "He called you my 'pretty Nayna.' 'Where's your pretty Nayna, Raj? Doesn't she want to visit a sick old man?'"

"I hope you told him it was on doctor's orders."

"I think he's decided he likes being a cranky patient." A tightening of his arms around her before he drew back.

Nayna wondered if he could see her heart, exposed and without barriers. "Where are your mum and sister?"

"They're with him. I was just waiting for you."

"Are Navin and Komal here too?"

"They spent the afternoon with him while I gave Aditi the task of getting our mother to nap—she's barely been sleeping." Raj stood and put his hand on the lower part of her back. "Aditi gained victory by crawling into bed, and, according to her, 'acting like a needy baby' so our mother would cuddle her."

Nayna laughed. "And napdom was achieved?"

"For three hours—for both of them."

Leaving the food on the table, the whānau room otherwise empty, Raj led her into the room where his father lay recovering. The older man had been given a single room to himself, which would've told Nayna the severity of the surgery even if she hadn't known the details. All the wires and tubes hooked up to him further underlined the seriousness of the heart attack and the emergency surgery that had followed.

Jitesh Sen's previously healthy brown skin was pallid, his breath shallow and ragged at times. But he smiled when he saw Nayna and patted at his bed. She went around to that side and put her hand in his.

He curled his fingers weakly around hers. "Beta, I've been waiting to see you."

"I didn't want to intrude," Nayna began.

"Intrude, schrimtrude," the older man said. "You're family. Isn't she, Sangeeta?"

Raj's mother smiled and nodded while Aditi said a cheerful "Yep." Both mother and daughter were seated in visitor chairs by the bed, though Aditi had somehow managed to create the full teenage-sprawl in hers.

"I have something to say." Raj's father looked at Nayna, then Raj. "I know you young people have your modern ways, but I'm an old man and I might not have a lot of time left."

"Don't say it, Papa," Aditi cried out, straightening in an alarm of arms and legs.

"The doctors are confident you'll make a full recovery," Raj added, touching a hand to his father's shoulder. "There's no need to worry."

The older man nodded but said, "Maybe, maybe. Or maybe I have only five years. Or maybe I have only one year. We don't know—I could get hit by a car tomorrow."

Raj's mother was nodding, clearly knowing where this was going. Aditi had her head in her hands, her curls bouncing every which way as she shook her head in slow motion. Nayna meanwhile was starting to have a strange prickling on the back of her neck. Because she'd seen this scene before—in a hundred Bollywood movies. She just couldn't believe it was happening to her.

She glanced up at Raj and saw that he was frowning. Her lover needed to watch more Bollywood movies. She'd make that a part of his education stat. But right now she could do nothing but listen as destiny careened toward her at the speed of light.

"What I'm saying," Raj's father continued after taking a sip of juice, "is that I know you two want to take your time before marriage, but I'd like to see my eldest son married and settled... Just in case." He pressed his free hand to his heart, his fingers trembling. "We don't know what the future will hold. Son, I want this happiness for you. And maybe, if we are very lucky, I'll get to see my grandchild before..."

Raj's eyes connected with hers, realization having dawned dark and heavy. "Dad," he said, "we—"

"No." Sangeeta Sen's voice was firmer than Nayna had ever heard it. "There's no problem in this, what your father's asking. He still has to recover, so it won't be a super rush like with Nayna's sister's wedding. You'll have time to prepare, have a proper wedding, invite all your friends. Four months' time, don't you think?"

"The venues will all be booked out," Aditi piped up, a small warrior fighting for Raj and Nayna, who were both shell-shocked. "Madhuri only got a spot because Dr. Patel knows someone."

"Adi, meri rani, did you forget that your uncle owns an entire golf course and the club building?" Sangeeta Sen smiled at her daughter. "He will find us a date in that time. Four months."

Raj's father nodded, his hand weak when it squeezed Nayna's hand. "I think I should be healthy enough by then." A smile. "I look forward to dancing at your wedding, son."

41

ADITI SPEAKS THE TRUTH

Raj and Nayna stared at each other across the table in the waiting room.

"What the hell just happened?" Raj said, shoving his hands through his hair.

Nayna, her head yet ringing from the shock, opened up the bag of takeout and pushed over the burger with all the fixings that she'd gotten him. "Eat first. Your brain needs fuel." He had to be starving by now, given the physical nature of his work and the fact he'd come straight from the site to the hospital.

Picking up the burger, Raj ate in silence. It didn't take him long to demolish it. Nayna passed over sweet potato fries, then the chicken-bite things she'd picked up, along with a pot of coleslaw.

He was just finishing up when Aditi wandered into the room and dropped into a seat that put her to Nayna's right and Raj's left

"Okay," she said after grabbing a burger for herself

from the bag, "did you guys seriously just get told to get married in four months' time or Dad will drop dead?"

Nayna almost choked on the water she'd been trying to drink.

But Aditi wasn't done. "I mean, it's a gold-medal guilt trip even by Indian-parent standards."

"He's probably just worried because he's come out of surgery," Raj said, sounding far calmer than he had at the start of the meal. "I'll talk to him again after he's healed a bit."

Mouth full of burger, Aditi shook her head. After finally swallowing down the huge bite she'd taken, she said, "No, they're serious. Ma's in there talking to Uncle Dhiraj, and before that she was chatting on about caterers and even the type of cake. The wedding hammer, it's a-fallin'."

RAJ'S EYES CONNECTED WITH NAYNA'S.

"Um..." Aditi stopped chewing. "You want me to go? Because you guys are getting all intense."

His heart squeezed when Nayna reached out and tugged on one of his sister's curls. "No, stay. We can talk about how this has turned into a masala picture."

Aditi's dimple popped out, his sister smiling in truth for the first time since their father's heart attack. "Oh. Em. Gee!" she said. "You're right! This is *so* Bollywood drama! The part where the dying father asks a couple to get married so he can see the event?" She shook her head and stuffed a fry into her mouth, talking around it. "All we need now is for Raj to be in love with someone else but feel forced to marry you because he doesn't want to break his father's heart."

Aditi's head swiveled toward Raj. "Nope, that plot point won't work—he's clearly crazy over you." Another fry inhaled. "The good thing is the father always survives in those and there's a big happily-ever-after."

Catching the hitch in his sister's voice, Raj brushed a fist against her cheek. "I spoke to Dr. Olivier while I was waiting for Nayna. He says Dad has a great outlook—he doesn't smoke, doesn't have diabetes, *does* have huge family support. A little care and he'll be around to create a Bollywood drama when it's your turn to get married."

"Babita auntie's husband had a quadruple bypass ten years ago," Nayna added. "He's in excellent health. Just complains a lot about how he can only smell ghee and not eat it."

Dimple flashing again, Aditi relaxed. "I can totally see Dad doing that. Especially since Ma's started a notebook full of heart-healthy vegetarian recipes. He's already trying to bribe me to smuggle him sausages."

Raj chuckled at his sister's words, glad to see her spirit returning. Aditi wasn't the quiet type, so to see her go so silent and hollow-eyed had been heartbreaking. Now he watched as Nayna drew her into a cheerful conversation about their favorite Bollywood movies, with Aditi nodding eagerly when Nayna suggested a movie date for a sweeping historical epic set to release in a month.

"Are you gonna make Raj bhaiya come?" Aditi asked, cheeky as a monkey. "Last time he took me, he fell asleep during the most amazing dance number by Hrithik."

"Sacrilege." Nayna gasped, her hand on her heart. "We'll just have to work on him until he sees the beauty of lip-syncing in the Swiss Alps in the middle of winter while wearing a sari."

Aditi snorted with laughter, and for the moment, Raj's world was okay... on the surface at least. Because even as Nayna gently took care of his sister's heart, he knew her mind had to be spinning, her thoughts a roar.

It was only when Aditi's friend Harlow arrived that he and Nayna had time alone. First, however, he shook hands with the tall and lanky boy who had grown significantly in confidence over the summer and who was turning out to be a young man Raj liked. Even better, both Jitesh and Sangeeta Sen were warming up to him. It helped that Harlow Chan kept his stick-straight black hair cut with ruthless neatness, wore wire-rimmed spectacles, dressed in pants that actually fit instead of hanging halfway down his butt, and was unfailingly respectful.

Aditi had also let it slip that, while Harlow had a year of high school to go, he'd already been offered an academic scholarship to the city's major university on the basis of his previous year's exam results. The boy had deferred the scholarship because he wanted to have his senior year.

Jitesh Sen had thawed enough at that to grumble, "Well, I suppose it's good he's not an idiot."

High praise from a protective Indian father on his seventeen-year-old daughter's friend who happened to be a boy—and who might end up more if the two kept on hanging out.

"Nayna." Harlow's face cracked into a huge smile when Nayna walked back into the room, having left to wash off a bit of sauce that had dripped onto her top when she ate a few of Aditi's fries.

"Hey, you. When did you get so tall?" Nayna hugged her best friend's stepbrother; she'd told him that Ísa was a huge reason why Harlow was so well-adjusted. Ísa Rain had basically adopted Harlow when their parents divorced, making sure the young teen he'd been at the time wasn't forgotten in the mess.

Ísa, Raj suddenly realized, would always be in his life. She was going to marry one of his closest friends. Which meant that even if all this crashed and burned, Nayna too would always be in his life. It would be the worst private hell he could imagine. To see her and to know she wasn't his. Perhaps to see her move on with another man?

His gut wrenched.

"We have to go now," Aditi stage-whispered to Harlow after a few minutes. "Raj bhaiya and Nayna bh—" She cut herself off at the last minute, but Raj knew the word she'd almost said. The word for a big brother's wife.

Recovering quickly, she said, "They have *big deal stuff* to talk about."

Alone with Nayna at last, Raj said, "I'll fix it." He had no desire for Nayna to be manipulated into marriage with him when she'd fought so determinedly for freedom and when marriage was a topic she simply never raised on her own.

Eyes shining, Nayna looked up at him and brushed his hair off his forehead. "You're right in what you said to Adi—your dad's just come out of surgery," she said. "The doctor said we're not supposed to stress him. Just go along with it."

"He's a stubborn man. Can give a mule a run for its money when he wants to be pigheaded."

Nayna's lips twitched. "Like father, like son?"

His glare had zero affect.

"Don't worry right now," said the woman who owned him body and soul. "You're already carrying too much on your shoulders." Rising up on her tiptoes, she pressed her lips soft and sweet to his, her hand cradling the back of his neck.

He hadn't made love to her for over a week now, and he ached for her. So much that after he drove his mother and sister home so his father could rest, he snuck out to Nayna's apartment and woke her up. She was still warm from bed when she opened the door, strands of her hair sticking to her cheek.

And she walked into his arms without hesitation.

He carried her to bed, stripped them both naked, then spent long moments simply stroking his hand over her skin while she did the same with him. Their kisses were deep and tender, the way she spread her thighs so he could push into her a gift. He went in slow, pulled back as slow, heard her breath hitch.

So he did it again, in no hurry to lose her hands on his skin, her voice whispering his name.

"Raj... The way you move..." A shiver rippled over her, her thighs clenching around his body.

He'd gained control since their first time together, rocked her through it, then caressed her until her back arched against his in sinuous feminine beauty, her body holding on tight to his as she melted with pleasure.

"Raj," she said again, her eyes heavy-lidded and her fingers brushing his lips. "My Raj."

The hour he spent with her grounded him in a way nothing else could.

She was in his blood and he'd marry her a thousand times over if she'd have him. But if she agreed to his father's demand, he'd never know if she would've chosen him of her own free will—the lack would forever be a shadow on their lives together. And if they didn't do this and his father died before anything was decided, Raj would never forgive himself.

42

THE BOSS'S GIRL

Nayna's parents visited Raj's father in hospital as soon as Jitesh Sen felt ready to receive more visitors. It was as obvious as the nose on Nayna's face that the Sharmas and the Sens genuinely got along—especially when it came to talking about their misbehaving offspring.

"All these modern ideas," one said. "As if they're the first couple to ever meet!"

"I blame it on television," another added. "I mean, the dramas! And always rebellion, made to look so romantic."

At which point, the four of them would inevitably fall into a spirited discussion about their shared passion for said dramas with rebellious characters. At least their conversations were joyful. From what Nayna had seen of Komal and Navin lately, their hospital reconciliation had quickly faded into a kind of stiff formality. The two put up a front for Mr. Sen, but—according to Raj—were otherwise living separate lives.

"Navin's moved into our old game room," he'd told

her. "They aren't screaming at each other, and Navin's home more to help with everything, but I think the damage is done." A shake of his head. "Far as I can figure, both of them broke more than one promise they'd made to each other. Why make promises at all if you're not going to keep them?"

If Nayna hadn't already been terrifyingly in love with him, that harsh question would've done it.

"Well," Nayna's grandmother said to her not long afterward, while the two of them were alone in Nayna's apartment. Her parents had dropped Aji off while they went on a big shopping trip to get some things for Madhuri's wedding—including an outfit for their father, who usually never wore a suit but had opted for a full sherwani for the auspicious occasion.

Of course, he'd also added, "Now that your wedding with Raj is also arranged, I might as well get both suits at once."

Nayna had allowed the statement to pass unchallenged; it was far too soon to rock the boat, what with Mr. Sen still in hospital.

"What is it, Aji?" She looked up from her laptop where she'd been running a search for Madhuri. Her sister had asked her to hunt down a specific cake topper she'd seen in a magazine a decade earlier.

Nayna had begun to see tiny brides and grooms everywhere she looked, but so far there was no sign of a sari-clad princess and an Indian prince down on one knee. Nayna was starting to imagine gluing pieces of various toppers together to Frankenstein it.

"How about a muffin to go with your tea?" she asked before her grandmother could reply. "I made a batch yesterday." She'd managed to find out Raj's favorite flavor —banana walnut—then spent her Saturday morning in the kitchen. It was a need inside her, to look after him, to ease the load in even a small way.

Putting most of the muffins in a large plastic container, she'd driven out to the site where he was working and called him to meet her in the parking lot. The security and safety signs made it clear no one was to enter the site without the requisite gear.

He'd walked out in dusty jeans and an equally dusty dark gray T-shirt, a battered brown tool belt around his hips. On his head had been a white hard hat that bore a couple of dents and scratches. His trusty work boots had completed the look. Sweaty and a little scowly from the strain of managing the business while worrying about his father, he'd looked better than any dream she'd ever had.

"I made you muffins," she'd said when he reached her, feeling suddenly and oddly shy. "Banana walnut. And extras for your crew."

A strange, unsmiling look... before he'd taken off his hard hat and kissed her so deep that her head spun. "You're destroying me, Nayna Sharma."

He'd just stepped back, Nayna's heart thunder and the unvarnished masculine scent of him in her lungs, when a skinny man with ropy muscles and tattoos on both arms poked his head out from around the safety fencing and said, "Hey! Are you the one who thinks the boss is a sexy hunk?"

As Raj groaned, Nayna had found herself laughing, her shyness disappearing under the force of her need to claim Raj. "Yes!" she'd called out. "And a hot fling!"

"Crikey." The man had scratched at his chin. "You

done all right, boss. I guess I better keep reading that Sense and Shampoo book."

"I think you need more work, Tino," Raj had threatened darkly.

The other man had grinned. "Nah! I'm having a legal-like smoke-o." But he'd wandered off to take his coffee break elsewhere, no doubt while spreading the news of the boss's girl.

Raj had kissed her again before he left, his eyes impenetrable in a way that haunted her. But later in the day, he'd messaged to say that his crew had demolished the muffins and asked for more. "Good thing I took out two for myself before the others smelled your baking," he'd written. "Tasted great."

A simple message. Pragmatic even. Certainly not romantic.

Except he'd added a heart at the end.

Nayna kept glancing at that heart every so often. Raj was a bluntly honest man, up-front and strong. He wasn't much for soft words. For him to add a heart to a message...

She hugged the warm glow of it close.

"Muffins later." Her grandmother's firm tone dragged her back to the present. "First, what are you going to do about this marriage business?" She took a sip of the tea Nayna had made her. "You know all four of them are talking about it anytime they're together." Putting down the teacup, she smoothed a hand down the dark green of her newest velour tracksuit. "That Dhiraj man has even found an opening in the bookings for his ugly golf building."

Nayna had never wanted to get married inside, much

less in a building designed in the seventies, with the attendant décor—complete with avocado-colored walls and orange linoleum that had been lovingly restored by Raj's Dhiraj uncle. Outside, in the air, where she could breathe, that's what Nayna wanted for her wedding when the time came.

Putting aside her laptop, she leaned forward with her forearms on her thighs. "I'm hoping they'll come to their senses when Mr. Sen's recovered. He's very emotional right now."

Her grandmother made a sound distinctly similar to a snort. "What he is, is a wily old goat."

"He was hurting and panicking when he asked us," Nayna began.

"He might've been," Aji conceded, "but he also knew this was his one chance to get his own way. I mean, imagine the good luck of having a heart attack just when you need to convince your son to hurry his wedding along. No point wasting such a golden opportunity."

Nayna stared at her grandmother. "I can't believe you just said that."

"Someone had to!" Aji huffed. "Now bring me that muffin."

After demolishing half of it, she picked up the thread of their conversation again. "Indian parents, they're very good at guilt."

"You're an Indian parent," Nayna pointed out. "And you're not—"

"That's because I'm your grandmother," Aji interrupted. "Ask your father how good I am at the guilt." Her eyes twinkled. "I asked Madhuri's doctor about this type of surgery, and he said it is a serious thing but that many,

many people have the surgery every day. Raj's father isn't on his deathbed."

Nayna slumped back against the sofa, swallowed hard. "But what if?" That was the crux of it and the real reason she hadn't pushed back so far. "What if he's one of the ones where it all goes wrong? Raj would never forgive himself if we'd denied his last wish."

Her grandmother finished off the muffin before saying, "Are Raj's feelings that important to you?"

"Yes." The answer didn't take any thought. "I see the future and I see him," she whispered. "He's the only man I can ever imagine myself marrying." It should, then, have been a simple decision. "I just... I just wanted a little time to grow into my own skin, a little time to be plain old Nayna Sharma before becoming Mrs. Raj Sen."

The wedding garland would bring with it the traditions and expectations that came with being the wife of a man who was the eldest son of his house, a man who was respected in the community for his acuity in business as well as his dedication to his family. Nayna loved all of that about Raj. Every tiny bit.

"I want to be Raj's wife," she said, the confession a rasp of sound, her throat was so tight. "But I don't want to be Mrs. Sen, the woman who never puts a step wrong and is a paragon of a daughter-in-law, a woman the community looks to and points out to their daughters as an example." Again, the feeling of constriction, the sound of cage doors slamming shut.

"But your Raj comes with tradition," Aji murmured. "As Mr. Darcy did with his great big estate and all the responsibilities it meant." A gentle smile that reminded Nayna of all the times Aji had watched the BBC adaptation of *Pride and Prejudice* with her. "To love one part of him is to love the other."

She closed a soft hand over Nayna's. "I think this boy, he is a good one. He doesn't deserve a wife who looks always to the past and mourns what she might've had." Aji wiped away the tears Nayna hadn't felt herself shedding. "If you can't go to him with an open heart, then love him enough to let him go."

43

AVOCADO-GREEN WALLS & THE TIME OF DISCO

H ER GRANDMOTHER'S WORDS WERE STILL ringing around in Nayna's head two weeks later when Jitesh Sen's health took a sudden turn for the worse as a result of a rare complication that landed him back in surgery. The surgery didn't last as long this time, but it was exactly as traumatic for the family.

When the medical staff brought him out onto the ward, he looked grayer, more diminished. Nayna knew that would pass, that he'd get his strength back, but she could see her own fear and worry magnified a thousand times over in the faces of his family—and in the faces of her own parents. They had truly come to embrace Raj's family as their own.

She waited until she was alone with Raj to bring up the subject they'd been avoiding of late. It was the next day, as the two of them walked a wide corridor in a part of Auckland Hospital that was drenched in natural light. Sangeeta Sen and Aditi had been granted permission to sit with Jitesh Sen for the next half hour.

"Let's get married," she said.

Raj's head jerked toward her, his dark hair tumbled and his eyes shadowed by purplish bruises. "It's not what you want."

Nayna closed her fingers over his fisted hand. "I told my grandmother that when I look into my future, I see you." That part of things felt right, so *right*.

Raj was hers and Nayna was *never* going to give him up. And she wouldn't look back. Her grandmother was right—doing that would fundamentally damage their relationship. She'd take this terrifying step into the unknown with hope and faith in what they were to each other. "I want to be your wife."

RAJ STAGGERED INSIDE AT THE words he'd dreamed of hearing her say.

Except it was all wrong. She wasn't running into his arms with all the passionate fury of her nature, was instead walking to him on a conscious decision fueled by her soft heart.

Would he ever have all of her? Or would she keep a small part hidden away? The secret wildness of her. A woman who wore skintight dresses and dreamed of hiking through the Amazon. A lover who'd kissed him under a subterranean sky. A brilliant accountant who struggled against the ordinary and the mundane.

He wanted to tell her no, that they would not marry until she had no more worries, no more doubts, until she looked at him and saw not the walls of tradition... but dizzying freedom. Except that his life and responsibilities —especially now—would make that a lie.

His fist tightened even further.

None of it mattered. His hunger to be trusted that deeply by Nayna was a selfish need—right now he had far heavier priorities. His mother was losing weight at a precipitous rate, unable to eat with his father so ill, and his sister had become withdrawn and quiet, not even messaging with Harlow.

Navin and Komal were locked in their own emotional meltdown, and—despite both staying close to home—neither was currently of any real help.

As for his father, the doctors assured them he'd make a full recovery, but that's what they'd said the last time.

Everything was going wrong.

"Raj." Nayna shifted so she was in front of him, putting one of her hands palm-down over his heart. "This is a new adventure—and we'll go through it together, like we did the cave." Her fingers rising to brush his jaw, her touch gentle and her scent in his every breath.

Before his father's illness, he'd been doing everything in his power to seduce her, convince her that marrying him wouldn't equal walls and stifling expectations, but in the end, none of it had made a difference. Because Nayna was doing what she always did—surrendering her own dreams to help the people important to her.

And the worst of it, the absolute *worst* of it, was that he couldn't say no.

This might be the last thing his father ever asked of him—Raj couldn't refuse the request and live with himself. He just hoped Nayna could live with the choice she'd made.

Cradling her head in his hands, he said, "I will do

everything in my power to make sure you never regret being my wife."

"I could never regret being with you." Fierce words.

Raj wished he could believe her, but he'd seen her joy in living life on her terms, heard her excitement as she looked up the distant shores she wanted to travel. Raj wouldn't be traveling anywhere for a long time, not with his father sick, Adi so young, and Navin suffering a personal breakdown.

There was no one to take over the business if he left, no one to ensure the livelihood of not just his own family, but of all those who worked for him. "We don't have to live on my parents' land," he promised her, because that was one thing he could give her. "After my father is on solid ground again, we'll buy our own plot and I'll build you a house all your own."

Nayna's smile was lopsided. "We'll talk about that later," she said, pressing a soft kiss to his lips. "Right now the only thing I'm worried about is having an avocado-green background to our wedding photos." She shuddered. "What're our chances of convincing your uncle to let us put on a coat of white paint?"

"Nil to zero," Raj said, silently vowing that he'd find her a better venue.

If he couldn't give Nayna freedom, at least he'd give her a wedding day filled with happiness.

Wrapping his arms around her, he held her next to his heart... and tried to forget his dreams of a Nayna who flew to him on her own wings, without manipulation or coercion or guilt. Just because she wanted to be his wife.

Needless to say, Nayna's parents were overjoyed when she and Raj became actively involved in the wedding preparations. Raj's parents were exactly the same. Rather than being in any way annoyed or angered, Jitesh Sen—still in the hospital—brightened like a light bulb when Raj announced that the golf clubhouse would not do.

Arms folded and voice unbending, Raj said, "Nayna deserves as beautiful a wedding location as her sister."

Falling in love with him all over again for fighting for her, Nayna was about to say something when Sangeeta Sen broke in. "Raj is right." A scowl between her brows. "I mean, how will it look for the Sharmas if one daughter gets a fancy wedding in a five-star hotel and the other only gets a *golf club*? No, no, what were we thinking?"

"Also, the place is like a seventies disco palace," Aditi put in suddenly, having apparently pulled up the location on her phone and found photos. "Look, Ma."

Sangeeta Sen blanched at what she saw. "Dhiraj said it was all renovated!"

Aditi's smile peeked out for the first time since her father's second operation. "That's the worst part. This article says it just underwent a million-dollar makeover!" Giggling, she walked over to show her father the pictures.

"Nothing wrong with green and orange," Jitesh said, his breathing uneven but a smile on his face. "Remember, Geeta, when we went dancing before we found our Raj?"

"Hush, Tesh." Sangeeta Sen brushed her hand over her husband's balding head, the love in the simple action bringing tears to Nayna's eyes. "But this isn't modern. Raj and Nayna are young, should have a modern place."

"True, true." Raj's father smiled. "Anything you want, beta, beti." After a sip of juice held out by his wife, he

NALINI SINGH

said, "It's even okay if we have to go out of town for a nice place. It can be one of those location weddings!"

Hauling down Raj by a grip on the front of his shirt once they were out of his father's room, Nayna kissed him all over his face until his lips finally began to curve. The weight on her heart that had refused to budge for two long days, ever since she'd agreed to marriage—and Raj had gone quiet—finally lifted.

"You're a wonderful man." She kissed his cheeks, then his jaw. "Hallelujah for no more avocado green!"

A giggle reached them.

Shifting on her heel, Nayna wrapped an arm around Aditi, who'd been taking photos of them, and said, "Give up the contraband."

Aditi held the phone out of reach.

Taller than both of them, Raj plucked it out of her grasp, then tapped in her unlock code with big-brother knowledge that had Aditi laughingly protesting her privacy. Nayna was looking at Raj when he saw the first photo, and her stomach, it went into free fall. God, his *smile*.

No, she wouldn't regret being Raj's wife.

IN CONTRAST TO BOTH SETS of parents, Nayna's best friend frowned when Nayna told her what was going on. The two of them were sitting on Nayna's couch, sharing a tub of colorful gumdrop ice cream, both of them in their pj's. Ísa had told her fiancé she was having a girls' night, and Nayna would've done the same with Raj if he hadn't called her earlier to confess he could feel his body reaching the limit after weeks of stress and low sleep.

Nayna had ordered him to go to bed at once. "I'll cuddle you later."

His laughter had curled her toes.

Now Ísa said, "You sure, Nayna?"

After digging out another spoonful of ice cream chunky with chewy gumdrops, Nayna pointed it at her friend. "I get to go to bed with Raj every single night. And I get to wake up with his smile every morning." Her insides went all melty at the thought of it. "I'm sure."

Ísa still looked troubled. "Will it be enough? Being a wife and living a steady, everyday life? I'm a homebody, but you always had other dreams."

"Yes, it'll be wonderful," Nayna said because she would permit nothing else. "As for steady and everyday... there *is* one thing I'm considering." She told her friend about her hunger to get involved with a start-up, help it rise.

Ísa listened intently, then tapped her lower lip. "I've got a possibility for you, but you'd be doing it for no money until the investors sign on—extra work around your actual job."

"I won't do anything risky workwise until Raj's father is better anyway," Nayna said. "You know how my parents will worry if I give up a stable job. The Sens are the same." And the last thing she wanted was to create more stress on any level. "So something I can do around my current work would be perfect. What have you got?"

"It's Sailor," Ísa began, excitement in her voice. "He's come up with an innovative new concept that I think has the potential to be huge."

Poetry-loving Ísa was the Dragon's daughter—and Jacqueline Rain had made millions in business. Love or not, Ísa wouldn't say something like that unless she believed absolutely in it. Nayna listened.

THE NEXT DAY, WHILE RAJ was lying next to Nayna, both their chests heaving after an explosive quickie squeezed in between the end of the workday and an upcoming visit to the hospital, his future wife mentioned her possible change in direction.

"Nothing's settled yet," she added, "but I'm excited about it."

"Then you should do it," Raj said at once, rolling over so that he was braced on one arm beside her, the hand of his other on her abdomen. "I love my work. I want the same for you." He never wanted Nayna unhappy—and at least in this, he could make sure her dreams came true.

"It'll be risky at the start," she said, closing her hand over his. "Pay's likely to be a pittance and the hours will be brutal."

"Money won't be a problem," Raj said, then stilled, suddenly conscious of her fierce need for freedom. "If you don't mind me stepping in to cover things while you get on your feet."

"No, I don't mind," Nayna said, poking a gentle finger into his chest. "As long as you keep on letting me prop you up when needed too. We're a team. No one-way traffic allowed."

The tension draining out of him, Raj said, "Yes, we're a team." It felt so fucking good to say that and to hear Nayna say it. "As for the hours, by then Dad should be fine, so it'll only impact me and you." He moved again, this time so he was braced full length over her. "I'll deal with the home side of things, you conquer the business world, and we'll meet in the middle. Naked."

His last word made her laugh and wrap her legs around his hips. As she tried to tip him over, the two of them wrestling playfully, Raj prayed that this was how it would always be, that his Nayna would find joy with him even when his responsibilities kept the two of them pinned to the earth.

44

OH, MADHURI. HOW COULD YOU?

TWO DAYS LATER AND RAJ'S father had been at home for over twenty-four hours and, Nayna was pleased to hear, was already up to short walks around the house. The rest of the time, he and Raj's mother apparently spent making wedding plans, both of them happy and engaged. Aditi often joined in to—in her words—head off any future disco ideas.

Relieved his family was heading back on track—Komal and Navin not included—Raj swung by to see Nayna after work, and the two of them put together a delicious dinner with zero drama and multiple kisses. That was when she discovered her gorgeous hunk could actually cook.

"Used to do it all the time when my parents were running the company," he told her while expertly adding spices to a chicken dish. "Aditi was only little, and Navin not even in high school."

"I assumed your grandparents must've babysat you."

"They did, but my aji's got arthritis, so I'd take over in

the kitchen when her joints got bad, while my aja supervised Adi and Navin. She'd instruct and I'd do as I was told." He let her taste the dish, smiled that slow, sinful smile at her moan of delight. "I figured out after a while that it was like building. Construct a good foundation and even bad décor won't mess it up."

"Keep talking sexy to me and I'll drag you off to bed in a second."

He turned off the stove, took off his shirt, and Nayna's panties just fell off.

AN HOUR LATER, HER BODY sated in a bone-deep way and a belated but delicious dinner in her belly, Nayna was closest to the door when someone knocked—Raj was grabbing an apple out of her fridge. "It's probably my neighbor." The elderly man often popped over for a cup of tea and a chat.

But the man on the other side wasn't harmless Mr. Franklin.

"Madhuri's run away." Dr. Sandesh Patel's words were a dousing of ice water, his eyes black chips. "She says she's in love with someone else."

Raj walked out right then. "Nayna, is—" His eyes fell on the scene in the doorway and on her ashen face. "What's happened?" He put the apple in his hand on her small hallway table.

"Her sister has run away." Sandesh thrust his phone at Raj. "Read this."

"Come in and shut the door," Raj said before turning his attention to the message.

Trembling inside, her head stuffy and too full, Nayna leaned up against Raj and scanned the message.

Dear Sandesh, I'm so sorry to do this to you, but I just can't go through with the wedding. I thought I could, but the closer it gets, the more panicked I feel. And I've finally realized it's because I'm not in love with you. I'm in love with someone else. I didn't mean to break your heart. Thank you for being so good to me. – Maddie

Raj put one arm around her. "When did you get this?"

"Just before I drove here from my office." Sandesh turned his icy gaze on Nayna. "Did you know?"

"*Sandesh.*" Raj's tone was harder than stone. "You do not talk to Nayna like that."

The doctor flinched, clearly unused to being addressed in that tone, but it seemed to get through. "No, I shouldn't. I'm sorry." The anger cracked, exposing desperation and hurt. "Why would she do this?" The words were a plea this time. "Did you know there was someone else?"

Having drawn several deep breaths in the interim, Nayna could think again. "No," she answered. As far as she was aware, Madhuri hadn't seen the surfer since her engagement. "She gave you no clue?" Anger began to simmer in her, that her sister would take such a damaging and impulsive action a second time around.

And to do it now? Only two weeks before her wedding?

"Nothing, and we had dinner just last night." Sandesh paced the narrow space. "I took her to the revolving restaurant in the Sky Tower because she likes to watch the sunset from there." His fingers trembled as he thrust them through his hair. "Afterward, we went for a walk along Mission Bay. It was fine. Everything was fine."

Nayna knew Madhuri and the doctor hadn't yet been intimate, so she didn't ask if they'd spent the night together. Sandesh Patel was old-fashioned in his courtship, and Madhuri seemed happy with that. She'd told Nayna how much she loved how he treated her. It just didn't make any sense.

"Have you tried to call her?" Raj asked.

"I set my car's system to dial her the entire way here. But she won't answer."

Digging out her own phone, Nayna sent her sister a message, figuring Madhuri was more likely to reply to that: *Are you okay?*

The answer came within seconds: *I'm safe.*

After passing on the message to Sandesh, Nayna typed another: *I need to talk to you, Maddie. What's going on? I'm going to call you.*

No response to the message or the call. Not then, and not in the frustrating quarter hour that followed as Nayna touched base with Anjali and Jaci. She had to be delicate about what she asked, because if Madhuri hadn't shared her plans with her friends, then Nayna wasn't about to betray her and have the information spread.

"Hi, Anj," she said with forced cheer. "Is Maddie with you? I'm trying to track her down to show her the cake topper I finally found, but I think her phone might be flat."

"It must be if she hasn't called you screaming in excitement" was Anjali's laughing response. "She's deter-mined to have that topper and that topper only. Anyway, I haven't talked to her today." A child's cry in the background. "Got to go. Send me a pic of the topper if it's the one Maddie wants. I can't wait to see it."

Jaci said much the same.

By the time Nayna hung up from that call, otherwise stiff and contained Sandesh Patel was close to going to pieces, but he remained unwilling to give up on Madhuri.

"I didn't go to your parents for this reason," he said. "I knew they would feel so much shame. I don't want that between me and my in-laws when Madhuri and I get married."

His voice broke, and Nayna could see him pulling himself together with conscious effort of will. "I thought, she's your sister. Maybe you can talk sense into her before this gets out. The wedding can go ahead and no one will ever know—I can understand if she's having jitters. I know she had a bad first marriage."

Yes, this man was very much madly in love with Nayna's sister. "I'll try to track her down," she promised. "But you have to understand, if she really is in love with someone else and doesn't want to come back, I won't force her." Angry as she was with Madhuri, they remained sisters, and Nayna's loyalty had to be to her.

Lines of strain on Sandesh's face, but he nodded. "No force. I waited a long time to marry, and I want a happy married life. But I need to understand why. Why did she say yes? Was it only because I'm rich and respectable? Did she ever care for me?"

Nayna felt the same need for answers and said so to Raj after he returned from driving Sandesh Patel home. Neither one of them had trusted the other man behind the wheel of a car in his current emotional state. His dark blue Mercedes was parked on the street in front of Nayna's apartment and should be safe enough in the residential neighborhood.

"This is what your sister did before." Raj's words held no judgment. "Do you think she'd repeat her mistake?"

"Before today, I would've bet everything that she wouldn't," Nayna said, her mind awash in memories of her conversation with Madhuri the night Sandesh and his family had come over—her sister had been so peaceful, so determined to put the past behind her. Not only that, but she'd displayed a distinct attraction to the doctor.

"Obviously," she added, "I don't know her as well as I thought I did." Nayna thrust a hand through her hair. "I called my parents and asked if Madhuri was there—Ma said she was off visiting out-of-town friends and wouldn't be home for a couple of days, but when I called the hotel Madhuri said she'd be at, they had no guest with that name."

Anger bubbled in the pit of her stomach. "She lied to my mother, she broke up with her fiancé by text message, and now she isn't answering my calls or messages." Nayna folded her arms, her hand squeezing her phone. "What possible explanation can she have for acting this way? If she wanted to call off the wedding, fine, but do it like an adult. Why cut and run?"

"Is it possible she needs a couple of days' time out and then she'll be back?"

Nayna pressed her lips together. "I have no idea. I don't trust my sister very much right now." It was the lie to their mother that caught in her craw the most; Madhuri had witnessed how Shilpa Sharma was at last breaking out of her shell to assert herself with their father. It had taken their mother decades and the near-banishment of a second daughter to find her voice.

If she discovered what Madhuri had done, it would not only hurt her, it would make her doubt her instincts at a critical time. "I am not going to wait around for her to decide to be an adult, but I can't work out where she might've gone."

"Navin watches true crime shows on TV sometimes." Raj rubbed at his jaw. "I saw an episode with him where a cop said most people who run tend to go to a familiar place. Especially when stressed—they don't have the emotional capacity to think of a brand-new place to hide."

Nayna's mind flashed to the image she'd seen on Madhuri's phone. Of that cottage by the ocean. A cottage with a name. "Wait." Grabbing her laptop, she got it going, then typed in "Seagrass Cottage," centering her search on New Zealand.

It was the first hit. A listing on a small local website that advertised vacation homes turned into short-term rentals.

Seagrass was located about two hours outside Auckland.

When she checked, she saw that today's date as well as tomorrow and the day after were blacked out. The place was booked.

"This is a long shot," Nayna said to Raj. "But it's where she went with her last boyfriend."

Raj leaned over her chair, his arms braced on the back. "Owner's number is listed, but there's no information about if there's a direct line to the cottage."

"I'll call the owner, say I'm trying to touch base with my sister and I think she's at the cottage." If Madhuri wasn't there, no harm, no foul.

If she was, however...

Nayna crossed her fingers behind her back and made the call. The owner was suspicious at first, but softened when Nayna stayed polite and threw in phrases like "family emergency" and "no cell phone reception."

"I still can't give out information on my guests, dear," the other woman said at last, but Nayna could feel her wavering. "And we don't have a landline out there."

That was when Nayna had a burst of genius. "She usually uses my phone number as her emergency contact on any forms that require it," she told the owner. "If that's on your records, would that ease your mind?"

The owner didn't say anything, but Nayna heard clicking on the other end. "Well, I'm so glad you mentioned that," she said at last. "Your name and phone number are right here on her reservation, so I think it's all right to tell you your sister is at Seagrass. I hope the news isn't too bad."

"Thank you so much for your help." Nayna asked a few more questions to ensure she understood how to reach the seaside cottage, then hung up.

Raj already had his keys in hand. "Let me call Navin, make sure he's home to deal with anything that comes up, then we can go. My grandparents are there too, but they're elderly. I don't want them panicking if Dad needs medical help."

His brother proved to be at home and willing to do what was necessary.

"Being half-drunk and out of reach while Dad was

undergoing major surgery screwed Navin's head on straight in at least one way," Raj said to her as they walked out to his truck. "He's become way more reliable."

Nayna waited to reply until they were both in the truck and belted in. "What about Komal?" Despite her strong negative reaction to the other woman the first time they'd met, after learning of Navin's partying ways, Nayna had come to have a certain sympathy for Komal.

It couldn't have been fun for a young bride to spend endless weekends alone while her husband hung out with "the boys." No wonder Komal had started going out to parties of her own. It didn't excuse her abrasive and often unkind nature, but it gave Nayna insight into the reason she might've become that way.

"Hard to tell," Raj said. "Komal's been picking up extra shifts at work, so I haven't seen her much."

"I guess their relationship is their private business," Nayna said. "I wish I could say that about Madhuri and Dr. Patel and Madhuri's lover, but this has the potential to devastate my parents and grandmother." Aji had been bragging about her granddaughter's upcoming nuptials ever since the engagement. "I can't sit by and do nothing."

And if the news got out, it would reflect badly on her too. More, it would create gossip about the Sens and whether their son was marrying into a family with bad blood.

Nayna's hands curled into fists on her thighs.

45

SEAGRASS TEARS

I N FULL FURY WHEN SHE got out of the truck two hours later, Nayna strode down the sandy path to the cottage without waiting for Raj.

The cottage was picturesque, surrounded by the waving seagrasses of its name, as well as other foliage designed to survive the saltwater-laced winds that came off the ocean that crashed gently to shore on her right side. She was about to knock on the door when something made her look to the water... and there was Madhuri, sitting on the sand in the dark, her knees tucked up under her chin and her arms wrapped around her legs.

Her hair flew back in the sea winds, knotted and wild.

She looked so very alone that Nayna's anger broke under the power of the love she felt for her mixed-up, beautiful mess of a sister. "Will you wait here?" she asked Raj, who'd caught up to her.

A nod. "I'll see if there's anyone else in the cottage."

Leaving him to the task, she took off her shoes and

socks and left them on the edge of the sand. That sand was soft and sparkling between her toes when she started the short walk to Madhuri, the grains yet warm from the sun. But the sea air carried enough of a chill that she regretted not bringing a cardigan.

Taking a seat beside Madhuri, who looked at her with a devastated face, her beauty buried under shadows and darkness, Nayna just opened her arms. Her sister fell into them, wrapping her own arms tight around Nayna and sobbing. She tried to speak, but her words were unintelligible. Nayna just held her, stroked her back, and waited.

Finally, when she'd cried herself out, Madhuri raised her head and, voice tear-rough, said, "Sorry about the mascara stains."

"I'll survive." She wiped her thumbs under her sister's eyes. "Are you truly in love with someone else?"

Fisting her hand in the sand, Madhuri watched it slide through her fingers. "I was stupid," she said. "Bailey messaged me. I hadn't bothered to tell him about the engagement, and he asked if I wanted to come out here for a good time."

Nayna frowned. "You hadn't seen him until all this?"

Avoiding the question, Madhuri said, "We were never serious, only friends with benefits." Her lips twisted. "I don't know if we were actually friends either, or just bed buddies."

Nayna didn't interrupt, though she was unable to see how a text from an ex had led to Madhuri breaking up her engagement.

"After he messaged, I called him, and I told him about Sandesh." Another fistful of sand, Madhuri watching the grains fall with too much attention. "And Bailey, he was jealous. I got all... I don't know." A shrug. "I went to him. And we had a night together."

"Was that last night?" Nayna asked, a bad feeling in the pit of her stomach.

Madhuri shook her head. "It was two weeks ago," she admitted, shame writ large on her features.

"*Maddie*."

Her sister kicked at the sand, squeezed her eyes shut, then opened them again. "Other than when we drove here, I only saw him two more times." She began to draw in the sand. "He's always been charming. Charming and funny and full of ideas. And Sandesh... He's so staid, so solid."

"I thought those were the things you liked about him."

"I got blinded, Nayna." Madhuri drew a heart in the sand, and in that heart she wrote *M Loves S*. "The shiny and the sparkly. That's who I am. No substance at all."

Frowning, Nayna took her sister's hand. "Those aren't your words. Who said that to you?" Who'd been so cruel to her sister?

"Vinod emailed me. Can you believe it?" Huge, tear-drenched eyes. "He heard I was getting married and wanted to congratulate me. I saw his name in my inbox, and all at once, I had his voice in my head, screaming at me for being useless and stupid. And I thought of how smart Sandesh is and my chest went all hot and painful, and then Bailey got in touch."

So help her, Nayna would punch Vinod if he ever had the misfortune to appear in her path. "Maddie, you can't let that bastard destroy your future. You make Sandesh laugh, and I've never ever seen him do that with *anyone* else. You give a joy to his life that he never before had. That's a gift."

Madhuri's lower lip trembled. "Ma and Pa will never forgive me for this."

"They don't know," Nayna told her sister. "Sandesh came to me."

Two more tears leaked out from Madhuri's eyes. "Do you think *he* could ever forgive me?"

Nayna considered her words with care. "I think that man would forgive you almost anything," she said quietly, "but if this wasn't a one-off mistake you made because of how Vinod hurt you in the past, if you aren't sure you can be faithful to him, you need to walk away."

She held her sister's eyes, no give in her voice this time because they were talking about a good man's happiness. "He's not the kind of man who would bounce back, do you understand? He's forty-eight years old, and this is the first time he's fallen in love. It's probably going to be the only time."

Her sister swallowed hard, her voice shaky. "I need help, don't I? Like from a counselor or someone?"

"Yes, Maddie, I think so." Nayna's heart squeezed at seeing the depth of the wounds on Madhuri's psyche. That her sister had also caused wounds on others, that didn't negate her own hurts. "I think the one thing Sandesh knows how to be," she told her sister, "is loyal. But don't break him, Madhuri. Because I really think you could."

Her sister began to cry again, and Nayna took her into her arms. This time, however, it was short, and then Madhuri leaned her head against Nayna's shoulder and said, "I kicked Bailey out an hour after we arrived. He'd spent that entire hour chatting about how, now that I was free, we would have fun like before. No strings, no drama."

A self-mocking laugh. "All the panic and confusion in my head suddenly cleared. I saw past the flash and the charm and I saw the immature boy within. And I realized what I'd given up when I left Sandesh." A shudder. "What should I do? Should I call him?" Her gaze begged Nayna for an answer.

Nayna thought of the distraught man at her door, the way he'd gone so painfully quiet by the time Raj took him home. "Yes. Put his mind at rest, tell him you're coming back. And ask him to book a hotel room."

Madhuri's head jerked up, nearly clipping Nayna on the chin. "What?"

"I think you two need time alone." Nayna smoothed Madhuri's hair back from her face. "Tell him to make sure the hotel room isn't within surveillance reach of an auntie. Pick an obscure bed-and-breakfast maybe."

"He's really old-fashioned, Ninu. Like the guys in those books you like."

"I know, but he's also heartbroken right now," Nayna pointed out. "If you want this to work, you need to be honest with him, tell him everything. And you need to forge a bond with him that's as honest. I don't mean sex necessarily. I mean being together, just you two."

Madhuri's lower lip trembled again, tears filling her eyes. "What if he tosses me away afterward?"

As her last husband had done.

As her own parents had done when she hadn't acted as they wanted.

Nayna's eyes stung. "I don't know Sandesh as well as

you," she said softly, "but he came to me rather than go to our parents because he wants to be able to forget this ever happened. That doesn't mean he couldn't turn out to be a bastard—and if he does, you call me and I'll get you out. But maybe it means he's willing to try."

It took ten more minutes of gentle encouragement before Madhuri picked up the phone and called her fiancé.

TWO AND A HALF HOURS LATER, they dropped Madhuri in front of a tiny hotel owned by an otherwise retired couple. Located approximately forty minutes from central Auckland, and to the west of the city, it was private, with small rooms, but had access to walking paths through native forest.

Madhuri's maybe-fiancé was waiting for her on the doorstep.

Dr. Sandesh Patel was no longer wild-eyed, but he had new lines on his features.

Madhuri got out of the truck, hesitated for a second, then ran straight to him, throwing her arms around him as she sobbed. Sandesh's own arms snapped around her at once, and in that moment, Nayna had hope. When his eyes met hers, she saw both gratitude and the same bright flicker of hope.

The doctor was a smart man. And from what Nayna had overheard during Madhuri's phone call, her sister had spilled everything already. Including the fears and torments that had led to her self-destructive and hurtful actions. That he held Madhuri so close now told Nayna he loved her. Enough to forgive. Enough to give her the safety and stability she needed.

Leaving the two, she got back in the truck with Raj.

"Nayna," Raj said ten minutes later. "You're sure?"

Her skin chilled. She knew at once what he was asking and why. "I'm sure," she said, emotion raw in her voice. "I want to marry you, Raj. I'm not Madhuri—I'm not mixed up and worried about my choice."

Raj nodded, but they didn't speak the entire rest of the way to her place.

His father's illness and their resulting decision to marry, Nayna realized with a numbness in her cheeks, would always lie between them. It didn't make any difference what she said. Raj would have to spend a lifetime knowing that his wife hadn't come to him on her own, free of all outside interference.

Nayna didn't know how to fix that.

Once inside her place, Raj took her face into his hands and kissed her until he was her breath, his body her only anchor in a tumbling universe.

Nayna didn't remember taking off her clothes or stripping him of his, but his big body was moving over her, branding her, all silken skin and heat. She moved with him, her hands clawing at his back and her voice throaty as she whispered his name. He stroked her, caressed her, pushed her over the edge not once but twice. And in all that time, he didn't speak.

Raj and Nayna, they'd lost each other in the silence.

46

THE VILLAINESS STRIKES

R AJ GOT HOME LATE THAT Monday after a hard day at the site, his body heavy with tiredness. Despite that, he planned to shower, then go see Nayna. He hadn't been able to go to her on Sunday, having already promised his grandparents he'd take them to visit various friends, and he hated how they'd left things. Madhuri's actions, her hesitation, it had stirred everything up again and he'd let it get to him.

He wasn't scared Nayna would run; she was too honest and loyal a woman to do that to him. But did she *want* to run? That was the worry that had blindsided him all over again, and it was *his* fucking problem. He had to get over it or he'd be responsible for the ruination of his marriage.

After locking his truck, he decided to look in on his parents.

He found them in the main lounge, watching their favorite drama. His father was looking encouragingly hale and hearty, though his recovery would be a long process.

They waved him in when he arrived, their expressions solemn. Then, for the first time in memory, they turned off the drama in the middle and asked him to sit. Chest suddenly cold, Raj took a seat across from them.

"What is it?" he asked, keeping an ear open for the rest of the household.

He had a gut feeling this was a private discussion he didn't want anyone else to overhear.

"Son," his father said, "I hope this is all wrong information, but Komal has a friend, and this friend said she saw Madhuri holding hands with another man on the beach."

For God's sake, that beach had been on the edge of nowhere. "Where is Komal?" He had to initiate damage control, stop his sister-in-law and her friend from spreading the news. The resulting gossip and whispers would hurt too many people, most of all his Nayna.

"Your brother took her out." His mother, always the diplomat, didn't add anything further, but it was obvious to Raj that his parents had made the suggestion and Navin had taken the hint.

"There's no problem," Raj said. "Sandesh and Madhuri are together right now."

His mother put a hand to her chest and exhaled. "Oh, I'm happy to hear that. I was worrying so much about Shilpa and Gaurav." A shake of her head. "Your Nayna is a lovely girl. Her sister though... But it's all fine, and we can focus on the wedding again."

Raj looked from one parent to the other, his chest yet

cold. "What if everyone finds out?" he asked. "What if Komal spreads the gossip?"

"That girl won't say a word." His mother's voice, sterner than he'd heard it since he was ten and decided to climb up to the roof. "I told her not to say a word, because this is about family, and we don't bring down family."

Rising to his feet, Raj lifted her up off her feet and gave her a huge kiss on the cheek. "Thank you, Ma. Dad." He knew his father would've been right there, backing his mother.

His father smiled and waved off his words. "Turn on the TV, Geeta. We can catch up."

"Raj! Your aji made your favorite green pumpkin curry," his mother called out as his father went for the remote. "You better eat some or you know she'll singe your ears."

He could just hear his grandmother's voice: *Oho! My food is no longer good enough for Mr. Big Construction Boss? I see. Now you only eat in fancy restaurants. And to think I went to the vegetable store especially to get this for you. How quickly children forget what we do for them.*

His lips curved. "I'll raid the kitchen after my shower."

Leaving his parents watching their show, he headed out the back door and toward his flat. He decided to call Nayna along the way, relay the Komal situation and that it had been handled by his mother. The phone rang and rang on the other end without an answer. He left a voice mail, then sent her a text. At the last minute, he attached a picture of his chest from back when they'd first been flirting.

Nayna could never resist replying to those, not even if she was mad at him.

But when he left the shower ten minutes later, his phone remained dark. Telling himself not to worry—she was probably finishing up some work and had her phone on silent—he got dressed and walked up to the kitchen of the main house.

Despite the name, pumpkin curry as his grandmother made it had no curry powder in it. The unripe young pumpkin was washed, then cut and cored without removing the thin green skin, before being gently sautéed until it softened. Other than a tiny bit of oil to brown the onions at the start of the process, the only other things involved were fresh chopped chili, crushed garlic, fenugreek seeds, and mustard seeds.

It was a simple dish, to be eaten with rice or roti, and one Raj had always loved.

But when he entered the kitchen, it was to the sound of a furious conversation in the main lounge. Not shouting, just hissed and angry voices. Frowning, he walked down the hall and looked in to see his grandparents sitting stiff-backed on the sofa while his mother paced the room and his father sat grim-jawed in his armchair.

Komal stood behind his grandparents, Navin beside her.

His brother had a sickened look on his face while Komal was smirking.

"What's going on?" Raj's voice brought everything to a halt.

"Your grandparents didn't understand the situation," his mother said at last.

The cold returned. "Tell me."

"Komal spoke to us," his grandfather said, his voice as stern as always, as stern as the lines on the dark brown of his skin. "She told us how disgracefully your betrothed's sister is acting."

Raj couldn't look at either his brother or his wife. He wasn't in enough control. How the fuck had Navin let this happen? And why would Komal go out of her way to throw dirt on Nayna?

"Dad," he said quietly, "why isn't Nayna answering my phone calls?"

His father's eyes snapped, nothing of weakness in him. "Ma and Pitaji and Komal went to her and told her about that new contract you're vying for, the multimillion-dollar one with Hari Shankar."

Hari Shankar was a major developer, the project on offer enough to triple their turnover. "What's that got to do with anything?" Raj asked, utterly in the dark.

"You know how conservative Hari is," his father reminded him. "Your grandparents told Nayna that we'd lose all hope of gaining the contract if it came out that your future sister-in-law was going around with other men. Worse, they said Hari would spread it around that we aren't the right kind of family to do business with and we'd lose everything."

It was as if he was living in the nineteenth century. "Hari Shankar didn't become a multimillionaire developer by caring about his contractors' personal lives." Outside of his visits to the temple and pious weekly prayer meetings, the man was a ruthless shark. "He wants the best and most cost-effective build, full stop."

"Yes, I know, son," his father continued, his jaw set in a way Raj had rarely seen. Jitesh Sen was the jovial joker of the family, not a man who'd ever been a harsh discipli-narian. "But Nayna isn't in our industry and wouldn't know it wasn't the truth. Your aja and aji told her that if she loves you, she should walk away."

Raj's hand fisted at his side. Before he could trust himself to speak, his grandmother said, "We were thinking only of you," and the edge in her tone made it clear she wasn't impressed by his parents' stance on the matter. "This isn't the kind of blood you want to bring into our family. Komal has let us know that that sister of hers already ran off with a man before. And then got divorced! It's possible that your—"

"*Aji.*" Raj shook his head at his rail-thin, silver-haired grandmother. "Nayna is the woman I love, and she's the woman I'm going to marry. If she'll have me after this." He locked gazes with his father and made the call he should've made right back when this farce first began; Jitesh Sen knew how much Raj loved him. This wouldn't change that. "You need to let us decide. You need to let Nayna decide if she wants to come into this family after the way she's been treated. As much time as she needs."

His father gave a solemn nod, his features stricken. "I'm sorry, beta," he said with a sigh. "Your grandparents haven't seen the two of you together as many times as we have. They don't understand what they're getting in the middle of—and they don't understand Nayna."

"Well," his aji said, "if that woman comes into this family, then you can forget about me. I'll be moving in with Dhiraj and his wife."

"If that's the decision you want to make, Aji," Raj said, well aware that his grandmother was used to getting her way by throwing down ultimatums.

He also knew she loved him. Despite her often anti-quated ideas, she'd never once brought up his adoption. As far as she was concerned, he was her eldest grand-child, and he loved her for that. But he would never give up Nayna for her. "I would've liked you in my life and in the lives of my children, but if you want to walk away, that's your prerogative."

Then he left to find his Nayna.

He was pulling out of the drive when he realized he didn't know where to go. The first place he tried was her apartment, but no one responded to his knock. When he checked with her neighbor, the old man told him that Nayna had been home, had visitors, then left. "I was hoping she'd come back soon, make me some of that chai, and help me download my emails," he said with a denture-white grin. "Nicest neighbor I've ever had."

After leaving Nayna's place, Raj swung by her office, but the villa was also shut up. And when he drove by her parents place, he saw no sign of her green MINI.

Gut in knots, he called Sailor. "Sail, do you know if Nayna is with Ísa?"

"No, Ísa and I are out of town visiting Ísa's sister. Everything okay?"

"Yeah," Raj said, squeezing the steering wheel. "Have a nice time." Hanging up, he sat in his vehicle and thought about where Nayna could've gone. She had always stood her ground. But Komal had poured poison into his grandparents' minds. Maybe Nayna had fallen for it.

No.

He refused to believe that of the woman who owned his heart. The Nayna he knew would give him a chance to make this right. She would *never* just leave him. Not when she knew how much the abandonment would hurt.

Turning the truck around, he drove back to her apartment complex and parked in a visitor spot. He'd only been there two minutes when lights flashed behind him as another vehicle pulled in. A familiar green MINI.

He was out of his truck before he remembered opening the door.

"Raj!" The startled word was all that Nayna had time to say before he crushed his mouth over hers and wrapped her up in his arms. Hands fisting in his shirt, Nayna rose on tiptoe and kissed him back as she always did.

No distance, no rejection.

His breath harsh and his eyes stinging, he looked at her and said, "Why didn't you answer my messages?"

"I forgot my phone at the office—and I was at the supermarket before I realized." Scrunching up her nose, she scowled. "I had the most *awful* meeting with your grandparents—Komal was there too, though she didn't talk—and I really needed double chocolate ice cream, so I drove out in a temper to get it."

Her eyes flashed. "I went to call you once I'd calmed down enough to talk, and that's when I realized my phone was at the office. I'd already bought the ice cream by then, so I came back here to put it in the freezer before driving to the office."

Gripping the back of her neck, he pressed his forehead to her own. "My grandparents, what they said—"

"If you wanted to get rid of me," Nayna interrupted, "you'd do it yourself to my face. You'd never send your grandparents, and you would definitely never send

Komal." She spread her hand over his heart. "Your parents—"

"They love you." Shaking inside, he couldn't make himself release her. "My grandmother threatened to cut me out of their lives if I stayed with you. I told her that was her choice. You're mine."

"Raj, no." Nayna shook her head.

"I am not willing to give you up for anyone," Raj vowed. "Not anyone, Nayna." He held the rich brown of her eyes, eyes in which he saw home. "As for our wedding, it's off the table until you're ready. No one in my family will ever again interfere. If you're never ready, then I'll continue to be your boyfriend even when we're old and gray, just like your aji and Mr. Hohepa."

47

LOVE. LOVE. LOVE

N AYNA'S BREATH STOPPED, HER LUNGS devoid of
air and the moment, it hung like a star against
the night sky.

"You have your freedom again, Nayna." Raj's hand
rough on her cheek, cradling her face as he so often did,
this big man who cherished her. "I will never ever allow
anyone to steal it from you."

A sudden rush of air, a crystalline clarity. "I don't see
walls when I see you," she whispered, the joy of the
moment incandescent. "I don't see a cage. I see my sexy
hunk and hot fling. I see the man who drove hours to find
my sister and who didn't hesitate when I told him I
planned to throw away my stable job for a wild risk. I see
you." And he was a man beyond price.

Raj was the husband she would choose, whether she
waited five years or five months. It would always be him.
By her side when trouble rose, *on* her side against the
world. "I want you to be my husband, Raj." A sense of

utter rightness settling inside her, an inner happiness brighter than the sun.

But Raj wasn't smiling. His hand trembled where it lay against her cheek. "You want the world, Nayna." It came out ragged, rough. "I can't take you to those faraway places. I have to stay here."

Because he was a good son, a good boss, a good brother. A man who took his responsibilities and his promises seriously. "You will be an amazing husband," she whispered, "and a devoted father."

And because she knew he had a habit of carrying too much weight on his shoulders, she got practical. "We'll rejig the schedule. We'll stay home, look after things, and while we're doing that, I'll work on Sailor's project. It'll take time to get that up and running, and I couldn't have traveled during the intensive early period anyway."

Kissing his jaw, his lips, his cheek, she said, "You use that time to train a deputy you can leave in charge when needed. We get your father strong, and we whip Navin into shape so he can be your parents' support here if they need it. Aditi will be older by then anyway, and I'm fully confident in her ability to kick ass and take names."

RAJ STARED AT NAYNA, HIS voice thick when he spoke. "You've thought about this." And everything she said, it made complete sense. She could fulfill all her dreams while making his deepest one come true.

Laughter from his dazzling lover. "Of course I have. I love you. It was only ever going to be you. So I had to figure out how to make things work."

Raj barely heard any words after the three that

changed everything. And she'd said it so simply, as if it were nothing extraordinary. As if loving him was so much a part of her it was no big deal.

Lifting her up with a grip on her waist, he said, "I love you too," then spun them both around in a circle while she laughed and wrapped her arms around him.

When he finally came to a stop, she wobbled dizzily on her feet for a second or two before saying, "Raj Sen, will you do me the honor of being my husband?"

Feeling young in a way he'd never done, Raj replied as solemnly. "Yes, Nayna Sharma. I will." Then he asked her to wait while he jogged to his truck.

When he returned with a small black twist tie, she laughed but held out her hand. He wrapped the twist tie around her ring finger with care, then bent to kiss the back of her hand. "A placeholder until you tell me what ring you want." Having a sister had taught him that jewelry was serious business—and Nayna would be wearing that ring for the rest of her life.

She'd agreed to wear his ring. He'd get her any one she wanted.

Eyes dancing, she pretended to admire his creation. "Very avant-garde."

Joy bursting out of his pores, he could do nothing but kiss her laughing mouth. He didn't even care when a camera flash went off.

"I expect an invitation to the wedding!" Nayna's elderly neighbor lowered his camera and surreptitiously wiped away a tear. "I'll put this in a frame for you."

Laughing, Nayna leaned in to kiss Raj again. And it was all so fucking perfect, with the stars in the sky and the moon peeking through the trees and Nayna's hair all tumbled around her and her taste in his mouth.

When she suddenly pulled back with a squeak, he said, "What?"

"Ice cream!" Wrenching open her car door, she picked up the grocery bag and peeked inside. "Not melted yet."

He waited while she ran upstairs and passed the bag to her neighbor to keep in his freezer for her.

"Now," Nayna said after Mr. Franklin had gone inside and she was back in Raj's arms, "let's go fix this mess your evil sister-in-law's made." A scowl. "I knew it had to be her stirring things."

Making a face, she added, "You know, the only downside of marrying you will be Komal. Promise me you'll never let her convince you I'm having an affair with the milkman." She poked him in the chest.

He grabbed her hand, hauled her close, kissed her because he could. "Komal is going to learn to avoid me whenever possible. I am done with her." He'd had sympathy for his sister-in-law because of Navin's antics, but this was beyond anything he could ever forgive. "And I know you'd hold out for the plumber."

He laughed when she pretended to beat him up for that joke—which he could make because he knew Nayna would never break her promises to him. Nayna Sharma's flaw was that she loved too much and too deeply. And Raj was lucky enough to be loved by her. It was a gift he would never take for granted.

"Come on, Mr. Funny, we have to vanquish a villain." Once in the truck, she said, "Afterward, we'll come back and have ice cream."

Raj's hands tightened on the steering wheel as his

heart expanded to fill his entire body. Nayna was putting on her seat belt but shot him a questioning smile when he didn't immediately pull out. Unable to explain what her simple everyday words had meant to him, he just ran his knuckles over her cheek before heading out.

All that time, his heart continued to grow and grow. Because Nayna had chosen to be his. One hundred percent in. Of her own free will. Their futures entwined. Ice cream, evil-sister-in-law, rides in this truck through the night, her asking him to wait while she ran into her office to grab her phone, muffins delivered to his job site, him fixing her plumbing, all the small, everyday moments of life, they'd have them together.

48

VANQUISH YOUR FOES (USE BLACKMAIL AS REQUIRED)

NAYNA HESITATED A LITTLE WHEN she and Raj walked hand in hand into his parents' lounge. Not only were his parents there, so were his grandparents as well as Navin and Komal. All of them silent and stiff as they watched a documentary on television. No one talking, a hundred angry thoughts unsaid.

Jitesh Sen was the first to see them in the doorway. His face lit up. "Geeta," he said. "Look."

Her smile luminous, Sangeeta Sen turned off the television and rose. "You sit," she ordered her healing husband when he went to get out of his armchair.

Then she came over and cupped Nayna's face in her hands. A kiss on each cheek, then a hug. Whispered words in her ear. "He will love you always. My Raj doesn't change his mind about the people he loves."

Nayna's eyes burned. Nodding as the older woman pulled away, she swallowed the knot in her throat. Raj hugged his mother; after that, he and Nayna went to greet his father. When they announced their engagement was back on, Jitesh and Sangeeta burned with joy.

But Raj still had something to say—this time to his grandparents. "We'll be getting married," he told the older couple. "Whether you want to be a part of our lives is up to you."

"Hold on there, Raj," his grandfather said, waving his cane. "Would you truly cut off your family for this girl?"

"If you force me to," Raj said, utter resolve in his tone.

"Well, I suppose you know her much better than we do. If she makes you act like this, she must be some kind of woman indeed." He thumped his cane on the ground. "Kushla, I'm too old to get into a feud with my eldest son and his son. And you know you don't like Dhiraj's flashy new wife."

Raj's grandmother sniffed. "Well," she said to Nayna, "I hope you don't think this means you'll always get your own way in this family."

Nayna wove her fingers through Raj's. "My future husband is a stubborn man. I think we'll be having a few disagreements."

Raj scowled down at her, but she laughed and leaned her body against him. When he looked at his grandparents again, he saw his grandmother's face had softened. She wasn't a bad person underneath the stern demeanor. She'd be all right once she got to know Nayna.

"I was just looking out for the family." Komal's voice cut through the warmth, a serrated razor.

Raj didn't trust himself to speak. Thankfully, he didn't have to.

Nayna bristled. "Since when does looking out for the family mean being vicious and destructive?"

Komal stood, her entire body rigid. "You can't speak to me like that!"

"Sure I can," Nayna said, calm but unbending. "You gave me that right when you poked your nose into my business." Temper in her eyes. "You can't sow seeds of pain and anger between Raj and me, or with his parents. But if you try, I will kick your posterior all the way back to the hole you crawled out of!"

Raj was attempting not to smile. His grandfather wasn't even doing that much—he had a full-out grin on his face. "Kushla! This one is like you!"

His grandmother sniffed again. "At least she knows how to be loyal."

"What, she's perfect and I'm not?"

"Jesus, Komal, let it go." Navin sounded tired. "I asked Komal for a divorce," he announced to the room. "That's why she did it."

Komal turned on her husband, all fury and wet eyes. "Why does she get to have the happiness?" Pointing at Nayna. "Why can't you love me like Raj loves her? What is so wrong with me that you have to go out night after night without me?"

Navin stared at her, stricken. "There is *nothing* wrong with you," he said. "I was just immature when we got married and I made mistakes and then you got so angry and I couldn't fix it and it was easier to avoid the problem and then it got worse and worse." Thrusting both hands in his hair, he stared at his wife. "I don't know what went wrong with us, K, but you know it's gone wrong."

Tears rolled down Komal's cheeks. "I loved you so much. And for your information, I never cheated. Not even when handsome, rich men hit on me while my husband wasn't around."

Navin swallowed. "I didn't either. I just... I wanted you to be jealous, so I pretended."

Nayna's fingers squeezed Raj's. When he angled his head down toward her, she whispered, "Masala picture, complete with dramatic reconciliation. Aditi is going to be so mad she missed this."

Raj would always be angry at Komal on some level. That type of breach of trust wasn't forgivable in his book. But when his brother got up and took her into his arms, he silently wished them luck. "Drama's fine for the movies, but loving you every day works better for me."

Nayna's eyes welled up. Pretending to punch him on the arm, she said, "Ditto."

"I think we need some privacy." That was Navin, about to lead Komal out of the room.

"Wait." Raj's mother stood up again. "First, I wish you both all the luck in mending your marriage. I've only ever wanted happiness for you."

Both nodded.

"But something else needs to be said," Raj's mother continued. "I was too angry before to do it. I've calmed down, but I still cannot *believe* our daughter-in-law would disrespect us by going to my in-laws after we specifically made our feelings on the matter clear." Her voice was cool, calm. "Is this what your parents taught you, Komal? To talk behind your elders' backs?"

Eyes swollen, Komal shifted restlessly. "I'm sorry. I was angry and sad and I struck out." She swallowed hard. "I won't ever do it again."

"No, you won't," Sangeeta Sen said, a tone in her voice

that had Raj paying intense attention. "I wish I could trust you to keep your word, but just as Navin has to win back the faith of his family, that's a trust you'll have to earn. Until then, I'll just say one word: Taveuni."

Komal went sheet-white under the brown of her skin, swaying on her feet. Navin grabbed her before she fainted, held her upright.

In the silence that followed, Raj's father scratched at his head and said, "Isn't that the island off the coast of Vanua Levu?"

No one answered.

When Komal could speak again, she blurted out a string of words. "I won't say anything else and I'll tell my friend who saw Madhuri not to say a word either." She was all but hyperventilating.

"Just in case you have another spike of meanness and temper," Raj's mother said, "you should know that I'll be sharing what I know with Nayna in the next few minutes —and I'm going to tell Raj too. Remember that the next time you want to make trouble for them."

Then she turned toward him and Nayna and, voice as scarily calm as it had been through the entire exchange, said, "Come on, I have to tell you Komal's secret."

A whimper of sound from Raj's sister-in-law.

49

WE TOLD YOU SO (AND TWO WEDDINGS)

AYNA SAT CURLED UP IN Raj's lap, his gorgeous, warm, naked chest cradling her while she fed him ice cream and ate twice as much herself. He stroked her thigh, her legs bare—she'd pulled on lace panties after they'd made love but hadn't bothered with pants. Up top, she wore a simple camisole. Raj was wearing his boxer briefs and nothing else.

She approved.

When she misjudged a spoonful and a drop hit his chest, she leaned over and licked it up.

He groaned. "You're a devil woman." He slid his hand up under her camisole, spread it on her stomach. "I can't believe you threatened to kick Komal's ass in front of everyone."

"I was so mad." Nayna fed him a little more ice cream. "But at least I remembered to say posterior instead of ass." Her lips twitched. "And your grandpa likes me now." The older man had given her a big hug before they left.

His grandmother was withholding judgment, but that

was all right. One thing at a time. "I don't want to tell my parents we're officially engaged, complete with a romantic proposal."

Raj raised an eyebrow.

Pointing a spoon at him, she said, "They'll smirk and be all 'We told you so' and 'We found you the perfect man.'"

He grinned at her description of him, and she stuck out her tongue. "Be quiet." Then she kissed him because she couldn't help it when he smiled. "Your parents won't say anything?" She'd felt drained after the drama and emotion of the day, needed some time alone with Raj.

"No—they know we're doing that tomorrow night, and they'll wait for everything to happen at a proper pace," Raj said. "Do you think you can take two or three hours off tomorrow during the day?"

"Sure, I'm not backed up anymore. Why?"

"I really want you to wear my ring." Solemn, intent words.

He could have anything he wanted from her when he got like that, his love an open secret in his voice, his eyes, his hands.

And that was how she found herself ring shopping with her sexy hunk the next morning, while trying to avoid being spotted by any aunties who might be prowling the malls and boutiques.

At one point she hissed at Raj to hide. "Babita Auntie's just over there."

Since Raj was too big to take advantage of the potted plant behind which she'd ducked, he bent down and pretended to tie his shoe, face averted from Batty Auntie's sharp eyes, until the danger was past.

"Phew." Nayna pressed a hand to her racing heart. "My mother wouldn't talk to me for a year if Babita Auntie learned we were ring shopping before Ma saw my ring."

Over the time that followed, she tried on lots of pretty rings, but nothing spoke to her. "I want color," she'd told Raj before they began. "Nothing too traditional."

"Any ring you want," he'd said, but in the end, it was Raj who found it. "Nayna, did you see this one?"

The tears came again the instant she laid eyes on the ring he'd pointed out, because he'd *listened* to her. This was no sedate, elegant, expected diamond. Set in two twists of platinum, it was a deep, deep pink ruby positioned at a sharp angle and bordered by equally angular diamonds cut to refract light.

"Yes," she whispered. "That's my ring." And this was her man.

It was past eight by the time they pulled into her parents' drive that night. Raj had arrived late after being held up on a site due to an emergency. The good news was the outcome had been positive. And now he looked incredible in formal black pants and a crisp white shirt under a black jacket. She kept staring at him.

"You like the suit, huh?" He smiled that quiet, sinful smile at her as he came around to open the door.

Smoothing her hands down his lapels, she sighed. "I like the suit." Another unnecessary smoothing. "But I also like the jeans and the tool belt—and the naked."

Hands on her waist, he scooped her down to the ground. "You can have the naked later. First, let's do this."

He closed his hand over hers, hiding her ring. Not that it mattered. The instant they walked into the lounge hand in hand, Raj in a suit, his hair neatly combed, and Nayna wearing a pretty dress, her parents started grinning like cats who'd gotten into the cream. Aji did a slightly better job of not looking delighted, but it was a lost cause.

"Ma, Dad," Raj said, addressing her parents as they'd asked him to, "we've come to ask your blessing on our official engagement."

Her father was up and shaking Raj's hand a second later while her mother kissed Nayna's cheeks and cried happy tears. "Oh, I knew you two were meant to be."

"Yes, you should listen to your elders," her father added.

Told-you-sos heroically suffered, Raj and Nayna went to Aji and knelt before her so that she could put her aged hands on their heads. "I wish only happiness for you," she said in Hindi. "Also, many great-grandchildren for me." Leaning in as Nayna's parents laughed, she whispered, "Tawhiri is winning that race. You two better start with triplets."

"There is one other thing," Raj said after the first celebration was over. "We're not going to rush our wedding. We'd rather focus on Madhuri's wedding first, then make plans for ours."

"Discussion" ensued.

Raj didn't budge. Neither did Nayna.

"I want a wedding that's mine," she said. "And I want to have time to figure out exactly what that entails."

"We're not compromising on the number of guests," her father finally said.

"No, Nayna, beta." Her mother held up a hand before she could argue. "You can have the wedding on the date you choose, and we'll do it how you and Raj want, but we've waited a long time for this. We plan to invite everyone we know."

Nayna glanced at Raj. He gave her a "best offer we're going to get" look and they both nodded. "Deal."

Exactly two weeks later, Nayna kissed her sister goodbye at the airport. A giggly Madhuri, mehndi on her hands from her wedding the Saturday past, waved until she and her equally delighted husband were out of sight. She'd made Nayna promise to involve her in all the wedding preparations for her and Raj's wedding—there was no question but that Madhuri and Sandesh would be flying back for it in six months' time.

"I don't think I've recovered from your sister's wedding yet," Raj murmured as they walked out to his truck. Her parents walked ahead. Aji had said her good-byes at home, plenty of tears included.

"Tell me about it." Nayna's feet ached still from all the running around she'd done pre-wedding. "But she got her dream wedding, complete with glittering chandeliers, that enormous waterfall cake with the perfect topper, and arriving by Rolls-Royce—and that makes me happy."

Raj squeezed her hand, which she'd slipped into his. Her hands, too, bore mehndi designs from during the lead-up to Madhuri's wedding. "I want this," she said, lifting her hand so he could see the red-brown lines of the delicate work.

"You can have whatever you want," Raj said before

pausing. "Except for a giant ice sculpture that begins to melt halfway through, almost causing a flood."

Nayna burst out laughing at the memory of how Raj and Sailor had sprung into action to avert disaster. The poor melting swan, in danger of imminent decapitation, had been whisked away with alacrity to provide the children running around outside with a source of much laughter and fun.

"Did Ísa tell you anything about her and Sailor's plans?"

"They're thinking a beach wedding." Nayna drank in the sunshine outside. "She gets this funny, sweet smile when she talks about it. I think the two of them must've had an important moment on a beach." Ísa had never told Nayna what, and Nayna understood. Some things were to be held close to the heart, shared with only one other person.

Having reached the truck, Nayna got into the back with her mum while her father got in the front passenger seat. The four of them talked easily as Raj drove her parents home.

"We have to finish packing for the cruise today," her mother said.

Up ahead, Nayna saw her father wince at the idea of a cruise, but he didn't say a word. Nayna had to fight to keep her grin off her face. It was about time her mother got her own way in their plans. "It's a week, isn't it?"

"Eight days." Shilpa Sharma sighed. "I need the rest and for someone else to cook and do the cleaning and the laundry. I love Madhuri, but she was a bridezilla."

Then Nayna's well-behaved mother made claws with

her hands, as if pretending to be a marauding bridal monster.

Nayna laughed so hard that she cried—and so did her mother. In the rearview mirror, Raj's eyes were bright. Her father was actually grinning.

Life, Nayna thought with a smile, was good.

IT ONLY GOT BETTER AS the months passed. Nayna was a bridesmaid at Ísa's wedding, alongside Ísa's sister, Catie, and Raj was a groomsman alongside two of Sailor's brothers and a plus-one. That plus-one was Harlow.

Sailor's older brother, Gabriel, stood as best man.

The sea crashed to shore beyond the wedding party while sand glimmered around them, the sunshine bright. Color cascaded from the flowers in Ísa's hair and in the clothing of her guests. Sailor wore a crisp black suit with a white shirt and a blue tie that matched the brilliant hue of his eyes and the ribbon tied around Ísa's living bouquet. That bouquet featured astonishing, lovely succulents and had been created by Ísa's soon-to-be-husband.

Raj and Sailor plus his brothers had, together, built a temporary wooden aisle and wedding platform, all of it in a sand-washed wood that appeared aged by the sea itself. Ísa had made the request and Nayna knew why. Catie was incredibly surefooted on her prosthetic legs, but Nayna knew she'd been stressing about messing up Ísa's wedding by tripping on the sand.

It was also why they were wearing shoes rather than going barefoot. Even on this most important day, Ísa thought of her teenage sister's happiness along with her own.

As it was, the aisle and platform had turned out exquisite. The men had outdone themselves by putting up four posts and connecting them at the top. That had provided the understructure for gauzy curtains and cascades of white flowers. Ísa and Nayna had done a lot of the decoration with Catie and, surprisingly enough, the Dragon.

With the wedding taking place on the edge of sunset, glass lanterns sat on the sand around the wedding platform, the candles within glowing softly. The seats for the guests were placed on either side of the aisle, simple wicker chairs with flowers woven into the backs. Many of the heavily muscled rugby players in attendance had given the chairs a serious side-eye before gingerly taking their places.

"You look so beautiful," Nayna said to her best friend as she fussed over Ísa's halter-neck dress with lace detailing. Ísa's red hair blazed against the rich cream of it. The lower half of the dress was flowy and floaty while the upper half was as delicate and pretty as spun sugar.

Face glowing from within, an inner peace in Ísa's eyes that Nayna had never before seen, her best friend said, "I'm so ready to marry him."

As Nayna stepped out with Catie, the two of them dressed in lovely, simple dresses of sea blue, she felt the same certainty about Raj. He was hers and she was his, and they'd have their adventures together.

His eyes caught hers as she walked up, and the intense look he shot her was unabashed in its appreciation. Beside her, Catie giggled. Nayna shared a smiling glance with her before the two of them took their places on the platform, ready to watch Nayna's best friend walk up the aisle.

The lanterns shone around them, but nothing could compete with Ísa's glow—or with the light in Sailor's eyes when he saw her. Nayna had to swallow back tears, was more than ready for Raj to put his arm around her when they followed the newly married couple down the aisle.

Catie was up ahead with Gabriel.

Raj kissed the top of her head as the guests rained flower petals down on a laughing Ísa and Sailor. "You like this a lot. Regretting our own plans?"

"Six hundred and fifty guests at last count," she reminded him, slipping her arm around his waist. "No way a beach would work. Most importantly, I get to marry you—I would do it even if all we'd been able to find were avocado-green walls. I just want to be your wife."

His jaw got tense in that way it did when he was battling strong emotions.

Rising up on tiptoe, she kissed that jaw. "I love you too."

He didn't say it then. He said it when they were alone and he was inside her and he was holding her in his arms and her breath was lost. "I love you, Nayna. You could break my heart into a million pieces."

Eyes hot, she wrapped herself around him as tightly as she could and just held on. And knew she'd have to show her love to him always. He was so strong, Raj, but he had this wound inside him. She didn't know if she could heal it, but she was damn well going to try. "You're mine, Raj, and I'm not letting go. Ever."

They came together tangled in a kiss.

50

HUSBAND AND WIFE

NOT LONG AFTER THAT, THEY came together as husband and wife.

This time it was Ísa who fussed around Nayna, checking that her dupatta was fixed perfectly over the simple coil of her hair—simple, that is, but for the strands of gold she'd had put in. The gold glittered through the fine gauze of her bridal dupatta.

Madhuri had nearly died of cheerful jealousy.

Edging the light gold dupatta was a band of gold embroidery. Her skirt was a deep pink with intricate gold embroidery, her fitted top matched—complete with borders at the bottoms and at the edges of the short sleeves.

Her jewelry was the same that Madhuri had worn—their mother's and grandmothers' pieces, along with additions that were gifts from Madhuri and Ísa. And Raj's ring on her finger. All things that meant something to her.

"You look like an Indian princess," Ísa whispered, her eyes dancing.

They both laughed at the memory of the seven teaspoons of sugar with which she'd punished Raj. "He keeps threatening to get me back for that."

"Nayna, meri bitia." Placing a hand on her head, her grandmother gave her one last kiss before walking out to make her way to her seat at the front table—right next to Mr. Hohepa.

Nayna's parents told everyone he was Aji's good friend. The "youngsters'" bemusement caused the two elders huge amounts of glee.

"Girls, it's almost time." Nayna's mother bustled in, resplendent in a deep aquamarine sari with white beading. She fixed Nayna's necklace, then turned to make sure Ísa's dupatta was securely pinned.

Her best friend was dressed in a half sari, the color a redhead-flattering vivid purple accented with blues, golds, and even a strip of green on the hem of the skirt. The dupatta, which picked up the accent colors, was made of netting and tucked in a way that complimented Ísa's curvy form. She wore jewelry matched to the outfit, and hidden under her long skirt were pretty heeled sandals. Mehndi designs marked her palms.

Madhuri bustled in then, gorgeous in vibrant yellow. "Come on, Ísa, it's time!" She grabbed Ísa's hand, but Nayna's best friend turned around to smile at her one more time.

"I'm so happy for you, Nayna."

Then the music was playing and Madhuri and Ísa and the other younger members of the family were dancing down the open-air aisle under the soft darkness of dusk, all of them laughing as they pulled off an upbeat Bollywood dance number that had the guests on their feet, singing and dancing along. Someone whistled and a friend of Raj's beat out a rhythm on a tabla set up in one corner for just this purpose.

Children ran out from the crowd to join in, and were joyously welcomed.

Aditi, on the groom's side, technically shouldn't have been in the group, but she was the one who'd choreographed the entire thing after Nayna told her what she wanted—and no way was she about to miss the big event. And this was Nayna and Raj's wedding, with their rules. Dressed in an outfit of shimmering cobalt blue edged with intricate silver, her dupatta silver with a lacy silver pattern, Raj's baby sister danced down alongside the others.

Madhuri had learned the steps while in her lounge in London, while several of Nayna's Fiji-resident cousins had got together at an aunt's house to do the same.

The rehearsal yesterday'd had them all in hysterics, but they were in fine form today.

Nayna, able to see them from her hiding spot, grinned. Yes, this was her and Raj's wedding, nothing solemn or stiff about it.

Her parents paraded far more elegantly up the aisle, both with huge smiles on their faces.

Raj's family—Aditi excepted—was already with him on the wedding pavilion built on the grass of the huge piece of land they'd managed to borrow thanks to Raj's friendship with the owner. It was gorgeous, with mature trees all around the edges. Huge wooden buckets overflowing with cheerful flowers dotted the landscape, and fairy lights strung across the area created a twinkling ceiling.

The wedding pavilion was raised so all their guests could see the ceremony. Rather than glitz, they'd gone for wild and joyous. The structure was a creamy white, but waterfalls of colorful silk fabric dropped from the roof in fairytale abundance to tumble over the edges of the pavilion. Velvet-covered cushions and a thick Turkish rug finished off the decadent space.

People sat at tables dressed with more bright silks and centerpieces that were a spill of floral joy. The small sparkly bags filled with snacks to tide people over through the beginning of the ceremony had been Madhuri's idea. Wait staff would soon begin circulating with more substantial eats.

Her parents and Raj's had insisted on paying for the ridiculously huge wedding, complete with catering. She and Raj had the feeling they were hoping for payback in the form of grandchildren.

Smiling inside at the idea of making babies with Raj, she took a deep breath and got ready. Her escort was made up of "brothers." Younger male cousins, all spiffed up in colorful sherwanis for the occasion and trying to be adult and serious.

Nayna had to fight the urge to pinch their cheeks and hug them close.

Her entrance music began.

Though hundreds of people stood watching her move up toward Raj, the wedding garland in her hands, he was the only one she saw. And then he was standing across from her and he was bending so she could place the garland over his head, and she was wearing the one he'd put over her head, and the ceremony had begun.

She knew it took a long time, but every time she glanced at Raj, he'd give her the smile that was just for her, and it was perfect. Their parents tried to glare at them to behave and be solemn, but their lips kept tugging up. Even the pandit just sighed and shook his head as he said, "Young people these days" and continued the ceremony.

During the part where the two of them were hidden under a heavily embroidered cloth so they were invisible to others, Nayna blew Raj a kiss, and he fleetingly touched his thumb to her lower lip. After which they had to behave and do what they were supposed to under the cloth, which was for Raj to put sindoor—vermillion powder—in the center part of her hair.

He did it with a gentle touch.

The rest of the ceremony passed by in joy after joy, but Nayna was never so glad as when she collapsed in bed with Raj that night. They'd managed to convince their parents to do away with the custom of "fetching the bride back." Lying on his back beside her, wearing only his formal pants, Raj lifted up her hand and traced the lines of mehndi down her arm.

"There's a secret hidden in the design somewhere on my body." Mehndi patterns covered her arms past the elbow, her feet, and her legs up to her calves.

He continued to lazily trace the lines. "What?"

"Your name."

A glance at her. "Really?"

"Yep."

His eyes narrowed, determination on his features. "I'm going to find it."

She ended up naked and sated and delighted as a result of his hunt. It was after midnight when he finally said, "There" and pressed a kiss to the crook of her elbow.

Nayna sighed, tugged him up so she could cuddle in his arms... and fell fast asleep in the embrace of the husband who'd always been meant to be hers.

51

SEVEN YEARS LATER

AARAV GLANCED OVER FROM HIS position in the pack on Raj's back. "Ma! Look!"

Nayna followed his small finger to see a colorful tropical parrot. "Good spotting!" She took a photograph, then plucked at her T-shirt. "I never realized marinating in my own sweat was a thing," she said to her husband.

The heavens opened up as if on cue, the warm rain washing away the sweat before disappearing as quickly as it had come. Her hand locked with Raj's by now, Nayna laughed along with him and their son. Three-year-old Aarav was as used to going with the flow as he was to trying strange new foods.

"It'll dry soon enough," said the man who was her everything. "I think you're steaming already."

"It's funny because it's not even a joke." She reached up to ruffle their baby's wet hair. "Hungry?"

When Aarav nodded, she dug out a kid-friendly fruit bar

from her pack, unwrapped it, and passed it over. The three of them continued on along the path in one of Indonesia's dense forests. It was far from their first adventure. They'd begun small only a year into their marriage, a couple of days here and there exploring their own backyard. New Zealand was a land full of chances for wonder and excitement.

It had helped that Navin and Komal, ensconced in their own home and weirdly happy considering their past, had slowly become reliable members of the family. Aditi, of course, could run rings around them even back then.

Then Raj's deputy had "graduated" his training and they'd been able to take off for a week at a time. Not more because Sailor's company was growing like crazy, and Nayna, as its chief financial officer, was working insane hours. But she met Raj in the middle as they'd promised one another, and they came out of that manic period whole and happy and rooted in one another.

A breather, her longed-for trip to the Amazon, before Aarav settled in her womb.

Their families had been horrified when they started traveling with a one-year-old, but Aarav was an adventurer at heart. He knew Maddie mausi and Sunny mausa lived in London with his twin girl cousins, while his aunt Adi was working on an engineering project in Australia, and he also knew that he liked guavas but not pawpaw. Lychees continued to be up for debate.

All their travels, every work challenge or opportunity, each family decision, Nayna and Raj had talked over and handled as a team. Nayna had begun this trip as CFO of a brilliant ethical-cosmetics company, but after talking it over with Raj the previous night, she'd decided to hand in her notice on her return.

It was time for her to jump into another start-up, help create their financial foundation. She'd spent four years as Sailor's right hand, left only when his company was rock steady and thriving. After three years with the cosmetics company, she felt it was in the same strong position. Her skills would be better utilized elsewhere.

Raj, meanwhile, continued to grow his family's business with slow, steady patience. It was a legacy he'd leave not only to Aarav but to Navin and Komal's son and daughter and to any children Aditi might one day have.

He was, and always would be, her anchor, her love, her heart.

"What're you thinking, Nayna with the sundar nayna?" asked her gorgeous husband who sent her half-naked selfies when she was least expecting them.

"That Mr. Darcy has nothing on Raj Sen." Rising on tiptoe, she kissed him to the sound of their son's laughter. "I love our happily-ever-after, and I love you."

"And me!" Aarav cried.

"And you," Nayna confirmed for their smiling baby.

Her man with the dark eyes full of intensity smiled, and his gaze held no shadows, no hollows, no whispers of pain. All she saw was love so deep and true that Nayna knew it would be there for her. Always.

Thank you for reading REBEL HARD. If you missed CHERISH HARD (Ísa and Sailor) and ROCK HARD (featuring Sailor's rugby legend brother, Gabriel), both are

now out. To stay up to date with my releases and get exclusive access to deleted scenes and short stories, please join my newsletter at: www.nalinisingh.com And if you feel like leaving a review, that would be wonderful!

If you're curious about the Hindi language words used in this book, it's a dialect/form specific to Fiji, so some words/spellings may not be as you've seen them previously. The food described in it comes from the same tiny cluster of islands in the Pacific—it tends to be simpler than dishes you would usually find in an Indian restaurant, not as heavy with creams and sauces, most likely because of the tropical climate. (I stole all the mentioned recipes from my mum, who is an incredible cook.) Also, yes, I have tasted kava and, as with Nayna, it made my tongue go numb.

—xoxo Nalini

ABOUT THE AUTHOR

New York Times and *USA Today* bestselling author of the Psy-Changeling, Guild Hunter, and Rock Kiss series, Nalini Singh usually writes about hot shapeshifters, dangerous angels, and sexy rock stars. With the Hard Play series, she decided to write about a sinfully gorgeous set of brothers and their friends, all of whom will make your blood pump and your heart melt.

Nalini lives and works in beautiful New Zealand, and is passionate about writing. If you'd like to learn more about the Hard Play series or her other books, you can find excerpts, behind-the-scenes materials, and more information on her website: www.nalinisingh.com.